THE DEMON'S DAUGHTER

THE DEMON'S DAUGHTER

PAULA ALTENBURG

Entangled Publishing, LLC
2614 South Timberline Road
Suite 109
Fort Collins, CO 80525
Visit our website at www.entangledpublishing.com.

Edited by Kerri-Leigh Grady
Cover design by Kim Killion

Ebook ISBN   978-1-62061-038-1
Print ISBN   978-1-62061-037-4

Manufactured in the United States of America

First Edition March 2013

For my mother Carroll, my sisters Andrea and Kathryn,
and my brother Brad

ACKNOWLEDGMENTS

It always amazes me how many people it takes to bring a story to life. I'd like to thank the staff at Entangled Publishing, in particular my editor, Kerri-Leigh Grady, for all her hard work. I liked the story a lot before she got her hands on it. Now I love it.

I'd also like to thank Catherine Verge/Cathryn Fox/Cat Kalen for being such a terrific friend. This new series wouldn't exist without her. While I'm on the subject of friends, thanks to Carolyn Stewart White, Melanie Young, and Suzanne Durkacz MacNeil for getting me started, way back in college. More thanks go to Anne MacFarlane, Victoria LeBlanc, and especially Deborah Hale, who dropped everything when I needed her to read this for me. Writer friends are the best.

PROLOGUE

YEAR 330 PD *(POST DEMON OCCUPATION)*
THE GODDESSES' MOUNTAIN

The mountain was on fire.

Only a few days prior, ten priestesses had dwelled in its catacombs. Now, none but Desire remained. The haven the goddesses had built against demons had proved to be no haven this day.

She shivered despite the intense heat, thankful that the demon fire no longer had enough force behind it to sear the entire world. That did not mean it wasn't devastating still.

She ran a hand over her shaved head—a symbol of her service to the goddesses—and tried to suck a few extra breaths into a chest almost rigid from exhaustion. Pain from her failing heart shot through her left arm.

A shriek rang from one of the deeper chambers, splintering the unnatural silence, and Desire hurried toward the sound. Murmuring a small prayer at the door, she crossed the gleaming marble floor to the shrouded bed where a woman, belly grotesquely swollen, panted through the last of a contraction. Desire had suffered three stillbirths of her own in her younger years, and could only stand by and watch helplessly now.

The contraction passed. The woman on the bed opened eyes of such a vibrant shade of indigo blue that Desire never failed to marvel at them. Sweat-dampened skin glowed golden in the muted light, the only indication that the woman was not what she appeared at first glance. In this world, the goddesses assumed mortal form and lived a mortal existence. Here, their lives were as fragile as any other.

Yet no goddess had ever before given birth.

After a few ragged breaths, the goddess's eyes again drifted closed. "I am dying."

Desire feared she was right. "As soon as the baby is born, you can rejoin your sisters," she said.

The goddess shook her head. "I can never rejoin them now. Not after what I have done."

"Have you done something so terrible?" Desire asked gently. "You fell in love. That hardly seems such a great crime."

The goddess grabbed Desire's arm. Her voice dropped, taking on an edge of formality. "Hear my confession, Priestess. I have lain with a demon."

"It is not my place to hear your confession," Desire protested. She tried to draw back, afraid to listen to secrets not meant for mortal ears, but the goddess would not release her. "You are above this."

Not only was she above it, she had been forced into it. Her sisters had demanded this of her, yet had turned their backs and fled when she needed them most. Desire felt the pain and depth of their betrayal as if it had happened to her.

"No one is ever above the laws of the universe. This isn't our world. Death is to be my punishment for what's happened here." Tears choked the goddess's weakening voice. "The child will be punished for my sins as well. It will be a monster. If it somehow survives the birth, you must promise to destroy it."

Desire had seen demon spawn born before, from demon matings with mortal women. They clawed their way into the world through their mothers' bellies and fed off their mothers' flesh. They were indeed monsters—but this spawn would be born of a goddess, not a mortal.

"You had no way of knowing that falling in love would result in a child," she said. "You should not be punished for that. Not even goddesses can tell their hearts whom to love."

"All of this—the destruction of the goddesses' mountain, and the danger to our people—is because of me. He will not rest until every last trace of me is banished from existence. He believes I betrayed him." Golden tears coated the goddess's lashes. "I may not be able to tell my heart whom to love, but I knew what to do to make him love me. He will never forgive me for it."

There was little else Desire could say. She limped from the room to the fireplace in the center of the greater common area, where the priestesses received supplicants and offerings, and scooped a bowlful of warm water from the reservoir. An artesian well provided plenty of fresh water, and the storerooms remained well stocked, so Desire would not have that to worry about in the days to come.

She carried the bowl back to the goddess and wiped the lovely, gleaming face with a soft cloth.

Soon after, a baby's cries replaced its mother's shrieks of pain.

"Look," Desire said in a hushed, awestruck tone, arms trembling from relief. She held the blanket-wrapped bundle up for its reluctant mother to see. "She is beautiful. Not a monster at all."

The goddess twisted away. "Destroy it," she said. "It is demon spawn. An abomination to the universe. It belongs to no world."

Something deep inside Desire twisted. She had wanted so much to hold a baby of her own in her arms and three times had been denied the opportunity, yet here was a mother with a beautiful, healthy child and she would not so much as take one look?

This small creature radiated nothing but innocence, and had come into the mortal world by natural means. It was no abomination.

Far from it.

"She is a girl!" Desire insisted. "See? Spawn are male. And she is beautiful. She is no spawn, nor is she a monster. If anything, she is a goddess." The baby in her arms puckered a tiny, rosebud mouth, then opened dark, astonishing eyes rimmed with thick black lashes. Love shot through her with all the fierceness of a bolt of lightning, and she knew she could never destroy something so wonderful. "Let me keep her."

"I cannot," the goddess said, but Desire sensed her hesitation. She was, after all, a goddess—and now, a mother. Both nurtured life. They did not destroy it.

Desire pressed her small advantage. "No one need ever know. I can raise her as mine. I feel nothing but goodness in her. I can teach her the ways of the goddesses."

The goddess bit her lip, her face alarmingly pale. "You forget that she has two birthrights, not one."

"But she is a female," Desire insisted. "Not a demon. If you would only touch her, or look at her, you would see for yourself."

Before the goddess could protest, Desire placed the baby on its mother's chest.

Instinctively, the goddess's arms came up to keep the child from falling. She cradled her daughter for long moments while Desire held her breath, until a single golden tear slid down the goddess's cheek.

"Keep her, then," she finally said, and Desire reclaimed the precious bundle. "But she remains my responsibility. I cannot leave the world unprotected if you are mistaken about her." She lifted a finger. "Bring me that coffer."

Desire took the small silver box from the shelf and lifted the lid for the goddess. Inside were two amulets. One, round and flat and carved from a red soil hardened with several layers of natural desert varnish, bore the symbol of a lightning bolt. The other, more delicate in structure, was crafted from a common mountain stone that glimmered with all the colors of the rainbow.

Desire recognized the rainbow. It was a favorite stone the goddess had once worn often, but now that Desire thought about it, she had not seen it on her in recent months.

The other amulet, however, was ugly and unfamiliar to her. It was not goddess-made.

"The rainbow," the goddess said, "is for the baby." A second golden tear chased the first. "I would like for her to have something of mine in case she should ever want it or need it. Let her know she was born of love, not hate. No child should ever have to live with such a burden. Not even a monster. The other amulet," she added, indicating the lightning bolt, "has been invoked by the Demon Lord himself to protect its owner against others of his kind. Keep it until you are certain you no longer need protection from her. Then, it is to be sealed in a container and dropped in the river so my Chosen may find it. He's to be her protector, if she ever has need of one." She ran the tips of her fingers over its surface. A flash of gold light suffused it, and she murmured a few words in a language the priestess did not know. "There. It has been invoked by a goddess now, too, so that only the two of you may wear it."

Desire did not like the lightning bolt amulet or the energy that pulsed from it. She slipped it into a small leather pouch she carried, not wanting it next to her skin.

The goddess looked at the baby with wonder in her eyes, then up at Desire. "May the goddesses watch over you both. And maybe someday, her father can find it in his heart to forgive me for my part in this."

The goddess's form on the bed began to fade, becoming a translucent, golden light that surrounded Desire and the child in her arms. In minutes, she vanished completely.

Tears filled Desire's eyes. She did not know what happened to immortals after death. They were not meant to die. In some ways it was better to be mortal and return to the earth, where at least something of substance remained behind.

The rains came soon after, extinguishing the fire, yet the goddesses did not return. Neither did the other priestesses, so Desire was left to maintain the temple alone.

In honor of the baby's mother, and the father her mother had loved, Desire called the baby Airie, a name meaning rainbows and lightning. And, when Airie turned six months of age, Desire took the lightning bolt amulet, sealed it in a watertight container, and threw it into the mountain river to be lost in one of its many eddies as the goddess had instructed. She had no need for protection from Airie.

Airie, however, might someday have need of the protector her mother had chosen for her.

• • •

Many miles away, across the vast expanse of desert, a blond-headed boy in the Borderlands played in one of the local springs fed by an underground river. He dipped his hand into a shallow pool, searching for freshwater mussels, and found a container wedged in the rocks instead.

From inside the container, he withdrew a red amulet marked with the carving of a lightning bolt.

He slipped its gold chain around his neck, liking the feel of the amulet's warmth against his skin. Ignoring the light goddess rain that had begun to fall, he went back to his game.

CHAPTER ONE

Year 352 PD
Inside Demon Territory

Hunter slapped the length of his toe-grazing leather duster, sending a shower of fine red silt into the air around him. It was a habit learned from his mother a long time ago in another life, and one he had never seen the need to break—removing the desert dirt before entering an establishment.

Even an establishment in a place like Freetown, where niceties weren't the rule of the day.

Dusk was settling in, and the saloon would soon prepare to close. No honest man stayed out after dark. If they weren't afraid of thieves, they were terrified of demons. Hunter wanted this meeting over with so he, too, could be on his way.

With his hat dangling by its straps between his shoulder blades, Hunter pushed open the swinging door. The dim interior of the saloon meant anyone framed in the doorway was backlit by the setting sun and virtually blinded. Sidestepping to the right, he brushed back his duster, keeping his hand close to the six-shooter at his hip. The short sword strapped to his back came in handy for those times when a gunshot might attract too much unwanted attention, but in a saloon, loud weapons made the better deterrents. And faster, cleaner kills.

A sword, however, worked best against demons if a man was willing to fight them up close. And Hunter wasn't known as the Demon Slayer for nothing.

The smells of ale-soaked pine, smoked meats, and stale tobacco thickened the air. He remained with his back to the raw wooden wall while his eyes adjusted to the change in the light. When they did, he nodded to Blade, the tall, stone-faced man behind the bar.

Blade, polishing the glass in his hand with a pristine white cloth, acknowledged Hunter with the slightest drop of his chin. Hunter let his gaze drift around the near-empty room, searching for the one he'd been summoned to meet.

A man with a long, ugly red scar down the side of an even uglier face slouched on a stool at the bar. Hunter noted and dismissed him. The women who worked in the saloon had already retired to the second floor. A few stragglers sat at well-spaced tables, showing signs of imminent departure. Once the front door was locked, it was locked for the night. Blade did not encourage overnight business, and anyone who wanted it paid a significant price.

A lone woman sat in the single booth in one shadowed corner of the room. Twisted and misshapen, dressed in a man's greatcoat and coarse woolen trousers, she hunched in her seat, unbothered by the other patrons. It wasn't her appearance that kept her from harassment. Being a priestess protected her far better than simple ugliness ever could, for priestesses served as the only law this side of the Godseekers' mountains. They were all that stood between the people and the demons, and in their own way, they were far more ruthless than the basest of cutthroats.

This one was the worst of the lot, and the client Hunter had come here to meet. Mamna was her name, and he didn't like her. He didn't like that she had made a deal with the Demon Lord, one that put her in her current position of power. He didn't like that laws were being written by a woman who had no use for other women.

And he did not like being summoned.

The nails in his boot heels echoed on the whitewashed floor as he walked to the priestess's table. He didn't miss the sneer of disgust twisting Scarface's lips as Hunter passed him. Men knew better than to show open contempt for the priestess, but anyone who dealt with her was another matter.

Hunter committed Scarface to memory. It was good to have an idea of who might try to plant a knife in his back. Or die trying.

He slid onto the bench across the battered table from the priestess. The amulet around his neck grew warm, but Hunter ignored it. It indicated the priestess had been in recent contact with a demon, a fact that did not surprise him as much as it left him with a bad taste in his mouth.

Hunter knew why Mamna wanted to meet with him in a public place. She wanted everyone in Freetown to know that she was conducting business with the Demon Slayer, and that there were certain laws in the land even the Slayer could be made to respect.

That was why Hunter had kept this meeting to a time when as few people as possible were likely to see them. He respected the law, such as it was. But he hated demons and all who associated with them, and Mamna knew it.

With watery, pale-blue eyes lodged in an aging face withered and burned from a hard life in a harsh desert, the priestess examined Scarface at the bar before acknowledging Hunter.

"If he takes offense at your speaking with a priestess, try not to kill him," she said. "But go ahead and hurt him a little."

Hunter allowed his own eyes to turn to ice. "I never kill unless I have to." It was a less-than-subtle reminder that, while Hunter might be persuaded to take a contract from the priestess, he would do so on his own terms. He rested one palm on the table, keeping his other hand out of her line of vision. "Why have you summoned me here?"

Scarface continued to watch him, but Blade, Hunter knew, would be watching Scarface on his behalf.

It paid to have good friends.

"There is a thief at large on the goddesses' mountain," Mamna said.

Hunter shrugged. "There are thieves everywhere. It was bound to happen sooner or later. Besides, the goddesses are long gone and their temple is abandoned. What difference will one thief make to anyone?"

Another subtle jab on Hunter's part. The priestesses—Mamna in particular—didn't like to be reminded of the goddesses' departure. It represented betrayal.

"The mountain is forbidden," Mamna said. She rubbed a gnarled hand over her shaven head.

"Then this thief does your work for you. If he's successful at his chosen profession, people will learn to leave the mountain alone, and he will have to move on."

"The thief is a woman."

Hunter laughed out loud. "More power to her." At the bar, Scarface tightened his grip on his drink and Hunter lowered his voice. "If she thieves on the mountain, she is more than likely one of your own."

"She is not a priestess."

Mamna sounded definite about that, and Hunter had to admit he was growing intrigued. A woman on the mountain who stole from trespassers? What kind of woman would she be?

A hideous one, no doubt. Probably bitter as the priestesses about it, too. Women judged themselves far harder than men, although from what he'd seen, beauty didn't get them much in this world.

Mamna pulled a small pouch from a pocket in her greatcoat and slid it to Hunter. He lifted the pouch. It was heavier than it looked, meaning it contained mostly, if not all, gold coins.

Which also meant he was being overpaid.

"There's more to this story," Hunter said flatly.

Mamna had the nerve to feign righteousness. "She is ambushing innocents, most likely supplicants to the temple. All you have to do is capture her and bring her here to face justice."

That did not explain the coins. Hunter disliked that Mamna might think his reluctance to accept this task sprang from not wanting to bring a woman to so-called justice. It would give her a weakness to use against him in future negotiations. He tossed the pouch in the palm of his hand. The coins clinked dully.

Gold. Definitely gold.

"This is a great deal of money for bringing in one woman." Hunter waited for an answer he believed, or at least one he was willing to accept.

At the bar Blade made a production of putting glasses away. "Closing time," he said to Scarface.

Scarface grunted. "There are two others still here."

"Those two have no need to fear demons." The shutters on the windows rattled to emphasize Blade's point. Everyone knew that when the wind blew from the west, demons rode with it, calling a challenge to mortals very few could resist. "I require a great deal of cash up front if you want to spend the entire night here. A great deal. So my next question is, how much do *you* need to fear them?"

Scarface tossed a few coins on the bar, hitched up the back of his dust-crusted trousers, and left through the swinging doors.

Mamna cleared her throat, drawing Hunter's attention back to her. For the first time, she appeared uneasy. "This is no ordinary woman."

Hunter regarded her for a long moment. "Rule number one— no surprises."

"There will not be any," she reassured him, which didn't reassure him at all.

He dropped the pouch on the table. It landed with a heavy thud. He pushed it toward the priestess with his fingertips. "Rule number two—don't lie to me."

Mamna ignored the pouch. She met his eyes. "It is claimed she has demon blood. If that's true, she must be turned over to the Demon Lord, as per my agreement with him."

Only a great deal of discipline kept Hunter from allowing the revulsion that shivered up his spine to show on his face. Men hated demons, and demons hated men, but spawn, who carried the blood of both, were hated by all. They belonged to no world. Even Hunter had no problem with the Demon Lord claiming one because a demon would not allow it to live either.

But the claim that the thief was spawn had to be true, and Hunter did not believe it was.

"Impossible," he said. "She's a woman."

Mamna's wrinkled face smoothed as her eyebrows lifted. "Is it impossible?" she asked. "Can you know this for certain?"

All Hunter knew for certain was that Mamna hated women more than anyone hated spawn, and for whatever reason, she wanted this woman dead. He did not believe her, and he should not take this job.

But if he didn't, someone else would. And to think of an innocent woman being handed over to demons was more than his stomach could handle.

Was Mamna testing him somehow? Could he afford for her to suspect a weakness about him that she would, in all likelihood, use against him in the future?

He scanned his memory for anything he might have given away in the past. He had left behind everything he'd ever valued years ago so that he would have no such weaknesses to betray. Only Blade could be considered a true friend, and Hunter had no concerns for him or his safety.

He also had no concerns over Blade's loyalty. Hunter had found him in the desert some years ago, fighting a losing battle with a demon driven wild by the taste of his blood. Hunter had killed the demon and saved Blade's life, although not before the demon had bitten a large chunk of flesh from Blade's right leg. While no longer as agile as he'd once been, Blade was still quite capable of taking care of himself, and a close ally.

No, Mamna had no hold on Hunter. He intended to keep it that way.

He reclaimed the money pouch and slipped it into an inside pocket. He rose to his feet, wanting this meeting to be over and done with so he could think.

"How much time do I have?" he asked her.

"As long as necessary." She shrugged. "No longer."

Which meant not much time beyond what she thought it would take him to travel, two or three weeks at most, but Hunter wasn't concerned about that. He'd take whatever time he deemed necessary, then a little more. It never paid to seem too cooperative.

Mamna hopped from her seat without a word of good-bye and shuffled from the saloon, the hem of her ill-fitting greatcoat dragging on the floor.

Blade closed the heavier exterior doors behind her. He then dropped an iron bar into place, barricading them in.

"Thirsty?" he asked Hunter.

"Please."

The wind picked up, and Hunter hoped the townspeople had gotten themselves locked up in time. On nights like this demons sought pleasure in their demon forms, and pleasure, to them, meant killing men and violating women.

While Blade slung a kettle on a hook inside the large fireplace to heat water, Hunter went around the room and latched all the shutters in place.

"Do the women have their windows closed?" he asked Blade. Three whores called the saloon home. They worked when they wanted, and with whom they pleased. Blade offered them protection and a roof, and in return, they helped with the cooking and cleaning.

"Of course."

The kettle hissed and soon began to steam.

"One of these days," Blade said, "that ugly little priestess will pay someone to plant a knife in your back."

Hunter grabbed a broom from behind the bar to sweep the floor. "Dying of old age is overrated."

"Perhaps. But you seem to have forgotten that living to an old age is not." Blade dropped a metal ball filled with fragrant loose tea into the hot water, then lifted the kettle from the fire with a long hook. He carried it to the bar. "What did the evil little troll want from you?"

Hunter told him, and he frowned.

"She's made it no secret that she no longer serves the goddesses. She has no reason to do demon work either. Neither do you. She's lying to you for some purpose of her own. You know how she feels about women. You shouldn't take her work."

Hunter had learned long ago to trust Blade's instincts. He'd also learned to work around them. He leaned on the broom and faced his friend. "If I don't take it someone else will, and they might not care whether or not this woman truly is spawn. What would you have me do—abandon those who are still innocent in this goddessforsaken world?"

Blade produced two sturdy mugs and set them on the bar. "I wouldn't have you abandon anyone. But how do you determine who is worth saving and who is not? That kind of choice does something to your soul." Blade took a cloth and wiped the varnished surface. "Sometimes I wonder if you've also forgotten what true justice really is."

Hunter often wondered the same thing himself. He had grown hard over the years, to the point where he did not always recognize the man who looked back at him from the shaving mirror.

Speaking of shaving…

He scratched at the scruff on his jaw.

"People are asking questions about you," Blade continued, interrupting Hunter's thoughts.

"That's nothing new." He was the Demon Slayer. That inspired questions. There was always someone trying to take his place.

Some days, he'd gladly let them.

"These questions are new. They have to do with your family."

Hunter went still. He tried to think if he had ever let anything slip, and could not come up with a single instance. He had never visited his sisters, nor spoken of them. Not in all the years since he had fled from the Borderlands. Not even to Blade.

He tried to dismiss his unease. "Forget about it. Everyone comes from somewhere. People wonder if I have anyone I might want to protect. If I have a weakness. They won't find any."

When he finished sweeping the saloon floor, he took a seat near his friend at the bar.

Blade passed him a steaming mug of fragrant tea brewed from desert lavender. Hunter blew on it, watching the ripples crease its mud-brown surface, then took a slow sip to savor the taste. Neither he nor Blade touched alcohol. In their businesses, men who drank did not live long.

"I have something for you," Hunter said.

He reached in his pocket and withdrew a thick chunk of plastic, an artifact that predated the demons to a time when the world was filled with large cities and millions of people. While the wind had buried most of the ruins, it often turned up little things such as this, and these items were worth money to the right traders. Whenever Hunter found any in the desert, he brought them to Blade, who in turn sold the artifacts and split the profits among Hunter, himself, and the women.

Blade took the artifact from him, rolled it around in his long fingers, then dropped it into a box hidden behind the counter. He continued to stand, taking a sip from his own mug of tea, his dark eyes brooding as he returned to the original topic of conversation. "I'll try and get to the bottom of whoever's asking questions about you."

Hunter felt himself relax. If there were anything for him to worry about, Blade would find out.

"Anything new since the last time I was in town?" he asked, wanting to change the subject.

"A few murders. Some changes in wealth. More migrants from the border regions, seeking their fortunes on this side of the mountains. Overall, no."

Weariness crept over Hunter. Not much ever changed in Freetown in that respect. The rich got richer, and the poor served the rich. Migrants came to Freetown seeking quick fortunes and often found servitude instead, assuming they survived the trek across the desert. One would have thought the priestesses, who'd once served the goddesses, would have a greater sense of philanthropy, or even basic kindness. Yet any gold they parted with came at a rate of exchange even desperate people should shudder to pay.

The coins weighed heavily in his pocket and on his conscience. That Mamna could so easily turn any woman over to the demons bothered him. How awful would this thief have to be in order for Hunter to look the other way?

She would have to be spawn. In which case, let the demons take care of a problem they had created.

He finished his tea. "I should go."

Blade cocked his head, listening to the howling wind. Driven sand rang like raindrops against the exterior walls and shutters.

"It's going to be a rough night," he said. "You're welcome to stay." He frowned, and Hunter knew he was still thinking of those questions about his past, and who might be behind them. "In fact, I recommend you do. The women won't mind. You might even be able to talk them into letting you use their bath."

"They would waste water on me?" Hunter's amazement was

only partly feigned. Even in Freetown, built on an oasis, water usage was tightly controlled. By Mamna.

Blade's eyebrow shot up. "It has a lot to do with your smell. They prefer their men clean."

Hunter spent most of his days in the desert alone so he was used to his own smell, but a bath would be welcome. It was hard to turn one down. But he was more uneasy about those questions regarding his past than he cared to admit, and while Blade could look out for himself, Hunter didn't like the idea of bringing any danger to the women. He was already too fond of them.

That last thought alone was enough to make him refuse to stay. "Thanks, but I'd better go."

Blade unbarred the door and Hunter slipped like a shadow into the dark and deserted street beyond.

Mamna and her priestesses founded Freetown not far from the ruins of a buried city rumored to have contained close to two million inhabitants in the time before demons. The ruins stretched across several miles of desert, and although they undoubtedly contained many treasures, no one entered them to find out—the shifting sands had left them unstable and riddled with deadly sinkholes.

But that was when demons numbered in the tens of thousands. Whoever the inhabitants of that lost city were, they had done their part against the invaders before falling.

Sand stung Hunter's cheeks, and he pulled a heavy cotton kerchief over his mouth and nose. He settled his hat back on his head, tugging the wide brim low to shield his eyes.

Even in the dark of a storm, the streets of Freetown weren't difficult for Hunter to navigate. He knew them well. A market served as the town center. Radiating from there, like the spokes of a wagon's wheel, spread the other main areas—the wealthy, the not-so-wealthy, the poor, and the various trade shops that serviced them all. Blade's saloon sat at the outer tip of one spoke, near the high wall surrounding the city. The wall was not meant to keep demons out. That was impossible. Rather, it allowed Mamna to be selective in the people who came and went.

Most people. Not Hunter. He had set up a shelter of sorts in a natural, rock-faced corral not too far out in the desert. He came and went as he pleased.

He headed for a hidden tunnel that burrowed beneath the outer city wall, more distracted than was probably wise, but the storm should have kept even the bravest of lowlifes indoors. He felt safe in letting his thoughts wander.

His mind kept going back to those questions Blade had spoken of. Hunter had not thought of his sisters in a long time. It was pointless to do so. When he'd left he had gotten as far away from them as he could, covering his tracks, and he'd never looked back. Only they knew why he had killed that first demon. No one else cared as long as he continued to kill them. Few men were brave enough to try. Fewer still survived a first attempt.

He caught a slight movement from the corner of his eye, an unnatural shift of shadow off to his left. Someone was following him.

He stopped, not bothering to pretend he wasn't aware. He unholstered his six-shooter, wondering if his stalker was alone, then pressed himself against the false front of a nearby shanty in an attempt to keep the wind-whipped sand from blinding him completely. He disliked using a gun, but tonight, the storm would drown out any sounds of a gunfight.

The attack, although expected, nevertheless took him by surprise, more because of its professionalism and choice of weapon than its ferocity. He sucked in his stomach as the knife in his assailant's hand slashed a six-inch gap in his shirt. He brought his gun up and fired, and was rewarded with the hiss of an indrawn breath. He drew his short sword from the sheath on his back with his left hand. He did not want to kill his assailant just yet. Dead men didn't talk.

Lightning-quick, the man came at Hunter again, but Hunter was better prepared this time. He slid to the side to avoid the thrust of the knife, and from behind his back he shot his sword's blade through the other man's extended arm.

Rather than pull away, the assailant fell forward. A heavy knife handle protruded from between his shoulder blades.

Hunter holstered his gun, reached down to jerk the blade free, and wiped it clean on the assailant's ruined shirt.

"Thank you," he said. He handed the knife hilt-first to its owner.

"You're welcome." The knife disappeared into the sheath Blade always wore strapped to his mangled leg.

"Not that I wasn't managing just fine on my own," Hunter added.

"You were doing okay." Blade rolled the dead man onto his back with the toe of his boot. Enough light remained for them to identify him as Scarface. "But increasing the odds in your favor never hurts." Blade's eyes met Hunter's. "Why would anyone risk angering Mamna by killing someone she's just hired?"

"That's what I was hoping to ask him."

Blade riffled through the man's pockets and came up empty-handed. "Nothing. The man's a professional."

"Maybe he's poor," Hunter guessed, without any real hope.

"Even poor people keep things in their pockets." Blade patted down the man's arms and legs and came up with an assortment of weapons. He held them out. "See anything here you want?"

Hunter waved him off. "You killed him. It's all yours."

The weapons disappeared into Blade's clothing.

"How did you know he'd follow me?" Hunter asked.

Blade shielded his face from the stinging sand with the crook of an elbow. "His hands were too clean."

That made sense, and was something Blade would notice right away. An assassin's hands were his greatest asset, and Blade took pride in his own despite the fact that he no longer worked for hire.

"Why didn't you warn me?"

"Because I didn't want to be wrong about what he was. And it was something you should have noticed yourself." Demon howls carried on the wind now, still far off in the distance, and Blade checked nervously over his shoulder. "Fresh blood is going to draw them here. Sure you don't want to come back to my place for the night?"

"I'm sure." Hunter grinned at him. "Scared?"

"Stiff," Blade admitted without shame. "While I don't mind getting killed, the being eaten alive part continues to bother me. I'm heading for home. I'd search this guy for markings if I were you, but I doubt you'll find anything. He's your problem now."

Blade left, and Hunter took a few extra minutes to search for any tattoos or markings that might give some indication of where the would-be assassin was from. He found nothing, but that could have been because of the poor light and blowing sand. Or it could have been because Blade was right. The man had no markings on him because he was a professional.

Then, because Hunter didn't feel like confronting blood-frenzied demons either, he headed for shelter.

CHAPTER TWO

Airie tipped her wide-brimmed hat to partially hide her face, hitched up her scratchy woolen trousers in what she hoped was a manly fashion, and stepped from the concealment of the forest into the world beyond. Her boots, three sizes too large, were the smallest pair she'd been able to acquire. If luck were with her, she would not trip over them and fall on her face.

This was her third visit in as many months to the mean little trading post at the foot of the goddesses' mountain, because she was hesitant to spend too much money all at once. To do so would attract unwanted attention.

She did not like leaving her mother alone for very long, partly because she had forbidden her to come to this place, and partly because Desire had not been well of late. But what else was Airie supposed to do? The offerings to the goddesses and priestesses had stopped a long time ago, and she and Desire had run out of many of the necessities and small luxuries they could not grow or raise for themselves.

A tingle of excitement coursed up her spine. The trading post was no more than a one-room log cabin, crudely constructed, but to Airie it represented civilization. There were times when she craved the company of other people far more than the almost forgotten sweets she planned to buy today in the hopes they might help improve Desire's appetite.

Airie stepped onto the sagging porch, her too-large boots thudding heavily. More than one pair of eyes turned in her direction. She dipped her head, resisting the urge to tug at her hat's brim again, and pushed past the small group of men gathered in the open doorway. She hoped the dirt she had rubbed into her cheeks and chin would disguise the fact that she could not grow whiskers.

The men let her pass without a second glance, moving off to go about their own business.

Airie's eyes had no difficulty adjusting to the darkness of the long, narrow room. Desire often marveled at her ability to see on even the blackest of nights, but to Airie it was as natural as breathing.

Three men stood near the squat wooden flour bin, deliberately blocking the room's center aisle. She knew at once that they were trouble and turned to leave, but in this instance her normally good instincts had come too late.

A man with bad skin approached the narrow counter running the width of one end of the room. Smoked meats hung from the crude rafters, swaying in the slight current of air he created as he moved beneath them, almost grazing them with his greasy head. Airie crinkled her nose. She rarely ate meat, liking the taste even less than the smell.

Another man moved to bar the door, and Airie barely resisted covering her nose. The meats were not the only source of offensive odors in the room.

The man with bad skin held a gun in his hand.

"If you want to stay open for business," he said to the boy behind the counter, "then you have to pay taxes."

The boy was young and badly scared. Airie could smell the fear on him, and that scent was not pleasant either. It stirred her anger. That, in turn, frightened Airie. Her temper could be too much for her to control at times. She clenched her hands into tight fists and tamped the anger down.

"Pay taxes?" the boy echoed, bewilderment touching his pale eyes, and Airie realized he was not quite right—that he was one of the world's special children, who needed to be cared for and protected.

All three men laughed and Airie wondered where the boy's father was. What would possess him to leave this simple child alone, in charge of a store in a land where theft was a way of life?

"Taxes. The money you have to pay if you want to be in business. You'll be paying it every month from now on," the bad-skinned man said. His words, high-pitched and slow, mocked the boy's diminished mental capacities.

Airie's temper cranked up a notch. It was clear there would be no assistance from the people outside. If they knew what was happening, they chose to ignore it.

Airie should, too. So far the men had paid her little attention. Although tall for a woman, she was slight, and no doubt they thought her the boy she pretended to be. She settled her hat more firmly on her head, hoping it would stay in place, wishing her mother would let her cut off the long, dark curls.

The thought of her invalid mother made her reevaluate the situation. She should stay out of this. If anyone saw she was a woman it would make future excursions to the trading outpost difficult, if not impossible, and then where would she and her mother be?

She reached for the handle of a broom resting against a shelf of dry goods, easing around so that her back was to it and no one could see her actions. If they threatened to harm the boy, then she would interfere. His life was what mattered. The rest was only money.

The boy opened a drawer and lifted out a tray of gold and silver coins. The man tucked his gun into his waistband and emptied the tray into a canvas sack, grunting his disapproval at its lack of weight. "This is it?"

The boy nodded and the men, seeming to accept that this was all they could expect, tossed a few more items from the counter into the sack and then were gone.

Both relieved and disappointed, Airie let go of the broom. Other patrons drifted inside now that the thieves had left, and she quickly gathered what she had come for. She took the merchandise to the counter.

The boy's fingers trembled as he collected the coins Airie passed him.

"Where is your father?" she asked, dropping her voice to little more than a whisper so it could not be easily identified as that of a woman.

The boy's eyes darted to the sides. "He heard they were coming and said that if he were here, they would most likely kill him. He told me to give them whatever they wanted."

Her lips thinned. So the man had left a child, a *special* child, to be murdered in his place.

"I could never have been as brave as you were," she said.

"You deal with what life hands you," the boy replied, shrugging off her praise, although she could tell by his smile that it pleased him.

Someone else wandered to the counter then, so Airie shoved her purchases into her backpack and returned to the sunshine outside.

Even though she knew she should, she did not head for home. Instead, she walked the perimeter of the outpost, looking for the three thieves.

They were shouldering their packs, preparing to leave. Airie followed, disliking that they were escaping unchallenged, although the small inner voice that sometimes spoke to her asked why this was so different from what she'd done so many times, herself.

The difference, she answered the voice, was that she took only from those who invaded her home. The goddesses' mountain was forbidden to all but their appellants. Anyone venturing near the sacred temple should know enough to leave an offering, no matter how small.

And the mountain, Airie soon realized, was the place the thieves were headed. Thoroughly outraged now, she continued to follow.

They had built a crude camp for themselves a few miles up a faintly marked trail. She wrinkled her nose in disgust at the mess they had made. Broken tools, scraps of past meals, and other offal desecrated the goddesses' ground.

The man with the bad skin set his pack against a ramshackle shelter woven from evergreen branches. The one with the gun had removed it from his clothing and set it near the sack of stolen goods while he counted the coins.

"That ought to keep the old hag happy for a few weeks," he said with satisfaction. He swatted at a blowfly taking up residence on his pocked cheek.

The other two men appeared to be unarmed. Airie chose a stout branch for a weapon, and with a practiced hand, weighed it for sturdiness. Now that the goddesses were gone, people forgot too easily, or no longer cared, that the mountain remained a sacred place. Her mother was too old and ill to confront men such as these, and it fell to Airie to take on her priestess responsibilities when it became necessary.

Her mother couldn't fault her for what she was about to do. She would drive the men from the mountain, nothing more.

She tugged at her hat, remembering at the last moment to keep her face partially hidden. She stepped out of the bushes.

"This is the goddesses' mountain," she said, her makeshift staff lying confidently across her palms in front of her. "You're trespassing. Are you prepared to pay the price?"

Incredulity crossed the leader's face. Airie paid him special attention. He was not as tall as her, but he was much heavier, and the extra weight on him could not be attributed entirely to fat.

The other two men split up and slowly circled behind her, flanking her on both sides, but she kept her eyes focused on the one in front of her. Her fingers curled around her staff, excitement pumping up her heart rate. She was not afraid, or even alarmed. Her reflexes were excellent. So was her strength.

"The goddesses are gone," the first man said. "It's time the mountain gives back to the people all that the goddesses once kept from them."

She did not bother to contradict him. Airie knew the goddesses' physical presences were gone, but all her life she had felt them in spirit. They remained close at hand, constantly watching and waiting, biding their time—but for what, she did not know for certain.

One man came in low, from the side, attempting to catch her off guard. With a whiplike flick of her wrist, she brought the staff over her head and down, rapping the man hard at the temple. His eyes rolled back, and he dropped like a stone. In a continuous motion, she brought the staff back and caught the other man in the ribs. He fell, clutching at his stomach, and retched into the dirt. Airie's chin shot up and her hat slid off, releasing a thick, dark braid of waist-length hair.

"A priestess, then," the leader said, sounding amused. He looked closer. "Too young to be a priestess. And far too pretty. Priestess spawn, perhaps?" He laughed, and it was an ugly sound. "What other services did the priestesses provide when they lived in the temple?"

Airie gasped at the crudity and irreverence of the remark. Desire was too good and kind to be the brunt of this heathen's humor.

The man advanced. "What services do *you* provide mortal man?"

Kill them, a dark, instinctive inner voice said.

Airie's temper reacted to the command, so quickly she could not catch it back to her. She felt the heat as an all-too-familiar, and frightening, red haze slid over her vision. Sparks from her eyes sprayed the man's face and greasy hair.

He drew back, terror twisting his features. "Demon spawn!" he spat out, tripping over his own feet in his haste to back away.

His companions, roused from senselessness by the sound of his shout, scrambled upright and stumbled after him. Long after they were gone from sight, Airie could hear them crashing through the brush in a headlong flight down the mountain.

Her normal vision returned, along with a rising dismay. She'd succeeded in ridding the mountain of parasites, but a little too well. Desire would not be pleased when she found out.

If she found out. Airie would have to lie to her, something she did not like to do, but sometimes it was necessary. Airie did not want her upset.

She picked up her hat, dusted it off, and set it back on her head. Then she cleaned up all traces of the thieves' desecration, tearing down their shelter and putting their trash in a pile before burning it all. She uncovered nothing of any value other than what they had taken from the trading post.

Airie doused the fire with dirt and slipped the canvas sack filled with money into her backpack before beginning the trek to return it.

While the boy was busy with another customer at the back of the store, she set the bag of money behind the counter.

By the time she began the long climb to the temple and her waiting mother, the sun had slid below the horizon, plunging the mountain forest into deep shadow.

Darkness did not bother Airie. She could see quite well in it and was unafraid of the mountain's nightlife. In fact, there was very little in her life for her to fear.

Demon spawn, the thief had called her.

While there was not much in her life to fear, the one thing that caused Airie more than a little concern was that the thief might be right, that she was spawn of some sort, and that sooner or later, the goddesses would shun her.

Because, as much as she wished to believe otherwise, it could not have been one of them who had counseled her to kill.

• • •

Desire waited patiently at the open door of the stone temple for Airie to return.

The doe flowers were in bloom. Their rich scent hung heavy on the damp, moonlit air, pink heads bobbing as the mountain breathed around them.

Her bones ached, and she longed for Airie to help ease her pain, but it was becoming more and more obvious to her that not even Airie's healing touch would work much longer. Her time was coming.

When Desire was gone, what would become of Airie?

The goddesses watched over her, Desire knew, deeply troubled by that fact. Their mortal forms might be gone from the world, and their gifts now limited within it, but their spirits could yet be felt—if one knew how to call to them. Desire shivered. She had once served them faithfully, and continued to pray to them, but she would deny them in a heartbeat if it meant keeping her daughter safe from harm.

Desire heard Airie before she saw her, singing as she climbed the night-shrouded path. The priestess smiled in the darkness. Airie was a true child of the earth.

But she was a child no longer and had not been for quite some time. She was a grown woman, and Desire did not know what was to become of her. When Desire died, no one—not even Airie—would know of her birthright.

Airie reached the top of the path. Tall, slim-waisted, and long-legged, with sable eyes and coal-black hair, she was the counter image of her golden mother, dark where the goddess had been fair. Yet they had the same features, and the same presence. From the way she carried herself to the healing power of her touch, Airie had the bearing of an immortal. It was impossible not to love her, although Desire knew from long experience how difficult goddesses could be to love at times.

Airie's wet hair, long and loose to her hips and slightly curling at the tips, told Desire she had stopped to bathe in one of the hot mountain springs. She wore a fresh change of clothes, the sleeves of her crisp white blouse rolled back to her elbows, her long brown skirt wrapping around her legs with her strides. From her fingers dangled the pack carrying the offerings she had gone to collect. Desire was not misled by the easy way she carried the pack. It would be full, and very heavy.

Despite the singing, Desire knew at once that something was wrong. The soft glow of happiness normally surrounding Airie was missing tonight.

Airie set the pack at Desire's feet, then bent down and kissed her cheek.

"You're in pain." Concern filled her voice.

"It's nothing," Desire replied. Just that one brief kiss had been enough to make her feel better, and to ease her aches. "Sit. Tell me about your day. You're late."

Very late, in fact. Far too late to have been collecting offerings, but then again, Airie often lost track of time.

She sat in the long cool mountain grass at Desire's feet, her head on her mother's knees. "I walked to the far side of the mountain, beyond the lake."

Desire's already erratic heart skipped a beat, then picked up a few extra to compensate. Airie had not gone to the far side of the mountain. If she had, she would have brought back sweetberries and some of the white cedar bark Desire often sprinkled on the fire at night to freshen the temple air.

The knowledge disquieted her. She loved Airie, and Airie loved her in return. Her nature was kind and gentle, but she was also fiercely protective, and there was nothing she would not do for Desire, or anything she loved, if she believed it necessary. Desire hoped it would not get her in trouble someday.

She chose not to challenge Airie on the lie. Instead, they both sat in silence, soaking up the sounds and smells of the evening. Desire stroked Airie's damp hair.

"When did you first notice my eyes?" Airie asked suddenly.

This time when it stopped, Desire feared that her heart might not start on its own again. She carefully considered her answer before speaking. "You were a baby."

And it had not been Airie's eyes she had noticed first. Desire had been outdoors when she smelled smoke and hurried inside to find the chamber on fire and Airie shrieking at the top of her young lungs. The crib was in ruins because she had torn it apart. The angry welts on her neck had told Desire she'd most likely gotten her head caught between its spindles. The flaming eyes were nothing compared to the destruction Airie had caused in her struggle to free herself.

Yet Airie had never turned her temper on another living being, not even the time she'd been stung by a bee as a small child, and Desire never regretted throwing away the protective amulet.

Airie lifted her head. "Were you afraid of me?"

"Not for an instant," Desire was able to declare in complete honesty. She had never been afraid for herself, or for anyone else. Any fear was all for Airie.

Airie was quiet for quite some time then, gazing out toward the west. Miles beyond the moonlit mountain, visible from the temple in daylight, the flatland settlements served as reminders that there were other people in the world. On calm nights settlement lights could be seen, but on this night a west wind blew, and a sandstorm swallowed the world. Windows would be shuttered tight against it, and against demons.

Here on the mountain, though, demons were not a concern. Despite the fire that had forced the goddesses to flee, the mountain remained forbidden to them.

Airie pointed into the darkness. "What's beyond the flatlands?"

This was a game they had played for years, with both of them making up the most ridiculous stories about the world around them, but Desire sensed that tonight it was not a game Airie played.

"You've studied your maps. The biggest settlement is Freetown. To the west of it lie the Borderlands, near the end of the world. To the north are the gold mines and mountains of the Godseekers. To the south lies the sea. We live in the east."

"And the boundaries surround them all." Airie's lovely face, normally all smiles, was unusually pensive. "The world is a very small place."

"Only what we know of it today. Before the immortals it was much larger, and given time, it will be again." Desire did not doubt that, but it was difficult to explain to Airie when she had never traveled beyond the mountain, nor studied the buried ruins of a very different civilization from the one she lived in.

"What brought them here?" Airie shifted to look at Desire as she asked the question. "If they're immortal, they have no need for a physical world to live in."

Desire did not like discussing this subject with Airie. She did not want her choosing sides between her two birth parents. She had tried hard over the years not to influence her with natural mortal prejudice. But Airie deserved at least some of the truth, and she would not deny it to her. Not as long as it did her no harm.

"Time," Desire said simply. "To the immortals it has no meaning, and the knowledge it can run out makes everything they experience within it that much more exciting." She paused, weighing her next words with even more care. "For the goddesses," she continued, "this world also provided a chance to escape. They came first, a dozen of them, a long time ago. They traveled the old world in its entirety, bringing life and prosperity with them, and it brought them great pleasure in return. Then the demons arrived, numbering in the thousands, to scour the world with demon fire in their hunt for the goddesses. Mortals tried to protect the goddesses from them, and fought back with fire of their own. Before they fell, they decreased demon numbers to the hundred or so that we know of today."

Airie did not look satisfied. "Demons make no secret of the fact that they hate mortal men, so why would they choose to remain?"

"They have no choice," Desire replied. "They follow the goddesses, and the goddesses, stronger against a hundred than a thousand, built the boundaries beyond which no demon can cross, confining them to the desert. No one knows what exists beyond those boundaries anymore, or if anything of the old world's past life remains. All we have of it in the new world are ruins."

Desire believed people were stronger and more resilient than the immortals gave them credit for. Someday, curiosity was going to win out over fear of the unknown, and those boundaries would fall.

Pensiveness touched Airie's tone. "If the goddesses protected mortals from demons, why did they abandon the world to them?"

This part was too close to Airie's story for Desire to be truly comfortable. "The immortals have always been at war," she said. "The goddesses did the best they could, but were too few in number. They came here to escape demons, and they left to escape them again."

Airie tipped her head to the side, still deep in thought. "I often dream of the desert, even though I have never seen it. It's a vast place filled with heat and sand, and holds the most beautiful sculptures carved from the earth." Desire caught her breath at the unexpected and unwelcome revelation that Airie had not outgrown her childhood dreams. Then she shifted their conversation yet again. "Do the goddesses mind me being here? In their temple?"

"You are my daughter," Desire said simply, evading the true question. "They watch over us both. Your talent for healing comes from them."

Airie plucked a slender blade of dew-slickened grass, twisting it around her fingers. "Tell me about my father."

This was the one topic Desire had never openly discussed with her. Always, when asked, she had told Airie that she'd been created out of love, which was all that mattered. That answer had satisfied her in the past.

But not tonight.

"I have a right to know," Airie said.

"But why do you want to know now?" Desire asked. Suddenly, she had a lot of questions she knew she should have asked Airie sooner. "What has happened to make you so interested?"

"Nothing," Airie replied, and Desire let it drop, but only because they both had secrets they did not want to share.

Sooner or later, however, they both would need answers. Desire intended to have hers. Ill health aside, the next time Airie went to collect the offerings, she would follow.

• • •

The Demon Lord came to rest on desert sand still scorching hot though the sun had set many hours before. He balanced his weight on thickset demon legs, furled his wings between powerfully muscled shoulders, and with a grinding of bones and joints, shifted into his mortal form. Plain cotton breeches were all he wore. Most times, he wore nothing. For this meeting, he preferred the priestess's eyes on his face. He was not blind to the way she watched him.

The winds were high, which did not surprise him. On nights like this one—when the stars and the moon shone their light on the world and the west winds blew—demons called to mortal women, beckoning them into the desert for games of pleasure. Few women who had been chosen to play could resist the call.

He no longer prowled for either women or pleasure. The game had been ruined for him. He came here now only because the priestess had summoned him.

He sniffed the air and caught a faint whiff of blood, the coppery tang unmistakable. Excitement curled in the pit of his belly. He followed the scent, striding easily across the sands and past plush cacti, the desert wind tangling his hair. Nightlife, both predator and prey, scurried away at his approach.

The woman was not quite dead by the time he reached her. Her skin was yet warm to the touch, and her lips gaped in a soundless scream. Long, sand-clumped fair hair, damp with sweat, pooled beneath her head.

She'd been pretty once, which did not surprise him. Demons hunted only the best. Now, however, swelling distorted her face and limbs, her distended belly ripped open wide.

The smell of fresh blood ignited a reaction in the Demon Lord that at one time, he might not have been able to resist. Time, however, had affected him in many ways that immortality had not. He had learned to control the strongest of his urges.

He formed a talon from one fingernail and slit her throat to end her suffering. The talon retracted.

The true cause of her death lay next to her, panting heavily and blinking owlish eyes. Its bulbous head, too large for a long, ungainly neck, lolled to one side. Wet wings glistened in the pale moonlight, curling and uncurling with each labored breath, its clawed fingers and toes moving in unison. It lapped greedily at its mother's blood. He did not bother to resume his demon form. It was not necessary, not with a newborn, although he did not underestimate it. Even now, mere minutes old, it held the potential to cause serious harm— and spawn were as likely to turn on their demon fathers as they were their unfortunate mothers.

He planted a slim, bare foot on the squirming body and, reaching down, ripped the head from the spawn's scrawny neck before it could bite or scratch him. The blue-green light of demon death rising from its body was fainter than that of a true demon, but evident nonetheless.

Immortals did not die the same way mortals did, not even a monstrosity such as this.

"Nasty business," a voice laden with distaste said from behind him.

The Demon Lord tossed the head aside and wiped his hands on the hem of the dead mother's tattered dress. "Nastier if it had lived. Demons seek their promised mates. Reproduction is sometimes an unfortunate result of an unsuccessful hunt." He faced her. "You summoned me. Have you learned anything?"

The priestess, Mamna, stayed well back, her hand covering her nose to filter the stench. Spawn smelled worse dead than alive.

"Nothing new. I've hired someone to bring her in."

The Demon Lord stilled, instantly wary. "Who?"

She hesitated too long before responding. "The Demon Slayer."

Anger built deep inside him, and he knew his eyes had flared with demon fire. The glow glittered off wind-polished particles of sand and shot red shards of light into the night. "You hired the Demon Slayer to do demon work?"

Mamna stood her ground beneath the heat of his gaze as

it scorched her homely face. The goddesses had not chosen their handmaids for their beauty. If anything, the handmaids had been chosen to highlight the beauty of the goddesses. But the handicap made the priestesses safe to wander on such nights, when no other mortal woman should dare.

Mamna was safer than most, although not because of her looks. His fingers curled at his sides. If anything should happen to the protective amulet she wore, she had cause for concern. Their uneasy alliance would be finished.

The existence of that amulet, however, was a secret they both kept for now, and for their own reasons. They knew far too much of each other, and neither wished for their weaknesses to be exposed.

"The Slayer has proven himself to be more than capable of besting a demon," she was saying, "and even though the thief might wear the form of a woman, she's still a spawn."

The fire in his eyes cooled at the priestess's words. She was right. There would be a certain advantage in having the Slayer involved if the little thief should get out of hand. But if she did get out of hand and the Slayer was forced to kill her, the Demon Lord might never know for certain if she were his.

He needed to know. He needed to know if she was the reason demons could no longer abandon this world and return to the heart of the universe, and to immortality. But more than that, he needed to know if she had been born to the one who had betrayed him.

Mamna claimed the spawn on the mountain was that of a priestess who had survived the fire. She said the goddesses had manipulated the spawn's birth, and she had never been told for what purpose. She was the one who speculated that a spawn in mortal form might be the key to why demons remained trapped in the mortal world.

He did not trust Mamna. She hated the goddesses with the same passion he did himself, and if she thought this thief could be used against them in some manner, not even fear of him would stop her. By leaving Freetown under her control for all these years he had bought Mamna's fragile loyalty, but she had her own scores to settle.

He would take no chances. "Spawn are mine," he reminded her. "She is to be turned over to me."

"And she will be." The ugly little priestess did not flinch. She knew better than to show fear to a demon.

"Very well," he said, "but make no mistake. I want her alive."

Assuming his demon form once more, he set free his wings. They billowed like sails, catching and filling, lifting him into the starry sky. He headed for his desert home, away from the unfortunate mortal mother who had once been lovely enough to catch the interest of a demon but was now nothing more than food for scavengers.

Mortal women could be exceedingly beautiful, the Demon Lord conceded. He glided on a bank of warm air. But it was fleeting, and nothing when compared to the light and essence of an immortal goddess.

One in particular.

His memory filled with the sight of her walking across the warm desert sands toward him that final evening, a smile lighting her golden face, her translucent white gown outlining the graceful curves of her body. Light had shone from her pores, and he had known at once she was meant to be his.

The memory brought him no joy. The smile and body he'd found so irresistible had masked treachery. She had fought her battle armed with the weapons she had known would fell him, and the victory had been well and truly hers.

In the end, she had proven stronger than he. All he could do now was destroy everything she had once cherished, and hopefully, regain freedom for what remained of his followers.

CHAPTER THREE

"What in the demons' land would possess you to use such a mount?" Blade roared. He leaped awkwardly out of range of a sticky, razor-sharp tongue. His hat landed in the dust.

Hunter swung his saddle onto the squat-legged sand swift's back. "Relax. Sally's already eaten. She's testing you."

"Testing or tasting?" Blade grumbled. He kept a wary eye on the lizard-like creature and stooped to retrieve his hat.

Hunter drew the saddle cinch tight. He understood Blade's suspicion. If not properly tamed, sand swifts were known to eat their riders, but Hunter had been raised in the farming region of the Borderlands. He knew how to break a sand swift, and once they'd been broken, they were fiercely loyal and protective. He never had to worry about Freetown's murderers and thieves when he left Sally tethered at the mouth of the canyon to watch over him.

Besides, adult sand swifts were no real threat. Juveniles were another matter. They lived in these canyons, hiding from the heat among the rocks and the shrubs, and were continuously hungry because of their rapid growth rate. They were no bigger than Hunter's fist, and their tongues contained a paralyzing protective property that adults of the species no longer required. They stunned their prey and then fed on them at leisure.

Hunter fastened down the last of his belongings and tested the straps. "Did you come out here to make fun of my mount?" he asked. He patted Sally's scaly neck. "Because I have a thief to catch and I'd like to get started before the sun gets too high."

The mountain beckoned him. He'd never been there, had never felt the urge before, although it loomed on the horizon, designed by the goddesses to be a constant reminder of their presence to mortals and demons alike. Probably not their smartest idea, given what the demons had done to it. And to them.

"I came to tell you I took a closer look at the money the assassin used to pay for his drink."

Blade held something out and Hunter took it, turning the small coin over in his fingers.

At first glance it was nothing special—a thin gold coin, unrefined and common, with a few tiny threads of impurities. On closer inspection, however, the gold had an odd, fiery cast to it.

"It's from the gold mines of the north," Blade said.

The north was the land of the Godseekers, the goddesses' favorites, and it was unusual for one of their assassins to be so far from home. Demons made certain any mortals who left the north did not do so through their territory.

Godseekers believed the Demon Slayer would help bring salvation to the world. Hunter believed they were all crazy.

He tossed the coin back into his friend's outstretched palm. "Godseekers have never tried to kill me before, although I must say, it's a nice change. I never much cared for being worshipped."

"Don't laugh," Blade said.

Hunter slammed his hat onto his head. "I'm not laughing."

• • •

A week later, and many miles from Freetown, Hunter still was not laughing.

Here he was, approaching a sacred mountain, hunting a woman on behalf of the very creatures he hated more than anything else in the world. He did not believe Mamna's claim that the woman had demon blood, although part of him hoped it was true. Then he could hand her to Mamna with an easy conscience, and maybe this knot in his stomach, the one that said he'd finally gotten into something over his head, might go away.

The sand swift lashed out with its tongue and caught a saucy graybird that ventured too close, methodically grinding it to pulp before swallowing. A ripple trickled down the length of its body that Hunter could feel beneath his thighs.

"Why a bird?" he asked, patting its scaly hide. "You aren't fussy. If you have to snack, why not on something that nobody likes?"

Once Hunter crossed the river that signaled the true end of the desert region, the land turned greener, with rolling foothills and grand trees. Here and there, thrusting through fields of long grass and overgrown brush, poked the blackened stone-and-mortar remains of burned-out settlements.

The last outpost he passed was nothing unusual, no more than a place for the poor and the greedy to congregate and moan about their lots in life.

But then came the mountain...

Sunshine saturated the surrounding air, warming the sharp scent of pine stinging his nostrils. Hunter breathed it deep into his lungs, and for the first time in many years, was stricken with a wave of homesickness. He had grown up on a ranch at the edge of the desert, and it was not the smell of the mountain that struck him so much as the freshness of it, and the peacefulness.

He had been a small boy when the demons set fire to the goddesses' mountain, but to this day he remembered the odd, greenish glow of the sky and the white fall of ash that had rained throughout all the lands for days.

The devastation caused here by the fire had been replaced by new forest growth, and while not as glorious as it once must have been, the mountain was recovering.

He rode up a narrow path that he guessed led to the temple. The path skirted a small lake cut from the rock, its waters clear and deep.

Movement on the other side of the path caught the sand swift's attention. Its broad head swung around, nearly unseating Hunter. He grabbed at the reins and slid from the saddle, putting the beast between him and whatever had distracted it, his free hand dropping to his six-shooter. He swore at his own inattention. Twice now, he had been taken off guard.

He was getting too old for this business.

He scanned the scarred rocks and trees, searching for what the sand swift had seen, and caught a flash of long black hair and a filmy white sleeve buried in the dappled shadows beneath a tangle of brush.

"I know you're there," he called out. "Show yourself."

The bushes rustled. "I need help," a woman said. "I've injured my leg."

Hunter, who'd bested demons in battle, was not about to fall victim to such an obvious ploy. If this was the thief he was hunting, it amazed him she had not been caught long before now.

The sand swift, however, was not showing any undue signs of alarm. When agitated, its tongue flicked whiplike back and forth, a warning for all to stand clear. Its mouth remained closed and its color stayed a steady greenish brown, not changing to the vivid purple signifying danger. His amulet, too, lay silent next to his skin.

Hunter relaxed, loosening his grip on his weapon but not on the reins. "I don't help thieves," he said.

"I'm no thief!" Indignation quivered in the feminine voice.

The bushes parted and her head poked through, and Hunter could not help but stare.

She had the face of a goddess, with smooth, golden skin and full lips a deep shade of ripe-apple red. Thick black hair absorbed and reflected the light. Her eyes, dark as a moonless night, gazed up at him in reproach for his lack of chivalry.

If this was his thief, she was not at all what he had expected. Or been led to believe.

Hunter quickly collected himself. He had seven—six now, he corrected the thought—beautiful sisters, and he was not easily swayed by a lovely face. Even though he had not seen them in a number of years, he remembered this feminine trick quite well. They played most men for fools.

That didn't mean a man could not enjoy being made a fool of every once in a while. He had loved his sisters. He liked women in general. But they were far from the fragile creatures they sometimes portrayed.

"I need help," the woman repeated.

Here was the test. "You have another leg, I assume, and two arms. Come out where I can see you first."

Her glossy hair hung in curls to her hips, he saw when she

emerged upright from the bushes. She favored her right leg, although it was hidden beneath her long skirt so he could not see an injury. He noticed no weapon, which meant nothing. The blouse and skirt could hide any number of interesting but dangerous things.

She dropped to the ground, drawing her knee to her chest and rubbing her ankle.

Hunter hesitated. She did not appear badly hurt, and that made him more suspicious. On the other hand, if she posed a real threat to Hunter, Sally would have indicated so by now.

Although granted, a sand swift's interpretation of a threat and Hunter's could be two vastly different things.

He dismounted, tossed the reins over the sand swift's neck, and walked toward her.

She bore an air of innocence difficult for most women in this day and age to feign. Even Blade's ladies, although lovely and kind, had faces filled with too great an understanding of a harsh world.

This woman's eyes contained not even the slightest hint of fear. She couldn't possibly be the thief. Not with this guileless, trusting demeanor. For an instant, he had an ugly vision of what it would mean to turn a woman this young and lovely over to Mamna, and by default to the demons, and it was not nice.

A memory of his sister's swollen belly, and the fear and pain etched on her dead face, also arose. Miriam might have given her innocence willingly to the demon she had professed to love, but their relationship had ended badly for her.

It had ended badly for the demon, too. Hunter had made certain of that.

He hesitated, looked at the sand swift standing calmly nearby, and then opted to give the woman the benefit of the doubt. "Where does it hurt?"

He crouched down beside her, eyes shifting to her ankle, and that brief opening was all she needed. The heel of her palm came up with lightning speed, connecting with the bridge of his nose. His head flew back and red stars burst from the blackness behind his eyes.

Acting on instinct alone, he rolled to the side and shot to his feet. He wiped his nose with the back of his hand, surprised to find she hadn't drawn blood, and equally certain she had held back. The blow had been well aimed.

She was on her feet now too, no longer favoring her leg. She was tall, he noted. Almost as tall as he was, but with the fine-boned delicateness of a woman, making the power behind the controlled blow she had delivered all the more surprising.

So much for guileless and trusting eyes.

He was more entertained than angry. He could accept that he had been played for a fool. She was good, he granted her that, and her restraint said she had not tried to kill him.

"I don't want to hurt you," she said to him. "All I want are your packs."

The pain behind his eyes ebbed to a dull, throbbing ache.

"And if I don't give them to you?" he asked, curious as to how far she would take this.

Faster than he'd imagined possible, one of her booted feet caught him high in the ribs, toppling him to the ground. His hip landed on his six-shooter, and he forgot the pain in his head in favor of new ones.

She walked to the sand swift and worked at the fastenings that secured his belongings to the saddle. The indifferent sand swift showed not the faintest trace of agitation or aggressiveness toward her.

So much for loyalty and protection, too.

Much of his entertainment from the situation vanished. So did his good nature. If she wished to be treated like a woman, she should act more like one.

He went in low, intending to hit her in the center of her chest with his shoulder to knock her down.

She was quick — but so was he. He grabbed her arm as she tried to sidestep, hooking her feet from underneath her with his ankle. With a twist of his upper body, he hauled her off-balance, rolled her over his throbbing hip, and hurled her into the deep waters of the small lake at the side of the path.

The thief came up gasping, her hair streaming down her face, her wet blouse transparent. Hunter took the time to enjoy her appearance, and let her know he did, while rubbing his ribs where she had kicked him. His hip, he suspected, was already blue.

Enough was enough. Now that they'd both had their fun, he had to decide what to do about her.

Wincing a little, he extended a hand to help haul her from the water. He braced himself, fully prepared for her to try and pull him in too, but he was not prepared for her strength even though he'd had a healthy sampling of it already.

He shot headfirst into the lake.

He got his feet beneath him and surged to the surface, flipping his hair from his eyes. His hat floated nearby. It was not a gentlemanly thing to do, but this was no lady. He gave her a hard push, sending her into deeper water. Then he grabbed a handful of her wet hair, and wrapping it around his wrist, hauled her head under water.

Her arms flailed, but she didn't strike hard enough to bruise. He collected his hat and settled it, dripping, back in place.

A few bubbles drifted up, then a few more. Hunter considered releasing her. Although Mamna hadn't specified alive—that was an assumption—and his ribs and hip hurt like hell, he did not really want her dead. Being a thief did not make her spawn. Everyone needed to eat. But he hated wet boots.

He counted to ten.

Suddenly, the temperature of the water began to rise. Then the surface of the water boiled, stinging his skin through his pants. He dropped his hold on her hair and paddled a few paces backward.

She burst from the water, sleek black hair plastered to her cheeks and breasts, anger crackling like a halo around her. He did not have a chance to enjoy it this time. The flames that shot from her eyes had him floundering for shore.

As did the amulet around his neck sputtering unexpectedly to life.

• • •

The woman who had been brought before Mamna for judgment today was especially lovely. For that alone Mamna would have condemned her to death.

But this woman had made condemning her particularly easy. She had arrived through the slave trade, destined for one of the remote mining areas, and was well aware of her worth on the market. She had spoken ill of the priestesses, and that was enough.

The amulet hidden beneath Mamna's clothing throbbed. Only the Demon Lord knew she possessed it, and even he did not know the source of its strength. If he did, he would kill her.

"Clear the circle," she commanded.

The guards stiffened, understanding what she intended to do a few beats ahead of the crowd, then hastened to do as directed.

Around the dais, a shallow trough had been carved from the

baked desert earth and lined with tile to hold water. Four points had been marked inside the circular trough—north, south, east, and west. The dais sat to the east, the land of the goddesses, and represented their mountain. The center of the circle was the desert, the land claimed by the demons. Tied to a pole at the center stood the woman on trial, limp from both fear and the morning heat.

Buckets of water, collected from goddess rain and drawn from the temple's cistern by the priestesses, were poured into the trough. The water would help contain the demon Mamna intended to summon with her amulet, but she would need to be quick before it evaporated in the dry heat.

The crowd had gained numbers, morbid curiosity drawing people out to see what would happen next. It had been several years since Mamna's last public demon-raising. Then, the man on trial had been savaged and partially eaten before Mamna had called it off.

The woman remained stoic, defiant by her silence, although her face had lost its color. Mamna might have found it in her heart to pity her if she had not despised her so deeply. Demons could be gentle with the innocent, and Mamna had it on good authority that this one was not one of them. Traders, before bringing slaves through the desert, spoiled the women to avoid having them stolen away.

When the trough was full, the priestesses stepped back and blended as best they could with the crowd. No one could now cross the circle, not that anyone would willingly try.

Summoning a demon took more of her amulet's power than she liked. The amulet, in turn, drew from Mamna. Sweat beaded her forehead, running down the sides of her face. Her shaved scalp itched under the cap she wore to protect it from the sun. Gradually, the sounds of the crowd and the condemned woman's heavy breathing muted to a dull background noise.

She directed her thoughts through the amulet and into the boundary beyond the mortal world, then from there, into the desert territory the demons had claimed. Once inside their territory, she searched for a demon. When she found one, she called it to her.

Its vague, shadowy form appeared, then solidified. It crouched on the ground before the dais, its wings folded tight against massive shoulders. Thick red bone plate covered its body. The tips of the horns on its bent head grazed the hem of her gown, but when it straightened and stretched, its true size expanded to something formidable. The amulet grew hot against Mamna's flesh in a spontaneous defensive response, and her skin seared beneath it. She ignored the pain.

The majority of the crowd withdrew several yards, widening the distance between them and the circle. A few brave souls who had seen demons raised before stood their ground, but looked ready to bolt at the first sign of danger.

The demon blinked flaming eyes filled with hatred, then swept them over the crowd before turning its attention on her.

Confident in the control the amulet gave her, Mamna did not flinch. She had faced the Demon Lord more times than she could count. This demon paled in comparison.

Her bent fingers gripped the arms of her throne. "You stand on priestess ground. By his command, you will do as I say."

Slyness entered its eyes. It rolled its head back and forth on its shoulders, examining the silent onlookers, then it slid a long, high-arched foot toward the circular trough filled with rainwater. Shrieks of terror rippled through the crowd, and the people closest to the circle trampled those behind them in a panicked stampede to escape.

Mamna watched the crowd with contempt. Then she recognized something was wrong. The amulet around her neck had lost its heat and the normally steady throbbing became erratic.

The demon's head whipped around, sensing the sudden shift in dynamics inside the circle, and she chastised herself for her inattention. This was not the time to show either fear or a loss of control.

She gestured to the bound woman who trembled and made small, animal noises deep in her throat.

"This woman is accused of treason," Mamna said to the demon, in a hurry to end matters she wished she had not begun. "Conspiracy against the leaders of Freetown is conspiracy against the immortals. She is yours to do with as you please. What will it be, Demon?"

It stared at Mamna. She stared back, unflinching. Slow seconds passed. Then it turned to examine the bound woman, choosing an easy reward over a confrontation it might not win. The woman had slumped forward in a faint.

"I will have her," the demon decided, and the glint in its hot eyes said it would not be easy for her when it did.

Mamna released the demon, thankful that no one could see the fright now licking her insides as it vanished. The amulet regained its steady beat, although it did not seem as strong to her as before.

She addressed the guards. "Turn the traitor loose in the desert. Give her no food or water."

If the heat or wild animals did not kill her first, then the demon would return for her. No mortal would dare go to her rescue now that she had been claimed by it.

Stone-faced guards untied the woman. As she revived, her low, panicked wails built to a crescendo of shrieks.

Mamna signaled for one of her priestess attendants to help her from the throne-like chair, which was far too big for her, but another formality she was unwilling to forsake. These were symbols of all she'd attained in the years since the goddesses had abandoned her.

Her legs, unsteady from a combination of age, deformity, and unease, wobbled as she passed through the heavy curtains covering an exit behind the dais. Pausing for a moment to hide from view within the folds of fabric, and ignoring the fading screams of the condemned, she drew the amulet from her dress and ran nervous fingers over its varnished surface.

Tiny fractures marred its previously smooth finish.

She tucked it away again, anxious now for complete privacy so she could examine the full extent of the damage, and thrust the curtain aside.

Mamna dismissed the hovering attendants with a wave of her hand. She would make this walk back to her city residence alone to prove she was unafraid.

As she stepped onto the weather-beaten, oil-soaked plank sidewalk, a tall, bone-thin old man dared to approach her.

"Excuse me," he said, twisting his hat in his hands.

His clothes were of good quality, although they had seen better days. That meant he had to be from the north, a region once wealthy because of its gold mines. But now that the goddesses were gone, demons made it dangerous for anyone wanting to do business to travel there. Northerners rarely found their way to Freetown.

More and more had been cropping up of late, she had noticed. The discovery was disquieting.

This northerner wore a small, amber-colored amulet around his neck that she recognized as something the goddesses had once given out freely to favored companions. She had one herself. It gave no protection from demons but grew warm if an immortal lurked nearby, which explained how he had survived a trip through the desert.

A Godseeker as well as a northerner, then. He had that certain light in his eyes, and the presence of the goddesses clung to him. They had serviced the goddesses as little more than male whores, and believed that gave them the same privileges as priestesses. They dispensed justice in the mining regions and their assassins were the best in the world.

She hated them.

She waited for him to continue speaking, too cautious to simply dismiss him before she knew what he wanted from her.

He lowered his voice. "The goddesses are returning. We must gather an army for them."

Godseekers believed the goddesses continued to favor them, even if from a distance, but this one had just witnessed Mamna summon a demon and condemn a woman to death. Why would he think she would welcome their return?

"The goddesses are long gone from the world," she said. "You feel the lingering touch of their presence, nothing more."

It was true. Once one had been touched by the goddesses, the goddesses could never be forgotten. She knew that far too well. And because this world had been touched by them, their presence would be felt here forever.

But the goddesses themselves were gone.

The light in the old man's eyes brightened. "One goddess remains," he insisted. "She will bring the others back. They will forgive you your dealings with demons if you join her army and fight for her. You will no longer be a slave to the Demon Lord."

Mamna tapped her fingers against her thigh, alarmed by the Godseeker's words. Sweat trickled down her back, and her sensitive skin itched under the rough hrosshair gown. She did not want him to be overheard or for such stories to spread. Had he not witnessed what happened to people who plotted against her?

"I am no slave to the Demon Lord. I command demons. They do not command me. The goddesses are gone," she repeated, more sharply this time. "I witnessed their departure myself."

He stepped closer, crowding her with his greater height and invading her personal space. Mamna did not care for it. It highlighted her deformity and challenged her authority. She scowled up at him, but he was so wrapped up in his message that he did not notice her displeasure.

"One remains on the mountain," he insisted. "She challenges trespassers and collects alms for the temple."

The noise from the market faded, overwhelmed by a roaring in Mamna's ears.

"An old priestess and her bastard, thieving daughter live on the mountain." Impatience frayed her temper, and her heart was now beating so rapidly she felt off-balance, as if all the blood in her twisted body had rushed to her head.

How had the spawn survived all these years in the crumbling temple of the goddesses, she wondered for the thousandth time since learning of the thief on the mountain. Worse, how could that silly old hag have kept it?

Desire might have had an advantage over the other priestesses in that she had not been born homely—she had become scarred later in life when her looks had not mattered so much to her—but she was still an old fool with a soft heart. She always would be.

Stubbornness set the Godseeker's jaw. "She is a goddess, not a thief. She is the one who will lead the Demon Slayer against the demons. This is our chance to fight back, and to send them away. This world does not belong to them."

Nor had it belonged to the goddesses, Mamna could have argued. An immortal was an immortal, regardless of any distinction. But the Godseeker's beliefs, like those of all fanatics, would never change.

"Even if you are right, she is still only one goddess while the demons are many. If they could drive the other goddesses from the world, then this one can have no hope of standing against them alone."

"She holds the will of all the goddesses," he insisted. "They left her here to finish their war. She will lead the Slayer against the demons. Godseekers can raise an army to help her."

Mamna was truly alarmed now. If the Demon Lord heard this talk of a goddess or her army and withdrew his protection, and the people of Freetown could no longer depend on Mamna for their safety, she would have nothing.

"If the goddesses had left one of their own behind, I would have known," she said.

Suspicion backlit the zealousness in the old man's eyes. "We thought you, of all people, would welcome this news."

Welcome it? She had betrayed the goddesses to the Demon Lord. She had told him how he could drive them from the mountain, and given him the means to do so. She had carried the fire for him. She had fanned the flames. He was the reason she owned Freetown. She did not, under any circumstances, wish for the goddesses to return.

Neither did she wish for the Demon Lord to discover how she had gathered the soil from the earth where he and his goddess lover had lain together, and given it to the goddess's sisters. When they fled the world she had kept the flaming rainbow amulet they had crafted, but it had been intended for use by a goddess, not a mortal. Now it was damaged, and only an immortal could repair and invoke it again.

But with the help of the amulet, a spawn might be encouraged to try.

Mamna had thought she would enjoy seeing the Demon Lord condemn his own daughter to death. She wanted the last reminders of the goddess he had once loved wiped from existence. But now she thought the spawn might prove more valuable to her alive. At least for a while.

Her unsteadiness eased.

She considered having the Godseeker killed so he could not spread this story of a goddess and her need for an army. One lift of her finger would make it so. But she discarded the idea. Another Godseeker would take his place, and that one might not identify himself to her before irreparable damage was done in Freetown. She might be better off finding out what she could from him.

"What is your name?" she asked.

"Fly."

Interesting. Many names, particularly in the north, were not given at birth but acquired over time, and based on the perception of the individual by others.

"Well, Fly. Have you eaten yet today?" she asked.

At the shake of his head, she gathered the stiff skirt of her gown in one crooked hand and shuffled in the direction of her home, carefully keeping the round heels of her shoes from catching between the planks of the sidewalk.

"Come with me," she said over her shoulder, "and I will see to your food and lodgings."

CHAPTER FOUR

"Airie!"

The single-worded command rang from the rocky edge of the lake, whip-sharp and reproachful.

Just like that, the flames died and Airie's vision cleared. She had never heard Desire sound so angry before, and it brought her back to herself faster than anything else could ever do. Water, warm now, swirled around her as she slogged, shamefaced, to shore, her wet skirt dragging heavily behind her.

The stranger had already climbed the rocks to stand near Desire. Water ran from his clothes and over the tops of his boots. His wet denim trousers outlined his muscled thighs and buttocks when he moved. He said something to Desire that Airie could not quite believe, although she hadn't misheard. Neither had she mistaken the revulsion in his words.

The spawn. Is she yours?

She expected a denial from Desire, some sort of reproof for the insult, but the words did not seem to register with her mother at all. Instead, the elderly priestess could not take her eyes from the lightning bolt amulet around the stranger's neck.

Desire stretched out shaking fingers to touch it. "Where did you get this?" she demanded of him.

He lifted one dark-blond eyebrow, as if puzzled by her reaction. "I found it a long time ago, floating in a container in a spring."

He had gentled his voice, much as he had when he'd asked Airie where her ankle hurt. Airie was not fooled by the false gentleness. The man had no scruples whatsoever and she did not like him standing so close to her mother, who was too frail to defend herself.

And he had called her spawn. Airie would never forgive him for the slur, more so even than that he had tried to drown her. She pulled herself up the rocks to shore, hampered by the wet weight of her skirt.

"How far did it travel," Desire was whispering, "and for what purpose?" Airie was uncertain if she spoke to the stranger or herself.

"He's a trespasser on the goddesses' mountain," Airie interrupted. "He has to leave."

Desire tore her gaze away from the amulet to look at Airie. "A small token is all that is required," she replied with mild reproof. "It's not necessary to take all of his belongings from him."

Airie's face flamed, and not from temper. Her mother had seen more than the dunking she had received. She felt a twinge of shame. She had not wanted for her to find out how she collected their alms. She blamed the stranger for that as well.

She turned on him. "Leave whatever you feel you can spare, and then be on your way."

The stranger, water dripping down the sides of his lean face, met her eyes with a look that mirrored contempt and a faint surprise, as if he could not quite believe who—or what—he was seeing, but found her distasteful regardless. "Then I'll leave you my name. It's Hunter, but I'm known as the Demon Slayer."

Desire's face went gray, and she grabbed at her chest just as a tremor rocked the ground beneath their feet. She stumbled and would have fallen if the stranger, who was closest, hadn't caught her in his arms and held her steady.

Airie righted herself. The tremor passed, and with a cry of alarm she reached for Desire. "Mother!"

"This priestess is your *mother*?"

Again, faint surprise, and this time a touch of horror, filled his voice. Airie ignored him, too intent on the woman in his arms to care about him or his reactions to her, although she filed them away to contemplate later. Right now, she feared the worst.

She stroked her mother's cheek, and beneath her fingers the ashen skin warmed, but still, Desire did not stir. Always, in the past, Airie's touch had brought her some degree of physical comfort, but not this time. She knew she had to do something—anything—no matter how insignificant, to try and bring her peace at the very least. Her mother was dying.

Take her home.

Airie heard the command with great clarity, and fear for her mother brushed her heart. She could not permit this woman who had raised her, and loved her, to die here on the mountainside. She needed to get her home, to the temple, where Desire could rest and feel the presence of the goddesses. They would summon her to them when she passed on from this life.

The stranger knelt and laid Desire's frail little frame on the cold ground. At the same time, Airie rose and began to peel off her own wet clothing.

"I'll get a blanket from my pack and—" His head swung around as he noticed Airie's actions. "What are you doing?"

Airie's fingers halted on the hooks at the waistband of her skirt. "I can't carry her against my wet clothing. She'll freeze."

The stranger's neck reddened and he busied himself at his pack. "Here. Put these on." He tossed a heavy shirt and pair of coarse trousers over his shoulder in her general direction. Airie caught them. "I have a blanket for the priestess."

She changed clothes quickly, not caring if her nudity bothered him, more concerned for her mother's well-being than his sensibilities. He had stared at her long enough when he thought she was a normal woman. He was uncomfortable now only because he thought she was something less.

She slipped her arms beneath Desire's shoulders and knees and lifted her easily. Again, the stranger started, but he said nothing about her strength.

"Here," he said curtly instead, reaching to take Desire from her. "If you aren't afraid of Sally, you can ride and hold the priestess. I'll walk."

There was a veiled antagonism in his attitude that kindled Airie's temper. She did not want him near the temple. She did not want him to be there if her mother did not survive because grief was an unfamiliar emotion to Airie. The prospect of it frightened her, and she was afraid of how she might react to that fear.

"You've done enough. I can carry her myself," she said, her tone sharp.

The stranger dropped his hands to his sides, but he did not budge. "You are using my clothes and my blanket. I want them back."

"Consider them your offering and leave."

"I already gave you an offering," he said. "I gave you my name."

Hunter. The Demon Slayer.

He had no shame, and they wasted precious time by arguing. He would only follow her if she walked away, and her mother could travel in greater comfort on the back of this creature he called Sally.

Without another word, she passed her mother to him and reached out a hand to take the creature by its lead to steady it.

"Careful!"

Hunter's warning came too late. The animal's tongue flickered out to encircle her wrist. It was rough and sharp, and under normal conditions might have torn flesh. Airie, however, was not so fragile. She rapped the beast's ugly snout with her other fist, and it quickly released her. She then scrambled onto its back with less grace than she would have liked, still holding its lead.

Hunter's frown darkened. He lifted Desire up in front of Airie, and as he did so, another tremor shook the earth, harder than the first.

"That does it," Hunter said when it passed, sounding grim. He took the lead from Airie's hand. "We're getting off this mountain."

"No!" Panic seized her. "If we take my mother away from the temple, the goddesses might not be able to claim her!"

"The goddesses are gone." He jerked the beast's head around, toward the foot of the mountain.

Despite the awkwardness of her mother's limp form in her arms, Airie made a move to slide to the ground. "If the goddesses are gone, why do I feel their presence in me? Why do they speak to me?"

"That's not the goddesses you feel or hear. Sit still," he commanded.

Airie clutched her mother tighter to her chest. Already, the first claws of grief tore at her heart.

"Have you no respect for the traditions of the priestesses whatsoever?" she asked him, hating that she had to beg but willing to do so for her mother's sake. She swallowed past a painful lump in her throat and blinked back tears of desperation. "Please," she whispered. "Does it not bother you that you're making a dying woman abandon her faith at a time when she needs it the most? Have you no decency?"

He stared at her, speechless. His eyes, the deep blue of a mountain lake's clear, crystal depths, swirled with such hostility that it took her aback.

"You're a—" His eyes narrowed. "You dare speak to *me* of decency?"

He swore under his breath, but he yanked the beast's head around, and they started up the steep path toward the temple.

• • •

Hunter continued to swear to himself as they climbed.

It was the underlying touch of disbelief he felt that fed his anger, he knew, because he had not bested a spawn. If not for the intervention of the priestess, she could have torn him to shreds or drowned him in the lake. His amulet had been useless against her.

The priestess's knowledge of the amulet had caught him off guard as well, almost as much as the fact that it hadn't reacted to the spawn's presence until her true nature emerged. His ribs creaked with every breath he drew, and he winced. It should have given him her demon strength. Why had it not?

Anger was the emotion he chose to cling to. It burned to think she dared challenge his decency. *His.* He should walk away now, while he still could, and leave this…this *creature* to whatever fate the mountain dealt her.

He shut his mind's eye against the nightmare vision of his sister's mutilated body, and the grotesque parody of human life that had scrabbled in the dirt beside her remains.

Was it possible for a spawn to be female? Were the stories so completely wrong, then? Were there more spawn like this one out there in the world, masquerading as mortal women?

The thought chilled him. Demons were one thing. They had their own world to return to if and when they could be persuaded to leave this one. But a spawn born to the mortal world, and mortal in appearance...

His initial attraction to her made him feel somehow unclean. Spawn were an abomination, tolerated in no world. He wondered what the Demon Lord would do to her before he killed her, because kill her he would. He did not permit spawn to live, any more than a mortal who stumbled upon one would.

If only she did not look like a woman, or behave as though she loved the priestess.

The path to the temple was easy enough for Hunter to follow, even without direction. They crested a rise and there it was—the gleaming white stones of its entrance marred by the scars of demon fire, despite time's obvious efforts to scrub them.

The entrance was open.

He moved to take the priestess from the spawn's arms, but the spawn slid easily from the sand swift's back and leaped lightly to the ground. She brushed past him and carried the old woman into the temple.

Hunter had never seen the inside of a temple before. The few he knew of were closed to outsiders, particularly men, so it surprised him that no complaint was made when he crossed the threshold behind her.

Then again, he could be no more of an intrusion than a spawn.

Light gleamed from the ceiling of the temple's main room,

brightening in response to the spawn's command. A fire that had no discernible source of fuel burned in a grating. A low settee faced the fire. The spawn lowered the priestess to its cushions.

The priestess was awake.

"Airie, fetch me my pendant," the old woman murmured, her voice scratchy and filled with pain, and the spawn rose to obey.

Hunter, standing close, caught the fresh scent of flowers in the spawn's damp hair. The scent disturbed him even more than her presence. Flowers, to him, were a symbol of all that remained pure in the world, and were out of place on a demon.

His head ached as he watched the spawn leave the room, unable to help it. She was beautiful, breathtakingly so, and he resented his natural male awareness of her. This was why so many mortal women fell victim to demons. Physically they were irresistible. Now he, too, had been touched by that allure. It was false, nothing more than bewitchment, and he'd do well to remember it.

"How do you control her?" he asked abruptly, forcing his attention back to the priestess. "You wear no special amulet for protection against her. Is it something about the temple, or the mountain itself? Have the goddesses left that much power here that they can protect you from her?"

And, if the goddesses' protection was for the priestess alone, what would happen if the priestess was dying, and the spawn was then able to roam free in the world?

"She's not a monster," the priestess replied quietly, but with gentle reproof. "She's a young woman who's been sheltered all her life, and she's afraid of what will happen to her once I'm gone."

As well she should be. Even if Hunter turned and left now, once the priestess passed on from this life it would only be a matter of time before the demons came after the spawn. When they did,

Hunter did not believe it possible that the goddesses' magic would continue to protect her.

The goddesses were gone.

"That fear alone should have been reason enough for you to destroy her when she was born," Hunter said. "There is no place in the world for her kind. What were you thinking?"

The priestess reached for the sleeve of his jacket, her grip as fragile as the rest of her, although her words were intense. "I was thinking that she was the most beautiful baby I'd ever seen and that I felt nothing but goodness in her. She was born of love, and indeed, I love her with all my heart."

The priestess had been lucky to survive a spawn's birthing. Countless other women had not been so fortunate. Countless more would not be either—not while demons wandered the earth.

He wondered if his sister had thought her spawn was born of love too, before it ripped her apart.

"You understand that the demons will kill her, don't you?" Hunter asked. "That by letting her live, you have made her death far worse?"

Pain that had nothing to do with illness crossed the priestess's face. "I'd hoped that by raising her to follow the path of the goddesses, she would be accepted for what she is. A young woman, with all the failings and graces of any other. She's kind and loving, and knows right from wrong, although she's not perfect and makes mistakes. I could not have asked for a better daughter."

"But a demon lurks inside her." He did not know why he persisted in trying to reason with her. The woman was dying, and he was not easing her journey. He should be ashamed. He was.

"*Airie* lurks inside her. She controls who she is. She sometimes loses that control, as she did today, but she's had little experience with the world beyond the mountain. As her experience grows, so will her control."

It was too late to make the priestess understand why Airie could never be allowed to leave the mountain alive, or that what he had to do, he did for both the world's benefit and also for Airie's own. If she were truly good, as the priestess believed, then he would be doing her a mercy because she could not stay isolated here on the mountain forever. He knew all about loneliness, and loneliness would eventually make her seek out other living beings. When she did, the Demon Lord would find her. Who knew what harm she might do to mortals before then?

"Take her with you."

"What?" At first, Hunter thought he had heard the priestess incorrectly.

"I've been praying for a sign from the goddesses." The old woman paused, caught her breath, and continued. "You can teach her control. You wear protection. I never needed it, but until Airie gains full control of herself in the outside world, there may be times like today when you will."

She did not know what she asked of him. If he took Airie with him, she would be passed on to the demons. It would be better for everyone involved if he killed her now. He would tell Mamna he'd had no choice in the matter, which was true.

"I'm sorry, I—" Hunter started to say that he would not make promises to a dying woman that he could not keep, but then Airie walked into the room and he could say no more.

She had changed her clothes and tied her hair into a long, heavy braid that touched her waist. She cradled a rainbow-colored stone on a golden chain in the palm of one hand. The strange overhead lighting of the temple caught the amulet's colors and shot them to the darkest corners of the room. She carried the amulet to the priestess and tried to press it into her thin fingers.

The priestess refused it. "It's yours now," she said to Airie. "Wear it always, and think of your mother often. Remember me in your prayers."

Hunter stood on the periphery of the room, uncertain what to do and feeling more of an unwanted intruder with each passing breath. Airie kissed her mother's cheek as the priestess's eyes slid shut. A short time later a dry rattle deep in the old woman's chest told him the end was near. Airie clung to her hand, holding it tight against her breast, tears streaming down her cheeks.

Hunter had seen death more times than he cared to remember. He'd experienced it first with his own sister. He had felt the gut-wrenching pain of its touch.

Never before, however, had he witnessed a raw grief such as this. Airie's was something he knew he would never forget, not so much for its intensity as its quiet dignity. It was as if she drew every emotion she felt deep within her body and held it there so it could not escape.

But it was the gentleness in the touch of a spawn for its mother that unsettled Hunter the most. He could not kill this woman and call it a mercy. Not while there was the slightest chance the priestess had been right about her.

She's kind and loving, and knows right from wrong...

He felt the jaws of a giant, invisible trap slamming shut around his neck.

He let her sit in silence for a long time, saying whatever good-byes she felt needed to be said, then placed a firm hand on her shoulder. Time was passing, and he could not forget about the earth tremors they had already experienced. This mountain was the last place he wanted to be if they began again.

Airie started at his touch, as if she had forgotten all about his presence.

"We have to go," he said. "Gather your things."

She looked up at him with dark, tragic eyes, and again he was struck by the illusion of beauty and innocence she presented. Instinct had him wanting to reach for her, to take her in his arms and offer comfort. Then his ribs twitched with pain and he remembered she was not all that innocent, no matter what her mother believed about her or how she presented herself. He called to mind an image of his sister and her torn remains, and of the monstrosity she had died giving birth to, and any pity he might have felt for Airie fled.

"I'm not going anywhere," she said. A hint of hysteria tempered her words. "I can't leave my mother."

Spawn or not, this was awkward for him, and as always when Hunter did not know what to do, he opted for plain, harsh truth. "Your mother is gone. She asked me to take you with me."

"I heard her." A shiver began in her as if she were cold, or in deep, physical pain, but then she pulled herself tight to contain it. "Don't worry. You won't need protection from me because I'm not going anywhere with you. If there's no place in the world for my *kind*, then I choose to stay here."

So she had caught his words. Hunter could not remember the last time he had felt himself blush—if ever—and the sense of being somehow in the wrong made him angry with her all over again. "You can't stay here. We'll have to make a place for you elsewhere."

When she looked at him, it was as if she saw inside him and had no liking for what she found. Coldly polite, her contempt lashed him. "Tell me, *Demon Slayer*. What are you doing here on the mountain? Are you on some sort of pilgrimage?"

He was at a loss. She was the criminal, not he. He had not thought about having to explain himself to her when he'd set out from Freetown. While he had not intended to tie her up and carry her across his saddle the way he often did when collecting bounty—past bounties had been male—some stupid part of him had assumed that since she was female, she would accompany him without resistance.

Before he could think of a believable response to her question, another tremor shook the room. He fell against her, knocking her from her chair. He managed to stay on his own feet, although with difficulty.

A second tremor, far more intense, rumbled deep beneath the temple floor, then rammed to the surface. Fine cracks shot up the walls, and the temple's odd lighting flickered and dimmed. A loud crack from beyond the open entrance sounded as if the whole mountain were splitting in two, and Sally, waiting outside, let out a frightened bellow. Hunter knew he had only a few seconds before the animal bolted, with or without him.

He grabbed Airie's hand and jerked her along behind him as he ran from the temple to the sand swift, adrenaline lending him enough added strength to override her protests. He hoisted her into the saddle and scrambled up after her.

The temple collapsed. A slide of boulders, dirt, and debris buried its entrance.

"My *mother*!" she cried.

Hunter did not waste time contemplating how they had been mere seconds from joining the dead priestess in her entombment, or the agony in Airie's voice. That would come later. Instead, he gave the sand swift its head.

The ground shook as they hurtled down the narrow path, packs bouncing and swaying.

He intended for them to make it off the mountain before it fell beneath them.

CHAPTER FIVE

The Demon Lord found the desert to his liking for several reasons, not the least of which was that it served as a natural barrier against mortal men.

Neither could demons bear the touch of rain, the gift from the goddesses to the mortal world. It burned like acid on demon flesh and bound them to the desert, where it rarely fell.

Demons were also solitary, and enforced confinement in any great number created conflict among them. Only when necessary did the Demon Lord summon them together in the cavern he had carved into the red desert cliffs as protection from the searing light of day.

He had summoned them now, and as he looked out on them, was reminded how pitiful their remaining numbers were. He had once drawn his strength from tens of thousands, enough to scorch this entire world with demon fire.

The stone platform on which he sat placed him well above the restless crowd. He rolled his shoulders. Prolonged periods in mortal form created discomfort, but overall, it was one better suited to this world than any other.

Mortality fascinated demon and goddess alike. Mortal existence was governed by the passage of time, and natural instinct encouraged the seeking of its fleeting physical pleasures. Assuming mortal forms provided access to pleasures demons had never before experienced.

Time, however, had begun to affect demons in other, less pleasurable ways. The Demon Lord held up one hand and examined it by the light of the torches. The flesh over the knuckles had stretched and slightly puckered through time. His hair, once black as onyx, now bore a few threads of silver. Quite often, after prolonged periods of inactivity, his joints stiffened and even ached.

Many, although not all, of those gathered around him were faring no better. The reality was, the Demon Lord found himself at the head of an aging army. Time had become the goddesses' most effective weapon against them, and he had to find a way for them to escape before it was too late.

If this spawn was the key to why they were trapped, as Mamna suggested, then there could be others like her too, and that was not to be tolerated. He wanted very much to know how a demon spawn could have survived all these years in the temple of the goddesses. And how a spawn came to be female.

He rose to his feet and stepped to the front of the platform. The horde below him gradually quieted. When they were silent and all he could hear was the sputtering flames of the torches, he spoke.

"The mating with mortal women ends now."

An angry murmur began at the back of the room and quickly spread throughout. One of the demons who had chosen to keep his natural form for this gathering nudged his way forward through the crowd.

Firelight glanced off bone-plated red skin as thick as a sand swift's hide. Ridges lined a curved spine. Two short, sharp-pointed horns sprang from the sides of a broad forehead. His name was Be'el, and in his demon form even the bravest among them thought twice before accepting his challenge.

Yet in his mortal form, women found him irresistible. Countless spawn had borne Be'el's telltale markings.

"We followed the goddesses to this world for the promise of its pleasures," Be'el said. "We fought for them. Now you wish to deny them to us?"

The Demon Lord had expected opposition, and from whom it would come, and he had prepared for it. He did not shift to his demon form, knowing it would insult and enrage Be'el that he did not. An added advantage was that in his mortal form he did not succumb easily to bloodlust, and he needed to keep a cool head.

He rolled his head from side to side, lifting his shoulders and swinging his arms in anticipation. "We came here to bring the goddesses to their knees before us."

"And we did."

There was a rumble of agreement. The Demon Lord waited for it to die down. "No. They ran from us. And now they are free to roam the universe while we are stranded here, trapped in time."

"Time." Be'el spat on the ground. "Time is nothing to us. If not for you we could rule this world, and all its pleasures would be ours for the taking."

"For how long?" the Demon Lord asked. "Until the last of us grows old and dies?"

"We are immortals."

Death was not a concept easily understood by them. Neither was time. Demons did not fear either. Freedom, however, was something they valued. So was power. To claim one meant to risk losing the other, because when an immortal was killed by another immortal, the victor owned the death. The dead became slaves.

Victory, however, came with its own heavy price. The dead did not give up freedom willingly. For Be'el to challenge him, he had to believe the Demon Lord weak enough to enslave. That belief could not be allowed to spread.

"We are bound by the laws of the universe," the Demon Lord said. "While we're confined to this world, we are as subject to time as any mortal. Too many of us have been lost here already."

Be'el grinned. "Then until we die, we should be able to enjoy all time's pleasures."

Again, there was a rumble of agreement. Louder, this time. Soon the crowd would grow completely out of control.

"Clear the floor," the Demon Lord commanded, and the rumble became a roar of eager excitement.

Demons emptied the area in front of the platform, pushing back to the far walls of the cavern. The Demon Lord leaped to the smooth rock ground. Many of the spectators scrambled to the platform for a better view of the fight to come.

The Demon Lord beckoned with cupped fingers for Be'el to approach him, and Be'el stepped into the clearing. He did not waste time, instead shooting out one massive, fisted hand in a roundhouse blow aimed at the Demon Lord's temple.

The Demon Lord's mortal form was lighter and more agile, and used the thin desert air with greater efficiency. He easily dodged the first blow, and the next, dancing around the floor on the balls of his feet and making Be'el chase him. Be'el roared with rage and frustration.

The onlookers, too, did not care for the Demon Lord's tactics.

Their discontent forced him to present one shoulder and absorb the next ham-fisted blow. He swallowed the pain, remaining upright with difficulty. A mortal form was not built for this type of abuse, but he needed to remind the others why he was Lord.

He commanded demon fire, but he did not do so on his strength alone. When he'd burned the goddesses' mountain, he had summoned it through the others.

This time, he wanted only enough fire to remind the others of who he was, and why. So he drew it through Be'el, not the others, forming a ball of red flame between his fingers that licked up his arms and shot from his eyes. A spray of sparks danced from the ground to the cavern ceiling. He threw the ball of fire at Be'el. It caught him in the chest, ignited, and sent him staggering. Then, he aimed a kick at the demon's knee.

It was Be'el's own bulk that toppled him. Once he was down, he rolled in an attempt to extinguish the flames, but the Demon Lord did not allow them to go out until the smell of roasting meat filled the cavern.

The Demon Lord let the fire die away as he shifted into demon form. He planted a clawed foot on Be'el's smoldering chest, and bending, slammed both fists into Be'el's ears hard enough to draw blood.

Blood was what the Demon Lord wanted, and now that he had drawn a little, he wanted more.

Be'el, however, was far from defeated, and age had slowed the Demon Lord more than he wanted the others to see. Be'el's feet caught him from below, lifting and tossing him to the side. The Demon Lord rolled as he landed, waited for Be'el to follow through with the attack, then grappled him into a headlock.

One of Be'el's claws scored a tear down his arm, and the

combination of fiery pain and the smell of his own blood made the Demon Lord lose the last of his control. He bit into Be'el's shoulder, cracking through protective plating and tearing the flesh from the bone.

The other demon howled in pain and anger. Demons, however, did not show fear.

Blood dripped from the Demon Lord's chin as he swallowed the mouthful of hot flesh. He crammed the claws of one hand into the wound and wrenched until the exposed bone popped free from Be'el's shoulder.

Be'el panted, his agony evident, but he did not cede.

The Demon Lord had to decide now if he would kill him, because this would be a fierce death for him to own. The more of them he possessed, the greater the risk they might someday manage to turn on him. Even in death they did not serve willingly. It was why demons did not fight demons.

But it was what made him Lord. If he did not kill Be'el, the others would not learn the lesson he'd intended to impart.

He had an arm wrapped around Be'el's neck. With a jerk of his elbow, he snapped it.

The cheers of the onlookers echoed throughout the cavern, bringing him back to the moment, and he tossed Be'el's limp body aside for the others to finish.

The blue-green haze of the dead demon's soul settled over him, slowly seeping under his skin to join the others already in his possession.

Breathing heavily, he shifted back to mortal form.

Two of his supporters had moved in to stand between him and the masses now that the fight was over. He had them kneel so he could stand on their shoulders, and they raised him tall above the rioting crowd. The slight amount of his own drawn blood paled to insignificance when compared to the spreading pool of Be'el's and the stench of cooked meat, but drawn blood meant there would be no holding the demons back this night.

He did not want them turning on one another. Their numbers were few enough. Let them turn on those the goddesses had favored instead. Let the demons destroy everything the goddesses had loved, and leave nothing for them to return to once the demons were gone.

"There will be no more mating with mortal women," the Demon Lord repeated, shouting over the crazed cacophony. He lifted a fist against their displeasure. "But do what you will with the men."

With that, he released them into the night to prey on those mortals who had not heeded the warning of the rising west wind.

The Demon Lord, however, did not follow them.

He abandoned the now-empty cavern to wander the cooling sands of the desert, and to allow the cut on his arm to heal. The winds cleared his head.

When he'd first come to this world, he had found the west wind as irresistible as the others did. He too had thought mortal women the most beautiful creatures in the universe.

Then he had seen a goddess in her mortal form for the first time.

The pull of the wind had been strong that night, he recalled. He had let it fill his wings and carry him far out into the night, closer than he'd ever before dared to go toward the mountain that was protected against him and his kind.

The desert and the world had still been new to him. He had reveled in the countless sensations—the sounds, the tastes, the touch—of everything around him. The universe was a complex place, and he had traveled it from beginning to end, but here, where time ruled, the senses overwhelmed him. To live was to know unimaginable joy and unutterable sorrow. The universe might be complex, but the world of time was full of extremes.

Something below him had caught his attention that night. A sparkle of starlight on water, perhaps. Or on wet, golden skin. A faint hint of her perfume. He had let the wind drop him to the sand, where he'd used his mortal form to carry him to the edge of a small oasis.

She had discarded her robe. Clad only in the moonlight and her long, fair hair, her skin shone gold against the pool's glassy black surface.

He had known her for a goddess the instant he set eyes on her. No mere mortal could be so perfect, or capture a demon's attention so completely. He had heard stories that a goddess was as irresistible to mortal men as demons were to mortal women, and had felt nothing but contempt for such human weakness.

Seeing her, however, made him understand. She was alone, she was vulnerable…and he should take from her what was his by right. A goddess was meant to be the other half of a demon's self, promised to him at the dawn of the universe.

The goddesses, however, had refused to be claimed.

Until now.

He took a step closer, and her head lifted from the water in alarm.

"Who's there?" she demanded.

The Demon Lord brushed through a small stand of cottonwood and without a word, entered the clearing.

Her eyes grew wide. "You're a demon."

"And you're a goddess." He let his desire smolder for her to see. The west wind had called to him for a reason this particular night. Here, at last, was the one he'd been promised. "Come to me. I won't

harm you."

She, too, felt the pull between them, and she hesitated like a gazelle deciding whether or not it should bolt. He moved closer, carefully, so as not to alarm her further, and reached out with one finger to caress the soft, damp curve of her cheek.

The spell shattered with that small touch.

But not, he thought bitterly, before she had captured him.

Her name was Allia, or so she had told him. To this day he did not know for certain what had drawn her into the desert on a night when the west wind blew. He did not want to believe that it was as Mamna had told him, that she had been sent by her sisters to seduce and enslave him.

He had no reason to believe Mamna spoke the truth other than that, somehow, Allia had shackled him to her in a way that he could not now escape. He dreamed of her often, and if his own kind knew how he longed for her, they would turn on him in disgust for the weakness it displayed.

Mortal life could bring great pleasure, yes. But it also brought indescribable pain. He needed his immortality back. He needed to be free again. If he could not have those things, then he wished only for the passage of time to ease this terrible sense of loss he had not been able to recover from.

The dead demons he possessed thrashed inside him, demanding he face the truth. Allia might not have been his, but he was hers. Regaining immortality meant he would feel this agony throughout eternity if he could not find her and reclaim her.

Across the giant dunes of the desert, past the playa and the mesas, the scorched mountain of the goddesses kept silent watch over the mortal world.

A faint rumbling began in the desert earth beneath his feet, and the Demon Lord stumbled back in surprise. To his utter amazement, the tip of the far-off, shadowed mountain folded inward.

Then it disappeared from the black, star-littered horizon as if it had not existed.

. . .

Airie could smell the fear of the animal beneath her.

The cracking of the earth and the crash of tumbling rocks and trees still had not abated, so she bent over the sand swift's scaly neck and held on as best she could. Unfamiliar with riding, she slid sideways. Hunter, seated behind her, wrapped his arm around her waist and tightened his grip to keep her from falling. He held the reins in his other hand, although he'd given the sand swift its head.

"The path is gone!" Hunter shouted in her ear.

Airie lifted her head to see what he meant. Fallen pine and rock choked the common path, the one used by the goddesses' faithful. It was impassible.

She pointed to her left. "This way. There's a deer path through here that I sometimes use."

Hunter jerked hard on the reins. The sand swift swung its ugly head, shifting direction too quickly, and smashed off the common path into the bushes. He fought to bring the panicked animal to a halt.

A branch slapped Airie across the face, knocking her from her seat. She landed on her back in a scratchy thicket, her skirt tangled around her knees. She looked up from her thorny bed to where the moon should have bathed the top of the mountain in its pale light. Shock numbed her. The mountain peak had imploded. There was no other way to describe it.

Hunter steadied the sand swift, brought it around to where

Airie lay, and offered her his hand. His face tensed when he looked toward the mountain.

"Don't look back!" he commanded her.

Airie took his hand and allowed him to pull her into the saddle, behind him this time, and once again they hurtled down the mountain at a speed that took her breath away.

Without warning, a chasm gaped open in front of them, cutting off their escape.

The sand swift reared on its hind legs. It twisted to the side, flipping itself over. Hunter rolled from the saddle in the opposite direction, pulling Airie with him, dragging them both clear before they could be crushed beneath the animal's considerable weight.

Airie scrambled to her feet. Panic clawed her throat raw at the terrible sound of the animal's screams.

The sand swift lay on its side, chest heaving, kicking its feet in terror and pain. A splintered pine, broken off by a falling boulder now resting a few paces from the chasm's edge, had impaled the poor animal.

Airie forgot her own fear in the face of its suffering. Ignoring the flailing, razor-sharp claws of the sand swift and the heaving earth beneath her feet, she stretched out her fingertips in an instinctive attempt to ease its pain.

Hunter lunged from his prone position to snag her skirt and stop her from getting too close to the dangerous animal, but Airie sidestepped him.

Making soothing noises deep in her throat, she placed her hand on the sand swift's belly. Immediately, its legs stopped churning and the clear lids of its eyes drooped closed.

Hunter moved to her side.

"Help me lift her free," Airie said.

He had not yet uttered a single sound. Airie paid no attention. He already thought she was a monster. What did it matter if she confirmed his opinion? She could not leave the animal to die in agony.

Between the two of them, they lifted the animal clear of the splintered and bloodied pine.

Once the sand swift was free, Airie probed the entry wound with her fingers. Nothing vital had been too damaged for her to mend, she noted with relief.

She sent warm, healing thoughts into the worst of the animal's injuries, along with her prayers. Severed muscles, torn tendons and mangled flesh knitted in response. When the worst damage was repaired, she concentrated on calming its mind.

Its trembling ceased.

Moments later, the sand swift was back on its feet, and in a rapture of affection, tried to lick at her face with its rough-edged tongue.

"Here!" Hunter said sharply, catching it in his fist before it could touch Airie's cheek.

The mountain's rumbling stopped, and a terrible stillness settled over the woods that Airie found equally frightening. She rubbed her hands over her arms, although the cold she felt did not come from the mountain air.

Something more was missing from the mountain than the usual sounds of animal life. Desolation tore at her, leaving her raw and bleeding on the inside. The presence of the goddesses was gone from her.

The passing of her mother had taken them from her too, and only an empty place in her soul remained. She was alone in a world she had been told would not want her, with a man who disliked and distrusted her. She wanted her mother, and she wanted to cry, but she would not do so again in front of a man who hated her for nothing more than being born.

Everything she owned had been abandoned in the rush of their departure. She had nothing—no clothes, no money—except for the amulet her mother had given her. She looked around. As for Hunter's possessions, only the saddle remained of the things the sand swift had carried. What wasn't smashed and useless had fallen into the newly formed crack in the earth.

"Is Sally okay for us to ride?" Hunter demanded of Airie.

Airie nodded, and they remounted.

Blackness and silence settled on the mountain. Fortunately the sand swift's night vision was as good as Airie's, and Airie knew the mountain well, although their descent was slow and frequently blocked by fallen debris. More than once they had to dismount to clear the way.

Other than to give direction to each other as they moved what they could and skirted around what they could not, she and Hunter did not speak.

• • •

Hunter had expected the scent of the sand swift's blood to drive Airie into a demon's frenzy. Instead, she had saved the creature's life.

Something about this was not right.

He wondered how a priestess, selected for service to the goddesses because of her plainness, had incited the lust of a demon. Her advanced age, ill health, and scarred face might have concealed the fact that she was beautiful in her youth, but she would already have been middle-aged by the time Airie was conceived.

Certainty had him gripping the reins tighter. He ducked his head to avoid a low branch, edging it aside so it would not strike Airie behind him. The priestess had lied to him, but about what, and for what purpose?

That Airie believed the priestess to be her mother, he did not dispute. That meant the priestess had lied to her as well.

Mamna, too, had undoubtedly lied to him.

He had no idea what to do next.

The heat from her clasped hands spread through his abdomen. When he turned his head, the fresh, feminine scent of her skin and hair engulfed him and made him ache in a way he could scarcely believe. One cheek rested on his shoulder, her weight against him suggesting she was close to sleep and implying a level of trust, however slight.

Guilt gnawed at him. He pushed it away. He was the Demon Slayer and she was part demon. If she trusted him it was because she had no one else to turn to, not because he had given her reason. He had no cause to trust her either.

Except that she saved Sally's life, his conscience rebuked him. And she loved her mother. As much as he wanted to, he could not deny that.

He could not wait to be rid of her.

They continued down the mountain in silence.

When the first fingers of dawn streaked the sky red, they came to a better-traveled path at the foot of the mountain. There, the land leveled off and the forest thinned. Hunter had avoided this path on his way to the temple, uninterested in passing through civilization.

He was interested now. What he had lost on the mountain had been necessities for travel, and he had to replace them.

"Where does this path lead?" he asked Airie, tossing the words over his shoulder.

"To a trading post." She straightened behind him. "I don't want to go there."

"Why not?" Hunter asked. Fatigue and frustration, as well as hours of awkward awareness of her pressed against him, sparked an already short temper. "Tried to sell them something you stole and got caught at it?"

"Yes."

That single syllabic response stopped him and made him wonder. What was the real reason she wanted to avoid the place? Even if it involved danger, her reason didn't matter. He had no choice. It was not safe to travel to Freetown without adequate supplies either. Settlements were few and far between, and the few there were, were heavily fortified. Walls did not keep demons out, but they did manage to keep out other mortals. Mortals on the outside meant demons did not need to bother with those inside.

"Would anyone at this trading post recognize you?" he asked, although they would have to be blind and stupid if they could not. She was unusually tall and very beautiful, and she carried herself like a goddess.

Or a demon.

She considered the question a few seconds before replying. "I don't know," she said. "I always went dressed as a boy."

"Then this time, you'll go as a woman. We won't be there long. But while we are, you're to do exactly as I tell you."

"I'd rather wait here for you." She made a move as if to slip from the saddle, but he reached back and grabbed her hip to stop her.

"I don't think so." She did not seem to understand that she was his prisoner and he could not let her out of his sight. The world had enough problems without another demon on the loose, especially one who was not at all what she seemed.

"I'm not used to riding," she insisted. "I'm tired."

The weary crack in her voice almost swayed him. Then he thought of her flaming eyes and how she had intended to rob him. While he could hardly blame her for doing what was necessary in order to survive, it made him wary of her motives.

He realized his hand was still cupping her hip, and that he had hesitated too long in responding. His next words surprised him because, although churlish and grudging, they were not what he'd intended to say. "Very well. We'll rest for a bit. But we stay together."

She dismounted stiffly, and again, he experienced a twinge of guilt. Throughout the long night she had not complained and had done her fair share in clearing their escape route.

He swung out of the saddle and turned Sally loose to forage for food in the brush at the side of the path. Airie paced, stretching her legs and saying nothing, but her gaze continually returned to the remains of the smoldering mountain.

Hunter could think of no distractions to offer. He reached into a pocket of his duster and found some hardtack, then thrust it at her. "Here," he said. "Eat something."

She stopped pacing. Her eyes, a soft, deep, feminine brown now, with no trace of flame, fixed on him. "Do I look like one?"

"Like what?" he asked, confused.

"Like a demon. I've never seen one."

"No." He slid the hardtack she ignored back into his pocket. Then, because he did not want either of them to forget what she was, he added, "At least, not right now."

Her gaze returned to the crumbled mountain. "This is the way

I always look."

He found that difficult to believe. Rumors to the contrary had spread all the way to Mamna, and he had seen the fire she contained for himself. It would be foolish to become distracted by her because eventually, her true form would emerge.

He could not claim she was trying to use the mortal one she wore to seduce him, however. Truth be told, she did not seem to like him at all. His jaw tightened. The thought of being judged by a demon and found wanting was far from an amusing one.

He did not like inconsistencies, and she was full of them. His aching ribs reminded him of her demonic strength, yet what sort of spawn cried over its mother, then healed a dying animal when common sense and self-preservation dictated it would be better to abandon it?

And what sort of man abandons a woman to demons?

He grabbed Sally's reins, unsettled.

"Break's over," he snarled. "Get back in the saddle."

Chapter Six

The Godseeker had refused to spend the night under Mamna's roof, and she had not encouraged him. He had told her, however, that more Godseekers were coming.

Some, she suspected, might already be here.

She had gotten what little information she could from him and he was of no further use to her. She had dropped a few casual remarks about the amulet the old man wore and its abilities, knowing full well that her words would spread. The value of the stone would ensure that the old man's days in Freetown were numbered. The amulet might alert him to the approach of demons, but offered little protection from mortal thieves.

She had not resolved a problem, merely delayed it, and her broken sleep that night reflected it.

She often dreamed of her time in the goddesses' temple—a collage of memories of thousands of thoughtless little kindnesses and cruelties—but there was always one particular dream that stood out above all the rest.

The goddesses, unlike their demon counterparts, were few in number, no more than a dozen, and they had grown tired of being relentlessly pursued by them. They had found peace and happiness in the mortal world, and possessed no desire to abandon it or its pleasures.

A question was raised. If mortal women touched by the goddesses became their servants, and mortal men became their slaves, what would happen if a goddess touched a demon?

A goddess might well find a demon as irresistible as he found her. Therefore, Mamna was tasked with watching over the goddess chosen to tempt the Demon Lord. It never occurred to any of them that poor, deformed, homely Mamna might not be able to resist a demon any easier than other, more beautiful mortal women.

It certainly had not occurred to Mamna. But she had fallen in love with the Demon Lord on sight, and his blindness to anyone but the chosen goddess had cut her far worse than any other slight experienced in a lifetime of humiliations. She had wanted to be treated with some of the same gentle kindness he had shown to one of her mistresses. She wanted her own chance to serve him.

Telling him of the goddess's deception had seemed the perfect opportunity.

He had been waiting for his lover in their usual place on the night Mamna finally gathered her courage to approach him. She kept her head down, her eyes on the cool, dew-dampened grass beneath her bare, misshapen feet.

"You have been betrayed," she had said.

At first, the Demon Lord had not believed her.

"Watch and see," Mamna declared. *"She will offer you a pendant, a small mountain stone of no obvious beauty or value, with all of the colors of the rainbow. She'll tell you it's a symbol of her*

love for you. She'll tell you it offers immunity against the goddesses, just as the amulet you gave her protects her from demons. But it is the same stone the goddesses give to their favored mortal men. It is meant to enslave you. It will bind you to her as surely as it binds them." Mamna held out her hand, raising her eyes to his. She had a handful of the same colored stones, some set in pendants, others as yet unpolished. *"Have you seen these before?"*

She could tell by the look on his face that he had.

Mamna withdrew to a nearby hiding place to watch what happened next. When the goddess had shown up with her offering, the Demon Lord rejected it with such violence that the protection of the amulet he had already given her was all that saved her.

The depth of his anger, however, had set the mountain on fire. Mamna had carried that demon fire onto the sacred ground for him, and the goddesses had fled before it.

All but one.

Any kindness he had shown his lover had not extended beyond that. What he had allowed his army to do to mortal men in the days that followed the departure of the goddesses still made Mamna shudder, even in her dreams.

Betraying immortals, she had discovered, was not for the timid.

Mamna never slept well after the fragments of those memories woke her in sweat-soaked terror, and tonight, when the shaking of the earth began, she was already wide awake.

The protective amulet she wore tucked beneath her nightdress remained silent, but she withdrew it for added reassurance that she was not under demon attack.

She rubbed it between her fingers. Its smoothness was gone. The fine cracks that shattered the desert varnish after she had summoned the demon that afternoon had deepened considerably.

Had it lost the last of its power?

Was that what this trembling of the earth signified?

She crawled from the soft, warm depths of her canopied bed and padded across the swaying floor. Thin shafts of moonlight beckoned to her through the slit where the two heavy brocade curtains did not quite meet. She inched the crack wider and peered outside with one eye.

Her bedroom window, crafted from cut glass and exorbitantly expensive, overlooked the manicured garden of one of the many fortified inner compounds designed to keep Freetown's wealthier inhabitants safe from thieves and murderers.

She pulled back one curtain and tried to see beyond the city's main walls to the east, where the mountain dominated the horizon, but the night was too dark.

The raised voices of people swarming in the street outside the compound reached her ears. They, too, wondered what the quaking earth signified. The last time, it meant the mountain burned and the goddesses had abandoned them.

The tremors slowly died away. Mamna watched for a long time as the crowds thinned, and eventually, the street emptied.

The earthquake might have something to do with the spawn on the mountain. It might have much to do with her damaged amulet as well. The timing was too much of a coincidence, and Mamna did not believe in coincidences.

She remained at the window for several more hours. When night shifted to morning in an explosion of sunshine, Mamna crawled into her bed to rest and think.

If the Slayer succeeded in bringing the spawn back with him, she now had a problem. She could no longer rely upon her amulet. Therefore, she had no method to control the spawn if he did succeed.

She smoothed the silk pillows. The Slayer quite possibly possessed the only remaining amulet that could be used against demons. He would not give it up willingly. That meant she either had to convince him to control the spawn for her, or she would have to take his amulet from him by force.

• • •

Hunter and Airie reached the trading post by midmorning. They rode into the main yard of a long, low, weathered building constructed of shaved logs. A creaky, sagging verandah lined with barrels ran its full length.

It was what Hunter would expect to find in a remote location once devastated by fire. The logs for its construction would have been hauled from the far side of the mountain where the fire had not been as rampant.

Here, though, on the westward face of the lower mountain region, signs of the fire remained. Fast-growing thickets of conifers had squeezed out much of the struggling hardwood in the forests, although a few saplings of the hardier varieties had persevered and thrived.

Homesteads were scattered throughout the mountains, so he had not expected to find the trading post completely abandoned. It sat well out of range of any possible landslides from the implosion and would have made a good gathering place. That it was empty indicated that people remembered those terror-filled days of the demon fires and preferred to take their chances in the desert.

A part of him was disappointed to find the trading post empty because he had expected Airie's appearance to trigger some sort of riot, and at the moment a good fight might be just the thing he needed to burn off some of the frustration he felt.

He entered the low-ceilinged building with caution, Airie behind him, making certain that it was, indeed, abandoned. Only the groan of the floorboards welcomed them.

"Take anything you think we might need," Hunter said, tossing her a sack from a pile he found beside the counter. He began to fill one of his own.

Airie caught the sack but did not move. "I have no money to pay for what I take. I left everything behind."

Hunter swept some dried meat from a hook on a rafter and dropped it into his sack. "You're a thief. This isn't a good time to develop morals."

"I am not a thief."

He stopped with his hand on a jar of preserves. "You tried to rob me."

"I asked only for what the goddesses demand from anyone who enters the mountain. You aren't exempt from that law."

He struggled to be reasonable. "Since the goddesses are gone and you aren't a priestess, I'd say that does make you a thief."

Her expression grew cold and remote. "My mother is—was—a priestess and therefore entitled to receive alms. She could no longer collect them herself. I did what had to be done."

The reference to her mother, reminding him of her loss and her reaction to it, did not improve his mood. She was a thief and a spawn. Those were the two most important things about her he needed to remember, and what silenced his conscience when he thought about her future.

"I'm not getting into a theological argument with you right now," Hunter said. "Fill that sack, and I'll leave money on the counter—although chances are good that some person other than the owner will come along and help himself to it first."

They filled both sacks and Hunter, true to his word, tossed a few coins on the counter. Airie looked at him. Hunter sighed, then placed a few more beside them.

"There. I've paid for both of us. To repay me for your share, you can tell me why you didn't want to be seen here." He wondered if she would tell him the truth.

Her cheeks turned red, and she avoided meeting his eyes. "There might have been a slight altercation with a few traders. And they might have decided to talk about it."

Hunter turned that information over carefully in his head. Wild stories of her had already reached Mamna. The fact that Airie reddened as she spoke of this particular incident suggested it had been worse than others.

But it bothered him that she could blush over it, and insist on paying for the goods they were taking, as if she really did know right from wrong. "Do I dare ask about the reason for this altercation?"

"Does a demon need one?" she threw back at him.

He grabbed one bulging sack, slung it over his shoulder, and turned away without another word.

They rode back the way they came, although as soon as they could Hunter intended to leave the common trail and find a place for them to rest. He was beyond tired. His muscles ached and his eyes scratched when he blinked. But he had no intention of being caught asleep by anyone returning to the small mountain outpost once the initial panic wore off.

They left the scarred mountain behind and entered the foothills, where the trail tended to curl around some of the more jagged hills. The forest remained thick, tapering off in the distance where the silver snake of the river and its delta divided the end of the mountain's foothills from the beginnings of the desert flatlands.

The river eventually entered one of the many canyons, where it disappeared into an underground waterway.

Hunter scanned the immediate landscape closely for any signs of those who had fled before them. The indications were there, but they told him that very few of the refugees were traveling together.

"Here," he said, pulling Sally to a halt and pointing into the forest. "See that little patch of light, way back in there? It's a clearing. We can make a shelter, and maybe get some sleep before nightfall." He preferred traveling at night when few others would dare because of the threat of demons.

They dismounted, and as he led Sally through the undergrowth, he took care to erase any traces of their passing.

Airie proved to be an able woodswoman, requiring very little direction, and building a shelter out of spruce boughs and saplings went quickly.

For Hunter, the difficulties arose once the shelter was complete. He had made it big enough for them both because he wasn't about to let her out of his sight, but how was he supposed to sleep and keep an eye on her as well?

He was not comfortable sleeping with a demon's spawn at his side, although even he had to admit that a spawn who healed animals was unlikely to pose a threat to a sleeping man. But he also knew the only reason she was with him now was because of the cracking of the mountain and their forced flight.

How, then, did he make certain she was with him when he awoke?

She did not know she was his prisoner, and he had no desire for her to find out just yet. Even though she was spawn, he could not bring himself to tie her up, or to him, which was what he would have done if she had been a man.

Airie tossed down the last armload of sharp-scented spruce boughs and made two separate beds on the floor of the shelter. Hunter unfurled the blankets.

"You aren't to leave this shelter without me," he said to her. "It's too dangerous for a woman alone. We don't know who else might be around."

She met his eyes, her response sharp and direct as if she'd read his thoughts. "It's fortunate, then, that I'm not a real woman."

"You give enough of the appearance of one for it to be a problem for you." A sense of wrongdoing on his part, which he did not like, intensified. "But by all means, do as you wish."

The boughs, when he collapsed on them, proved so comfortable that he immediately closed his eyes and decided to take his chances on Airie disappearing before he awoke. If he found her gone, he could simply track her down again.

Right now he wanted sleep more than anything.

• • •

Airie watched him sleep, her hand curled under her cheek and her arm resting on top of the prickly matting. The day had vanished far too soon, and night now rapidly approached.

He looked much younger when he was asleep. In fact, he was probably no more than five years older than she, ten at the very most.

He had darkly tanned skin, and bleached, shoulder-length hair spoke of many hours spent in the sun. His eyes, when they looked at her, were a shade of blue that could chill like winter's ice or heat with the intensity of a clear summer sky, depending on his mood. Several days' stubble, a few shades darker than his hair, covered his cheeks and chin, but did little to hide the sharp angles and planes.

She knew from the hours she had spent in the saddle with her arms wrapped around his waist that solid muscle underlay an otherwise long and lean body.

Compared to the men who frequented the trading post, she supposed Hunter was a fine and rare specimen of mortal man.

But he had called her spawn and a monster, and Airie had yet to forgive him for that. She'd wept again over the loss of her mother and her home while he slept, but now she was ready to move forward.

Grief had kept her from taking note of the route they traveled. She had not asked him where they were headed because she did not care. She had made up her mind as to what she would do, and Hunter's opinion on that wouldn't matter because she did not trust him any more than he trusted her. He had not explained what had brought him to the mountain, and she knew he had not happened there by chance.

He opened his eyes and blinked, slowly adjusting to the dim light and foreign surroundings.

Then, his eyes settled on her. She wore only her thin chemise and cotton knickers, and the length of his scrutiny told her he noticed them.

"We should grab something to eat and be on our way," he said, but he did not move.

Airie's mother had warned her constantly of the dangers of two women living alone, even under the protection of the goddesses' temple, so most of her small extended world knew her as a boy. No man had ever looked at her in a way that made her so self-conscious.

She rolled from her bedding and stretched her stiff limbs. She had no need to worry about protection from Hunter. He saw her as an abomination. Any other impression he might give was a product of her imagination, brought on by the frightening knowledge she was now all alone.

"We also need to talk about what will become of you," Hunter added, continuing to watch her with unreadable eyes, but following her line of thought.

"We don't need to talk," Airie said. "I know what I'm going to do."

"Oh?"

"I'm going to Freetown."

She had thought it through and weighed the advantages and risks. She was young and strong, and reasonably well-schooled. At least, she believed so. The priestesses had once been educators, although only to the finest and most promising girls, and while Airie had no idea if she would have been selected as a student under normal circumstances, her mother had been pleased with her efforts. She could cook, she could clean, and she could sew. She might even be able to teach. Surely she could find work to support herself. Her needs were few.

She could control her demon temper and blend in.

He raised himself to one elbow, propping his head on his hand.

"Why Freetown?" he asked.

Because it was the only town Airie knew of in spite of all that Desire had taught her. She had heard it spoken of at the trading post. It sounded big, and anonymous. She could make a place for herself there. More than anything, it allowed her to remain close to her mother.

"I have to go somewhere," she said.

There was a long stretch of silence.

"What kind of work do you think is available to you in Freetown?" he asked.

The way he posed the question made her feel ignorant, which in turn left her defensive. "I can do anything any other woman in Freetown can do."

"I don't doubt that."

Airie turned her back on him and the subtle hint of sarcasm he conveyed. His opinion of her and what she was—or wasn't—might not matter, but it stung nonetheless. The makeshift bedding rustled, and his discarded blanket landed beside her.

"Since I'm going to Freetown too, we may as well continue to travel together," he said.

The level of relief she felt at that statement surprised her. They did not like each other. They did not trust each other. She had not forgiven him for the things he had said, and neither of them felt any need to impress the other. The trip would be awkward at best.

But she would not be alone.

"Thank you," she said.

Hunter tugged on his boots. "If you want to thank me, you can try to remember two things the women in Freetown don't do. They don't light themselves on fire, and they don't get into *slight altercations* with men."

Airie reached for the overskirt she had removed before going to bed. He was so arrogant she could not resist a gibe. "Then those are two things I can teach them to do."

"Goddesses help them," Hunter muttered to the toes of his boots.

• • •

The early morning sun soon dispelled the chill of the night.

The Demon Lord wore his mortal form. Morning meant it was time for him to move underground, yet he continued to sit on his heels in the warm, sandy shade of a spiny soaptree yucca, his attention on the smoking remains of the mountain on the horizon.

As part of the exchange for his protection, Mamna had agreed to keep him informed of any unusual activity on the mountain. He considered its peak disintegrating into dust and rubble to be unusual, and had waited several days for her to send word to him of what had happened. So far, he had heard nothing.

Perhaps he was too impatient, but he did not believe so. He expected a certain degree of loyalty from his followers, and he disliked being at the mercy of a woman who had once betrayed her mistresses. He had never fully trusted Mamna because of that, and now she was becoming an even greater cause for concern.

He would send someone else to the mountain to see what had happened. He would deal with the priestess later.

The white, bell-shaped yucca flowers around the cliff's entrance bobbed on their long stems, nodding their approval.

"Agares!"

The demon was one of several who had remained behind after the fight with Be'el. He was indolent and easily bribed, and remarkably nonconfrontational for a demon.

Agares appeared at the front of the cavern, naked, also in his mortal form. Although it was easier for demons to bear the touch of the sun this way, the Demon Lord sometimes suspected wearing mortal form accelerated the ravages of time.

Agares, however, showed few of time's ill effects. His thick dark hair was untouched by gray, and his eyes were unlined.

"I'd like you to find out what has happened on the mountain," the Demon Lord said.

Shielding his eyes with his hand, Agares looked to the smoking horizon. "The top has blown off."

The Demon Lord tossed the stick aside and rose to his feet. "I meant that I want you to go there and see why."

"I know what you meant." Agares' eyes shifted to his, his expression calculating. "It's daylight. I would have to travel in mortal form. And the goddesses' protection of the mountain may as yet be unbroken. What if I can't get close enough to see?"

Asking Agares to travel in mortal form during the day meant the Demon Lord would have to grant him permission to hunt, and Freetown lay directly in his path. The agreement with Mamna would be broken, at least in part, and if Agares could not get close enough to the mountain to discover for certain what had happened, it would be broken for nothing.

Perhaps not for nothing. It was past time to renegotiate that agreement.

"Do what you must," he said to Agares. He would deal with Mamna when or if the need arose. "The Demon Slayer may be near the mountain. If he is, he may also have a woman with him. If he does, follow them. I want to know where he takes her."

"Who is this woman?" Agares asked, anticipation as well as curiosity now lighting his eyes.

The Demon Lord did not intend to reveal who she was, or what she might be. "She is from the mountain. Someone Mamna is interested in. Therefore, she is of interest to me. She may already be dead," he added. "The Slayer may be as well, if they were caught in that blast."

Agares grew more animated, no doubt at the possibilities for pleasure such freedom would give him. "If they are alive, I could kill the Slayer and bring the woman to you."

A part of him rebelled at the thought of this particular woman at the mercy of Agares, because he did not expect Agares to bring her to him untouched. Why that should matter to him was something he did not care to explore. If she were spawn, she was as good as dead. If she were not, then she was nothing to him.

The Demon Lord shrugged. "The Slayer has to lose a fight sometime. The odds say so."

The odds, however, were not in Agares' favor, and they both knew it.

Agares scowled up at the sun. "I hate traveling the desert in daylight."

"I will send someone else."

"No." Agares did not intend to pass up on this opportunity to hunt. "I will set out immediately, before the sun gets too hot."

Even in mortal form, a demon could cover considerably more ground than an ordinary man. Agares would be beyond Freetown well before noon.

• • •

Airie's decision to go to Freetown made things easier for Hunter. He did not have to force her but could travel with her as a companion.

Over the next few days, as they crossed from goddess territory into the desert, there were no signs that any of the fleeing refugees had begun to return. Hunter had not expected it. Not yet. But they would, soon enough.

He preferred to travel at night so that no one they did happen upon could get a good look at Airie. Beautiful women were a valuable commodity, and while she could, indeed, do the work any other woman did in Freetown, he doubted she knew what that work would entail. She would not be paid directly for it either. Even Blade's ladies were not. Blade gave them back the money they earned, not because any law required it of him, but because it was his choice to do so. Women had no rights. Not in Freetown, nor anywhere else.

Despite what she was, Hunter could not avoid feeling a certain amount of pity for her. She knew little of the world beyond the mountain. It was not the same one her priestess mother, sheltered in the temple for many years, had once known and taught her of. That made Airie, despite her unfortunate heritage, very much an innocent.

His grandmother had once told him that good and evil were mortal measurements that could not be solely assigned to either goddesses or demons, because the immortals were as flawed as anyone. He could picture her still, puffing on a pipe and rocking in her twig chair on the front verandah of the old log farmhouse his grandfather had built for her in their youth.

Goddess or demon, call them what you want, this world wasn't made for the immortals, she had said. *Neither belongs here. But they have yet to find a place of their own in the universe, and until they do this world will have to suffer their presence.*

Hunter was done suffering. The world was not made for immortals, and it was not made for their spawn either.

But Airie cried for her mother in her sleep, a fact that continued to disturb him. She had also healed Sally. So far, other than her eyes and an ability to boil water with them, she had not done anything that could be considered threatening or dangerous.

What if the priestess was right? What would Hunter do then?

They made their way out of the foothills in near pitch blackness with Airie sitting on Sally behind him. The press of her thighs against his and the occasional warmth of her hands low on his abdomen when she needed to stabilize herself in the saddle did not permit him to maintain a distance from her, either physically or mentally.

He was aware of every movement she made and breath she took.

The moon had not yet risen, but the sand swift was sure-footed. It was used to traveling the many arroyos and canyons of the desert.

"Stop!" Airie cried. She slid from the saddle before he or the sand swift had time to react. She ran as soon as her feet hit the ground, dashing toward what looked to Hunter in the negligible light to be a pile of discarded rags on the side of the road.

They were not rags, Hunter saw when he dismounted and followed her. A tiny hand emerged from the pile to clutch at Airie's sleeve, and his heart sank. This was not an unusual sight for him, although in the past he had always made the discovery after they were dead and there was nothing left for him to do but bury them — unwanted children, too small or sickly to sell into slavery, often abandoned to die.

This one was both small and dying. It was a boy, and a very young one, although it was possible he was so malnourished he had simply failed to thrive.

Hunter tightened the barrier he had built around his heart. Death was a far better fate for the child than the alternative.

"Leave him," Hunter ordered, deliberately harsh. "He's too close to death."

Airie stooped, scooping the frail child into her arms. The smell of him made Hunter lift his neckerchief over his nose and take a step backward, even though he'd thought he was long immune to the aroma of the unwashed. Desert travel did not lend itself to good personal hygiene practices. The child was undoubtedly ill. He reeked of it.

"I can save him," she protested, smoothing thin, dull-blond hair that appeared gray in the darkness of the night.

Hunter understood how she felt. Once upon a time, a very long time ago, he too had believed that life was meant to be preserved at all cost. Experience, however, had taught him that sometimes there was little kindness in doing so.

The child's head lolled against Airie's breast. His cheeks were hollow, speaking of slow starvation. Hunter rubbed his eyes with his thumb and forefinger because his own head had begun to ache.

"Think about what kind of life you're saving him for," he said, trying to sound compassionate even though he knew his words were not. "He's already been starved to the point of death once. If you save him, it will happen again." Or, if someone else did find him and take him in, he would end up sold into prostitution because he was too small for labor, Hunter could have added. Better the child meet death here and now, rather than damaged and disease-riddled later. Hunter took another cautious sniff of the air. If he wasn't diseased already. What if he carried contagion?

"He won't starve. I'll take care of him," Airie said.

She laid her palm against the child's cheek, and even in the night Hunter saw a warm flush begin to blossom. A sense of inevitability assailed him, but he tried to reason with her anyway. "You have yourself to worry about. How can you look after him, too?"

Her eyes, dark and determined, met his over the child's stirring form. "By doing whatever I have to," she replied with quiet resolve.

She had no idea what she was saying, or what it was she might have to do. Hunter tried again to make her see reason. "It's not up to you to decide who lives or dies."

"It's not for you to decide either," came her quick retort. "But if someone possesses the means to save a life, then there's really no decision to be made, is there?"

Being raised by a priestess had left her far too naive, and that naïveté now created all sorts of unwanted dilemmas for Hunter. If he allowed Airie to save this poor, unwanted child, what, then, would be his future after he turned Airie over to Mamna? How would the child's ultimate fate weigh on Hunter's already overburdened conscience?

His preference to walk away from an unpleasant situation rather than confront it introduced questions about himself, and what he had become, that he was reluctant to examine. Blade was right—deciding who was worth saving had done something to him.

The child coughed once, opened his eyes, and looked up at him with such innocent trust that Hunter knew he would now be saddled with two troublesome traveling companions, not one.

Airie waited in tense, pleading silence. If he said no he would have to force her to continue on without him, and that was another fight he wished to avoid.

Deep down, he did not believe he could walk away either.

It was easiest to blame her for that. "Keep him, then," Hunter said sourly. "But he's your responsibility, not mine. And the first chance you get, you're giving him a bath. He makes me scratch just looking at him."

The sand swift had been standing patiently nearby. Its tongue remained firmly in its mouth, probably because the child smelled too awful to taste.

"Thank you," Airie said with a relieved whisper. Those two simple words shamed him, which in turn stoked an already ill temper.

He was not the demon here. He did not enjoy feeling like one.

She positioned herself cross-legged on the ground, the child in her lap, and stroked his cheek while crooning soft words under her breath. Listening to her, Hunter realized she was praying.

She looked up at him. "Can I have a little water and a piece of dried bread?"

Hunter got them for her. She broke the bread into small fragments and dipped one in the tin cup, then held it to the child's lips. She was patient, repeating the steps several times until the child had swallowed enough to satisfy her. She gave him a sip of water, cradling the back of his head in her hand as she held the cup to his lips.

He was two, perhaps three, years of age, Hunter could now see, and his stomach twisted into a sickening knot. Even if he didn't turn Airie over to Mamna, the child was a burden she could ill afford and decreased her own chances of survival. He was not doing a kindness by permitting this.

He could not bring himself to do otherwise. The child's circumstances were no fault of his own.

"We need to go," he said, taking the cup from her hand and putting it back in a saddlebag.

When he turned, she was beside him. Her lips curved in a tentative smile, the first he had received from her, bright in the clear light of the rising moon. Impulsively, she kissed him. It was a light touch of her lips to his cheek, and over in an instant, but it shot an unanticipated lick of heat straight to his groin and stole any more protests he might have made.

"Thank you," she said again, her words infused with a breathless warmth that left a knot in his gut.

Before he could recover, her attention was once more on the child still in her arms, and he was forgotten.

He helped Airie remount, in front of him this time. He settled into the saddle and slipped a free arm around her waist to steady her and the child. Her skirt had slid up to bare her long legs, warm between his and impossible for him to ignore.

He jerked at the reins, even more unsettled by an unwelcome and surprising truth.

It was not thanks he wanted from her.

CHAPTER SEVEN

Blade limped around the end of the bar, wiping the counter and half listening to the conversations going on around him. The youngest of the whores took her turn waiting on tables. The gown she wore, a bold, shiny blue, was too tight at the hips and chest and exposed one long leg when she moved.

He would have to talk to Ruby about the way the girl dressed when in the saloon. He preferred to avoid trouble.

Noon was a busy time for business, more so these past few days because people were edgy about the fall of the mountain. Everyone wanted to drink. Some chose to eat. In fact, the spicy smell of Ruby's stew reminded Blade to grab a bowl before it was gone. No one wanted to discuss what the collapse of the mountain meant. Conflict between the immortals was never good.

Blade tossed the cloth beneath the counter and watched Ruby disappear upstairs with a client.

They had been friends a long time. He really should marry her and give her security. He owed her that much.

While most people remained cautious of saying anything too loud that might draw unwanted attention, a few could always be relied on for indiscretion. Blade had discovered a long time ago that being a cripple made him invisible. At one time the limp had embarrassed and humiliated him. Now it worked to his advantage, and he was not above exaggerating it. People assumed he was simple because he was disabled, so they were often indiscreet.

"Mamna isn't getting any younger," he heard someone declare. "What if the next time she raises a demon it escapes her control? What will happen to us when she's gone?"

He limped closer, careful not to appear unduly interested in the conversation.

"The Demon Slayer was seen meeting with Mamna," a second man said. "I heard he can fight ten demons at once. Maybe he plans to take her place."

Blade hoped Mamna had not heard that kind of speculation. She would not care for it, and neither would Hunter. But he, too, could not help but wonder what would happen to Freetown if Mamna were gone.

Perhaps it was time he planned for a different future than saloon keeping.

The first man spoke again. "I heard the Slayer is really a demon. That he hates them because he once challenged the Demon Lord and lost."

"If he'd lost to the Demon Lord, he'd be dead, wouldn't he?"

That was another rumor Hunter would not care for, Blade thought. Although neither of them was inclined to share any details of their past, of one thing he felt quite certain. Hunter was not a demon.

A different conversation by the fire caught Blade's attention.

Three travelers, one of them heavyset with bad skin and a loud mouth, had pulled their chairs close to the hearth as if they owned the place. Blade made a mental note to keep an even closer eye on his till. They had the look of tax collectors, technically illegal here in the city but sanctioned in the outer territories, and tax collectors were good at putting their fingers in places they did not belong. Particularly when no one would dare protest.

"I hope the mountain fell on her," said the loudest of the three. He gave an exaggerated shudder. "Monsters like that shouldn't be allowed to live."

"What monsters are you talking about?" a stranger at another table, a northerner, judging by his clothing, interrupted him to ask.

Blade had noticed an increased number of men from the north in Freetown of late. He wondered what it meant.

"There's a demon on the mountain," the loud one replied. "At least there was. She's buried under a ton of dirt and stone by now." He said the last with an air of satisfaction.

"You've made a mistake, my friend." The inquisitor turned back to the men at his own table, no longer interested in what had to be a fabrication. "Demons aren't female."

The loud one laughed, and the two men sitting with him looked uncomfortable at the turn the conversation was taking. No one liked to be called a liar, or worse, stupid. He did not think the loud one was either of those. Blade moved closer so as not to miss anything but stayed within a few steps of the shotgun he kept behind the bar.

"This demon was female," Loudmouth said. "We saw her up close." The two other men nodded, and a few more people around them shifted their chairs to pay more attention. One of the trio had a long, fading bruise down the side of his face. Another had a split lip and moved carefully, as if his back and shoulders hurt. Blade recognized damage caused by some sort of bludgeon. Demons did not use bludgeons. They had no need for them. So why would these men make up such a lie?

"How could you tell it was female?" someone asked.

"It started off in mortal form. Then its eyes glowed red and it turned into a demon. Big one. Hideous. We were lucky to make it out with our lives."

Blade noted the two companions did not nod in agreement over the description of the so-called demon. They kept their eyes down. Their loudmouthed leader was lying about at least part of his story.

Blade made a living out of reading people, and he believed they had indeed been attacked by a woman. She would need to be a strong one to inflict the damage he saw. She'd also have to have considerable fighting skills.

But why was Loudmouth making up stories about her being a demon?

"You should tell Mamna," a wide-eyed believer advised him.

Loudmouth looked smug. "Mamna already sent the Demon Slayer to finish it off. If the mountain didn't kill it, the Slayer will."

Blade did not like what he heard, or the conclusions that could be drawn from it. Hunter had gone up on that mountain well before its lid blew off. A Godseeker had tried to ambush him. And Mamna was about as trustworthy as a sunstroked goldthief snake.

The room went silent. Bringing Hunter into the conversation changed several opinions. "It must be a demon then, if the Slayer went after it. He wouldn't do any other kind of work for the priestesses. I heard he once turned down an offer of twenty gold pieces to go after a wagonload of Mamna's stained glass stolen by outlaws near the Borderlands. He said he wouldn't risk his life for anything so useless."

"Whatever he's after on the goddesses' mountain," someone declared, "it can't be a demon, male or female. No demon'd dare go near it."

A few people agreed, but even more looked uncertain.

One older man, with a wrinkled face resembling sunbaked dirt, shot a wad of chewed tobacco into a nearby spittoon. He wiped his mouth on a dust-crusted sleeve. "Something had to blow the top off that mountain."

One of the whores waiting tables swatted away a groping hand, gathered some empty plates off a table, and with a sway of her hips and swish of her skirts, carried them to the back of the saloon to the kitchen.

Blade watched her go, lost in thought.

Whatever had happened on that mountain, he did not like that Hunter had been sent into the middle of it.

• • •

The desert was far from the oceans of endless sand Airie had expected to see. There was sand—plenty of it—but also pillars of granite and basalt, and patches of shrubbery.

And in vast stretches, underneath the earth, odd ridges and patterns could be discerned that were too symmetrical to have happened by chance. They never rode too close to them, though, but skirted around.

"They're remains of settlements from another time," Hunter said when she asked what they were. "Before the demons came. Those are old rooftops you see."

"Can we look closer?" she asked. They had passed ruins in the foothills too, but these appeared enormous by comparison.

"No. They aren't safe. The ruins have caused sinkholes to form under the sand, sometimes thirty or more feet deep. If you fall in one you'll never come out."

Airie had to content herself with imagining how they once must have looked.

They had been traveling for more than a week now, and she was both excited and panic-stricken that they were nearing their destination.

She had chosen to walk so she could explore. Hunter rode, carrying the child on the saddle in front of him without complaint, a small blond head bobbing against his arm as the rolling motion of the sand swift lulled the little boy to sleep.

Hunter persisted in calling him Scratch because he claimed he made him itch. She did not bother arguing the point, even though he might equally have called him Shadow since he followed Hunter wherever he went.

He must have had a real name once, but so far, guessing at it had produced no results. She would choose a special one for him when they began their new life. To her, he was a gift from the goddesses as compensation for the loss of her home and her mother, and she loved him already. When she held him he brought a sense of peace to her heart. He should have a powerful name to reflect that.

For now, Scratch was as good a name as any. She would not think about where he might have come from, and what he might be, because she knew beyond doubt that he was not mortal. At least not entirely.

Airie found clusters of dull crystals scattered in places where the wind had worn the ground bare, and held one out for Hunter's inspection. He was unimpressed with her find.

"It's called desert rose," he said.

She stroked the brittle edges of the stone petals with her

fingertips. "It's beautiful."

He looked away. "It's a clump of gypsum that has no value."

"Other than that it's beautiful." Airie slipped it into a pocket of her skirt.

By midafternoon, Hunter had not shown any indication he planned to make camp. That meant there was no need for one, and that their journey was almost over.

Soon, they crested a rise.

"Is that Freetown?" she asked, lifting a hand to shade her eyes from the glaring sun.

Hunter grunted a *yes*.

From this distance, where she could look down on the city, she felt a certain degree of disappointment. It looked shabby, dirty, and crowded inside those fortified walls, and ridiculous when compared to the wide open, vast spaces surrounding it. Very little green touched the streets, an absence disconcerting after a lifetime living in the mountains. "What's that in the center?"

Hunter looked to where she pointed at a tall spire rising well above the surrounding buildings. "A temple."

Airie's drooping spirits lifted. "They have a temple to the goddesses?"

"This temple is to the priestesses, not the goddesses."

She did not understand. "How can priestesses have a temple?"

"Because they call it a market. But no matter what they choose to call it, it's where people go to worship them."

He was in a strange mood today, and Airie did not know what to make of it.

"I thought a city this size would have more people traveling to and from it," she said. The road leading to Freetown did not look well-traveled to her.

"It's a desert city surrounded by demons," Hunter reminded her. "Supplies are brought in from the border regions on a regular schedule, and only after careful planning. Smart people travel as part of large wagon trains."

Yet Hunter traveled alone. She wondered why, and if it were always so with him.

Instead of following the road to Freetown, Hunter turned his mount off the trail and into rougher terrain. He held a hand down to her. "You'd better ride with us the rest of the way. There are lots of little things living under rocks and bushes that don't like to be disturbed, especially during the day."

Airie stepped into the stirrup and swung onto the sand swift's back behind Hunter. She slid her arms around his waist and tickled Scratch, who rode in front, making him wriggle away from her fingers. "Where are we going?"

"My cabin."

She did not dare ask why. Instead, she rested her cheek against the back of his duster so that she shared the shade of his wide-brimmed hat. His shoulder muscles moved with a fluid rhythm as he guided the sand swift with the reins. She liked the way he smelled of desert and sun-warmed skin, and the feel of his flat stomach beneath her clasped hands.

It was easier to enjoy his company this way, when he was not watching her. She could pretend he did not resent her, or find her presence a trial.

They led the sand swift through a long crevice leading into a small, hidden canyon, where Hunter had blocked off one end to create a natural paddock. At the front of the paddock he had built a cabin beneath a rocky overhang. Fine lines of erosion ran like tears down the canyon wall's rock surface, feeding into an underground cistern used to collect rainwater and minimize evaporation. Everything was neat and tidy.

And isolated.

"Why don't you live inside the city?" she asked.

"I prefer my own company."

Airie had never spent a lot of time around people, so she did not know which she'd prefer. At the same time, she had never been completely alone. Her mother had always been with her.

She wondered what she and Scratch were supposed to do now. Hunter had made no secret of the fact that he did not like having her around.

"Thank you for everything," she said, feeling clumsy and inadequate, but eager to escape him. "We can walk to the city from here."

Hunter set Scratch on his feet and the little boy went off to play in the fine sand accumulated at the base of the canyon's rock wall.

"It's too late for that today," he said. He did not meet her eyes. "Distance can be deceptive. Freetown's a lot farther off than you think. You'll stay here for now. Help me with the packs."

He'd left them in a pile on the ground where he'd unsaddled Sally before turning her loose. He caught up Airie's small, makeshift bag and headed for the cabin, the loose back flaps of his leather duster rippling around his ankles as he strode across the flat sandy floor of the canyon.

Airie started after him.

"Why is it too late to go into the city today?" she asked, touching his arm to get him to face her. His steps slowed but did not halt.

"Because I need to make certain it's safe," he replied. "Because the gates of the city will be closing soon. And because I may have a…contact…for you, who can get you started on a new life."

Airie examined his words. Something was wrong. Hunter had been surly all morning—even more so than usual—and now acted as if he did not want to see her go.

He had never apologized for the names he had called her, or admitted to being wrong, so why would he choose to help her?

She wanted to say she had no need of his contact and could make her own arrangements, but the sight of Scratch playing in the sand stopped her from doing so. She did need Hunter's help, and that contact of his, for Scratch's sake if not her own.

"Thank you," she said.

He stopped at that, his back stiff, and whirled to face her. "You have nothing to thank me for."

He left her standing in the middle of the canyon's mouth, uncertain of what to do next and feeling utterly alone and abandoned. He did not want her thanks. She was not welcome in his home, but neither was she free to leave.

So what was she?

She played with Scratch for what remained of the afternoon, keeping him out of Hunter's way while he worked, until the wind picked up and darkness settled.

Hunter came to the door of the cabin. "Come inside."

Airie brushed at Scratch's clothes, removing as much sand from them as she could. Hunter watched her, his expression unsettling, so she turned her back to him.

"Here," he said in her ear, and Airie started. He moved very quietly. She was unused to anyone getting so close without her being aware of their approach. He nudged her aside. "You need to peel off his outer things and shake them."

The child lifted his arms obediently over his head so Hunter could remove his shirt. As he did, Hunter got a strange expression on his face.

Hunter held up a small, bright yellow box that had no openings in it that Airie could see. She did not recognize the material it was constructed from. The little boy always had an assortment of rocks and other treasures he came across hidden in his clothing, and she would set them aside for him to reclaim later in case he remembered.

"Where did he get this?" Hunter asked.

"I have no idea."

Airie held out her hand to take it from him so she could have a better look, but he pulled it out of her reach. He carried it fifty feet into the canyon to a more open space, and set it on the ground, his movements careful. He picked up a large rock, hefted it for weight, and walked back to Airie and Scratch.

"Cover your faces," he said.

He threw the rock at the yellow box. The box exploded with a loud bang, sending clumps of dirt and fragments of rock into the air to shower around them. Airie drew Scratch against her to shield his face, while Hunter wrapped his arms around them both to shelter them with his body.

When the dust settled, the box was gone. A hole, almost a foot deep and three wide, had replaced it.

Airie's heart thumped hard in her chest as she thought of what that might have done to a small child if it had gone off in his pocket. And to Hunter and her too, for that matter. "What was that?"

"It's a bomb," Hunter said, "from three or four hundred years ago. I've found similar things planted around the old cities. The wind sometimes unburies them." He frowned, but as if puzzled, not angry. "I didn't think we passed close enough to the ruins to find anything, let alone something like this." He shrugged. "No harm was done. I have soap and water inside the cabin. You can give him a bath before we eat."

Airie wished she could dismiss it as easily. She could not remember seeing him pick up the box, but promised herself she would be more vigilant in the future as she led him off for his bath.

The inside of the cabin was as neat and tidy as the yard, only very small. There was a counter and cupboard for food and cooking, a potbellied stove, a rough wooden slab table with a single low bench, and a narrow bunk along one wall. A wicker rocker took up an entire corner, and a few clothes hung from hooks on another wall.

"I'm mostly on the move," Hunter said, a faint edge in his tone.

"Don't you worry that you may come back some day and find someone else living here?" Airie asked.

He hauled a small tin bucket of water off the stove and handed it to her. The water was clean and looked fresh.

"There's an underground river that flows beneath this canyon and feeds into Freetown," he said, seeing her surprise at the water. "My well is hidden." He passed her soap and a cloth from a cupboard under the counter. The cloth, too, was clean. "And no, I don't worry about finding someone else living here," he said in answer to her question. "No one in their right mind would try. Demons would find them out here."

"You live here."

He didn't answer that.

She bathed Scratch in a basin on the table. When she poured a pitcher of water over his head he crumpled his face and scrunched his shoulders, making her laugh until she noticed Hunter watching her again. The moment grew awkward, and he turned away.

She dried Scratch thoroughly and wrapped him in one of Hunter's old undershirts. The worn cotton fabric felt soft and smooth to the touch, and smelled of fresh air.

"If you want to wash up, I have a shower outside." Hunter's gaze slid away from her face. "It's not very private, but the water will be warm. I filled the tank earlier."

Airie had been raised by her mother to believe her body belonged to the goddesses, and it was her duty to care for it, but it was what was inside that made it special. Modesty and vanity had never been important to her. She did, however, wish to feel clean again.

Hunter kept the covered tank, and a large basin that sat beneath it, behind the cabin. The basin had holes in it for drainage.

"You stand in the basin," he said, showing her, "and release water over you by pulling this cord." He passed her another of his undershirts and a pair of trousers before he left. "These will have to do for now. Tomorrow, you can wash your clothes."

Airie, who was used to cold mountain lakes, found the spray of water glorious, but her hair created a problem. She dragged her fingers through it to remove the worst of the tangles, and left it loose for the desert air to dry.

The undershirt Hunter gave her fit well enough, but the trousers were too large at the waist. She fastened the buttons, then rolled the waistband down so that the trousers sat comfortably low on her hips, and turned the cuffs up several inches so they would not drag in the dirt.

When she was done, Hunter took his turn bathing.

He reentered the cabin with his shirttail hanging free and his blond hair, dark and wet, loose so that the tips dampened the fabric draping his shoulders. The amulet he never removed dangled from a gold chain around his neck. He'd shaved earlier, and it surprised her how different it made him look. How much more approachable he seemed.

The goddesses had been kind when they crafted him. It was too easy for her to forget he was the Demon Slayer, and that his reputation was both deserved and widespread. Even on the mountain Airie had heard of him, and how demons trembled at the mention of his name.

Perhaps that was why she trembled at the sight of him now.

She fed Scratch his supper while Hunter sat at the table and watched. When she finished, he held up a long-toothed comb and a leather hair lace, his expression unreadable.

"Come here," he said, patting the bench between his thighs.

After a brief hesitation, Airie did as he said. He ran the comb through the heavy length of her hair, untangling it as best he could, and then to her surprise, he twisted the strands into a complex braid.

The caress of his knuckles against the nape of her neck did little to relax her. Tension coiled in her stomach and made it difficult to draw regular breaths. She felt foolish to be so affected by a simple, everyday act her mother had done for her many times.

Yet this was not the same.

When he was done they sat side by side on the bench at the table, and ate by lamplight. Shadows in the corners made the room seem smaller than it was, and the meal more intimate.

Hunter was not inclined to talk. His thoughts appeared to be miles away. While they were traveling, Airie had not worried about making conversation. They had little in common. This, however, was his home, and despite the fact that he had insisted she stay here, she felt an obligation to be polite.

"If you give me the name of your contact in Freetown, Scratch and I will be on our way in the morning," she said. "I'd like to get started before the worst of the heat." The heat did not bother her, but she could not make a small child walk in it.

Scratch had fallen asleep on the floor behind her, and she bent to stroke his baby-fine hair.

"Not tomorrow," Hunter said. He stared at his plate of half-eaten corncakes. A damp swath of hair shielded his expression from her. "I have things to do here first, but as soon as I find the time I'll go to Freetown and speak with them for you. After I've done that, I'll take you into the city."

"That means you'll have to make two trips," she protested.

He jabbed his corncakes with his fork. "Then that's what I'll do."

Everything about the stiff way he held his body, and how he did not look at her when he spoke, made her uneasy.

"What aren't you telling me?" she asked.

"I told you before. Freetown is not a welcoming place, especially for women."

"You told me nothing of the kind. You said the women don't have altercations with men." *Or light themselves on fire*, but she thought it best not to mention something she would prefer he forgot.

"They don't argue either." The corner of his mouth curled upward as he spoke, and he tipped his head sideways to look at her.

He was trying to distract her by making light of it.

Airie placed her fork on the table beside her plate and dropped her hands to her lap. She examined her fingers, her thoughts spinning further and deeper in unpleasant directions that led to only one possible conclusion.

"Am I a prisoner?" she asked.

Her quiet question crouched like a hungry wolven between them, and he hesitated a breath too long before answering. When he did, his response sounded forced and overly emphatic, and did nothing to ease her disquiet.

"Of course not."

Her supper flipped over in her stomach at his blatant lie. She turned on the bench, jerking her knees sideways from beneath the table so she could stand. Hunter seized her wrist.

"Why would you ask me that question?" he demanded. "Did I do something to make you think you are?"

She had given the possibility no thought before now. She felt stupid for not having done so. "You think I'm a…demon."

"You're only half demon. That makes you spawn."

She could not say the word herself. It was impolite, a derogatory term, and he used it so casually it could not help but hurt.

"Are they such different things to you?" she asked. "Demons and the other?"

"No," he admitted. "They're not."

She drew a shaky breath. What gave him the right to insult her this way? What had happened to him to make him so rigid in his prejudices?

She was not perfect. But neither was she the monster he professed her to be.

"My mother was mortal, and a priestess. I was raised to respect life and the teachings of the goddesses. I think for myself, and I make my own choices. What I am and what you believe me to be are very different things."

"Are they?" he said. "In Freetown, women have no right to protection other than what men or the priestesses offer them. If you reveal yourself there, you won't survive. Can you swear to me that you can control the demon in you? Even if you feel threatened? Because I've seen proof to the contrary."

"Of course I can control it." She knew she could. What she

could not always do was hide it. Her anxiety increased. She would have to learn to do so, for Scratch's sake if not her own. "It was different with you."

"Really?" His eyebrows went up. "In what way?"

"You're the Demon Slayer. I felt threatened."

"You didn't know I was the Demon Slayer at the time."

"I sensed it," she lied.

He laughed softly. The pad of his thumb scuffed against the delicate flesh of her wrist, which he had not released, and her anxiety shifted to an awareness of him as a male. She had never been touched like this before, in a way that stole her breath and made her feel awkward. She did not know how to interpret his mood or his actions.

"What are you sensing about me right now?" he asked.

This time, she answered honestly. "That you're playing with me."

His expression closed over. "Perhaps I am. Would you like me to continue?"

No. Yes. While she had never been averse to a challenge, she could not decide because she was uncertain of the rules of this game. "I have a feeling that playing with you would prove far more dangerous to me than I could ever be to anyone."

"Maybe. Maybe not. You haven't answered my question."

He was very beautiful, she thought. The clear, deep blue of his eyes on her made it difficult for her to think.

"If you continue to play," she said, "I insist on an equal chance for victory. I intend to defend myself."

She leaned closer and dragged a finger down the side of his cheek, then along the line of his smooth-shaven jaw, and watched his flaring pupils with interest. She kissed the corner of his mouth, then his lips, before straightening to put space between them again.

He did not smile at her as she had hoped he might. Instead, he continued to regard her with an unreadable expression that held a hint of hunger. Excitement shivered down her spine.

"You've made your opening move. Now, it's my turn." He cupped her chin in his palm and drew her mouth to his.

His kiss was far different from the light tease of hers. It made her heart beat faster and her limbs shake, to the point where she wondered if he could feel them, too.

Heat flushed through her as she became lost in the sensations the touch of his mouth aroused in her. Even though he held her face lightly, she could not have pulled away from him if she wanted, which she did not.

She had closed her eyes.

"Look at me," he commanded, his breath soft against her mouth. When she opened her eyes, the blue of his had darkened to midnight in the lamplit interior of the cabin. "Do you still want me to keep going?"

She could not speak.

Idly, he hooked his finger through the chain around her neck and lifted her rainbow-hued amulet in his palm. He held it next to the one he wore, then looked more closely at them both. He turned them back to back and with a faint click, they attached like two magnets.

She did not know what to make of that. Neither, it seemed, did he. A thoughtful frown crossed his lean face as he worked to twist them apart.

Once free, he rose from the bench and reached to take their empty plates from the table.

He straightened. "I don't believe you can control your demon instincts. But I do believe you can make a man forget about them."

CHAPTER EIGHT

Hunter unrolled his bedding near the mouth of the canyon, careful to scour the ground around him for any potential and unwelcome poisonous sleeping companions.

Out of long habit, he placed his short sword alongside the six-shooter beneath his bedding. He had left his repeating rifle in the cabin for Airie. It was more for his peace of mind than hers. He doubted she knew how to use it.

He'd had no business playing such games with her.

Hunter pulled the collar of his shirt tight around his neck against the cool night air, then hunched down with his back against the canyon wall so he could sit and think. The winds were light. It was not a night for demons. His amulet lay silent against his skin.

It had been a rough day for him, filled with guilt and indecision. He should have taken Airie directly to Mamna, but he found he could not do so.

The flare of her eyes when he kissed her had been far more erotic and sensual than abhorrent, as it should be. The unexpected fit of their two amulets had also caused a strong jolt of desire for her in him.

He could not lie to himself any longer. She was beautiful and alluring, and even though she was spawn, against all common sense he wanted her for himself.

Perhaps it was because he had yet to see her in full demon form. Maybe then he could hand her over to Mamna. As it was, when he looked at her he was stricken with the memory of a beloved sister who had been equally innocent, and betrayed by someone she had trusted and believed she loved.

He closed his eyes. Airie trusted him, at least up to a point. She thanked him for any small crumbs of kindness. It left him feeling little better than the demon who had ruined his sister.

He kicked at a tuft of desert weed with the toe of his boot. He would give her a week to reveal her true self. He could find a reason to keep her here with him for that much longer.

The decision gave him some peace.

He settled into his bedroll, soon so close to sleep he almost missed the black sole of a boot descending toward his throat.

Acting on instincts honed by years spent hunting demons, he grabbed his assailant's foot and twisted it to the side, toppling the boot's owner. In seconds, he was free of the bedding and on his feet, his short sword in one hand and the six-shooter held steady at the stranger's head.

The spread-eagled assailant threw up his hands in surrender. "I wish only to talk to the Demon Slayer."

The sliver of moon gave off enough watery light for Hunter to see the man. Running a blade through his heart would cause Hunter no loss of sleep, especially now that he had Airie and a small child to protect.

"You should try approaching in daylight," he replied.

The man laughed under his breath. "During the day, the goddess is with you."

Hunter pressed the tip of his sword into the assailant's flesh, although he was careful not to draw blood just yet. When he did draw it, he would kill the man. It would be far kinder than setting him free in the desert with the scent of fresh blood on him.

Then again, Hunter would have to be in the mood for kindness. "You've been following me. I don't like to be followed."

Neither did he like that the man knew of Airie, even though he was mistaken in what he thought she was. He could not be blamed for that, Hunter had to admit. She was beautiful enough to be taken for a goddess.

The man seemed untroubled by the sword in his side, the gun at his head, and the unfriendly tone of Hunter's voice. "You have a choice to make. If you choose wrong, the Godseekers will kill you."

"They can keep trying. So far, they've been unsuccessful." Hunter pressed the point of his blade deeper. "You have to the count of three to tell me who you are and what you're doing here."

"I am called Runner. I spread the word. The world needs to know about the goddess who leads you."

It came as no surprise that the man was a fanatic. His assumption about Airie, however, was so far from the truth that Hunter was tempted to enlighten him.

"No goddess leads me." He thought about that for a moment. "But let's say one did. Why would that make the Godseekers want to kill me?"

"The goddess has come from the mountain to lead the one who wears the Demon Slayer's amulet."

Ah. Now it all made a strange kind of sense. If a Godseeker wore his amulet, the Godseeker would become the Demon Slayer—the one their so-called goddess led into battle—and they preferred that the goddess be accompanied by one of their own.

Blade was right. They had gone from worshipping Hunter to wanting him dead. He could not wait for the bloodthirsty bastards to discover the true nature of the goddess they were so determined to revere.

"Give us the amulet so the goddess may lead us, instead," Runner said.

Hunter thought it over. "No. You'll have to kill me for it. Although," he added, "you're welcome to the goddess if you want her." That might solve his current dilemma. The Godseekers would care for Airie as if she truly were a goddess.

At least until they realized their mistake.

"You would give her—" the Godseeker began, but was interrupted when an amber object around his neck began to glow in the darkness like a miniature sun.

Hunter had seen this type of amulet before. These had been gifts from the goddesses to the mortal men who pleased them, and they warned of an immortal's approach. That meant at one time, Runner had been a favorite of the goddesses—or at least knew someone who was.

Resignation washed through Hunter. The stone sensed Airie's presence. The glowing amulet would confirm what the Godseeker wanted to believe. He would not be able to convince him now that she was not a goddess.

Sudden heat scorched his skin and Hunter glanced down in confusion. His own amulet glowed golden and grew hot against his skin. Hunter's head went up, and he scanned the night sky for demons.

In that split-second shift of his attention, the Godseeker rolled free of the tip of his sword and vanished into the shadowy desert night. Hunter, unwilling to shoot him in the back, let him go.

But where was the demon?

He cocked his head, listening for sounds of its approach, and then realized he had made a mistake. The demon would not come after him when it could have a woman like Airie, and she was at the cabin, alone with a small child.

Worry hit him, hard.

Hunter slid the six-shooter into the waistband of his trousers and tightened his grip on the sword. A gun might be useless against demon hide, but a sword wielded with a demon's strength was not.

He loped toward the cabin as quietly as possible, counting off the minutes in his head since the amulet had flared, and prayed he would be in time.

He was unprepared for the scene he found.

• • •

Hunter had sounded as if he'd prefer to sleep outside, so Airie had not argued.

But once he was gone and she had Scratch tucked into bed, she found she was too restless to sleep and with too many things on her mind. She did not want to think about Hunter, or the meaning of his puzzling actions and words. The future, too, was a frightening unknown to her.

Instead, she wandered onto the verandah and into the darkness, intending to sit and enjoy the moonlight and the sounds of the night in the hopes of finding a small measure of peace. She sat on the stoop, her bare toes peeping from under the cuffs of Hunter's too-long trousers, and absently played with her amulet, running the stone back and forth along its chain. Since Hunter had touched it to his, it felt different to her in an indefinable but important way.

A wolven howled in the desert, then another. Goose bumps chased across Airie's flesh, although not from fear.

Now that she was here, and her childhood dreams of the desert a reality, she found it could not compensate for the loss of the goddesses who no longer responded to her, even though she prayed to them faithfully every day. Could it be as she had feared? That with her mother gone, the goddesses had turned from her?

She rose, troubled, intending to go back inside. A soft breath of wind began to rise, scattering dust before it.

A low voice called to her from the shadows. "Well, well, little angel. What have we here?"

The voice was deep and very masculine, holding a hint of quiet amusement, and Airie spun around with her heart thumping madly beneath Hunter's undershirt.

A man approached until he stood not twenty feet from the foot of the steps. Tall, broad shouldered, he had dancing gray eyes that begged for a smile, and a mass of curling black hair. His chest and feet were bare, a pair of faded cotton trousers his only clothing.

Airie's breath caught, disliking that a stranger had gotten so close when she had a small child's safety to consider. She looked around.

Where was Hunter?

"Smile for me, angel," the stranger coaxed her, a wide grin cutting across his handsome face and displaying white, even teeth.

It would be very easy to become lost in that smile, Airie thought. The voice, too, mesmerized her. Some of her suspicion began to fade. How could someone so beautiful be anything but harmless?

He came closer, and she found herself descending the wooden

steps to face him, although warning bells rang wildly in a far off, secret part of her head. She tried to dismiss them but found she could not. Not entirely.

Something about this was not quite right.

She had not intended to permit him to get this close. Uncertain how he had managed it, she took several cautious steps backward. His smile widened as if he sensed her increasing nervousness.

He halted and lifted his hands, palms outward, in a gesture of placation. "Don't be afraid, little sweetheart."

She was not afraid. Sensing it would be dangerous for her if she were, and that he would take advantage of any weakness she exhibited, she chose to confront him with boldness instead.

"Who are you?"

"My name is Agares."

His gaze on her was too warm. She had liked that hungry look when she received it from Hunter earlier. Now, she was not so certain she did.

Hunter.

Airie struggled to dredge up an image of his face in her mind. When she did, there was no heat in his expression. Instead, he was scowling.

He would not like this.

There was no uncertainty in the thought at all, although she did not know why it should matter to her, only that it did. She sensed real danger, too, something she had never felt from Hunter.

"The desert is very beautiful, Airie," her mother had once warned her. "But nighttime brings out its predators, and demons are the most dangerous predators of all."

Now she understood what her mother had meant when she called them predators, because this demon Agares was stalking her.

A dark voice spoke to her. *You know what you are. You can play this game. You can stalk, too.*

The voice of her instincts was right. Her own smile flared. "I'm not afraid of you, demon."

She saw the glint of surprise in his eyes, quickly hidden, although not fast enough. He had expected shy, feminine resistance to his demon charm. Had known what to do to overcome it.

A hot ember of anger tingled to life, shooting ripples of fire through her flesh. This was a game he had played with mortal women many times before. He did not yet realize that Airie was not mortal.

And that he, too, could be a demon's prey.

You know what you are. She did. At least she knew what part of her was, and right now, it spoke to her.

"Come to me, Agares," she said, the soft, seductive words barely recognizable to her as her own. Her extended hand and naked arm gleamed with a fiery golden light.

He dragged one foot forward, then the other, while she waited for him. Let this demon discover what it was like to walk into danger, unable to resist it.

He reached to take her extended hand. Then, quick as a goldthief snake's strike, he seized it.

Too late, as she tumbled into his arms, Airie discovered that even though she might be able to compel him, he was a demon nevertheless—and with a great deal more practice at it.

She was the one playing with fire.

"Whatever you are," he murmured, his lips hot on her cheek and ear, an enormous erection pressing into her hip, "the evening has become far more interesting."

In a contest of wills, her instinct insisted she was his equal. In one of pure strength, she was not as certain. What she would not offer freely, this demon planned to take from her by force, and she did not know if she could fight him off.

A hand moved to her breast, startling her out of uncertainty. She did not like to be touched in this manner. Not by a demon who was not meant for her. How *dare* he touch her this way?

Angry red flames clouded her vision as the fire inside her built to an uncontainable level. She had to release it, or it would consume her.

Her blazing eyes seared his neck and chest. He reared back, releasing her, roaring with pain and surprise. He shook the hand that had touched her so intimately as if it, too, had been singed. He stared at her, and past her anger and his sudden caution, Airie saw recognition.

"How…" he breathed, then self-preservation kicked in. He shifted, changed, and within seconds, assumed his demon form.

The handsome face disappeared, swallowed by a mashed snout, long, wolven-like jaw, and fiery eyes. Bony plates covered the thick red hide of its hunched torso, protecting vital organs. The sheer size of it should have inspired awe in her.

Airie's anger, however, was far from spent. The demon had touched her. She would touch it, too.

It towered over her, but she faced it without flinching. *Fear is for mortals,* her instincts whispered.

It dipped its head toward hers. She had no ready weapon. As the ugly snout neared her face, she stooped, grabbed a handful of sand, and threw it at the demon's eyes in an attempt to blind it, even as her other hand slashed out to seize it by the windpipe. The fire in her palm sheared through its thick hide, and it bellowed as it tried to shake itself free of her grip.

She did not let it go, instead redirecting her fire into its throat to cut off all air. A talon sliced her arm open as the demon struggled, but she barely noticed the sharp sliver of pain. Instinct again warned her of its intentions. By drawing fresh blood, it hoped to summon a battle rage in an effort to gain an advantage on her.

It would not get another opportunity to try.

The fire on her skin cauterized the cut on her arm, sealing it shut before it could bleed. Airie squeezed her fingers around the demon's windpipe, completely enraged and beyond reasonable thought now, and watched with hungry triumph as life slowly seeped from its eyes.

"I will own your death and your strength," she said. "You will do as I say."

A green-blue haze shimmered in the air around it, then moved to envelop her, too. *I am yours to command.*

The submissive words shook her. They could not have been meant for her. She did not take life. *Any* life.

She might have demon blood in her but she was not a monster, and she would not become one. An echo of her mother's voice overrode any urgings of her demon instincts. *You control your anger. It doesn't control you.*

Airie released her grip on the demon's windpipe and it staggered backward, scratching at its throat and gasping for breath.

Cunning returned to its blood-red, glowing eyes. It looked to where a familiar presence watched from the black shadows, and for the first time since the demon approached her, Airie experienced real fear.

Hunter stood close by.

The demon sensed him, too.

. . .

Not one hundred feet from Hunter, Airie stood in the arms of a half-naked man, who had one hand on her breast and his mouth on her cheek, near her ear.

Stunned surprise, followed by a sharp stab of male jealousy, secured Hunter to the spot at the sight of a demon touching Airie so intimately. A desire to kill came over him, and blood pounded behind his eyes, but as he started forward, a small hand slid into his to hold him back.

Hunter's vision cleared. Scratch, his little face solemn, looked up at him, his tiny fingers wrapped tight around one of Hunter's.

Hunter's thoughts settled, became less chaotic, and he tore his gaze back to Airie. As difficult as it was for him to stand by while she fought a battle of wills with a demon, he needed to know if she could stand strong against temptation when his sister had not.

Could she deny one of her own kind?

He tensed when the demon backed away from Airie to assume demon form, and he pushed Scratch behind him, out of the way of danger.

Hunter started toward Airie, then froze when she dashed sand in the demon's eyes and grabbed it by the throat. He watched her fingers tighten, sending fire into its flesh, and saw the demon's eyes cloud over. He recognized the telltale bluish-green haze that accompanied the death of a demon.

And then, she released it.

Hunter's heart skipped several beats. What was she doing? Why had she stopped?

The demon lifted its head and looked in Hunter's direction.

"Hunter!" Airie cried. "Look out!"

Instead he looked at her, afraid she'd somehow been harmed, a distraction that cost him.

The demon drove itself at him on widespread, leathery wings, striking him in the chest with splayed feet, knocking him thirty feet backward into the canyon wall to send the sword spinning from his hand. Air exploded from his lungs on a painful and protracted exhale. Hunter slumped to the ground, stunned by the impact, only alive thanks to the amulet.

The demon landed and paced toward him, an ominous shadow in the dim light, growing steadily larger as it approached.

Hunter wheezed into the dirt as he tried to reach his sword, feigning more serious injury to lull the demon into false confidence even as the amulet siphoned strength from it to him.

He caught a flurry of movement from the corner of one eye. Airie had grabbed a shovel standing against the side of the cabin and now brandished it like a cudgel, the rough wood rolling easily between her palms.

She had diverted the demon's attention from him. Hunter, abandoning his search for the sword, brought his elbow up to ram into its groin. The demon backhanded him across the face in rebuttal, and Hunter's head snapped back.

Airie delivered a sharp crack to the back of the demon's head with the flat of the shovel.

It turned on her.

"Get back!" Hunter shouted at her. She had not been able to kill it before, and he did not want her to have to do it now. Not on his behalf. He hauled himself to his sword and grabbed its hilt.

Airie, however, like a golden, glowing, avenging goddess, rammed the handle of the shovel into the demon's stomach. When it doubled over, she swung the flat end up and under its chin with enough strength to bring it to its knees. The metal blade of the shovel was bent.

Scrabbling in the loose dirt, it got its clawed feet beneath it and launched itself into the sky. Its dark shadow blocked out the splinter of moon before it disappeared from sight.

Hunter's gaze never left Airie. She could not know how impossibly beautiful she appeared in this moment, with her golden skin on fire and yellow flames, not red, now dancing in her dark eyes. He wondered at the significance, if any.

The flames died. She dropped the shovel and hurried to Hunter's side.

"Are you hurt?" she asked.

He had not protected her, and that left him furious, but he was not certain with whom. He spit a mouthful of coppery blood onto the sand. The demon had drawn blood, yet it had run away. It knew what Airie was, as well.

Nothing good would come of this night.

Frustration and worry fed into his anger, and that was the emotion more easily expressed. He directed it at Airie. "The next time I give you an order, you do as you're told."

She drew back the hand she had been about to place on his arm. It took her a moment to find her voice, and when she did, it was soft and full of hurt. "I was afraid for you."

Hunter could have handled the demon on his own, but it did not change the fact that she had come to his rescue with no regard for her own safety. He should be grateful, not angry with her.

And yet it was his anger he continued to lash her with, flaying tiny pieces off her with well-honed words. "The demon escaped. Now it will bring others. I would have killed it if you hadn't interfered.

You should have killed it when you had the chance."

She twisted the front pockets of the old pair of trousers she wore with her fingers. "I don't kill."

He could not stop now. He plowed forward, digging in deeper. "Not for any reason?" he demanded. "Not even if to kill is the only way to rid the world of something that doesn't belong here?"

"As you would have killed me if my mother had not interfered?"

The quiet observation, filled with scorn, cut him down. He could think of nothing to say, no way to refute it, because he did not know if it was true or false.

Turning on her heel, she marched with stiff dignity back to the cabin. The door closed behind her, and he heard the wooden lock bar *snick* into place.

He kicked the shovel she'd left on the ground as hard as he could. Then he gathered up his bedding and moved it to the front of the cabin so he could guard the door in case the demon should decide to return.

He remembered Scratch. At some point in all the confusion, the child had vanished.

That was another problem Hunter needed to consider in more depth. The boy seemed to have an uncanny ability to disappear when he chose. How else had he managed to get out of the cabin without being seen? Hunter started to search the yard for him but soon gave up when common sense told him Airie would have come running by now if he wasn't already safe inside the cabin with her.

Instead, as Hunter tossed and turned on the hard ground well into the early hours of the morning, he wondered about something else.

What had brought a demon this close to Freetown on a night the west winds did not blow?

• • •

"A demon was not a part of our deal."

Mamna, seated in the lush garden beneath her living quarters, sheltered from the morning sun by heavy arbors of palm and thick drapes of multicolored, sweet-smelling desert blossoms, regarded the angry assassin with cool eyes.

Calling this man before her an assassin gave him far more credit than he deserved. He was a hired thug. True assassins were harder to come by, and not as easily intimidated into service.

"I don't control what demons do beyond these city gates," she replied without inflection.

Runner slouched in his chair across the delicate, round glass table from her, his dark expression brooding. An artesian well fed a fountain nearby, spilling water from a pitcher cradled in the arms of a winged cherub. The soft noise of the water effectively distorted any conversation that might otherwise be overheard.

As a rule, Mamna conducted most of her private business from within her compound because she was too easily recognizable to most of Freetown's population. Being born with her physical disadvantages made it difficult to find that delicate balance between being seen and unseen. Even if people had never met her, they had heard her described. The irony was not lost on her. When she had served the goddesses, she had gone unnoticed for decades. Now, people could not help but stare. Mamna could never decide which she hated more.

The only exception she made regarding the location when conducting personal business was for the Slayer, who refused to do anything by anyone's rules but his own.

In truth, she was more than a little disappointed in the Slayer.

She'd thought he hated demons and their spawn beyond anything. She had assumed he'd be immune to a beautiful face, if that face belonged to one of them. She had also expected the amulet he wore to offer some protection against the irresistible appeal of an immortal.

But the Slayer, it seemed, was as susceptible as the next man to a pretty face, proving to her that physical beauty remained the most powerful asset a woman could possess. It made her hate this spawn even more.

This so-called assassin before her was also proving to be a disappointment. She had sent Runner to see if the Slayer had brought a woman off the mountain with him. She wanted to know if he'd captured the spawn, or if he had killed her outright. She had told Runner to approach him, to repeat the tale the Godseeker had given her, and to relieve the Slayer of his amulet if at all possible.

She wanted to be certain, however, that she would not be implicated in any attack on the Slayer. Shifting suspicion onto the Godseekers worked well for her.

"The woman was unafraid of the demon," Runner said with undisguised admiration.

This was the part of the tale Mamna found most difficult to understand. Why would a spawn have come to the Demon Slayer's defense?

How had he persuaded her to travel with him willingly?

"Tell me again," she demanded, trying to make sense of his words. Perhaps the spawn had plans of her own. If so, Mamna would take care of those.

Runner tipped his wide-brimmed hat back with the blunt of his thumb. "She spent the day playing with a small boy in the yard. The Slayer called them inside to eat. She stayed in the cabin. He moved to the yard for the night. They did not seem all that friendly toward each other. Which surprised me, at least on his part," Runner's boot tapped the clay tiling, "because that is one gorgeous woman. The Slayer doesn't seem to appreciate his good fortune."

Mamna ignored that last comment, and the trace of envy that accompanied it. She had lived with the goddesses. She had a history with the Demon Lord. She knew all about mortal infatuation for the immortals. Given the spawn's parentage, it stood to reason that she would have been born with at least some of their allure.

But that the Slayer did not seem to be interested in her as a woman was what puzzled Mamna. If not for that purpose, then why else would he keep her with him instead of turning her over immediately?

"Where did the child come from?" she wondered out loud. Could it possibly belong to the spawn? If so, who, or what, was its father?

Runner had no interest in the child and dismissed him. "The Slayer doesn't believe she's a goddess," he was saying. "He was clear on that. Maybe your Godseeker gave you false information."

Mamna ran her finger around the lip of her dainty porcelain teacup. "The Godseeker told me what he believed to be true. That doesn't make it the truth. She is no goddess. The woman is the daughter of an old priestess, and nothing more than a thief who needs to be brought to justice."

While she had no patience for the ramblings of aging men who'd once been favored by the goddesses and who wished to recapture a place in time that could no longer be revisited, she could not deny that both the story and the spawn had become serious problems for her.

Part of Mamna's bargain with the Demon Lord was that she

would watch for, and tell him, of any goddess activity on the mountain. She did not want him to discover that the thief on the mountain was indeed his, for while he had once loved the goddess as much as he was capable of loving anyone, he believed she had willingly abandoned him. If he discovered she had refused to leave him, and instead had died in childbirth, what would he do to the one who had fed him those lies to the contrary?

Mamna had no way of knowing what the old priestess had told the spawn of her actual parentage. She did not know what the spawn, in turn, might have told the Slayer. That the spawn appeared to possess a predominantly mortal form was yet another complication, because it would make it easier for the Slayer to overlook or disregard what she really was.

Runner continued reciting his story. "I approached the Slayer and gave him your story. The demon arrived. I pretended to run away, then went back to watch. She helped the Slayer drive off the demon."

The sun had shifted, and Mamna's legs were no longer in the shade. She straightened the folds of her light linen trousers, unable to adjust the position of her chair without help and refusing to ask for it.

If the demon had not been hunting for pleasure, what purpose did it have for being so close to Freetown?

Because that had been another part of her bargain with the Demon Lord—the demons could hunt on the west winds, but other than that, they were to leave Freetown and its surrounding areas alone.

Her amulet was weakening, and the Demon Lord no longer respected their bargain. She had to regain control over the Demon Lord. To do that, she had to get the spawn away from the Slayer.

The sun burned too hot for her. She would get a message to the Slayer asking for a meeting. If he brought her the spawn, she would forgive him. If he came alone, she would have him killed, and deservedly so for taking payment and not delivering the promised results. Once he was dead, she would concentrate on recapturing the spawn.

She picked up the teapot and filled both cups, preoccupied with another, more pleasant, thought. If he came alone and she had him killed, she would have his amulet. It did not offer the same type of protection as the one she owned, but hers was damaged and his was better than nothing.

And she worried that soon, nothing was all she would have.

CHAPTER NINE

Something was wrong.

Hunter jerked on the sand swift's harness, pulling it to a halt a short distance from a bend in the arroyo he'd been following.

The overhanging rock and occasional scrub offered only slight protection from the desert heat, and Sally was out of sorts. To make matters worse, the animal had developed an attachment to Airie that made it reluctant to travel too far from her side.

Hunter, on the other hand, wanted to get as far away from Airie as possible and for as long as he dared. He had not expected or planned to find the demon that had attacked him.

That had been his excuse to escape the accusations in her eyes.

But now he had found something out here in the desert, and the circling of vultures in the barren sky overhead and the sand swift's sudden increase of surliness did not bode well. Neither did the smell.

He tugged his neckerchief over his nose and mouth and slid to the ground, wrapping the reins around the saddle horn and holding Sally by the bridle to leave his hands unencumbered. He could hear nothing, which was another bad sign.

The amulet around his neck flickered dully, then darkened again, confirming what he'd already suspected. Demons, one or more, had been at work here but were now gone, and the arrival of vultures meant other natural scavengers would soon follow.

The weight of his sword against his leg offered a measure of comfort. So did the repeating rifle he carried in his saddle scabbard. The amulet gave him no protection from any coyotes and wolven emboldened by the safety of numbers and the prospect of an easy meal.

He should turn around and walk away while he could. Whatever was ahead was beyond saving.

Sally didn't protest as they neared the bend in the arroyo, however, so Hunter felt confident he faced no immediate danger. Morbid curiosity won out over common sense, along with an urge to reinforce his hatred of anything demon. Including their spawn.

He rounded the bend.

Although he had been prepared for it, still, what he found was no easier to accept. He inhaled sharply.

A small wagon train, no more than five units all told, had made an attempt to cross the desert through demon territory. They had chosen the flat-bottomed arroyo as an easier path to travel than the drifting desert sands, as well as for the moderate protection it offered from anything flying the skies above.

Hunter wrapped the sand swift's reins around a thorny bush and approached the wagon train cautiously, even though he knew there would be no survivors. Pity and anger filled him at the sight of the blackened remains of a campfire that would have acted as a beacon to anything hunting at night. Its scattered ashes indicated that, when the attack began, they had tried to circle their wagons, an action which would have been of little help against an enemy that struck from the air.

He had seen similar scenes before. These had been small-time, inexperienced traders trying to make fast money. He'd occasionally hired out his services to escort such wagoners through demon territory in the past. Their wagons would have been filled with whiskey, worth its weight in gold in a place like Freetown, isolated as it was from the rest of the world. The wagons would be empty now. Demons, pleasure-seeking bastards that they were, liked alcohol almost as much as they liked women.

The hross that had hauled the wagons, long-legged, sturdy draft animals with enormous, thick-hoofed feet suited for the hot sands of the desert, had been cut loose. Their tracks showed where they'd scrambled in panic up the embankments of the arroyo.

The dismembered and partially eaten remains of the wagoners, however, littered the campsite. Hunter's stomach lurched. He knew from Blade's experience that demons cared little if the men were alive when they started to feed. It was not about hunger. They hated men, believing them to be poor copies of the immortals, and held them in little regard. This was their way of showing contempt.

He would have liked to bury what was left of these people, but the ground was too hard, and he did not have that much time. The sky had begun to darken on the horizon, and an arroyo was not the place to be when the rains came. It would not take long for it to revert to a river.

The river would have to take care of the wagoners' remains.

A vulture, its droopy eyes gleaming, dropped to the ground and hopped toward a trail of drying flesh. Hunter turned away, fixing his gaze on the abandoned wagons instead. He would see what the demon had left behind with regard to staples.

Two of the wagons were empty, much as he had expected. The third, however, came as a surprise. It contained common household goods.

Hunter's stomach plunged lower, bile burning his throat. This wagon had belonged to settlers, probably too poor to join a proper wagon train, and with hopes of earning back the cost of their passage through trade. He flipped open the lid of one of the trunks. It was filled with women's clothing.

Thoughtful now, and already suspecting what he might find, he leapt from the running board on the wagon box and looked beneath it. A young woman, more of a girl, lay curled on her side, her arms tucked under her head as if in sleep, a crusted pool of dried black blood staining her dress and the ground around her. A narrow gold wedding band circled one slender finger. A stray blond curl escaped her bonnet to lie against her waxen cheek.

Hunter knew what had happened to her. When the demons had struck, her husband had shot her. He did not blame him for it. She would have had to watch the slaughter, and since as a married woman she was not untouched, the best she could have hoped for was to be raped and abandoned in the desert. Worst case meant she, too, would have been torn apart, like the others.

If her husband was at fault for anything, it was for bringing her into demon territory in the first place.

Hunter looked at the sky, still clear above him, and decided taking the time to bury her would be worth the risk to him. He could not leave her for the vultures and the coyotes.

He carried her body out of the arroyo, and using the sand swift to haul stones from the dry creek bed, spent the next several hours erecting a crude cairn over her remains. Sand from the rising wind stung his eyes, and he wiped his face with his sweat-soaked neckerchief. Despite the scorching rays of the sun, he had discarded his hat and his shirt while he worked.

The makeshift burial complete, he turned back to the wagons. The woman's clothing, he would take with him for either Airie or Blade's women to use. They did not need to know where he'd gotten it. Any nonperishable food he would take with him as well.

As he returned to the wagons one last time, he spotted something lying on the ground near one wagon wheel. He stooped, brushing the dirt away with his fingertips.

It was an amulet. Hunter picked it up. It had been carved from desert sandstone to look much like the one he wore, although it was a very poor copy and had no real power. His lips thinned. He had seen many fake amulets over the years, but this was the first that was meant to match his own.

His fingers squeezed the fake amulet, crumbling it into pieces. Whoever had worn it had led these people to their deaths, letting them believe they had protection from demons. Whoever it was, he had gotten what he deserved.

The young couple had not.

Hunter crammed the food and clothing into his empty packs, removing his duster from one and putting it on as he did.

Raindrops began to fall. He needed to get out of the arroyo and find shelter. Part of him worried about Airie, who was unfamiliar with desert weather and its dangers. What if she had decided to explore the canyon?

What if she had decided to head into Freetown without him and got caught in the storm?

He should not worry about her, but he did. He settled his hat on his head to shield his face from the rain as he and the sand swift passed the newly erected cairn.

He knew what Airie was but at some point had finally accepted that it made no real difference to him. He'd had seven sisters he had loved beyond reason. One of them was dead. He could not willfully put any woman's life in danger. He had to find her a place where she could be safe.

But it was one thing for him to protect Airie from danger. How would he keep her from becoming a danger to others?

• • •

As Airie unpinned their bedding from the clothesline where she had hung it out to air, she kept an eye on the darkening sky. Heavy black storm clouds gathered on the horizon, shifting the colorful sandstone carvings peppering the desert landscape from shades of fire to a dull, lifeless gray.

Hunter had been gone for hours now, and in spite of everything, and his terrible moodiness, Airie was worried about him.

He was hunting the demon she had allowed to escape. She knew he had not liked that she'd interfered in their fight, but she had not been able to stand back and allow him to battle the demon alone.

Neither had she been able to talk to Hunter about how the demon had approached her first. She could not bear to see disgust for her in his eyes.

She folded a blanket, bending to lay it in a colorful woven basket, brushing strands of long dark hair that had worked free of its braid away from her face. She had no problem with fighting. She'd done it often after the offerings had stopped and her mother grew sick, and Airie needed to feed and clothe them both.

But she had been raised to believe that life was sacred and not to be taken without reason. Hatred such as Hunter possessed for demons and their spawn was foreign to her. It was a terrible emotion that led to unforgivable acts.

Airie had only ever been cherished. She had only known love and given her love in return. Until now, she had never been hated.

And it was for something she could not change.

The sting of sand on the rising wind prickled her skin. She sniffed back the sudden threat of tears. She missed her mother.

Scratch had been playing a game with two sticks, shuffling a stone back and forth in the dirt. He set the sticks aside and came to stand beside her, his worried little face turned up to the sky and his tiny fingers clutching at her skirt.

"Hunter will be back soon," Airie assured him, stroking his head. "It's just a little rain coming. Nothing to worry about."

She hoped she was telling him the truth. Rain in the desert was unlike rain in the mountains. She did not know what might happen once it started to fall.

She lifted Scratch in her arms and kissed his cheek. He patted her face, his eyes looking deep into hers for reassurance. Here was one person who did not see a demon when he looked at her, and she loved him all the more for it. The two of them had much in common.

She did not see a demon when she looked at him either.

"Do you know what raindrops are?" she asked him. "They are the goddesses' tears. When it rains it means the goddesses are thinking of us. They cry because they take all of our sorrow for themselves and leave us nothing but happiness. Their tears make things grow for us, so we can have life."

The rain was well timed. It reminded her that tears for her mother helped wash away the pain of loss, but eventually, the memories would strengthen and grow bright.

She carried Scratch to the cabin and set him on the step under the shelter of the verandah roof, then went back to gather her bedding and the basket. As she picked up the basket the sky opened up and the rain fell in thick, dirty sheets, the fine, wind-driven sand mixing with the drops of moisture.

Airie raced for the cabin. It was only a distance of a few feet, but she was wet to the skin by the time she reached it. She carried the basket on one hip, and seizing Scratch's hand, hurried him inside and shut the door against the storm. She dropped the basket on the table.

The rain pounding on the roof and the walls was loud, and Scratch covered his ears against it. Airie cuddled him in her arms. She loved the rain and did not want him to develop a fear of it. The poor little soul had been damaged enough.

She had an idea. She was wet already, and Scratch always seemed to be dirty. The rain was not cold.

"Lift up your arms," she said to him, and then peeled his shirt over his head. She stripped down to her shift. "Come on."

They dashed back out into the rainstorm. At first Scratch didn't like it, turning his face into her shoulder, but then Airie began to dance with him still cradled in her arms. Before long he was down on the ground, ankle deep in the slippery mud and squishing it between his toes.

Airie showed him how to slide in it by taking a running start and letting her feet shoot out from under her. They were drenched and soon very dirty, and the smile on Scratch's face was worth every minute of it.

As they played, it was impossible to see more than a few feet in front of them through the heavy rain. Airie understood why Hunter had built the cabin at the mouth of the canyon rather than deeper in, and she was glad he had taken Sally with him, because much of the canyon floor was a river now and the sand swift would have been trapped.

She tried not to worry about Hunter. He had survived on his own for years. He could look after himself.

Unease ate at her. She had no illusions that she and Scratch were anything more than a burden to Hunter despite the fact that so far, he had refused to take them to Freetown. He would do so eventually.

When he did, what was to become of them?

She needed guidance. The only source she knew to turn to, that she'd ever been taught to seek out other than her mother, was the goddesses themselves.

The rain was their gift to a burning land. She cleared her mind, lifted her face, and murmured the prayers her mother had taught her.

The rain gentled but did not stop. Without the driving force of the wind to mix them with sand, the drops cleared from opaque to glass. They shimmered and danced to fall around Airie like curtains of tiny, glittering crystals.

A figure appeared, outlined in the backdrop of rain, and Airie caught her breath, afraid at first that the demon had returned. Her immediate concern was for Scratch.

But the figure was that of a woman, and Airie's concern turned quickly to awe.

She was in the presence of a goddess. At least one of them had not turned from her.

The goddess's lips moved as if attempting to speak, but Airie heard nothing other than the patter of the rain on the mud-slickened ground. The goddess stretched out a hand in invitation and Airie accepted it, her own fingers trembling. The goddess's touch had no substance to it, and yet that it was real, she did not doubt.

The rain parted around them, leaving them isolated in a sparkling oasis of sunlight. The goddess was golden and glorious, dressed in a gown crafted from a rainbow of colors, and the warm hunger in her eyes as she examined Airie from head to toe was palpable.

All worry for the future was forgotten, banished by an opportunity Airie had never believed could be hers. Hope grazed her heart and overrode any disinclination to beg.

"Please," she implored, "can you tell me if my mother is at peace?"

The goddess went still. "She wants you to know that she is with you." An indefinable expression flashed across her face. "And that she loves you."

Airie closed her eyes and absorbed the goddess's words. She had never been given a chance to properly mourn her mother. She had left no offerings with her body, or dressed her in fine clothes so she could stand with pride before the goddesses she had served. Airie had left her alone, discarded in a temple even the goddesses had abandoned.

But now she knew beyond doubt that her mother was at peace, and Airie owed it to her memory to try to do something worthwhile with her life, as she would have wanted.

The sorrow she had struggled to control since leaving the mountain surged through her, then abated, although it did not disappear completely and never would.

"Thank you," she whispered.

A flash of pain crossed the goddess's face before her expression closed. "You have no reason to thank me. I am a part of you, and I owe a great debt to your…mother…for that. You are the product of her upbringing, not mine, and I've tried not to interfere before this.

But now, if you need me, I'll be here for you. You have only to ask."

Airie heard the slight hesitation in the soft-spoken words and her worry returned, not only for what was to become of both her and Scratch, but also as to whether she would be able to overcome the taint of her parentage.

She would not let the past overwhelm her future. She might not be able to change the fact that her father had been a demon, but her mother had been nothing but the personification of goodness and strength. She would make her mother proud, although it would not be easy. Airie had no illusions about herself or her flaws.

"I don't know what I will do without my mother to guide me," she confessed.

Tension stiffened the goddess's features, making her appear uncompromising. "You must make a choice," she said. "Not now, but soon. You were born on this world, but you were not born to it. It is not yours. If you wish to make a place for yourself here, you must be welcomed in it. If you don't do so soon, you will then have to choose between worlds. Will you choose the world of your mother or that of your father?"

Airie did not understand. The words made little sense to her. "I choose this world," she said.

"You have not yet earned any choice," the goddess replied. "You can make none until you do so. If you want to be a part of this world, you must make it yours."

The rain began to thin. Airie had hoped for more guidance than this.

Bursts of light shone from the goddess's pores. "The immortals watch you. But they do not favor you. It is up to you to earn their respect." She began to fade with the thinning droplets of rain, her form growing more translucent. The golden light dimmed. "Desire did very well with you," she added, her intent gaze memorizing Airie. "Know that your mother loves you."

The rain ceased and the goddess was gone.

As Airie glanced at the rain-soaked mud and rivulets of water streaming down the craggy canyon walls, sudden panic filled her.

Scratch was gone as well.

• • •

The rainstorm had forced Hunter to seek temporary shelter in a yucca grove, which meant he'd had no real shelter at all. His miserable day was complete.

Once the storm let up enough for him to judge that the slippery terrain was again safe for travel, he and the sand swift started for home.

He rocked in the saddle, settling his hat farther back on his head. Water trickled from its brim down the back of his neck. Why that irritated him he had no idea, because he was already soaked to the skin.

He'd had plenty of time to think while he waited for the rain to abate.

Perhaps the Godseekers really were the best ones to take Airie in. They would assume her differences stemmed from immortality. They would care for her and keep her safe. He would tell them of how she had healed Sally and Scratch, and they would believe he brought them salvation. He was the Demon Slayer. They might try to kill him for his amulet, but they would not doubt him.

Before he gave her over to the Godseekers, he would need to return Mamna's gold. The thought of doing so gave him great pleasure. It had weighed too heavily on him.

He finally crested the bluff overlooking the canyon. Sally picked her way down the other side of the steep, muddy slope, aware from past falls that the potential for landslides had greatly increased and that the rocks were no longer secure.

Hunter wiped water from his face, puzzled by what appeared to be two shadows in the canyon where there should not be any at all. Not in this weather. One shadow belonged to Airie. The owner of the second was unidentifiable from this distance because of the rain.

What quickly became obvious to him, however, not only from the halo of unnatural golden light surrounding Airie but also from the sudden responding warmth of the amulet around his neck, was that Airie was not speaking with a mortal.

Hunter had seen very few demons in mortal form before and wondered if that was what protected this one from the rain, or if its protection came from the hypnotic golden light around Airie.

What if the falling of the goddesses' mountain meant the rains were no longer able to keep the demons away?

His heart lurched in his chest. The thought of Airie facing another demon alone caused him far more concern than it should, since this demon appeared to pose no immediate threat to her. If it had, his amulet would warn him. Instead it sent a gentle heat seeping through him, chasing away the dampness that had permeated his skin for miles. Sally, too, would have charged to her defense.

But unwelcome memories of his sister, vibrant, beautiful, and trusting, surfaced. His fingers tightened on the reins and his vision blurred. A demon had seen Airie the night before. That it might return for her should come as no surprise. She, too, was a beautiful woman.

He had been a fool to leave her alone.

Instinct had him ready to dig his heels into the sand swift's sides and urge it forward so he could ride to Airie's rescue, but a mean, suspicious part of him made him draw back on the reins to see how she would respond to one of her own kind this time.

She stretched out her hand to the faint figure before her as if in supplication, and Hunter's shoulder muscles bunched in response as he watched.

The rain eased, then stopped entirely, and suddenly, he saw she was alone.

His relief disappeared an instant later as her hand went to her chest, clutching into a fist over her heart. She spun around in frantic circles, searching for something that was no longer there.

He had seen enough.

He gave the sand swift its head and within moments he was at her side.

The man in him admired the picture she presented even while the part of him that hated demons wished she did not look quite so appealing. Clad in a thin white cotton shift, its wet fabric clinging to her curves and far too transparent, she swiped damp curls off her flushed cheeks and tucked them with shaking fingers into the long, thick braid of coal-black hair she wore. She looked fresh and innocent, except for the fear filling her wide brown eyes.

Fear was an emotion he did not associate with Airie. Remorse wrenched at his heart, twisting and squeezing. He had left her alone and something bad had happened.

He slid from the sand swift's back and caught her by the shoulders, searching her face. He wanted to ask what the demon had done to her but didn't know if he could stomach the answer. She was alive, and that was enough.

It was more than could be said for anyone else who had faced a demon that day.

Airie threw herself into his arms, sending him stumbling

backward a step. He quickly regained his footing. His equilibrium took him a few seconds longer to retrieve.

"Thank the goddesses you're back," she cried, sounding both anxious and relieved, burrowing her face in the crook of his neck. "I only took my eyes off him for a few moments, and now he's gone. We have to find him."

Hunter's arms tightened around her. Did she think he would help her find this demon? Did she think he would do anything other than kill it if he did?

She was crying now, with intense, shuddering sobs that he had never heard from her, not even on that first night after her mother had passed away. He had not been kind to her then. She hadn't seemed mortal to him, not even in her grief. He felt helpless in the face of it now.

He held her close and rocked her, resting his cheek against her crown and rubbing the heel of his palm in slow, awkward circles between her shoulders. She smelled of fresh air and innocence, and deep down inside, the protective shell Hunter had erected around his memories of another life where innocence was cherished began to crack.

"He's just a little boy," Airie was saying into the collar of his shirt, and the circling motion of Hunter's hand stopped as the extent of his stupidity sank in.

She was talking about Scratch.

Of course she was talking about Scratch.

But then what of the demon?

At the moment, Scratch was the more immediate problem. The demon would have to wait.

"Airie," Hunter said firmly. He eased her out of his arms. When he was sure he had her attention, he asked, "Where have you looked?"

"Here. In the yard." Dismay filled her eyes at the realization that she had glanced around, but not searched.

"He's got to be somewhere nearby, then. He couldn't have gotten far."

"He was afraid of the rain," she said. Her breath hitched. "I wanted to show him there was nothing to fear."

He wondered if Scratch had been more afraid of the rain or the sudden appearance of a demon, but he didn't say it. Not yet. Later, he would have a talk with her. She might be half demon, but she knew nothing about them.

Her mother had been right. Airie had little to no experience of the world beyond the mountain and the temple. In many ways, she was as defenseless as Scratch.

Hunter started for the cabin. "Perhaps he tried to find cover."

He checked first beneath the steps, where there was a small crawl space of the right size to attract a child wanting to hide. Nothing. He looked inside the cabin, under the bed, and inside the cupboard, where it was less likely he could fit. He then searched the corners of the yard where an outcropping or crevice might conceal him.

After that he, too, began to worry. Where could the boy have gotten?

Airie watched Hunter with an expression of hope and trust on her face. She expected him to find Scratch, but other, more alarming thoughts niggled at him. Coyotes and wolven roamed the canyons. There was also the danger of sinkholes if one did not know how to avoid them. He had a habit of picking up things he should not. Worse, what if Airie's demon had not been alone? What if another had made off with the boy while she'd been distracted?

Sally waited where Hunter had left her. He crossed the yard to her side and unloaded the packs. Steam rose from the saddle. Already, the heat of the sun and the dryness of the earth wicked away excess moisture.

The desert would be in full bloom for a few days following the rain. Airie would love that. Once he found Scratch, he would take them out for a ride so they could enjoy it.

After that, he would make plans to get them to the Godseekers. He could not look after them out here. He couldn't watch over them. He did not lead that kind of life.

Most importantly, the Godseekers lived to the north, well out of demon territory, and after she was far away, perhaps the one now pursuing her would forget her. He could not bear the thought of Airie in the possession of a demon, or anyone else.

Not when he wanted her for himself.

"What are you doing?" she asked.

He continued to place the supplies he had retrieved from the ill-fated wagon train in a neat pile, his movements mechanical. His mind had gone blank. It took him a few seconds to remember. "I'm going to search for the boy."

He did not even know where to begin. The desert was vast, expanding in all directions, and he had no idea which direction Scratch might have taken. The rain would have washed away any traces. But he could not stand there with Airie looking at him with such expectant trust and do nothing.

What had he done to deserve this?

He grabbed the bony prong of the sand swift's neck and put his foot in the stirrup. He was about to swing his leg over its back when a small noise behind him caught his attention.

Scratch crawled from under the steps, rubbing at his eyes with the knuckles of one tiny fist as if he had been startled from a deep sleep.

With a cry of relief, Airie swooped him into her arms and showered his sleep-ruddied cheeks with kisses. The sand swift shied to the side, tipping Hunter to the ground and flicking its tongue in an excited reaction to her joy.

Hunter, too, was relieved. He'd developed an unexpected affection for the child. But as he got to his feet and wiped the dirt and drying mud from his clothes, a growing unease dominated his emotions. The boy showed up in unexpected places, often carrying things he should not possess. Whenever Hunter thought to ask questions, however, or investigate, he became distracted by other matters.

Not this time. As soon as he could, when Airie was not so emotional, he would discuss this with her.

Because he had looked under those steps and Scratch had not been there.

CHAPTER TEN

Agares was drunk.

Because of that he could not retain his mortal shape, and as a demon, he was less than impressive and not nearly so agile.

The Demon Lord eyed him with resignation and disgust. Getting information from Agares in his current state would be difficult.

It was now night. The storm had passed hours before, and already the scents and sounds of a desert newly awakened filled the air. Agares blinked piglike, bleary eyes. Leathery wings drooped over his bulky shoulders, and his elongated snout dipped abruptly toward his heaving chest. He crouched on a rock near the entrance to the Demon Lord's desert fortress, in imminent danger of passing out.

Before Agares did so, the Demon Lord needed to hear what more he had to say. Other than that he'd happened on a wagon train of unfortunate travelers hauling whiskey intended for Freetown, so far, he had passed on nothing of value.

The Demon Lord also wore his demon form. The long, talon-like toes of his bare feet gripped the earth as he balanced his weight on well-muscled legs.

"What happened before the wagon train?" he asked again, for the third and final time. His patience had ended.

Awareness dawned in Agares's eyes as he finally seemed to appreciate the precariousness of his position. He made more of an effort to drag himself upright and shook his head in an attempt to clear it. Droplets of blood-red saliva glistened on his muzzle. The words rumbled from his chest.

"The mountain is gone and there are no signs of the goddesses. Except for the one with the Slayer." The rumbled words turned to sounds of pleasure. "She could rival the fairest of them, and yet the fool has not touched her." He paused as if an unwelcome thought had only now occurred to him. "At least, he had not touched her as of last night."

The words of a drunken demon were not to be accepted without reservation. However, the comments about her beauty and innocence caused him concern.

"There are a lot of beautiful women in the world," the Demon Lord said.

"Not like this one." Agares's eyes focused. "She fought with the strength of a demon." He zeroed in on the Demon Lord, his tone faintly challenging. "I claim her as mine."

He should have been prepared for this, but he was not. Neither was he prepared for the way he felt about it. Was Agares claiming her for a lover? Or for another reason entirely? Did he believe she was the one he had pursued throughout time, just as the Demon Lord had known when he found his?

While it was possible this spawn belonged to one of the priestesses who had inhabited the temple as Mamna claimed, the

Demon Lord could no longer pretend to believe so. The goddesses had been every bit as promiscuous as demons. If she belonged to one of them, he needed to know who the father had been. What if she were his?

The thought was too painful to bear. He did not doubt that if so, she was a trap of some sort—as was her mother, and for that, she would be his to destroy.

Mamna was the only one left who could tell him for certain, and she was not to be trusted.

"You cannot claim her," he said to Agares.

The other demon's expression sharpened and grew ugly. "I had permission to hunt."

He was drunk, but he was not stupid. Eventually he would come to the correct conclusion that the woman was spawn. He would also wonder at the fact she was a female, something unheard of before now. And he would begin to question where she had come from. By trying to claim her, Agares had sealed his own fate.

"Then you should have taken her from the Slayer when you had the chance. Now, I am curious." The Demon Lord's voice rocked the ground in command. "Find another."

"I don't want another. I want this one."

Even sober, Agares was not an impressive fighter. As he launched himself from his perch, the Demon Lord rolled away, taking the brunt of the hit on one shoulder. The crest of a wing bent, sparking his already uncertain temper.

The fight was brutal but short after that.

In the end, the Demon Lord stood over Agares's savaged remains, breathing heavily. Thirst for blood clouded his thoughts and his vision, and it took time for him to recover as blue-green light settled into him. This was yet another demon death to claim as his. The additional burden was not a welcome one.

He dragged the mutilated body a short distance into the desert where the burning rays of the sun would turn Agares's mortal form into ashes and dust.

His problem had not been resolved.

He had dispensed with Agares before finding out where the Slayer was harboring the spawn. Unfurling his wings, he leaped into the night sky.

Since the Slayer was known to hate spawn as much as he hated demons, if he was keeping her alive, it meant he intended to use her in some way. But against the demons or Mamna?

As the Demon Lord sailed silently above the desert's darkened landscape, he decided it was past time he confronted Mamna and received the truth. If he had to beat it out of her, then so be it. He had grown tired of her demands and become impatient with her motives. She would not hesitate to use the spawn to her own advantage—and only she knew what that advantage might be.

A short while later he circled the night sky above the gated walls of Freetown.

He rarely ventured here. He did not like men. When he looked at them, in particular the ones considered old in mortal terms, he saw what the future held for him, and he did not care for it.

On clear nights, as tonight, guards patrolled the walls of the city. He laughed to himself without humor. They served no real purpose other than to be Mamna's eyes and ears against her own kind, since demons attacked from the sky and did not stop at the walls for permission to enter.

He selected the most ostentatious dwelling in Freetown and peered through its windows, finding Mamna's sleeping quarters with little difficulty. He cleared the railing of her balcony, landing lightly on his feet.

Then he shifted to his mortal form and stood at the window, staring out at the city and waiting for her to awaken.

• • •

The day's rain had brought a welcome respite from the heat and caused her garden to flourish.

Mamna's dreams, therefore, were pleasant at first.

A noise at the window jolted her from sleep. She sat upright with a start, her hand clutching the lacy coverlet to her bony chest. The fractured amulet grew hot against her skin. Terror settled in when she recognized the man silhouetted against the moonlit sky.

She had awakened to a nightmare.

This was it, then. The beginning of the end for her. She wondered what she might say or do to make him spare her life.

He climbed through the window, his long, bare legs and feet sliding easily over the frame. He straightened, wearing nothing but a short pair of breeches that barely covered his muscled thighs.

Mamna averted her eyes, but as a false pretense to modesty. Despite the fact that he had begun to age—although slowly—he remained a beautiful man. She both hated and feared him, but she loved him as well. She had long ago given up hope that her love would fade, or ever be returned by him. Instead, she allowed jealousy and resentment, and hopes for revenge, to twist and taint it. She could find no other way to bear it.

He walked to the canopied bed and drew back the filmy curtain, looking down at her with inscrutable eyes. His smile sparked a fear that liquefied her insides.

"Why do you suppose it is," he asked, "that I can get so close to you tonight despite the amulet you wear?"

He was a demon. He fed on her fear as she struggled to hide it. Grasping her throat, he tried to tighten his grip, but when he could not, he ran a finger beneath the chain around her neck and gave a light tug.

Mamna dared not brush his hand away, instead covering the amulet with her palm so that he could neither see nor touch it. He already knew it had weakened. She did not want him to see to what extent.

He straightened, apparently tiring of his game. "The mountain has been destroyed. Why did you not send word to me?"

"I don't know what happened to it, myself," Mamna managed to reply, and with honesty. "The Slayer would have been on or near the mountain at the time. He will be able to tell me what happened when he returns."

The Demon Lord's eyes narrowed. "If the Slayer was on the mountain, how can you be so certain he survived?"

He was trying to lead her into revealing something, but she did not know what it might be. Whatever it was, she suspected it would mean the difference between life and death for her.

"He is the Slayer," she replied, gripping the coverlet tighter. "If demons cannot harm him, a mountain is unlikely to do better."

"When will he return?"

"After capturing the spawn." That, too, was the truth.

He continued to watch her, his face dark with suspicion. She kept her own bland.

Long moments passed.

"This is your final chance to tell me the truth," he said, breaking the silence. "Is the spawn mine?"

She dared not show fear. If she said yes, he would kill her. He would probably do so no matter what. Not even the amulet she wore could protect her if he was truly enraged.

She wanted to wound him. "How is it possible to know that for certain?" she asked, almost spitting the words. "The goddesses were whores. They gave amulets to their favorites. How many of these do you think I have seen on mortal men?" She withdrew from the small table beside her bed the stone she'd worn during her service to the goddesses and tossed it at him. It struck his chest and fell to the floor, disregarded. "These buy them the bearer's loyalty. I have seen hundreds of them. Thousands. Do you think your whore was any different than the others? Or that you were the only one of your kind she slept with?"

He laughed as if amused instead of angered by her words. His amusement soon faded, and his eyes became harsh. "Perhaps not mine, then. But was the spawn hers?"

"I couldn't say for certain," Mamna admitted unwillingly. She was too cautious to lie outright. "She went into seclusion after you turned from her. Only her scar-faced handmaid was allowed to attend her in those final weeks before the fire." She twisted the knife. "The goddesses sent her to trap you," she reminded him. "Who is to say a pregnancy wasn't part of that plan?"

The fleeting glimmer of pain in his eyes said she had managed to hurt him at last.

"Since my *whore*, as you call her, kept herself hidden, then it stands to reason she had something to hide. But over the years you seem to have forgotten to mention that detail to me." He leaned over the bed, his demon form flickering like a shadow around him as a reminder to her of what he was, and of what he was capable.

Hot waves of anger washed off him, banishing the coolness brought on by the rain, and the air in the room became stifling. Terror seized her again and for an instant, she thought she was dead.

"When the Slayer returns, the spawn is mine. If she is not handed to me at once, keep your amulet close, Priestess, and prepare to use what little power remains to it. Demons are no longer restricted to riding west winds as a warning to mortals. What you are about to learn is something you had best never forget."

He let the curtain around the bed fall back into place and crossed to the window, pausing with his hand on the sill as if about to say more. Instead, he vaulted into the darkness and was gone.

Mamna closed her eyes. Her fingers, still clutching the coverlet, had long since gone numb. The amulet cooled, although it remained warmer than normal, and she suspected if she checked she would find even more new cracks.

Her relief at her own survival was short-lived, soon followed by dread. He wanted to believe the goddess had betrayed him because to believe otherwise meant that he had betrayed her in return. If he found out that the spawn was indeed his, there was no telling what conclusion he might draw or what he might do in response.

Mamna knew two things. He did not make idle threats.

And the last time she'd seen him this angry, he had set a mountain on fire.

• • •

"You baby him too much."

With bare feet propped against the wall, Hunter sat at the table, his long, sun-streaked hair, still damp from a shower, grazing his shoulders. As she moved about the small cabin, restlessly tidying, his eyes followed her.

Airie did not know what to make of his scrutiny. Her presence bothered him, more so than usual, and the knowledge left her feeling awkward and too aware of his presence. She knew he disliked her for what he believed her to be, but the look in his eyes this evening was more complex than usual.

It was as if he wanted something he could not—or should not—have.

He had also been staring at Scratch most of the evening, but his face when he did so was easier for her to read. He worried that she would not be able to look after a little boy on her own.

So far, she had proven him right. It did not help that Scratch was not a normal child. As much as she did not want to see it, she knew he was not.

But normal or not, he was still a child.

"He *is* a baby," she pointed out. She tucked the blankets around Scratch as he lay on the small cot and stroked a gentle knuckle along his cheek. The steady light from the oil lamp on the table gave his skin a soft, golden glow. In sleep, he looked so innocent. Her heart constricted with residual panic at the thought that she might have lost him. Hunter was right to worry about her ability to care for him. "I would never have imagined a little boy could disappear so quickly. I'll have to find work that allows me to keep him close, at least for the next few years."

Hunter's feet hit the floorboards. "You should think about finding a family for him. There's always some homesteader in the north needing a boy to help out with manual labor."

In her head Airie knew he was right, but her heart told her differently. She could not give Scratch up now. They were both alone in the world. They were both different, and they needed each other. She'd already fallen in love with him. How could she abandon someone she loved and who needed her?

She did not respond to Hunter's words or look at him. She did not want to talk about this, or her concerns. Instead she said, "We should give him a proper name. We can't call him Scratch forever."

"Airie." He sounded tired, resigned, but not unsympathetic. "Let someone else give him a name. You saved his life. Now give him a chance to have one worth living. Give yourself one, too. It won't be easy to look after a little boy while trying to start out. It won't be easy for him either. Not if you baby him all the time."

It wasn't what she wanted to hear. "Caring for him isn't babying him."

Hunter's lips curved into one of those brief smiles. It transformed his face, making him seem less intense. The odd, troubled expression he'd worn all evening disappeared.

"I had seven older sisters. Believe me, I know babying when I see it."

"*Seven*?" This was the first real bit of personal information he had shared with her, and Airie seized it, her annoyance with him vanishing in an instant. This explained why he was good at braiding hair. "I can't imagine what it must have been like, growing up with so many sisters. You're very lucky. Where are they now? Do you see them often?"

"I haven't seen them in years." He ran his fingertips over the table's surface as if polishing the worn wood with them. Airie held her breath, hoping he would reveal more. "One of them is dead. I don't know about the others." He looked up at her, catching her off guard with his next words. "Who were you speaking with when I rode into the canyon this afternoon?"

Understanding, followed by sympathy, overcame surprise. He was trying to distract her because he did not want to talk about his sisters anymore, especially the one who had died. His face when he'd mentioned her said it all.

Airie thought it best if she didn't know for certain what had happened to that particular sister. The possibilities were too ugly and might explain why he had taken such an immediate and intense dislike to her.

Aside, of course, from the fact that he insisted she had tried to rob him.

She debated the value of honesty in her response to his question. It might make him think more kindly of her to know that a goddess had spoken to her without horror or fear. The goddess had told her she would have to earn the respect of the immortals, so making an effort to earn Hunter's respect as well would do her no harm. He had been good to her when she'd thought Scratch was missing. It was possible they might even become friends.

Her cheeks warmed. She remembered the way she had thrown herself into his arms. Her temper was not the only thing her mother often said she needed to learn to control. She had always been too impulsive.

But he had not pushed her away. Perhaps that explained the strange way he watched her this evening. He worried she expected too much from him.

The possibility that she might disconcerted her.

"I wanted to show Scratch that rain is nothing to fear," she said. "My mother taught me it means the goddesses are thinking of us—that it is their offering to us, because it brings life. When it started to rain I called out to them, hoping they might hear me, and when I did, a goddess responded."

"I see."

The quiet, thoughtful statement reminded her of the few times she'd been questioned by her mother with regard to her activities when collecting alms—as if he wanted to believe her and was going to pretend that he did, although they both knew better.

Wind pattered against the walls and Scratch sighed in his sleep. "I'm telling the truth."

"I know you believe you are," Hunter replied. "But what you saw was an illusion. The goddesses are gone."

He had once called her a spawn. Now he called her a liar, and worse, he thought her naive. That hurt almost as much. "This was no illusion."

"This is the second one to approach you. Demons are shapeshifters, Airie. They can take on mortal form. It is one more way they prey on women—by appearing to you in a form that makes you susceptible to deceit." He got to his feet and the room grew very small. "Promise me the next time one of these *goddesses* appears to you, you'll call for me." He moved closer, his eyes penetrating in the lamplight. "Promise me you won't talk to them without my permission."

The audacity of the request burned within her. She did not need his permission to speak. "How could I make such a promise? How could you expect me to?"

He looked at her as if choosing his words. "I came across the remains of a small wagon train today. One or more demons attacked it. There were no survivors."

Pain sliced through her. This explained why he'd been so out of sorts and distracted all evening. She was half demon and therefore served as an unpleasant reminder to him.

She did not feel half demon. She felt one hundred percent Airie. "Do you blame me for what happened?"

He stared at the sleeping child for a long time before looking at her. When he did, he was blunt.

"No. But others would have. Try to understand why I don't want anyone to find out what you are, Airie. People in Freetown won't welcome you. Not if they know." She could tell it pained him to say it, but that he felt it was for her own good to hear. "And now that a demon has seen you, you aren't safe from them either. I could take you up north. You'd be well out of demon territory there."

"You think those people in the wagon train were killed by the demon I allowed to escape," she guessed, and saw by the way his eyes flickered from hers that he did. The possibility that she was to blame for those deaths sickened her. She'd wanted to help Hunter. She had given no thought as to what her revulsion for killing anything might mean to others. Her fingers curled in the front of her dress, creasing the fabric. "You must hate me."

"No. What happened to them had nothing to do with you. They were killed by ignorance, greed, and stupidity." He sighed, then spoke to himself, his frustration evident. "You are nothing like what I expected."

"What *did* you expect?" she demanded. He had never told her why he had been on the mountain, and she was uncertain whether she wanted to know. She wished she could take back the question. There had been enough honesty between them for one night.

He reached for her hand. His touch was not unwelcome so much as bewildering. She did not know how to interpret the small gesture. The slight squeeze of his fingers on hers brought back the awkwardness she'd experienced all evening as he pretended not to watch her.

"I expected a thief." He picked up the lantern with his other hand. "Come outside so we can talk without waking the boy."

He drew her with him, and hanging the lantern from a hook on one of the verandah's pillars, created a warm cocoon of light that enshrouded them between the thick layers of night shadows. He sat on the top step and she sat down beside him, smoothing her skirt neatly beneath her.

He continued to hold her hand, brushing the backs of her fingers with his thumb as if distracted by the feel of her skin. She wondered if she should withdraw her palm from his but decided against it, liking the sensations he created.

"I'm not a thief," she reminded him, breaking the silence between them.

"While you may not think so, there are others who would disagree. They live in Freetown." He laced his fingers through hers before resting their joined hands against his thigh, pulling her closer to him so that their shoulders touched. He seemed unbothered by the intimacy so Airie relaxed, ever so slightly, against him.

"How can people living in a town with priestesses have forgotten the goddesses and the alms that are theirs?" she asked him. Her mother would not have allowed people to forget. "Anyone who enters the mountain is expected to leave offerings."

"They aren't called offerings if you take them by force," Hunter observed, his tone dry. "They're called loot."

She refused to admit his point was valid. "They could also be called the price of a lesson learned."

He shrugged. "Fair enough. Let's call them that. But if you go ahead with your plan to settle in Freetown, you will find there are a few lessons for you to learn as well. And I doubt if you'll like their price."

"I don't understand." She tried to put more distance between them, but he slung one arm around her shoulders so she had to tilt her head to the side to avoid pressing her cheek into his chin.

"Do you know what sort of life women lead in Freetown?" he asked. His voice took on a quality difficult for her to define. "Did your mother teach you nothing of men?"

"I would think I've proved to you that I can defend myself."

She felt the rumble of a laugh build from deep in his chest. "In some ways I'm sure you can. In others, I'm not as positive."

His arm slid from her shoulders to encircle her waist, and he bent his head. He meant to kiss her. Her palms came to rest on the thick cotton front of his shirt, although she didn't push him away.

His lips found hers.

She remained motionless beneath the gentle caresses that rained lightly at first, and demanded nothing from her. The heel of his hand began to move in slow circles, rubbing the small of her back, but again, demanding nothing.

The scent of freshly laundered clothing that had been dried in the desert sun lingered around him. She breathed deeply, remembering how kind he had been to her that day, and she closed her eyes. The tip of his tongue brushed her mouth, and her lips parted slightly. She tilted her head back, relaxing against the strength of his arm as he cradled her. His other hand found her hip. Kisses, not so light now, trailed along her jaw before dipping lower. She sighed, the roughness of his unshaven cheek teasing the delicate skin of her throat, sparking a sense of restlessness in her that she did not know how to resolve. She wanted to touch him too, to kiss him in return, but she also wanted to stay just as she was. She liked what he did to her.

He lifted her onto his knees. "Put your arms around me," he said. "The way you did this afternoon."

She opened her eyes. It took her a few moments to understand what he referred to. At the time she had been so afraid for Scratch she hadn't thought about what she was doing. She'd merely reacted with profound relief to Hunter's arrival.

But she remembered the way she had felt at the time. All her worries had dissolved. She had trusted him to find Scratch, and he had. He had made her feel cared for and protected.

"I never thanked you," she said, dismayed.

Again, a slow rumble of laughter that never quite escaped shook through him. He found her amusing. "You can thank me now."

His eyes challenged her. Airie had a sudden awareness that an imbalance existed between them, and that she was obligated to him in some way. She had never gotten the impression that he wanted her to be obligated to him before. He had refused her thanks several times. Until now, he'd seemed to want to be left alone. She did not know what had changed in him, but something had.

She nestled sideways between his thighs and slid her arms around his neck, pressing her face into his collar. With great daring, she touched her lips to the skin at the base of his throat and felt tightly tensed muscles flinch beneath the light caress in response. It indicated to her that she wasn't completely at his mercy.

Emboldened, she tasted him with the tip of her tongue. His rumble of laughter became a low purr of surprise.

"Thank you," she said, tipping her chin to look at him.

The wick in the lantern sputtered above their heads, sending its smoking flame dancing. He sifted his fingers through her hair, then held her head in his fingertips.

"That was nice enough," he admitted. His eyes smoldered with heat. "But I'm sure you can do better."

His lips again found hers, although this time, they weren't as gentle and demanded more. One of his hands cupped her head. The other traced its way down the side of her breast. She gasped as his touch lingered, lifting its weight in his palm. Her restless tongue met his.

In the back of her mind, a cautious voice warned that this was how a demon had played with her. Another, more adventurous one urged her to enjoy the sensations that the touch and the taste of him aroused in her.

She returned his kiss, clumsily at first and then with more passion. Her hands grew impatient, and she fumbled with the buttons on the front of his shirt until she was able to ease them inside. She traced raised welts crisscrossing his ribs with her thumbs, and she frowned.

"Demons," he said in response to her touch, as if that one-word explanation should be enough.

It was not.

"Why do you do this to yourself?" she asked, her palms resting flat on his bare skin. "You can't rid the world of them single-handedly. They are too many, while you are one man. Who is to say that, sooner or later, they won't come for you?"

Sighing, he raised his head and looked up at the night sky, but he didn't release her. Instead, he trapped her hands with his elbows so she couldn't withdraw them from his shirtfront.

"They don't belong to this world," he said, "and I will do what I can to drive them back to wherever they came from. They won't come for me because they would have to cooperate in order to do so, and they have no more love for one another than they do for mortal men. They think only of pleasure."

Was that why she enjoyed Hunter's touch? Was it the demon in her, seeking pleasure?

He straightened her clothing. She had not noticed he'd begun to undress her.

"The goddess told me I would have to make this world mine," she said. "Do you think that means I don't belong here any more than demons do?"

He took so long to reply that hurt wrenched her heart. "Your mother had a lot of faith in you. She worked hard to prepare you for life on this world. I would have to say the real question is where do you belong?" He eased her from between his thighs and onto the step beside him and buttoned his shirt. "You know nothing of men, Airie." He shot her a soft, rueful smile. "Although a few more minutes of this and you'd have learned far more than I'd intended." His smile faded. He lifted a handful of her hair and touched it to his lips before letting it slide through his fingers. "Freetown is not the place for you. Let me take you north."

Her mother might have had faith in her, but it seemed Hunter did not. She felt betrayed, which was foolish. A few light kisses held little meaning. He was correct. She knew nothing of men.

Not this one, at least.

"My mother is buried on the mountain," she replied, quiet but firm. "If I go anywhere I'll go back to be near her, but not until I have at least tried to make a place for myself in Freetown. She did not raise me to choose a path because of its ease."

He started to argue. His mouth opened, then closed, whatever he'd been about to say forgotten as he stared over her shoulder at something in the distance.

Airie turned to see what had caught his attention. An orange glow lit up the night.

The sky over Freetown was on fire.

CHAPTER ELEVEN

A small group of northerners had made it through the desert to Freetown unmolested by demons, and they wanted to celebrate in Blade's saloon.

Blade eyed them from his position behind the bar. Godseekers. Six of them, all drunk. Only one of them was an assassin, and he made up the seventh in their party. He did not associate with the others. He sat off to one side, drinking little, absorbing as much from his surroundings as he could. He wore his sandy blond hair overly long so that it hung in his eyes.

No one else would have known him for a Godseeker assassin. Blade, however, had spotted the weapon he wore tucked into the collar of his shirt when he'd bent over to adjust a knife in his boot. That inability to conceal small details meant he was not experienced.

There were two ways to become a Godseeker assassin. The first was by reputation. The second, recruitment.

And recruits were better trained.

Blade guessed this assassin had maybe eighteen winters behind him. He'd probably earned a reputation around his hometown, made a lucky kill, and decided to turn it into a profession.

Well, they all had to start somewhere. Blade had been about fourteen, and his first kill was an uncle who beat him. He'd practiced with knives for months beforehand because that had been one big, mean son of a bitch, and he knew there would be no second chances.

He polished shot glasses with his apron and listened to the Godseekers talk. They had not come to trade, and if their trip was not for profit, then it had something to do with the fall of the goddesses' mountain.

The Godseekers were not the only ones celebrating in the saloon this evening. A wagon train, very large and filled with traders, had been spotted crossing the desert. Since demons hunted alone, they tended to avoid the larger trains as not worth the effort. For a frontier like Freetown, isolated as it was, the arrival of traders was crucial. It took careful planning to move a wagon train the size of the one that had been reported, which meant it would not be leaving Freetown any time soon either. The saloon would be busy in the coming weeks.

A glass smashed on the floor, and one of the women moved to clean it up. Blade watched her work. The six Godseekers who were drunk weren't being discreet this evening. There was going to be trouble, and Blade hated trouble. One of them hoisted his glass in the air. "To the goddess."

A chorus of "To the goddess," rang out in response.

Blade limped to the table. He made his voice friendly. "Perhaps you should keep it down. The head priestess can become a little ill-tempered when she's reminded of the goddesses, and public places have eyes and ears."

One man spat on the floor in contempt. "We've crossed the

desert to greet the goddess born on the mountain, and to join her in her fight to drive the demons from this world."

Blade's fingers itched for his knives. "You'd be better advised to help her avoid them instead. A single goddess does not stand a chance against them. They are too many."

"She will lead us. She will lend us her strength. We'll be her army." They all nodded in drunken agreement.

"Then I hope there are more of you coming with that wagon train." Blade had lived too long in the desert to expect fanatics to see reason. He turned away.

"She will have the Demon Slayer with her," someone said. "Once he has joined her, other men will follow."

Blade turned back to the men at the table. "If that's your plan, then you need to rethink it. Driving the demons from this world is not the Slayer's goal. He wants them all dead. And he works alone."

He didn't bother to wish them luck in making converts for their army in Freetown. He doubted if they would have many. People here had lived too long in fear, both of the demons and of Mamna. They were broken.

So was he. He returned to his position behind the bar.

One of the women who worked in the saloon picked up a tray filled with drinks from the counter. Worry touched her eyes as she looked from Blade to the table filled with fools.

"You don't like those men, do you?" she said.

He shrugged. "Liking them or not is a waste of my time. They're dead men if they continue on as they are."

She bit her lip. A pretty blonde, she drew the attention of a number of prospects in the room.

The saloon had grown more crowded.

"Stay away from the boy sitting alone," Blade advised her. He had never interfered with her clients before, and he could tell it surprised her.

Her eyes widened in curiosity. "Why?"

"Because," he said, "he doesn't know shit about the world beyond the north. And he's not going to be satisfied with a half hour of your time."

She turned her head and met the boy's eyes. He smiled at her, and Blade knew he had wasted his breath trying to warn her.

"He's handsome," she said, and the undercurrent of wistfulness he heard in her tone made him wish he'd said nothing.

Who was he to keep her from spending time with someone her own age, pretending to be something she should have been but was not?

"I've misspoken." He filled a row of shot glasses with practiced efficiency while the girl loaded them one by one onto a tray. "What you do is your own business."

A short while later he watched her go upstairs, hand in hand with the boy.

He wished the evening was over, but it seemed to be just getting started. People came and went, the opening and closing of the door drawing in wafts of air still fresh and cool from the earlier rain. The steady stream of customers told him the winds did not blow from the west. If they had, the streets would be empty, and so would the saloon.

Soon, he was too busy to worry about things over which he had no control.

A disturbance broke out at the front of the saloon. The door flew open and several people gathered around it, pointing at the night sky.

Patrons spilled onto the steps, then into the dusty street. Blade followed more slowly than the rest, partly because of his limp and more because he wanted to keep an eye on the drunkest and meanest in the crowd.

Out in the street the drunks, however, were not what caused him the greatest concern. Against the backdrop of the city's wooden palisades and the deep cobalt night sky, bright orange fingers of flame lit up the heavens.

From out of the flames swept a demon.

· · ·

"It's a wooden city," Hunter said. His thoughts had leaped immediately to Blade and the women. "A fire will spread fast. I have to go."

Airie touched his arm, her fingers light. Her face was tense and pale in the flickering light of the lamp overhead. "What can I do to help?"

"Nothing." He started to shake her off, to go inside for his sword and his weapons, but then he stopped. He was no longer alone. He had the safety of both Airie and Scratch to consider. What of them?

He could not leave them unprotected. Not with a demon pursuing her. Neither could he take them across the desert at night. Torn, and wasting time his friends might not have, he shot another look at the burning sky over Freetown.

It was too late for him to help them. The town would burn to the ground long before he arrived.

A thick gray mass rolled over the horizon, blocking the flames from view and obliterating the stars, again plunging the night into darkness. Hunter recognized the changing texture of the sky, and what it meant, even under the blanket of the night.

"Is that rain?" he said out loud, incredulous. "Twice in one day?"

It was unheard of in the desert.

Airie stood motionless beside him, murmuring words under her breath he could not understand and would rather not know. He suspected they were connected to the demon side of her.

A howl of rage split the night sky, echoing across the desert sands and shaking the earth.

The flame in the rocking lantern swelled, growing too large for the chimney to contain and cracking its glass. Fire licked the dry timbers of the verandah post, threatening the roof, and with a curse, Hunter tore off his shirt to beat at it.

"Get Scratch!" he said sharply to Airie.

She roused at his command. She stepped up beside him and raised her cupped hand, holding it to the spreading flames. The fire blazed brighter, then, reversing its course, skipped from the smoldering wood to the tips of her fingers and into her waiting palm.

She curled her fingers closed and the fire vanished.

Hunter had thought there was little left in the world that could render him speechless. She had a talent for both fire and healing.

Darkness, and a faint whiff of smoke, embraced them. Another roar filled the air.

"What is that noise?" Airie asked, covering her ears, tension rippling around her. She edged closer to Hunter, and he slipped an arm around her shoulders.

"That," he said grimly, "is the battle cry of a demon."

• • •

The Demon Lord swooped from the fire-seared sky over Freetown, flames shooting from his eyes and the horned tips of his wings.

The first strokes of demon fire scorched the tops of the city's palisades. A building burst into crackling flames.

Mamna would be taught a lesson. He had placed her where she was. Had given her position and power. He couldn't harm her directly, not yet, but he could take everything away that he had given her, and she needed to be reminded of that.

This was the last time she held things from him.

The sight of mortals spilling into the streets to stare up at him, slack-jawed and uncomprehending, enraged him further. Bells rang at the walls and more people swarmed outside to see what was happening.

The goddesses had favored these creatures. That alone was enough to make him hate them. That one goddess in particular had found them to her liking was more than he could bear. He had once loved her more than his own life and arrogantly assumed he had been loved in return.

A part of him had hoped she would return to him. That she would confess her role in her sisters' deception and beg for his forgiveness. But if the spawn were his, and had survived all these years in the care of a priestess on the goddesses' mountain, where demons were unwelcome, Mamna was undoubtedly correct. The spawn was a weapon to be used against him and his kind. He would turn his anger on those Allia had loved in his stead. Mamna, too, would learn he was not to be defied.

He plunged downward, his attention on those mortals foolish enough to remain in his path. They scattered before him, scrambling over one another and screaming in terror.

A spray of bullets from a shotgun bounced harmlessly off the Demon Lord's bone-plated body, ricocheting into the crowd. It did not slow him, but the boldness of the act had him seek out the shooter.

The man lifted the shotgun again, but the weapon jammed in

his hands. His eyes widened when he saw the demon's attention on him. He tossed the shotgun aside and turned to run.

The Demon Lord's claws grazed his shoulder, tearing a chunk of flesh and muscle from bone and knocking him to the ground, shrieking in pain and terror.

The scent of fresh blood drove the Demon Lord on. He banked to the left, coming around for another kill as two men, more brave than wise, stopped to help their downed companion. The Demon Lord tore the head off one and grabbed the other in his talons to carry him high, then dropped him, screaming, to the earth.

Fire had caught the roof of a second building by now, and licked up the side of a third. The Demon Lord plunged through the flames to emerge in a display of splendor. He would show the world what they faced if they disregarded his presence. It had been too long since they'd last seen what he was capable of.

Are you watching, Mamna? Do you see what happens when you conspire against me?

The first sheets of rain struck, fierce and unexpected, pocking his thick hide like drops of acid. Smoke and steam sizzled in the air as the fires of the burning buildings died beneath the onslaught.

He tumbled backward, his wings beating the sky, and forgot the mortals bleeding to death in the street.

Goddess rain.

The Demon Lord shot above the roiling clouds and the downpour, and circled the city. Goddess rain had been called against him.

Him.

Whoever had done so would die. Demon numbers might be small, no more than a hundred all told, but they would still be enough to destroy this entire world again if he chose. Not even the boundaries would stop him.

The battle cry he let loose shook the heavens.

First one, then another, and eventually a score of demons responded to the Demon Lord's summons, filling the night sky above Freetown. They took turns darting under the clouds in an attempt to ravage the city, but each was forced back by the rain.

Frustration filled the Demon Lord. He had once brought this world to its knees. Even now, the goddesses protected it.

Once his initial anger was spent and reason returned, he called the demons back. As long as the rain fell they were unable to take action, but it could not linger forever.

He had his demons circle the city for the remainder of the night. Then, when the moon slipped away, the morning sun dissipated the darkness, and the rainfall eased to a gentle mist, the Demon Lord sent them home.

Night would return. When it did, so would the demons. And in greater numbers.

He was not ready to destroy what was left of this world, he decided. Not until he had the truth about the spawn from the mountain.

• • •

With the first light of day, Hunter had everything packed and ready to leave. The problem then became Airie.

She would attract far too much attention in Freetown.

His feelings toward her remained mixed. He had already decided to tell Mamna that he had not found any thief, and that she had undoubtedly perished when the mountain collapsed. He would return the gold that made him feel unclean.

But Airie's demon blood could not be ignored. She attracted

their attention as well. Taking her to Freetown meant exposing everyone to even greater danger.

However, he could think of no other option. He needed to get her into Freetown unobserved. Though he had his doubts about it, she had said she could pass for a boy. They had no choice but to try.

He handed her some of his clothes. "Here," he said, "wear these."

When she was dressed, he had to admit that she was tall and lean enough, and the clothes suitably bulky, for her to fool the unobservant. His boots, however, proved too large, so they stuffed socks in the toes. He tried not to smile. She walked like she'd spent too many hours in a saddle.

Her hair posed another problem.

"We could cut it," she suggested with such enthusiasm his smile escaped. He suspected she had proposed it before, more than once, and her mother had refused to allow it.

Cutting it would make things far simpler. However, when he looked at the gleaming black masses of curls, he could not bring himself to do so. Once the weight was removed those curls would become ringlets, and he would have to cut it too short to compensate.

He was glad she had not shaved her head, as the priestesses did. He liked it as it was.

"Your braid will work better," he said. "We can tuck it inside your shirt and tie a kerchief around your neck. Lots of men wear braids, although not quite as long and thick as this."

He helped her tie her hair. The smooth tresses slid like silk over his palms, and he could not resist pressing a light kiss to the gentle curve of her neck when he was finished. A flash of sunlight lit her eyes as his reward.

He would have liked to kiss her with more thoroughness. Last night it had been very difficult for him to stop. The next time it would be twice as difficult, if not impossible, and he believed she would not protest, but because she did not understand the repercussions.

He was not certain he did either.

Instead, he found her an old hat he'd intended to throw away, and the disguise was complete.

He inspected her. Since he already knew her, he would never be fooled. But unless someone looked closely, for all intents and purposes, she could indeed pass for a boy.

A very effeminate one.

There was little to be done about that. His options were to escort a strikingly beautiful woman into town, or a strikingly beautiful boy. He was less likely to have to kill someone over a boy. He hoped. "Let's go."

The trek into the desert was unbearably hot although neither Airie nor Scratch seemed to mind. Hunter and Airie took turns carrying the little boy on the sand swift's back since it would look strange for two men to ride tandem.

Occasionally, Scratch squirmed to be let down so he could walk too, most often when Airie was on foot. She held his small hand and sang to him, swinging his arm as they trudged along the wind-bared trail.

Other, less-traveled trails converged with the main one they followed at several points. Around midday, Hunter spotted a telltale cloud of dust in the air ahead of them that signaled a wagon train of significant size.

A new plan occurred to him. If the wagon train was reputable, he could inquire about having Airie and Scratch join it so he could ride ahead into Freetown. If he gave her detailed instructions, she could meet him after dark at a predetermined location inside the city gates.

The plan had merit. He had been worried about bringing danger to Blade's home. The former assassin would have no difficulty in defending himself, but his crippled leg made protecting the women under his roof more complex, and Hunter disliked abusing their friendship.

A quiet entry into the city would be best for everyone.

As they drew close enough to see the wagons at the tail end of the train, Hunter, who was walking, caught the bit with his fingers and drew Sally to a stop. The sand swift shook its flat snout, leathery sides heaving, displeased at the delay when it scented both food and water so close.

"Wait here," he said to Airie. He lifted Scratch from the saddle. "I want to see what's ahead."

She dismounted too, her long legs sliding elegantly to the ground, and he groaned out loud. She looked at him with puzzlement in her dark eyes, his reaction arresting her movements. "What's wrong?"

He set Scratch on his feet. "You move like a woman."

Airie thought about it. "I do," she admitted. "I'll try to remember not to do so in the future."

His lips slid into a slow grin. "Only when you're dressed like a man. Otherwise, having you move like a woman is preferable by far." He nudged the boy toward the shelter of nearby rocks where he could escape the worst of the midday heat. "I won't be long."

By the time Hunter reached the lead wagon, the entire train was within sight of Freetown's gates. He saw at once that its wares included a brace of slaves and almost turned back. The term slave was somewhat misleading. They were almost always women, intended for trade in the mining towns where life was hard and pleasure scarce. Hunter never dealt with such traders, although his reluctance at the moment stemmed more from uncertainty as to how Airie might react than from any personal preference.

Then he thought of Mamna and the demons and decided he would take his chances. Airie would not have to travel far with the wagon train, only a few hours.

The wagon master, a middle-aged man with skin eroded by the elements, and a thick dusting of red desert sand on his face and clothes, rode a long-legged, black-haired hross alongside the wagons. He kept a sharp eye on the wagon train's progress.

His eyes noted the amulet Hunter wore around his neck as Hunter approached.

"Slayer," the man acknowledged him, touching the wide brim of his hat with the tips of two fingers.

"Master," Hunter nodded in return. He squinted at the cloudless blue sky. "It's a beautiful day."

"It is that."

They exchanged a few pleasantries while the wagon master's hross flicked its ears back and forth in displeasure at Sally's proximity. The sand swift responded by licking its rump with her sharp tongue, creating immediate chaos. The hross hauling the wagons closest to them shied away from the sand swift, too.

It took a few moments for the men to regain control of the animals.

"I acquired two young travel companions on the trail," Hunter said to the wagon master once calm was restored. "Brothers. One is a small child, perhaps two and a half or three years, who can't walk very far on his own. The older boy is maybe sixteen and stronger than he looks, but he's already carried the little one a long distance in this heat and refuses to leave him behind. They're both too tired to walk any farther, and my sand swift can't be trusted to carry them." He patted Sally's neck and she obliged him by darting out her tongue at the wagon master, who expertly dodged it. "Would it be possible for the boys to hitch a ride the rest of the way into Freetown with you? Neither one of them talks much, so they're no bother." He would have to warn Airie to remain silent so as not to give herself away.

The wagon master knew better than to ask why Hunter cared about the welfare of two boys who supposedly meant nothing to him, nor had Hunter expected him to express interest in anything other than compensation, but the wagon master was not a fool. His request for payment was high.

The only gold coin Hunter possessed belonged to Mamna, the weight of it heavy in his pocket and still sore on his conscience. He contemplated paying the wagon master from it and telling Mamna when he returned the remainder to her that he had retained a small fee for his troubles, but returning it in its entirety was the wisest option. He wanted to be done with her, once and for all, and under no obligation—either real or imagined.

"Your price is too steep, my friend," he replied, injecting a note of careless regret into his words. "The boys will have to walk the rest of the way on their own. I hope they make it before nightfall." They both knew the gates would be locked at that time.

He tugged on the sand swift's reins as if to withdraw.

"Wait a moment." The wagon master rested his arm on his knee, the reins loosely wrapped around one wrist. He spat in the dirt. "Word has it that Freetown was attacked by demons last night. That only rain held them off. We aren't stopping any longer than necessary in a place the demons have marked. If you stay with us for protection while we're in Freetown, then escort us the rest of the way across the desert, I'll take those boys into town for you."

Hunter had expected a deal such as this. If the demons were banding together, not even the size of this wagon train—which snaked several miles back down the trail—guaranteed the traders safe passage.

The Demon Slayer would be no guarantee either, although better than nothing.

"You would have to pay me more than offering a short ride for two boys," Hunter replied, and named a price equally as high as the wagon master's original. He did not want to seem too eager for this deal, but in truth, he was. Leaving Airie alone in Freetown had never been part of his plan, not that he'd had much of a plan to begin with. He was rushing to Freetown out of fear for his friends.

At least now, with a wagon train to accompany, he had a way to get Airie safely across the desert, and to the north.

"The boys can ride in the last wagon," the wagon master said, once he had agreed to the price. He eyed Sally. "Try to keep the sand swift from eating any of the hross."

Hunter went to collect Airie and Scratch.

After giving her instructions as to where to meet him once they had passed through the gates, Hunter deposited them both in the last wagon.

The wagon belonged to a trader carrying stained glass and other high-end building materials. The goods were of little interest to thieves, who would go for practical items such as food and tools, and was why this wagon brought up the rear.

Its wagoner wasn't pleased with having the extra weight added to his load and therefore was not inclined to make idle talk, and after a short time riding beside them, Hunter no longer feared Airie's disguise might fail.

Satisfied he had secured their safety, he rode ahead, anxious to learn what had happened in Freetown during the night.

CHAPTER TWELVE

Mamna's hold over the citizens of Freetown was based on their fear—of her, and of the demons. She spent the early hours of the morning wondering how she might turn this attack to her advantage.

The warm puddles from the rain had long since evaporated by the time she took her lunch in a garden exploding with colorful blossoms and rich, earthy fragrance. Irrigation was unnecessary today, thanks to the goddesses' rain.

The delicate pastries turned to dust in her mouth, and she pushed her plate away in annoyance. She would thank the goddesses for nothing.

The head of the night watch had waited all morning to speak with her. She called for one of the servants to admit him.

He walked stiffly along the narrow path, his wide shoulders nudging aside the tendrils of greenery and draping flowers. He stopped by her chair. It was several seconds before she acknowledged him.

"One civilian was torn to pieces, another decapitated. Three guardsmen were killed by fire on the ramparts," he said to her when she did. His face remained impassive. "The walls are scorched but still stand strong. Three buildings burned. The rain came in time to prevent any more from catching fire."

"What is the mood in the streets?" Mamna asked. She took a sip of her drink as if unconcerned by his words, but a slight tremor in her fingers gave her away. She set the glass down abruptly.

"Uncertain." The head night watchman clasped his hands behind his back and did not look at her. "There is talk that the demon attack was provoked by the rain earlier in the day. The fact that the rain came again in the night is considered further proof of provocation."

"Who do people believe is responsible for this provocation?" Mamna inquired, sounding no more than faintly curious, as if the matter bored her.

"They believe that only a priestess could call the goddesses' rain."

Mamna doubted that even a spawn could accomplish such a feat. The rains came at will and were no more than a coincidence. However, the Demon Lord would most definitely be provoked by anything connected with the goddesses, particularly in light of their recent conversation.

He would return tonight, and with reinforcements. How far did he plan to go in teaching this lesson?

She needed to divide the loyalty of those reinforcements. To turn them against him. At the very least, she had to distract them. If the Demon Lord called his fire again, her amulet would not be able to prevent the destruction of the city. The goddesses themselves had been unable to withstand it.

"Is it true that a wagon train approaches from the north?" she asked, shifting the conversation.

"Yes," he said.

The head night watchman's response was too slow. She did not care for people who considered their words before answering when she asked them a question. It meant they had something to hide.

"Lock the gates against them, then." That should provide a distraction if the demons decided to return when the sun set. "The gates can be reopened tomorrow morning."

He had no response for that other than to nod. Mamna dismissed him. She would find another way to distract the citizens and silence their belief that the priestesses had antagonized the demons. She would find someone to blame and hold them accountable. Then, she would find a way to appease the Demon Lord.

She sat back thoughtfully, her hand coming to rest over the amulet beneath her clothing. She needed the demons in order to maintain her position in Freetown. She did not necessarily need the Demon Lord. Wanting him was pointless and foolish. She was long past wasting time on silly dreams.

His daughter had two birthrights. The spawn would have traits of both parents. What if a priestess offered to support her in replacing the Demon Lord? What would the spawn be willing to do in exchange for such power?

· · ·

"They've locked the gates."

The wagon master's anger when he delivered the news was palpable, thick and sour on the hot afternoon air. A vein flexed at his temple.

Hunter looked at the sky. It was three hours to sundown. The gates should not be closed yet, let alone locked and barred.

Blackened scorch marks ran along the top of the palisade where demon fire had touched it the previous night, before the rains came.

"Did they say anything?" he asked.

"Only that the gates will be reopened in the morning."

Hunter kept his eyes away from the end of the train and the wagon where Airie rode with Scratch on her lap. Being dressed as a boy would not be of much help to her during the coming night hours. She was unclaimed and, therefore, doubly attractive to a demon. Her presence would bring disaster on these people.

Hunter should claim her first.

The thought rose unbidden, but if he were honest, not for the first time. If he claimed her, she would be less attractive to a demon. It would not be able to prey so easily on her innocence, to lure her, to make her believe that it loved her.

The thought of Airie bearing a monster that would tear her to shreds, as his sister had been, sickened him.

The wagon train ground to a halt. Several of the men strode forward to find out what caused the delay. People were hot and thirsty, and they had counted on Freetown for fresh water. Many had already run out, and weary after days spent rationing, had grown reckless with their supplies. Not only that, no one wanted to spend a night in the open when demons would most likely return, and in great numbers.

A small, hostile crowd formed.

"We could offer up some of the women," someone suggested.

The wagon master turned on him. "Are you planning to pay for them? Because I can guarantee the traders who own them will not part with them cheap."

A spark of anger caught fire inside Hunter.

"You know what the demons will do to women," he said.

"The lives of a few slaves compared to those of three hundred," the wagon master replied, sounding tired. "If we don't make some sort of offer, the demons will take whatever they want when they return tonight, including the women, regardless. What would you have me do, Slayer? Not even you can fend off an entire army of demons."

Hunter had nothing to say to that. The wagon master was correct.

He turned the sand swift and rode back to the last wagon, where Airie sat. It was too late for them to put any distance between themselves and Freetown. Their only chance for safety would be within the city walls. He would have to take Airie and the boy in through the hidden tunnel, but he could not do that with everyone watching.

He could not abandon these people to demons either. He would have to get Airie and Scratch to safety, and then return, without his movements being observed and before the next attack.

The timing would be difficult. He didn't think he could manage it before the first wave of demons attacked.

"What's happening?" Airie asked when he approached, her dark eyes wide and curious. "Why have the wagons stopped?"

"The gates are locked."

The shortness of his reply, and the anger he did nothing to hide, worked to keep her from asking more questions, but he could sense her concern. She glanced toward the gates and the activity of the wagon train's men in front of them.

"Come on." He slid from the sand swift's back. "The little one should stretch his legs." He reached up to take Scratch from her arms.

She vaulted one-handed off the side of the wagon and landed

catlike on her feet. If he hadn't been in such a foul mood he might have laughed. There had been nothing feminine at all about her dismount.

He stepped close to her, set Scratch on the ground, and issued orders in low tones. "Take the boy and head around the left side of the wall. About three hundred feet in, you'll find a cluster of sage buttressed against the footings. Pull the sage aside and smooth away the sand. You'll see a handle and a trap door. There's a tunnel beneath." The tunnel was known to the priestesses—Mamna had ordered it built and it was frequently used by both her and the men she hired—but it would never do to have the wagoners alerted to it. Hunter could not smuggle three hundred people into the city, even if he'd been so inclined. "Go inside, but don't go all the way through. Wait there for me. I may be a few hours." He eyed the blue sky, deepening to purple and then to red along the horizon. "Maybe longer."

He could see the stubborn determination rising in her eyes, reminding him of the girl from the mountain who had hidden in the bushes to ambush and rob him, but she had done it for her mother's sake. She knew what was coming at nightfall and she did not want to leave him behind.

She had fought a demon for him. She'd also held fire in her eyes and the palm of her hand. That would prove more difficult to disguise than her gender.

"Please," he added, not wanting to sort out his feelings for her. "Think of him." He looked at Scratch, who squatted at their feet and was chasing the trail of an insect through the sand with a dried twig. "I can't help these people if I have to worry about the two of you."

"But I can help," she said.

"No." Hunter could think of nothing he wanted less than that. She had already caught the attention of two demons. To expose her to many, many more—and possibly reveal her parentage to all of Freetown, as well as the wagon train, in the process—was not to be contemplated.

He knew he was becoming too protective of her, and at some point she was going to have to stand on her own, but that time was not now.

She caught the inside of her lip with her teeth. She took Scratch's grubby fingers in hers and averted her face. "But I'll be worrying about you."

She uttered the words so softly he almost did not hear them. How long had it been since someone worried over his welfare? Did it matter?

He had chosen this life. He had known what to expect. Still, he would have liked to hold her and ease her fears. He could hardly do so with her dressed as a boy.

Colorful sage and stands of cottonwood ringing the palisades offered some privacy from prying eyes as Airie led Scratch away. Hunter watched them out of the corner of his eye, making certain no one followed them.

Once he was certain she had done as instructed, he again went in search of the wagon master.

"There's a small canyon not far from here," Hunter said to him. "It will offer some protection for the night, but it's not very big. The wagons will have to remain behind."

"We can't abandon the wagons." The wagon master took off his hat and rubbed his face with his sleeve. The sun remained fierce in the heat-rippled sky, although it would set in a few short hours. "We traveled prepared to fight demons. We have barrels of pitch, and bows and arrows."

"You didn't travel prepared for a demon war. Bring a wagon with the pitch and weapons to the canyon, then, but nothing more. The demons won't bother the rest. They're hunting mortals."

"What of the people inside the gates?" the wagon master asked. He slapped his hat back on his head. "Can they be trusted to leave the wagons alone, too?"

Hunter understood his reluctance to have anything happen to the wagons. These people had traveled a great distance, many of them carrying all they possessed, while others had invested heavily in trade goods in the hopes of making their fortunes.

"As long as the gates remain locked, no one can leave the city. And if the demons attack, then yes, I can safely say the wagons will not be touched." He looked at the sky. "But we don't have much time left. With any luck," he added, although he didn't really believe it, "the demons aren't interested in the canyon. Their focus seems to be Freetown."

The wagon master reluctantly agreed. He had no other choice.

Hunter took charge of the weapons, leading the wagon to the small canyon where he stabled Sally when he came to Freetown. There were too many people in too confined a space for a sand swift, so he led Sally to the trail and slapped her hindquarters with his hat, sending her lumbering for home.

Hunter returned to the canyon, averting his eyes from the long line of slave women in chains who trudged listlessly past him to sit against one of the interior rock walls. He was doubly glad Airie was not here. She did not need to see this.

The canyon narrowed near the top, and shielded from the sun, it was several degrees cooler than the open desert. It would also retain heat better throughout the night, and offered protection from an aerial demon attack. Even so, it was going to be a very long night.

The wagoners built a fire to heat the pitch. After that, there was little for anyone to do but watch and wait.

All the while, Hunter worried about Airie. He did not like her being alone and without protection. If he were going to get her out of the tunnel and to Blade before demons attacked, he had to act now.

Armed with a sword, a backpack filled with things Airie might need, and several well-hidden knives, he sought out the wagon master.

"I'm going to check the area around us and make certain nothing approaches on foot," Hunter said.

He then slipped through the neck of the canyon. Once out in the desert, he ran.

Night had already fallen.

• • •

The tunnel was black inside, very narrow, and smelled of sour, stale dirt and other, even less pleasant things.

Airie sat on the ground and cuddled Scratch on her lap, burying her nose in his hair and breathing his little boy scent. Dark places held dark creatures, tiny but deadly, and she did not want him inadvertently provoking anything. He liked to examine things too closely sometimes. She wondered where he came from.

Kissing his cheek, she murmured, "Poor baby."

He snuggled deeper into her arms and fell asleep within seconds, his thumb in his mouth, leaving Airie with her thoughts.

She was not patient, particularly when afraid, and she was afraid for Hunter. He had refused her help. He still did not believe a goddess had spoken to her.

She removed Hunter's hat and set it on the ground beside her, pulling her braid free of her shirt with relief. Her hair itched her skin.

Several hours passed before she heard a scraping noise, then Hunter lowered himself into the tunnel, and Airie could have wept with relief.

"We don't have much time," he said to her. "I have to get you both to a friend's place. He lives nearby. He'll watch out for you until I return."

"We can leave Scratch with him," she replied, "but I'll stay with you. I can help."

"We'll talk about it later." He took Scratch from her. He was awake now, although silent as usual. "Follow me."

The tunnel was short. Hunter eased open the trap door on the other end of it, listened carefully, then slid it aside. They emerged onto a street, near the back door of a silent building.

Airie could see quite well in the darkness. She looked around, curious. The street was long, straight, and wide enough for a single wagon to pass through. They stood at the end nearest the city wall. Another, narrower street, more like a path, looped the wall's inner perimeter.

Footsteps thudded above, approaching on the wall. Hunter grabbed her hand and pulled her into the shadows, out of sight, as a figure swinging a lantern came into view.

The guard paused above them, angled the light in different directions, then after a few long moments, continued on.

"Night watchman," Hunter whispered to her. He examined her. "What happened to your hat?"

She had forgotten it on the floor of the tunnel. She made a move toward the tunnel entrance. "I'll go get it."

"Never mind," he said, his words stopping her. "We need to hurry. There's no one around other than the night watch."

There wasn't, she noticed, examining the street where they stood with growing unease. It was as if the entire city had been abandoned. She had seen more signs of life back home in the mountain's sparse trading posts than here.

And suddenly, a presence inside her grew restless. Her skin itched as if it were now too small for her body, and stretched unbearably tight. Compulsion, as if someone called her name, drew her toward the west end of Freetown and away from the direction Hunter indicated they were to travel.

She reached for his fingers to lead him. "We have to go this way."

Hunter shifted Scratch in his arms so that the little boy sat on the crook of one elbow. "Impossible. The demons will be here at any moment and I have to cross open desert to get back to the wagon train. The sooner I drop you off with Blade, the better."

The compulsion grew stronger. Not even the threat of being separated from Scratch helped her to fight it.

Airie shook off Hunter's hand and darted away. She heard his spurred boots clicking on clay cobblestones behind her, then his soft swearing. "Damn it all, Airie, we're announcing to the entire city where to find us. Slow down and try to make less noise."

She halted in the shadows of a long archway that led into a small cobbled courtyard encased by four two-level buildings. Inside the courtyard, a small crowd had gathered. In the midst of the crowd, one speaker stood out. A faint amber light glowed at his collar.

"The goddess will come," she heard him say. "I feel her presence."

The glowing amulet he wore around his neck was what had

drawn her to him. The goddess who spoke to her had responded to it.

Now that she knew what compelled her, she found it easier to resist. The light infusing the amber amulet flickered and went out. Murmurs of disappointment spread through the gathering.

Hunter pinned Airie to the wall of the archway with his body. One of his knees blocked her path.

"Godseekers," he breathed into her ear. "We don't need this kind of trouble right now."

Who were these people? Why did Hunter consider them trouble?

Why was she so drawn to them?

"If the Demon Slayer is with her," the spokesman continued, "we will ask him one last time to join us. If he refuses again, we will kill him."

"I don't remember being asked to join them," Hunter muttered beneath his breath. "They went straight to trying to kill me."

"Why?" Airie whispered back, confused.

"Because of my amulet. Whoever wears it becomes the Slayer."

The goddess's denial flared at his words. *That is untrue. The Slayer is champion. There will be only one.*

And Hunter had been chosen.

Scratch, still in Hunter's arms, squirmed to be let down. The moment of inattention he caused was enough for Airie. She pushed past Hunter and stepped boldly into the courtyard, guided again by the tug of compulsion on her amulet.

"Who's there?" the Godseeker's leader demanded from his place at the head of the gathering.

Airie's skin warmed. She looked at her hands in faint wonder, flipping them over to examine her palms. Her skin was glowing.

Her head went up and her voice rose so that all present could hear. "No one harms the Slayer."

The words rolled from her chest like a clap of thunder, startling her as much as anyone. The goddess had spoken, joining her thoughts and her voice to Airie's.

Her audience stilled, gaping at her in wonder and fear. One by one, they dropped to their knees.

Airie turned to Hunter, who had stepped beside her, his hand on the hilt of his sword. Scratch remained hidden in the alley. She sensed him behind her in the shadows.

"Congratulations," Hunter said to her, his eyes on the men in the gathering. "You have just been deified. Next time, let me speak for myself."

But from the corner of his eye he was looking at her strangely now, too. The soft golden glow from her skin warmed the angles of his face so that she could read the caution creeping into his eyes.

She didn't like it.

The glow of her skin dimmed with the shifting of her mood.

"She has come to lead us," the Godseeker said, starting toward her through his small crowd of followers.

"No, she has not." Hunter stepped in front of Airie to protect her.

The Godseeker reacted as if the move were a threat. He dropped his hand to his hip in a blur, too fast for Hunter to react to the gun being drawn on him.

Airie's world slowed, the faces around her distorting, sound waning to a dull background roar. Her own movements, however, remained lightning-quick. She pushed Hunter aside. The bullet shot past her ear to embed in one of the buildings behind her.

He tried to kill the champion. This is not to be tolerated.

Anger set in. She felt the heat rise in her eyes. She turned her head, needing something to burn, and narrowed her gaze on a target.

The Godseeker's boots smoldered.

With profound disbelief on his face, he danced as he tried to kick them off.

"Stop it, Airie!" Hunter shouted, grabbing and shaking her, startling her so that she lost her concentration. The Godseeker got his boots off his feet. Smoke rose from the insoles, but they did not catch fire.

She was not yet finished. "If you wish to fight demons," she said past Hunter to the now silent gathering, "you first need to know your allies." She let her eyes flare again. "And your enemy."

Hunter backed away from the mute Godseekers, pushing her behind him and into the alley where Scratch sat in wait on the cobblestones. Hunter lifted him and turned to Airie.

"Start running," he said to her, his voice quiet and grim. "And do not utter one more word until I say you can."

CHAPTER THIRTEEN

Blade carried the bucket of food waste into the small, unlit compound off his kitchen, heading for the alley beyond. A skittering of loose gravel immediately inside the locked gate let him know he wasn't alone.

He stepped out of the thin wash of light streaming from the open doorway behind him and reached for the knife he carried beneath one arm, but a long, low whistle stayed his hand.

Hunter.

The light from the kitchen was enough for him to identify the wriggling bundle Hunter carried in his arms, and Blade could not have been more surprised if his friend had appeared naked and dancing by moonlight before him.

What in the name of the goddesses was Hunter doing with a child?

Blade cleared his throat. "Well."

"Well, what?" Hunter plunked the child on the ground at his feet.

The little boy looked up at him, all wide eyes and wariness. The dark expression on Hunter's face left Blade with no idea what to say next.

"Hungry?" he asked the child, figuring that to be a safe topic, and if the answer was yes, one easily addressed.

The little boy nodded.

Ruby appeared in the kitchen doorway, no doubt wondering what was taking him so long.

"Well," she said, echoing Blade's surprise. She glanced sharply from Hunter to Blade. "We don't deal in children." Her tone left no doubt as to her opinion of those who did, an opinion Blade shared.

Surely Hunter wouldn't—

A woman moved out of the shadows into the soft light, surprising Blade even more than the child Hunter had carried. Hunter owed his life to his ability to move silently, so Blade wasn't concerned that he hadn't noticed his presence until Hunter wanted him to. But it bothered him that he had not been aware of the woman's.

She was very tall, but with a delicate femininity of frame. Her hair was as black as pitch, long and thick, and tied in a simple braid that dangled neatly to her narrow waist. Long legs, trim hips and high breasts didn't escape his attention, although the men's cast-offs she wore were far from flattering.

Yet it was her face that took his breath.

She had the smooth, golden features of a goddess. He'd never forgotten their visits to his childhood village, infrequent though they had been. No one who had seen them could possibly forget.

Ruby had crossed over the threshold to stand in the compound beside him. "Put your tongue back in your head," she said in an amused undertone. "You've seen women before."

"The little boy's hungry," Blade replied.

Ruby smiled at the woman. "I imagine you are, too." She extended her hand in welcome. "I'm Ruby."

"Airie."

Airie took the offered hand and when she did, Ruby started at the touch, as if she had received a jolt of some sort and wasn't quite certain whether she liked it.

The older woman recovered her hand and her poise with equal speed. "Let's go get you both something to eat, shall we?"

She stepped aside. Airie took the boy by the hand and led him into the light and warmth of the kitchen.

Blade watched them disappear inside, then turned his attention back to his friend. "Who is that?"

"That," Hunter said, slinging the pack from his back and dropping it to the ground with a grunt of pure weariness, "is a demon."

Blade drew back and stared through his kitchen doorway in shocked disbelief. "No."

"Oh, most definitely yes," Hunter said. "And keep your voice down. She has the ears of one, too."

Blade's initial disbelief turned from shock to a slow-burning, incredulous anger. "So you brought her here? To my home?"

Hunter mounted the single wooden step and closed the door to the kitchen, throwing them into darkness, shaking like a man badly in need of a drink despite the fact that he never drank. Not to Blade's knowledge.

"She's not one hundred percent demon. I don't know what she really is, except that she is the spawn I was hired to bring in. After we saw the fire last night I had to find out what was happening with you, and leaving her behind wasn't an option. What would you do in my place?"

Some of Blade's anger faded with the dawning awareness that Hunter's shock and disbelief surpassed his own.

What *would* he do?

Blade had no ready answer as Hunter sat on the back step and told him everything, starting with his first meeting with Airie, their flight down the mountain, and ending with the altercation with the Godseekers.

"Let's say she really is half demon," Blade said, although the thought of it made him ill. "Do I want her here? Do I want her near the other women?"

Hunter lifted his shoulders in a shrug of bewilderment. "She healed Sally with the touch of her bare hands. She saved that scrawny kid, who was starved to the point I could have sworn he was the next best thing to dead, and the next day he was fine. She wouldn't let me leave him behind, although you and I both know that would have been the kindest thing to do." He sighed, letting his hands drop. "She set a Godseeker's boots on fire. Although to be fair, he was trying to kill me."

Blade remembered Ruby's flash of surprise as she touched Airie's hand. He would ask Ruby about that later, and about her impressions of her. Ruby's instincts regarding people were usually sound.

"Can she be a…good demon?" Blade asked hopefully. Hunter shot him a black look. "Then why have you brought her here?"

Again, Hunter lifted his hands helplessly. "I wanted her to be safe."

Blade did not want any demon, good or otherwise, male or female, in his home. But the memory of the woman Mamna had condemned to death would not leave him, and that she would turn Airie, too, over to the demons was not in doubt. What the demons would do to a spawn was not either.

But what the demons would do to a spawn who looked like Airie before they killed her was the uncertainty that made Blade hesitate. That was the real reason Hunter had brought her here. Uncertainty had made him hesitate as well.

"You should have killed her when you realized what she was," Blade said.

"I know." Hunter passed a hand over his face. "But it's too late for that and now, I can't turn her over to Mamna with an easy conscience. Not until she does something…I don't know. Demon-like."

Setting a man's boots on fire wasn't demon enough?

Blade sensed his friend's tiredness despite the thick darkness. It was unlikely that he'd had a moment's rest since first meeting Airie, and how he'd managed to get her to Freetown was a complete mystery. She did not act as if she had come against her will.

"What do you consider 'demon-like'?" Blade asked. He settled on the step beside his friend, his leg aching fiercely. "Will she have to kill someone? Because you and I have both killed people, but you and I have never brought anyone back from the dead. What demon display would it take to make you turn her over to Mamna?"

"I don't know!" Hunter all but snarled. He kicked a heel into the dirt. "I don't know what I'm supposed to do with the boy either."

Responsibility for others wasn't something men like Hunter wore with ease. It fit like a poorly made shirt, too tight at the neck and shoulders. Blade knew all about it. "You've gotten yourself into a lot of trouble this time."

"What's worse, I've brought the trouble to you."

Blade was honest. "And I can't say I'm happy about it. But what's done is done, and until you come up with some plan, we aren't going to sleep at the same times. I'm not letting a demon run free around here without one of us watching her."

"Thank you," Hunter said, relief thick in his voice.

"Don't thank me yet," Blade warned him. "These two aren't the worst of your problems. Sooner or later you'll have to deal with Mamna, and that's the one thing I can't help you with."

"Can you keep Airie and the boy for me for the night?" Hunter rose to his feet. "I have to go back. I left the people from the wagon train in the canyon where I usually camp. They'll be frantic by now. I've been gone too long as it is." He rubbed the back of his neck.

"You think the demons will come back tonight?" Blade asked. He tried not to think of the man's screams as he'd been torn apart in the street the night before. He tried not to remember his own when the demon had torn flesh from his leg.

"Yes. So does Mamna. The gates were locked about three hours before sundown," Hunter replied. "I'm guessing she wanted to offer them a diversion."

Blade looked at him. "You don't have to go back out there. You don't owe those people anything."

Hunter handed the pack to Blade. "Give this to Airie. I do have to go because I made a promise to them. Besides," he added with a lopsided grin, "there will be demons to kill."

"I'll kill this one if I have to," Blade warned his departing back.

Hunter froze but did not turn around. He appeared to be thinking Blade's words over with careful consideration.

"I know," he admitted finally, then opened the gate and stepped through it. "But you won't have to." He latched the gate behind him.

Blade sat for a long time on the step listening to the cold desert night, hoping his friend's instincts were good ones. If he did have to kill her, it would be the death of a friendship as well.

• • •

Who was Mamna, and why would Hunter turn Airie over to her?

At first she had tried not to listen to the conversation outside because she suspected it would not be one to her liking. But the tone of Blade's voice, and the reference to Mamna, had turned her skin to ice. That Hunter also did not trust her around his friends — that he thought she might somehow harm or endanger them — hurt her deeply.

Yet she could not deny the possibility existed. While she knew a goddess walked with her, she also possessed demon blood, and it made her temper difficult to control.

The goddess was silent now. Airie had very little control over that relationship, either.

The gate latched behind Hunter, and she turned her attention back to the lovely woman named Ruby with the gleaming red hair. She puttered around the large kitchen, exuding a gentle kindness and chattering quietly to Scratch, who sat on a bench at the long wooden table.

"Does he not yet speak?" she asked Airie, glancing up from a small plate of some sort of stew she'd set on the counter to cool. She ladled up another plateful from the pot on the stove and gestured for Airie to sit, then placed it in front of her.

"No," Airie replied, and wondered if it was as unusual as she suspected. The slight frown on Ruby's face indicated it was. Airie touched his hair, brushing it back from his cheek. "Perhaps he has nothing he wants to speak of. I don't know what his life was like beyond a few days ago."

"He's young," said Ruby. "He'll forget his past life, and he'll speak when he's ready."

The man named Blade limped into the kitchen, his presence a dark cloud of thunder that nevertheless did not diminish Ruby's light.

He had straight black hair that met his shoulders, dark, brooding eyes, and a hawk nose over a harsh mouth. Despite an overall leanness, his arms and chest were well muscled beneath his linen shirt. He could not, however, disguise the pain that she sensed had been a constant companion to him for a very long time.

Airie understood chronic pain. People dealt with it differently. The pain, she suspected, Blade could endure. Its limiting effects, he could not. Sooner or later his lameness would eat away all that he had been and leave nothing but bitterness behind.

What a waste that would be. This was a man whose friendship Hunter valued. Ruby, too, obviously respected him. Airie could help.

He limped to a large chair near the stove and eased himself into it.

"What happened to your leg?" she asked him. Ruby stiffened.

His eyes met Airie's. "I battled a demon and lost," he said, his words flat and cold. Dispassionate. "It ate most of my thigh."

Ruby gasped. "Blade!"

Airie had heard Hunter tell him what she was, and the anger in Blade's response. She had braced herself for a revelation like this. Not much wonder he hated her and had said he would kill her if he had to.

It did not change the fact that he was suffering and she had the ability to help him.

Scratch slid from the bench and toddled the short distance to Blade. He did not wait for assistance, but climbed onto the man's lap without invitation. Blade's surprise and uncertainty as to what to do next defused the tension permeating the room. He did not seem to know what to do with his hands. Wincing, he set them under the little boy's arms and shifted his weight off his injured leg.

Airie needed to touch Blade in order to determine the extent of his injury, and Scratch had given her an opportunity to get close. That it was an old injury would make repairing it more difficult, although not impossible. It would depend on how willing he was to accept her help.

During her mother's last days, she had refused help from Airie. She had known she was dying, Airie now knew, and Airie could not cure what nature decreed. Only slow it.

Demons, however, were not natural to this world, and she believed she could heal an injury caused by one. But only if Blade let her.

He continued to watch her, his hostility not as open, but neither was it completely hidden. Airie pushed the food around her plate with her fork.

"You're tired," Ruby guessed, noticing her lack of interest in the meal. "Let me feed the boy, then I'll show you where you'll be sleeping." She looked at Blade, daring him to argue. "They can use your room. You'll stay with me."

Scratch remained on Blade's lap while Ruby fed him, and as he held the boy, the man's mood seemed to shift. It softened. And saddened.

Airie's heart ached for him. Blade wanted this. He wanted domestic, and normal, and he believed he could never have it. He was wrong. He could have this if he wanted. His leg was not what kept it from him. It was the excuse that kept him from having to try.

Even if she healed the physical wounds, he would have to deal with the deeper scars on his own.

The kitchen was warm, and a knot in the kindling snapped, sending sparks crackling around the inside of the stove. She yawned and started to rise, intending to take Scratch from Blade and use that as an excuse to get close, but Ruby was faster. She lifted Scratch from Blade's arms.

Blade stood too, and without warning, his weak leg went out from beneath him. He tumbled to one knee, Ruby helpless beside him, her arms filled with little boy. Blade's hand hit the stove's hot surface palm down as he fell, and he swore.

Airie darted forward and grabbed his burned hand.

"Don't touch me!" Blade growled. He tried to jerk his hand free from her grasp, but Airie was strong and refused to release it. Blisters, thick and watery, had begun to form. She poured healing into his hand. And then, she extended its reach. She did not ask his permission. He would not want the help of a demon, not even a half one. His revulsion for her was plain, and made her hesitate, but for no more than a second. She could not bear to see him suffer when there was no need for it.

The extent of the damage done to his leg filled her with a deep sense of dismay. She closed her eyes. Not much wonder he, too, hated her for what she was. It was a testimony to his inner strength and whoever had tended him that he had survived such a wound.

That he could walk at all defied belief.

A flicker of awareness for what she was doing dilated his eyes. "Stop," he said, his voice harsh and tight. "I don't want this."

He did not want the help of a demon, was what he meant but did not say.

Despite his protests she continued to knit the nerves and tissue, and reconstructed what she could. His skin remained scarred. She would leave him that much because she knew he would want the reminder of an important event in his life. But he did not wish to be a cripple. That, she could take away.

Finally, Airie opened her eyes to meet his.

He was angry, she saw. Furious, although he hid it well. Ruby stood nearby, clutching Scratch to her breast, uncertain what to do or whom to help. Worry etched her brow. Blade's gaze shifted from Airie to her, and when he saw the expression on Ruby's face, some of his anger faded. But not all.

"Take them away," he ordered Ruby, not rising from his one-kneed position on the floor. He held his burned hand to his chest. His breath came in small gasps, as if he were in great pain, but Airie knew any pain he experienced was no longer physical.

Ruby wanted to go to him, but Airie read her indecision. After a visible struggle, she seemed to decide that he was best left alone.

"I'll be right back," Ruby said to him. "Don't you dare try to move."

Ruby handed Scratch to Airie, lifted a lantern from one of the hooks on a ceiling joist, and ushered her up a staircase at the rear of the kitchen.

The saloon had three stories, unlike many of its meaner neighbors. Three women lived in rooms on the second floor. Blade kept the attic for himself.

The room Ruby led her to was large but spare. A double bed filled one corner. A sturdy wardrobe stood in another. A cushioned bench lined a deep window well beneath a skylight. Airie could see the night stars above her. A screen in the third corner indicated a chamber area.

"There are clean linens in the wardrobe," Ruby said, distracted and obviously in a hurry to return to Blade. She lit a lantern on the nightstand. "A nightdress, too. If you need anything else, my room is directly below this one. It's the first off this set of stairs."

"I didn't hurt him," Airie said, wanting badly for this woman to think well of her before Blade told her the truth.

"I know you didn't," Ruby said. She smiled, although a little sadly, Airie thought. "I knew the minute you touched my hand."

She left, closing the door behind her, and Airie no longer felt as if she had done something good.

. . .

Disregarding Ruby's instructions not to move, Blade pushed himself to his feet and steadied his breathing.

In and out, in and out.

He looked at his palm in the flickering light of the lanterns hanging about the low-ceilinged room. It was unburned. A recent nick on one of his knuckles was also gone.

But it was the absence of pain for the first time in almost a decade that left him dizzy and made his knees unable to hold his weight. He staggered into his chair and probed his bad leg through the heavy fabric of his trousers with nerveless, shaking fingers.

He was afraid to look. Beyond a doubt, the leg was whole.

He could hear the soft voices of the women above him, drifting down the stairwell. Ruby would be back soon and Blade was not ready to face her.

Beneath the counter, he kept his array of knives. He rose, starting to limp to collect them, and realized he no longer needed to do so. A fresh wave of dizziness assailed him, and he grabbed for the table. He shifted his weight to his bad leg.

It held him.

He gathered the knives and slipped them into his clothing with practiced speed, listening hard for Ruby's footsteps on the stairs. Then he walked to the door, gingerly, remembering those mind-crippling days after the demon attack when he had thought he might never walk again. Only Ruby had kept him from taking his own life. She had also forced him to take his first steps.

His brain disengaged, overwhelmed. He had to get away, to think, but he had nowhere to go. He strode into the small courtyard off the kitchen, then crossed to the gate with increasing confidence.

Once outside in the empty street and under the protective cover of night, he simply walked.

Instinct led him to the city wall and the hidden tunnel Hunter used for his comings and goings. Blade slipped into the tunnel, needing the privacy, not knowing what to do next and feeling as if his entire world had keeled on its side yet again. He'd made a new life, far different from the first. He rested his back against the dirt wall, then slid to the ground.

He sat in the darkness and wept.

• • •

When the first demons appeared on the horizon, blocking the moon with their numbers, Hunter was well within sight of the small canyon.

He quickened his pace, and as he ran across the shadowed desert, he thought about strategy. Demons did not play well with others. Of the estimated hundred or so in existence, probably no more than thirty would form any kind of alliance. Even that would be of short duration because they would turn on each other as easily as on men.

A force of thirty demons was still formidable. Three times the size of a mortal man in their demon form, with bone plating protecting their few vulnerable areas, they could tear an inexperienced fighter apart in seconds.

While Hunter's amulet gave him his opponents' strength,

outsmarting them was up to him, and demons were not stupid. *Sluggish thinkers*, was how Blade once described them. Perhaps it was because their demon form was predatory, distracting them with the scent of blood and the heat of battle.

If the wagoners drew demon blood first, it might create enough of a distraction in the demon ranks to help them survive the night.

Hunter called out to alert the wagoners of his identity so he would not be shot, or run through with a blade or an arrow. He ducked into the mouth of the canyon.

"They're coming," he said, telling the men on watch what they would not have been able to see over the canyon walls. "I have a plan."

They would begin with flaming arrows. Hunter needed the majority of demons kept at a distance while he lured one or two from the sky. Then, he would draw blood.

He waited at the mouth of the canyon, the archers behind him and the hot pitch nearby. The first demons appeared, and the first volley of arrows flew.

One of the demons broke free of the others, as Hunter had hoped. It landed on the desert floor, out of range of the arrows. "Slayer!"

Hunter, his sword in his hand, stepped out of the canyon. The desert night was cold. Stars sparkled in the sky. There was no sign of rain tonight, and the archers were keeping the rest of the demons mostly at bay. This one had gotten through because they had followed his instructions to allow it.

Adrenaline surged. He enjoyed fighting too much. Eventually, that would be his downfall.

The demon on the ground shifted. Became mortal.

"Slayer," it called to him again.

Its voice was hypnotic, even to Hunter, who was a man and supposedly immune to it.

Not immune, he thought. Rather, not so deeply affected, and not in the same way. It had challenged him, and he had responded.

His sister had not stood a chance against this. Neither would Airie in the end, despite any demon traits she might have inherited.

The night was silent except for the steady hiss of released arrows and the whisper of wings.

Hunter, his sword in his hand, strode out to meet the one who challenged him. The moon and the stars lit up the desert landscape and he could see his opponent quite clearly. With long black hair and direct eyes, he was larger than Hunter, heavier, better muscled.

Of course he would be. He was an immortal.

Hunter's amulet glowed fiercely, blistering his skin, a warning that even in mortal form, this demon was dangerous.

"Tell me, Slayer," the demon said to him when Hunter stopped a few yards away. "What have you done with the spawn you were hired to bring to me?"

The question should not have surprised him. Mamna had hired Hunter on the Demon Lord's behalf, although he had not anticipated facing the Demon Lord directly.

Now he knew what had instigated the attack on Freetown. The demon had even less patience than the priestess.

And Hunter had a far greater problem than returning a few gold coins. The thought of Airie in this demon's hands turned his stomach to stone.

He spread his legs and moored his feet more firmly in the dirt, bracing himself for attack. The demon was unarmed, but that did not make him harmless. "She's dead."

"She was seen." The demon remained unmoving, watchful. "I

would imagine she's very beautiful. Tell me about her."

His attention shifted to the glowing amulet around Hunter's neck. Hunter saw shocked recognition flash across his face, quickly gone. The demon had seen it somewhere before. Or, perhaps, he simply knew of its reputation, although only one demon Hunter had ever encountered had survived to carry any tales.

That was the one who had dared to touch Airie.

He would not admit to her existence. "When the old priestess died, the mountain would no longer tolerate a spawn's presence and it collapsed, taking her with it. She is dead."

"She is not dead." The Demon Lord's features hardened. "I want her. If you don't give her to me, I will burn the city to the ground. I will show no mercy."

"Why do you care about her?" Hunter asked. "Why is she so special to you?"

"Because she is female. The only one of her kind."

It was the wrong answer to give him. Years of contained anger and pain over the loss of his sister resurfaced. Hunter would never pass Airie over to demons. He tightened his grip on his sword and advanced.

His amulet flared another warning, hotter this time. He tried to determine the source of the Demon Lord's strength, and its level, but could not.

A second demon broke free from the legion soaring above, landing lightly behind him. He now had two demons to face. The amulet indicated that the Demon Lord remained the greater threat, so that was where he kept his attention.

And then a shadow, moving silently across the dark desert, came to his aid, running toward them in a crouch. The knives flying from its fingertips with unnerving precision were aimed at the second demon and the vulnerabilities between those bony plates. Several of the well-aimed blades hit their marks, and it grunted in surprise as blood poured from the wounds. It turned on itself, biting and clawing at the protruding knives, and retreated into the night sky where other demons would track it.

Hunter went after the Demon Lord, who dodged the first strike with ease.

"Enough dancing," Hunter said. "Fight me."

The Demon Lord smiled. Anyone else would have felt terror. Not Hunter. Airie had been threatened, and that was his only concern.

"I don't think so, Slayer. Not tonight. This is your final warning. I want the spawn." He flashed a feral grin. "Then, you can have your fight. When it's over, I will give her your head as a gift." He shifted, resuming his demon form, and shot into the night sky to rejoin the others.

Blade, panting, stood nearby.

"I'm not used to running anymore," he complained, resting his hands on his knees in an effort to catch his breath.

Hunter had a few questions about his ability to do so now, but this was not the time, because he suspected he knew the answers. He had seen Airie's skill in healing.

He bent to retrieve Blade's knives. "I suggest you get used to it," he advised, "because we have to move fast." He looked at the blood, then at the sky. "More company's coming."

They spent the remainder of the night in the canyon, taking their turns with bows and arrows. Blade was not as good with this weapon as he was with his knives, but Hunter's aim was respectable.

The demons were playing with them. Hunter wondered if they also toyed with Mamna. Was that why the Demon Lord left

Freetown alone tonight? To intimidate her into handing Airie over to him if she got to her first?

Hunter did not for a moment believe the Demon Lord wanted Airie because she was the only one of her kind, although no doubt it was part of her value. But Mamna wanted her, too. What was the connection?

He was missing something.

During their allotted breaks, he and Blade sat together. Blade polished his knives with sand to remove the demon blood. Hunter did not dare ask him about his leg, but for his friend's sake he was not sorry.

They did, however, speak of Airie.

"The Demon Lord wants her alive," Hunter said. "Even if she's spawn, I couldn't turn any woman over to demons."

"Have you touched her?" Blade asked. Hunter shot him a dark look. "I don't mean in that way." He paused, reconsidering his question. "You haven't, have you?"

"No," Hunter said. "Not that it's any of your business."

Blade frowned as he worked. Each cleaned knife vanished into his clothing.

"She healed my leg," he finally admitted. "I felt nothing but good in her when she did."

"What do you suppose the women who bore spawn felt in their demon lovers?" Hunter asked. "She set a man's boots on fire."

"His boots. Not him. And the man tried to kill you, did he not?"

"He did." Hunter traced a figure in the ground between his bent knees with a small rock. "I want to believe the best of her. But she's half demon. That won't change. No one who knows it will ever accept her."

It was unlikely the Godseekers would welcome her as a goddess now. She could not return to the mountain, nor stay in Freetown. He was left with few options with regard to her safety.

Hunter had considered himself a loner for many years now. An outsider. And yet, he had places he could go if he chose. Even family, if he needed them. What would it be like to be in Airie's position—alone, unwelcome, and feared by all?

Little wonder Scratch had become so important to her. He adored and trusted her.

The dissonant howl of frustrated demons echoed off the canyon walls. The enslaved women huddled closer, no doubt afraid that one of them might yet be chosen as a peace offering, but despite the unnerving noise, Hunter knew the wagoners were holding their own. A few more hours and the ordeal would be over for another night.

"Are you afraid of her?" he asked Blade, his thoughts again returning to Airie.

"I wouldn't have left her unguarded in my home if I believed she was a threat to anyone." He looked at Hunter. "Are you? Afraid of her?"

Hunter could not shake the Demon Lord's words from his head. "I'm afraid *for* her."

Blade slipped the last of his knives back into his clothing. "Then you, my friend, have a problem."

He did indeed. Airie terrified him, although not on a physical level. His fear of her went much deeper than that. He thought of her constantly. He dreamed of her. His compulsion to be with her, to protect her, was great, and Hunter was not a man given to impulse. She had a beautiful smile and a kind heart.

But how much of his attraction to Airie was because of her, and her innocence, and how much was because she was demon?

That was the true source of any fear of her he had.

"Do you find her attractive?" Hunter asked Blade abruptly.

His friend froze, the sidelong look he sent Hunter filled with speculation. "Will an honest answer get me killed?"

"No. Possibly," Hunter conceded, correcting himself. He could not be sure, and he wished he had not asked the question.

"I can resist her. I'm not as certain the same can be said for you." Blade stood, ready to take another turn with a bow and arrow. He tested his leg as if still not quite trusting its soundness. "Do the world a favor," he advised. "If you want her, then act on it. Don't think so hard about the reason for it. And don't tempt other men by asking such questions. Not unless you're willing to lose her to them."

The thought he'd had earlier returned. He could claim her as his. She fit well in his arms and went into them willingly. She trusted him. When he considered it in greater depth, who better to protect the world from a spawn than the Demon Slayer?

But a small, ugly part of him could not forget that he would be making a spawn a permanent part of his life.

He returned to his position at the mouth of the canyon, aimed a flaming arrow at a shadow above, and released it. A scream rang out in reward. The demon he struck reared back, wings beating hard, its feet scrabbling at air, although it did not fall from the sky. Hunter watched it break rank and fly off, an arrow protruding from beneath its ribs.

Now that his mind was made up, he could not wait for this night to be over.

Airie awaited him.

CHAPTER FOURTEEN

She sat by the window all night, watching the sky, with Scratch on her lap. When he fell asleep, she moved him to the bed, then returned to the bench in the window well.

She knew the instant Hunter returned.

She heard him enter through the courtyard and the back door, but he did not immediately come upstairs. Low voices rumbled in the kitchen two floors below, although not loud enough for her to distinguish what was being said. Something heavy scraped across the tiles.

The wait was agony. What if he was hurt? What if he needed her?

Then, he stood in the doorway.

Airie flew across the room and into his arms, the too-short nightdress she had found in the wardrobe tangling around her shins. Relieved beyond measure that he was safe and in one piece, she rained kisses along the lean lines of his fresh-shaven jaw.

That was what she had heard in the kitchen downstairs. The

washtub. He'd stopped to clean off the violence of the night.

Ruby appeared behind him, her fiery hair loose around her shoulders, wearing a thin cotton robe over her own nightdress. Her slipper-clad feet made very little sound as she eased past Hunter into the room. She gathered a sleepy Scratch into her arms and returned to the door.

"You'll both sleep better if you don't have a little boy under your feet," Ruby said, a slight smile on her lips. "I'll take care of him."

"Let them go," Hunter said when Airie tried to protest.

Something unsettling in his eyes as he looked at her made her obey. It did not frighten her. But it made her cautious.

The door closed behind Ruby, the soft *snick* of the latch echoing loudly in the sparsely furnished room.

"What's wrong?" Airie asked him.

"Well-timed rain showers. Godseekers shouting about the return of a goddess. Miracles." He traced a finger along her cheek, then brushed her lips with his thumb. "Forget I said anything. They're not important."

But she could see they were important to him.

"I told you that the goddesses hear me when I call to them. That I spoke with one," Airie reminded him, her tone soft. "I told you the rain chased the demons away."

"You told me, but I wasn't listening to your meaning," Hunter said. "I've heard it now."

He was speaking in riddles. She pulled away from him. "Then you can explain it to me because I don't know what it is you think you've heard me say other than that the goddesses bring rain."

He would not let her withdraw, capturing her hand. "Please, Airie," he implored her, tiredness apparent in his whole manner. It blanketed his features and shadowed his eyes. "I need you near me. Innocence is such a rare thing in this world."

A few short days ago he had called her spawn. While she disliked that he thought of her as such, she did not care for him thinking her innocent either.

And yet she knew she was both.

Perhaps it was the demon in her that made her more daring. It had been a long, frightening night of worry, and she was glad to touch him. If it was her innocence he wanted, he could have it. She had no real interest in preserving it.

Not where Hunter was concerned.

She pressed against him, her hands on his chest, and lifted her lips to his. Heat shot to her apex on contact, sparking into flames that spread through her body until fire consumed her. She made a soft sound of pleasure.

The effect on him was like setting a struck match to dry kindling. His tongue thrust between her lips, boldly stroking the insides of her mouth.

She met his tongue with the tip of her own. He tasted warm and sweet, and Airie wanted more of him. Tangling her hands in his shirt, she fumbled with the buttons. His hands covered hers, helping her, then the shirt dropped to the floor.

The pads of his fingers caressed her bare flesh at the open neck of the wide-collared nightdress she wore. He inched the smooth fabric off her shoulders, then hesitated. He broke off the kiss.

"I need you to understand what we are doing," he said to her, his breathing unsteady as he struggled to speak. He closed his eyes, then opened them again to meet hers. His thumbs swiped across her collarbone so that she had difficulty focusing on his words. "If we go much further, I won't stop."

"I don't want you to," she said. "I'm not stopping either."

He dropped a kiss to her forehead, and suddenly, she wanted him. All of him. She wanted him in her, as close as they could possibly become. She shrugged out of the nightdress. It slipped from her shoulders to pool at her feet. She stepped out of it, then kicked it aside.

Hunter cupped her face, tipping her head back so that she met his gaze. His eyes were blue and very intense, and any concern she might have had as to whether or not he found her attractive solely because of her demon blood vanished.

"You are so beautiful," he said to her, with just enough wonder in his tone to stoke the fires of desire. She'd never thought of herself as such, had never had a reason to think about it, but he made her feel as if it were an indisputable fact.

She liked that he thought of her that way.

One of his palms slid down her arm to her waist. His fingers trailed across her bare hip, then he tugged her against him. Again, he kissed her. Slower this time, deeper, and so thoroughly she lost all sense of their shifting surroundings.

He had drawn her to the bed. Soft morning light enveloped them as he pressed her into the rough blankets, the springs of the mattress groaning beneath their combined weight. He shrugged out of his trousers, sliding them off his muscular thighs and casting them aside.

She had never seen a naked man before, although she'd been told what to expect.

He lay down beside her and propped his head on his elbow, looking at her with understanding. "Go ahead and touch me," he invited her. "Wherever you'd like." Desire darkened his eyes. "If you're not ready for that, close your eyes and I can touch you."

"I'm ready." She smiled at him.

Teasing the arch of her foot along one of his calves, she enjoyed the texture of his skin. Her hand went to his hip, then the tips of her fingers traced the curve of his buttocks. The amused expression on his face disappeared.

He bent his head forward and placed a kiss on her neck. The next kiss feathered her breast. Then he drew the rosy bud of her nipple into his mouth, tracing the tip with his tongue, and she gasped with pleasure.

She touched the hard planes of his stomach and he sucked in a breath. She drew her hand away, uncertain of what his reaction meant, but he caught it.

"You surprised me, is all," he said. "Surprises are good." She ran her hand lower, felt tufts of curls, and encircled him with her palm. He let out a low groan. "*Very* good." He kissed her mouth, his tongue tracing her lips. "And very surprising."

He reached between them and wrapped his fingers over hers, showing her how to move her hand. She loved the sounds he made as she did so, his eyes closing in deep concentration as she found a rhythm that pleased him.

He released her hand and moved his own to the mound between her thighs. He inserted a finger, stroking her gently to the same cadence she caressed him, and she cried out in amazement.

"I told you surprises are good," he said, sensual satisfaction curving his lips as he watched her face.

She could no longer speak, lost in the sensations he'd created, arching her back to press against him and force his touch deeper inside her. He shifted his hips so that she could no longer hold him in her hand. He leaned over her, guiding the tip to her opening.

"I'm sorry, Airie," he said. "This often hurts the first time." He slid his entire length inside her in one thrust, then lay still, holding his weight on his arms until she could breathe again. "Give it a moment. You'll get used to the feel."

He distracted her with silly words, mixing them with tender kisses. His tongue again found her mouth, thrusting in and out, until suddenly, she realized he'd started to move inside her as well.

Any pain was forgotten, replaced by an indescribable pleasure. Sweat beaded on his forehead as he established a slow, deep tempo that gradually built. Within moments she was writhing beneath him, begging him for more, to make it faster.

"Airie, honey, if I do that, it will be over too soon for you." Pleasure and regret mingled in his eyes as he gazed down at her.

"I don't care," she gasped, the slow build of an impending climax clenching her muscles around the hard length of him. Color exploded behind her eyes and she cried out, wrapping her legs around him. He gave in to her demands, thrusting harder and deeper, and groaned as he came, although Airie barely heard him past the waves of pleasure engulfing her.

Hunter did not withdraw afterward, but anchored his weight so that he did not crush her and watched with an air of intense satisfaction while she recovered. He traced the curve of her cheek with the backs of his fingers.

"The first time is the worst," he said.

Airie caught his hand in both of hers. She pressed his fingers to her lips. "If that was the worst, then I don't dare dream about how wonderful the next time will be." He frowned, and some of her pleasure dimmed, replaced by uncertainty. "That was presumptuous of me," she said. "I enjoyed it so much that I assumed you did, too. You don't have to do it again if you don't want." She tried to push away from him.

"Stop." He pinned her down and kissed her until she went quiet beneath him. "I'm flattered beyond belief that you enjoyed it. Believe me, I did too, every bit as much, if not more. I'll be able to think of nothing else now until the next time, which may be far too soon for you.

"But did you know," he added, continuing to frown, "that your eyes are on fire?"

. . .

The fire in her eyes quickly cooled.

He had made a mistake, he saw at once, both in what he had said, but more importantly, what he had done. Claiming her had not diminished her appeal. In fact, the opposite was true.

The shift was not subtle. Sensuality seeped from her, her bare skin gleaming like brushed gold beneath the spray of morning sunshine on the rumpled bed. Gone was the innocent beauty, replaced by a glowing, well-satisfied woman who was too desirable by far.

He could not say he fully regretted it. He wanted her again. And he wanted her far from demon territory, where she would be safe. But first he had to explain because she had misinterpreted his words.

"Your eyes are beautiful. I like that I can make them flame." He said the last with more satisfaction than he had intended to reveal, but it achieved the desired effect.

Her smile returned, more radiant. "For the most part I can control it. But you make me forget."

She made him forget things, too. Important ones. At their first meeting, her eyes had shot fire when he'd thrown her in the lake. They had also flamed when she confronted the Godseekers.

Which brought him back to the matter of his second mistake. He had awakened a level of sensuality in her that could only be attributed to her demon blood. The effect was magnetic and did not appear to be lessening with the passing moments. Regardless of where she eventually settled, her mixed heritage would never go unnoticed. Not by men, and most assuredly not by demons.

But better for her to be noticed by mortal men, whom she could defend herself against, than by demons, whom perhaps she could not.

Absently, he stroked her neck and shoulder while he thought matters through. His fingers brushed against the amulet she wore, and his own warmed pleasantly in response. The two fit together. He wondered if they magnified his and Airie's reactions to each other.

Natural or not, whatever the source of his attraction to her, he had already made the decision that she was his. He'd convinced himself that he would be protecting mortals from her. In reality, Airie was the one who needed protection the most.

He had to get her away from demon territory and that part of her heritage. He would take her to the Borderlands, to his childhood home. It would not be far enough—a demon had managed to find his sister there—but it would be a start. He was tired of fighting demons. His sister was dead and nothing would bring her back, while Airie was alive and he had the ability to keep her that way.

He no longer cared who had fathered her. She had been raised well. Her tendency toward petty thievery aside, she was open and honest. She had empathy for others. He liked those qualities in her, and they had nothing to do with sexual attraction, although that, too, was high.

"We're leaving tomorrow," he announced. "You, Scratch, and me. As long as we stay here, you're in danger."

She had started to drift off to sleep. Her eyes, now their natural dark, chocolate brown, fluttered open. "What do you mean?"

He did not want to explain. He twisted a lock of her hair around one finger, rubbing it with his thumb. "You asked me what I was doing on the goddesses' mountain."

She sighed and rolled to her back, dragging the sheet with her to cover her breasts. His hands ached to hold her.

"I don't want to know," she said, staring at the ceiling.

All the more reason to tell her. Guilt consumed him. "I was hired by a priestess to bring you to her. She intends to turn you over to the Demon Lord."

Airie tilted her head, her soft exhalation of breath heating his skin. "And you agreed to do it because I am spawn."

Her calm understanding cut him, almost as much as her use of the slur. It sounded ugly coming so casually from her lips. How many times had he wounded her by using it himself in the same manner?

"I agreed to it because if I didn't go after you, she would have found someone else to do so. I couldn't in good conscience see a woman turned over to demons."

"Unless the woman was spawn," Airie added. Her fingers tightened on the bedding, the tips whitening.

She spoke the truth—that was to be his justification. He despised himself for it.

"I tried to keep you from coming here," he reminded her.

"Yet here we are." She shifted to face him. "What will you do with me?"

"You aren't listening." He wanted the fire back in her eyes. "I said that you, Scratch, and I are leaving."

"When the goddesses and the Demon Lord all want me dead? Why would I want to endanger the two of you?"

"Mamna does not represent the goddesses." Hunter needed her to understand that. "She's an evil, hateful little woman who has made a position for herself by using the immortals to her advantage." He cupped her chin so that she had to look at him. "I don't believe they want you dead. You told me that a goddess speaks to you. What of that?"

Airie's gaze remained steady and unreadable. "You were right, and I was mistaken. It is a demon."

Hunter drove a hand through his hair. He had done nothing to make her believe in her own worth. He had a lot to atone for.

"Do you trust me?" he demanded.

Airie bit her lip.

"*Do* you?"

She finally nodded, and the weight crushing his lungs eased.

"I never told you what happened to my sister. I've never told anyone." He swallowed against the painful lump in his throat that always accompanied her memory and forced himself to continue. "We grew up in the Borderlands. She was closest to me in age, and very beautiful, even more so than my other sisters. I'd gotten used to them sneaking in and out of the house to meet boyfriends over the years, so when she started doing it too, I didn't think anything of it. Not until she got pregnant. And even then, when she begged me not to tell, I kept her secret for her. We lived so far from demon territory the possibility never occurred to me. I thought the father was some local boy."

He brushed the backs of his knuckles up and down the side of her neck, and she closed her eyes as if knowing how the story would end.

"She disappeared one night, and when I finally tracked her down in the desert, the spawn had already torn her to shreds. I killed it. In demon form, they carry the markings of their fathers. I tracked the father down, and I killed him, too. Now you know why I hate spawn, and why I hate demons."

Airie looked away. "I see."

"No, you don't see," Hunter replied. He shifted one leg, turning Airie to face him. "You are not spawn, and you are not a demon. You are Airie—nothing more, nothing less, just as your mother said. And nothing will ever change that. I won't allow anything to happen to either you or Scratch. We will find a place for the three of us. In the meantime, stay here, stay out of sight, and let me take care of everything."

He kissed her, felt her lips part, then deepened it briefly before drawing away. She had been up all night, waiting for him. They were both exhausted. He had things to do, but nothing that couldn't wait. Right now he wanted to make certain she slept.

He settled onto a pillow and spooned her against him, her back to his front, his hand covering one of her breasts.

Once Airie fell asleep, he would return Mamna's gold. Then they would prepare to leave. He ran through the things they would need in his head. Crossing a desert of demons with her was not going to be easy.

Staying in Freetown, however, would be disastrous for everyone.

CHAPTER FIFTEEN

Hunter dressed, then watched Airie sleep for a long time.

She was golden-skinned and painfully lovely, with her long black hair loose across one naked shoulder and shining in a shaft of sunlight. The rainbow-hued amulet around her neck gleamed, exuding contentment. The one he wore emitted a similar sensation. He wished he could share in it.

He felt as if he had stolen something irreplaceable from her. He had taken what he'd wanted, had told himself it was in her best interests, but by doing so, he had tied her to him without regard for her wishes. He could not let her go now, and while he no longer had any objection to having her as a permanent part of his life, who was to say she wanted him always in hers?

He left her sleeping, and with his boots in his hand, crept silently down the back stairs to the second floor.

As quiet as he tried to be, Blade heard him.

He stopped Hunter at the landing, beckoning him into the hall so their voices would not carry. He looked like hell, but Hunter did not ask why. They had both spent a long night and another approached. Hunter knew he looked no better.

"Where are you going?" Blade asked him.

"To return Mamna's money." He met his friend's gaze. "Then Airie, the boy, and I are leaving. It's not safe for anyone with her here."

Blade inclined his head. "That's probably wise."

Hunter doubted if it could be called wise to take a beautiful, half-demon woman and a small child on a cross-country trek through the heart of demon territory, particularly when demons now hunted without the west winds as warning.

It also ate at him to leave Freetown, and Blade in particular, without his skills as the Slayer to help them, knowing that an attack was imminent.

"When I get back we should talk about what will come tonight, and how to protect people against it the best way possible," he added.

Again, Blade nodded.

Hunter yanked on his boots and left through the saloon at the front of the building to avoid the women he could hear laughing together in the kitchen.

He wondered how Mamna would react to the news of Airie's death.

• • •

She made Freetown unsafe for its inhabitants.

Airie huddled at the top of the stairs with her chin resting on her bare knees, hugging her legs, listening to the voices of the two men a floor below.

The grimness in their tone when they spoke of Mamna also

made her uneasy. Why would a priestess want to turn Airie, who had been raised in the goddesses' very own temple, over to demons the goddesses despised?

It forced her to examine an unpleasant reality. Despite Airie's belief that at least one of them continued to favor her, it meant the goddesses despised spawn, too. There could be no other explanation.

Did you know that your eyes are on fire?

Pain filled her heart. No matter how he felt at the moment, deep down she would always be spawn to Hunter. When he looked at her, he would forever be reminded of the death of a sister he had loved. She doubted she could live with that tragedy lingering between them.

She also doubted he had ever intended to take a half demon as a lover, and did not delude herself into believing that he could have lasting feelings for her. Her demon's allure might be enough for him now, but it would never be enough for Airie. Always, she would wonder when that false attraction might wear off, and she would worry over it.

She wanted a place in the world, but she wanted one that was real and not based on demon illusion. Hunter would hate himself when he realized what making love to her had meant. And worse, he would come to hate her.

Airie did not think she could bear to watch his feelings for her turn to hate when hers had slowly and irrevocably been turning to love.

She also did not want to be the reason he left an entire town defenseless. He could help these people, and so could she. She was the one the Demon Lord wanted. If she left the city, the demons would have no reason to attack Freetown.

Hunter would try to follow her, she knew. She would have to

put as much distance between them as possible. She was not even certain what direction she should take, but thought if she followed the wagon train's path, she would eventually find a place she could hide.

It was also difficult for her to think of leaving Scratch behind. She blinked back a few tears. She could not take him with her. Hunter had been right about that, too. She could not care for him. But Ruby already loved him and would see to his welfare.

Ruby had left Airie a clean change of clothes on a chair next to the bed. She dressed in a simple brown skirt that tied at the waist and a long-sleeved, light cotton blouse. The skirt was several inches too short and the blouse too tight across her breasts, but Airie cared little for clothes other than that they be clean and reasonably comfortable, which these were. She would have loved to replace Hunter's old boots with the socks stuffed in the toes, but those could not be helped.

She took a few coins from where Hunter had hidden them. She would buy what she needed in the market.

She tied her hair in its braid, then made her way out to the street unseen by Blade or the other inhabitants of the saloon.

• • •

The Slayer had come to her.

Mamna received him inside her home, far more worried that demons or Godseekers might see them together than whether or not they were overheard by her servants.

She needed the spawn. Her amulet had not yet failed completely only because it had not been truly tested. When the Demon Lord decided to attack Freetown, the people would soon see the full extent of their vulnerability.

And hers.

She worked to control an anticipation born out of rising desperation. It was possible the spawn did not have any immortal abilities. Perhaps being born on a mortal world precluded them. Or the immortality of one parent canceled the other's.

Either way, Mamna would soon possess something the Demon Lord wanted. That would be its own reward.

Hunter entered her front parlor, stooping his head slightly to avoid the crystal chandelier affixed to the ceiling in the center of the room. He wore no hat, his sun-bleached hair and tanned skin appearing clean and polished. Her eyes narrowed. He seemed different. More at ease. Less like the coiled snake she normally dealt with.

He tossed a familiar drawstring bag onto a polished mahogany sideboard. "I wasn't successful. I've come to return your money."

Although his decision was not unexpected, Mamna nevertheless felt anger and tension supersede her anticipation. The spawn was her final hope. The Slayer would not take that from her.

Without another word of explanation, or begging her permission, he turned to leave.

"Wait."

He paused, the eyebrow he raised in polite inquiry infuriating her. She had paid him well. How dare he stand in her presence and pretend not to have the very thing she wanted?

She choked back her anger. "What happened on the mountain?"

His eyes became glittering, blue chips of ice, cold and difficult to read. "I never reached it. I was a few hours away when the summit collapsed. I met a number of people fleeing for their lives, but none of them was a woman fitting the description you gave me. I assume she died in one of the landslides. Those were especially spectacular, even at a distance."

"You're lying."

His expression hardened. "Careful what you say to me, little priestess. I've returned your money. I owe you nothing."

She was not afraid of him, although she knew many who were. Or should be. "The spawn was seen with you."

"By whom?" the Slayer asked, as if the answer was of little significance to him. "A poorly skilled assassin named Runner who pretends to be a Godseeker? A demon who slaughtered a small wagon train of innocent people in one of the arroyos? Perhaps another one of your reliable witnesses who tells you whatever you want to hear?" He retrieved the bag of coins, opened it, and withdrew five gold pieces. "On second thought, I deserve some compensation." He slipped the gold pieces into his pocket and returned the bag to the sideboard. "Call me if you ever have legitimate work. Otherwise, I suggest you rely on your other resources."

She should applaud his performance. This was why he was the best. The man had no fear. But someone had called the goddesses' rain. A half demon could not do it.

A half goddess might.

"So you know nothing of a woman who set a man's boots on fire?" she asked.

"No. Although I know of several women who possess matches."

There were no tells in his body language. He stood at ease, his hands loose at his sides, giving nothing away.

He had the spawn. She had until nightfall to claim it. Certainty galvanized her into recklessness.

She laughed quietly. "Now I know what is different about you. You've slept with her." It was a stab in the dark, but a very slight dilation of his pupils gave him away. If she had not been watching for it she might have missed it. The unwelcome discovery enraged her more. "You foolish, mortal man. You have no idea what you have done."

He shrugged, neither confirming nor denying it.

"Did you know that the Demon Lord made me an offer for her as well?" he asked. "Last night, when I helped those wagoners fight off the demons you'd abandoned them to?" He pretended to think. "Let's say I do have her hidden somewhere. Why would I want to turn her over to either one of you? Why wouldn't I want to keep something so valuable for myself?" His cold eyes pierced her. The temperature in the room seemed to drop ten degrees, and Mamna almost shivered. "Good luck in your battle with the demons, little priestess. I can live with my choices. I suspect you are the one who has no idea what she's done."

A haze of red rage colored her vision even as fear eviscerated her. She no longer dared to summon demons, not that it would matter if she did. He was the Demon Slayer and none could defeat him.

She had to persuade him. Otherwise, he would walk out the door and everything she had worked for would be gone.

"The spawn is the key to ridding the world of demons," she said, the truth drawn from her with great reluctance.

"Then why would you want to turn her over to them?" He waved a hand around the room. "You've made yourself queen of a small empire based on your relationship with demons. Once that relationship is gone, you have nothing. Why would you want to be rid of them now, after all these years?"

"I'm an old woman," Mamna said. "I'm too tired for what is coming. My deformity shortens my life. Once I'm gone the demons will be able to do as they like." She met his emotionless eyes with an equally flat look of her own. "And they like to kill mortal men."

She could see his mind working, thinking over what she had said, sifting the truth from the lies.

"There have been hundreds of spawn. Many more than this one could have survived. Why her in particular?"

"Her conception was arranged by the goddesses to trap the demons inside of time because they believed age would eventually defeat them. Instead, the Demon Lord used its birth to draw demon fire to the mountain. The fire was meant to destroy the spawn as well. He had no way of knowing that a priestess would save its life."

She did not tell him the whole truth. While the goddesses had planned to trap the demons, they had not anticipated the birth of any child. And Mamna had been the one to suspect, correctly, as it turned out, that the Demon Lord's unborn spawn might be enough to draw his fire to the mountain. It was she who had intended for the spawn to be destroyed in it. The Demon Lord was never to have known of its existence.

She had not counted on the laboring goddess calling rain to save its life.

A muscle worked in the Slayer's jaw. "And now that the Demon Lord thinks she's alive, he wants her dead. How fortunate for you both that she died in the mountain's collapse. You can give him the happy news."

She drew a gun from beneath the cushions of her chair and aimed it at his chest. "I want the spawn."

He spread his arms wide. "Shoot me," he invited. Steel glittered in his eyes. "Then you can explain to people how you killed the Demon Slayer on the eve of a demon attack, when you admit you are too tired to protect them. Demons will be the least of your worries."

Her finger trembled on the trigger. "I could kill you and take your amulet."

He drew it over his head and held it out to her. "Go ahead, then. I'll even give it to you, and you can fight demons on the city's behalf. Guard your back against the Godseekers, however. They seem to want one of their own to fight at the head of their army."

She wanted to kill him but did not dare, not with the Demon Lord in his current rage. Without the Slayer she, too, would be vulnerable.

"I could take the amulet from you and give it to the Godseekers," she said.

"You'd give power to people who continue to worship the goddesses?" He slipped the amulet back over his head. "I don't believe you would do that."

She had lost. He would not help her.

Fear of the immortals, and the threat of impending ruin, weakened her hold on the gun, and she dropped it to her lap so he would not see the shake in her hand.

"The spawn has two birthrights," she spat at him. "Aren't you the slightest bit interested in the other?"

"Not in the least." He spun and headed across the tiled floor to the door.

"Her mother was a goddess," Mamna shouted after him, no longer caring who might overhear, "who whored herself to a demon. And in the end, she betrayed all of the immortals. Enjoy your spawn while you can, Slayer. Being a whore will come naturally to her. So will betrayal. What makes you think she would be loyal to you?"

"If she is part goddess," Hunter said, his hand on the door latch, "that would make you her servant, would it not?"

The door closed behind him, leaving Mamna shaking with fear and anger and having no firm plan for the coming night. Scouring the city for the spawn, then convincing it to do as she wished, would take time that no longer existed. She did not doubt that after tonight, despite the presence of the Demon Slayer, Freetown and the majority of its inhabitants would be lost.

Why should she die with them?

Perhaps it was time for her to make her way to the Borderlands where the demon presence was not so strong. She pressed a hand to the cracked amulet beneath her clothing. It might get her across the desert if the demons remained distracted.

But before she did, why not tell the Godseekers of the false goddess in their midst?

The Slayer would then have far more than demons to contend with.

• • •

Hunter had explained the layout of the city to Airie, so she had no worries about becoming lost in it. All major streets led to the city center and ended at the outer wall. Once she left the market she had only to find her way back to it, then follow the street that encircled it to the tunnel and make her escape.

Layers of desert dust coated the board sidewalks and the wooden fronts of the buildings of Freetown. Dust, in fact, layered everything, although the sun shone bright and hot overhead, and the sky was an endless blue.

Yet there was an odd tension in the streets, as if people struggled to maintain a pretense of normalcy during the day despite what happened at night.

She was not oblivious to the stares she received as she walked— she, too, had seen the golden cast to her skin that she could not control—but she held her head high and pretended not to notice the stares even as her spirits plummeted.

Was she fated to be so very different, then?

Once in the market, the majority of stares disappeared as people's attention gravitated toward a high platform in the middle of a large, open courtyard.

Airie saw a few of the traders from the wagon train in the crowd, although they did not recognize her dressed as a woman.

"What's happening?" she asked a man with heavy white eyebrows and thick, gray-streaked hair.

He spared her half a glance, then another, longer, look, as if not quite able to believe what he saw. His eyebrows disappeared into his shaggy hairline.

"Slave auction," he mumbled, before sidling away from her.

The crush of bodies, combined with the heat, fast became stifling. Hundreds of voices, all talking at once, blended into a dull, distorted roar that made her ears ache and her heart beat a little faster.

The majority of the spectators were men, she realized. The market might not be the best place for her right now. Hunter had warned her of a woman's status in Freetown. No vendor stalls had been assembled. She could see nothing for sale that she might need. Whatever sort of market this was, it was not for her.

Airie tried to push back the way she came, but the number of people had now swelled to the point that departure was impossible.

The crowd carried her forward, not away, and she was swept to its front where ten or so naked women stood shackled together at the back of a platform. Most kept their heads down, averting their faces, although a few held their chins high and stared at the crowd in defiance.

The despair behind it was what caught at Airie's heart. Anger kindled to life in her. She could ignite the platform. She could burn the entire city to the ground. Both options tempted her.

But, as her skin glowed more brightly in response to her thoughts, a gentle voice spoke.

Rain is a part of you, too, the voice whispered. *You don't need to pray for it, any more than you pray for fire. They are both yours to command. But remember, you alone own your actions.*

Hunter was wrong. The goddesses did speak to her. The knowledge gave her a sense of confidence that she had lacked of late. Airie closed her eyes and lifted her face to the sky.

Bring me the rain.

Within seconds the sky darkened and opened up, and a downpour began. Chaos erupted as people scattered and fled, seeking shelter. Soon, the streets were flooded with rushing torrents of dirty water.

Someone draped an oiled leather duster over her head to protect her from the driving rain, and Airie could see once again. She wiped water from her face with her free hand and looked into steady, familiar blue eyes.

She waited for recriminations. Braced herself to receive them. But this was an action she gladly claimed and could not regret, because no matter what else might happen, she was different, and that would not change.

If she could not accept it, then how could she expect anyone else to do so?

A huge grin creased Hunter's face.

"Nicely done," he said, and he kissed her deeply as the deluge continued around them.

• • •

The wet taste of her, the wary hope he saw in her eyes, made him wish they were not standing beneath his coat in an open market, even though at the moment it felt as if nothing existed beyond this private world.

She called rain on behalf of the goddesses. She had called it that night at his cabin, when the sky over Freetown was on fire. She'd offered to call it again to protect the wagon train from the demon attack. She had told him a goddess had spoken with her. She could heal with a touch.

He did not need Mamna's word to know the truth. Why else would a half demon be permitted to live on the goddesses' mountain unless she was half goddess, too?

He thanked those same goddesses that he had gone back to Blade's with the supplies he had purchased and discovered her missing. He had stumbled on her scant seconds before she opened the skies.

Considering what she had witnessed, and what he knew of her, rainfall was not the reaction from her he would have expected. It was very welcome nonetheless. Goddess rain meant they would have added protection when crossing through demon territory.

Unfortunately, it would also act as a beacon.

The rain continued to fall, although more gently now. She was soaked to the skin. There was little that could be done about that as he hustled her through the empty streets. Word of her presence would already be spreading, and the unseasonal rainstorms would confirm it. With the newly acquired golden glow to her skin, and the subtle sensuality, she looked every inch a goddess now. Even Ruby had remarked on it.

"Did you see what was happening in that market?" Airie demanded as they hurried along, indignation quivering in her tone.

"I saw." And there was little to be done about it. He had tried to warn her that her expectations of Freetown were too high, but she'd had to see this for herself.

If anything were to convince him she could control the demon side of her nature, this was it. She had behaved magnificently.

Desire would have been proud. The priestess had been right all along. In the ways that mattered most, Airie was no different from any other woman. If anything, she was better.

He had not quite come to terms with her birthright. But he would, given time. She had been born on this world and Hunter would help find her a place in it because that place now included him.

They reached the small compound behind the saloon. Hunter hustled her through the gate and into the kitchen, where he found Blade sitting at the table.

Blade paused with his coffee cup halfway to his mouth, surprise in his eyes. He looked from Airie, with her clinging wet clothes and golden skin, to Hunter.

"Don't ask," Hunter said to him, then turned to Airie. "Go dry off. I'll join you in a few minutes." He took her hand to draw her back to him again, and looked into her troubled expression. "You had better be waiting for me this time. Don't think I don't know you were running away," he added softly. He kissed her, a gentle brush of his lips against hers that instantly made him want her.

Banked fire sparkled in her eyes.

He watched as she left the room. When she was gone, the door closed tight behind her, he slid into a seat beside Blade at the table and dropped his forehead into his hands.

"I found her at a slave auction in the market. She took exception to it."

"Was she noticed?" Blade asked.

"What do you think?"

He shrugged as if it were of no matter. "So what is your plan? The city has been sealed off. The gates are closed and guards have been posted near the tunnel."

Hunter rubbed his tired eyes with the heels of his palms. Demons waited outside the walls, and Mamna waited within. The situation was not good.

He did not see that he had any real choice. He had spent years fighting demons, and had been wrong to think he could leave Freetown undefended against them. He could not have lived with that on his conscience.

And he most definitely intended to fight for Airie. Whether he took a stand here or elsewhere made no difference. Wherever they went, the Demon Lord would come for her. Her mother had been a goddess. He wondered what that might mean to the Demon Lord, if anything.

Regardless, the Demon Lord had threatened Airie's life. That meant he would die.

"I'll stand and fight them," Hunter said.

Blade was frowning. "Not even the Slayer can fight that many demons."

An idea began to form. "What if he heads the goddess's army?"

"Airie certainly looks like a goddess," Blade said slowly. "Do you think enough people saw her today for word to spread quickly?"

"Enough saw her for word to have reached the Borderlands by now," Hunter replied, only partly joking. "Although it might be more credible if she hadn't set one of the Godseekers on fire."

Blade tapped his thumb on the table as he stared at the wall, lost in thought. "They've already been hard at work spreading their message in Freetown. What if we can convince them that you're ready to lead them on their goddess's behalf, then get them back out on the streets to spread the word that the Demon Slayer now heads their army?"

"Good idea, but the Godseekers I've met lately have all tried to kill me," Hunter said. "I'd never get close enough to speak with their leader."

"I might not, either. They recognized me." Blade pushed away from the table. "But I think I know someone who can."

· · ·

The youngest whore, Sapphire, had been reluctant at first to admit she knew where the young Godseeker assassin was staying. But private words from Ruby had made her confess.

While Blade went with Sapphire to find him, Hunter joined Airie.

She sat on the bed wearing only her shift, watching Scratch play on the floor. Hunter threw himself on top of the blankets beside her, wanting nothing more than a few hours of sleep with her in his arms. The springs creaked beneath his weight.

The child was too quiet, Hunter thought. He knew very little about children, but with so many older sisters, he'd had a few nieces and nephews to compare him against. That had been a long time ago, however. His memories might not be accurate.

"Why were women about to be auctioned off in the market?" Airie asked him before he could question her about why she had left the saloon in the first place. Her eyes sparkled with fire.

It was odd that not so long ago, he had viewed the fire in her eyes with suspicion. Now he recognized it as passion, and an integral part of her personality that he had come to appreciate and value. It entranced him. He did not fear it.

He traced a finger along the outside of her thigh, from her knee to the curve of her hip, lifting the edge of the thin cotton shift in an attempt to tease a smile from her.

"Freetown supports the sale of women to outlying areas," he explained. "They usually end up as wives to men who work in the more remote mines."

"Priestesses would never allow such a thing," Airie said, sounding as if she wanted him to confirm the truth of her statement.

He wished he could do so, because he liked it that she was so ignorant of the more terrible things that went on in a virtually lawless land. Immortals had once ruled it completely. Now, it was struggling to find a new path.

"The priestesses are the ones who began the tradition." Hunter rolled to his side and rested his head on the heel of his hand so he could better see her face. "At first, they claimed it was because they wanted nothing within the walls of a newly established city to draw demons to Freetown. After a few years, they said the slave trade honored the hardworking men of the north by giving them wives made in the image of the goddesses. When all is said and done, the real reason for it is that Mamna hates women. And because she can do whatever she pleases."

"How could the priestesses have strayed so far from the goddesses' teachings?" Airie asked in dismay. "My mother observed their rituals until the day she died. She never taught that the goddesses were perfect, but said they bring new life to the world, as mortal women do, and for that alone, we should respect and honor them." Airie looked at him. "Perhaps I could talk to Mamna. Try to find out what went wrong."

She was such an innocent. And a little too honest for what he was about to suggest.

"It's too late for talking." He stopped playing with the hem of her shift and braced himself. "Blade and I have a plan for fighting the demons when they return."

"I can call rain against them," Airie offered. "That will chase them away, just as it did before."

"Chasing them away is no longer enough. They will return. The time has come to take a stand. The Godseekers believe you're a goddess, and we can use that to our advantage."

She went still. "Go on."

"Blade has gone to speak with them. He'll tell them I'm willing to lead their army—which I am—and that I fight on your behalf." Which he did. "We need you to speak with them, too, and persuade them that you are who they believe you to be."

"You want me to pretend that I am a goddess so I can convince people to die fighting demons?" She folded her arms. "No."

Dismay settled like a stone weight inside him. If he had not been so tired and overwhelmed he would have realized she did not know she was half goddess as well as half demon. A small-spirited, selfish part of him did not want her to discover it either. Its full meaning had not quite sunk in. When it did, he suspected their future together might not be as inevitable as he had assumed. The priestess had been partially correct about one other thing—it was not that he thought Airie could not be loyal to him. Rather, why should she wish to be his?

He did not know what to say, or how much to tell her, to win her support. Godseekers, who expected to be addressed by her, would soon descend on the saloon. He was bone-tired already from too little sleep, and he had another long night ahead of him. First, he had to persuade Godseekers to fight beside him rather than try to kill him.

Dismay turned to frustration. It was her life he was trying to protect now, even though turning her over to the demons would end this standoff for Freetown. He betrayed his own kind for her, and she did not understand. She was not mortal, and mortals owed her nothing.

He, however, would walk through fire for her.

"Have I ever asked so very much of you," he said, "that you can't find it in you to help me now when the people of Freetown need me the most?"

He might as well have slapped her. The hurt in her eyes made the sensation a thousand times worse.

"I'll gladly help you save lives. But I'm half demon," she said quietly. "Fighting them, driving them away, is one thing. Killing them seems wrong to me. I don't want anyone to die, mortal or immortal. There must be another way."

For her sake, he wished there was because he had never considered what a mixed heritage might mean to her. Killing demons was what he did, and what he would continue to do as long as they remained in the mortal world.

But he would not force his battles on Airie, or tear her in opposing directions.

"You don't have to do or say anything," Hunter said. "Make an appearance, that's all I ask."

She finally nodded, and some of the heavy weight inside him eased, but he saw the doubt lingering in her eyes. He took her in his arms. Whatever happened with the demons when night fell, he would make certain Airie played no real part in it.

What happened in the future, however, remained to be seen.

He now knew who her father was, even though that was something else of which she was unaware.

That was good, because Hunter intended to kill him.

CHAPTER SIXTEEN

Steam rose from the muddy streets to disperse almost immediately in the dry desert air, the red earth cracking beneath the hot sun.

The creosote-soaked sidewalks had dried enough that they were no longer greasy, although treacherous pockets of water continued to pose a hazard to the inattentive.

Mamna drew the hood of a tan-colored canvas cloak forward so that her face was in shadow. The cloak was not for disguise, an impossible feat because of her deformity. She wore the cloak because her bald scalp and face burned quickly and required vigilant protection.

Snippets of conversation overheard on the streets told her many people held out hope that the rains would recur to save them from the next demon attack. She could have told them that goddess rain, falling in demon territory, would not withstand demon fire for long. The only thing that had saved Freetown from devastation already was the Demon Lord's desire to possess the spawn. Once he had it, the lives of mere mortals would be forfeit.

Mamna, however, was no mere mortal. She counted on enough strength remaining in her amulet to protect her from demons until she reached the Borderlands.

She was too easily recognized to leave the city through the gates, and she wanted no one to know of her departure. Several hours remained until sundown. Once night fell she would escape through the tunnel and put as much distance as possible between her and Freetown while the demons were occupied. Before that, she would leave the Slayer a parting gift.

The Godseekers had made their presence in the city widely known. They had taken shelter in a four-house rooming complex near the city's outer wall, one mostly used by teamsters accompanying the larger wagon trains. Several requests for a meeting had been sent to her. Until now, she had ignored them.

Mamna found the entrance to the rooming house complex and walked through the narrow, arched tunnel into the cobbled courtyard. It was almost empty.

She remained in the shadows as two people crossed the open area ahead of her. She recognized the crippled saloonkeeper from the establishment where she had met with the Slayer. A woman accompanied him, pretty and probably younger than she appeared, but who nevertheless had the hard-edged look of an experienced whore.

It seemed Mamna was not the only one who had business with the Godseekers this day. She was willing to bet that the saloonkeeper was here on behalf of the Slayer, because as far as she knew, whores did not make house calls to public rooming houses with notoriously thin walls.

The saloonkeeper and the whore entered the house on the far side of the courtyard.

Suspicion about the Demon Slayer's activities had her traversing the uneven cobblestones after them, then pausing to listen at the outer door of the house they had entered. She heard voices inside, but they sounded muffled and far away. Cautiously, she eased open the front door.

The voices, more distinguishable now, drifted down from the second level and included the higher pitched tones of a woman arguing with someone. Several doors opened and closed, there was movement, then more voices drifted down to her. A flight of stairs facing the entry rose a dozen steps to meet a small landing, then turned to the right and continued upward and out of sight. She stopped at the base of the stairwell, resting one boot on the first rise, and deliberated as to whether or not to proceed. As far as anyone knew, she still ruled Freetown. She could come and go as she pleased and answered to no one. That did not mean someone would not take the opportunity to kill her if it arose, and no one knew she was here.

But what was the Slayer up to?

She took another step.

"There aren't enough of us," a man said above her. "It's too soon." Another, quieter voice rumbled low in a response she could not quite capture. "The Demon Slayer has made it clear he doesn't share our beliefs. He's prepared to fight demons, but not to lead an army against them." A second, longer pause followed. "If he gives me the amulet I will lead them myself. We serve the goddess, not the Slayer." Then, "Let me think about it," and, "Yes, I know time's running out."

She did not recognize the speaker's voice. It was not that of Fly, the Godseeker who had approached her. As far as she knew, Fly was dead.

A door clicked open, then footsteps descended the stairs, and she scurried into the parlor where she pressed against the wall beside the door. She watched three people depart—the saloonkeeper, a younger man, and the whore.

One man remained behind. He turned to go back upstairs.

She stepped into the hall and pushed back the hood of her cloak so that it draped around her hunched shoulders. "Godseeker. I would like a word with you."

He was a tall man, and as handsome as she would expect of a northerner, although his dark blond hair carried more than a hint of gray. A familiar amber stone glinted against the open throat of an unbuttoned white linen shirt, the shirttail untucked from a pair of thigh-hugging, faded blue trousers as if he'd dressed hastily. He wore a shoulder holster with a very expensive pearl-handled pistol.

His eyes were slate gray and very direct. "Mamna, I assume?"

Irritation made her sharp. "It would be difficult to assume otherwise, given my appearance. Your name would be…?"

"Pillar."

"Pillar," she said. "Can we speak in private?"

He ushered her into the parlor and opened the shutters a crack to allow for more light before closing the door.

Mamna chose a black hrosshair sofa to sit on, then removed the heavy tan cloak and laid it next to her on the roughly cushioned seat. She had her own pistol in its pocket for protection, and she wanted it close in case she should need it.

The room possessed faded wallpaper that puckered at the seams and lifted in several places where it joined the ceiling. The woodwork around the long window and door had been painted too many coats of white without proper stripping beforehand. The overall impression was one of clean and tidy neglect.

"I've already met with a Godseeker," she began, in a preemptive effort to avoid any questions as to why a priestess had seemed so reluctant to meet with the goddesses' chosen. "His name is Fly. He spoke of an army. Is this correct?"

Pillar went to stand near the window, his gaze drawn to the courtyard outside as if he waited for something. Or someone.

"Fly went missing several weeks ago," he said.

"I'm sorry to hear that."

Pillar shrugged. "He was premature in discussing an army. Unfortunately, it's not as well-organized as we'd hoped it to be when this moment arrived."

She deliberately misunderstood what moment he meant. "This isn't the first time the Demon Lord has used fire," she said. "The other night was a test, nothing more."

Pillar made a dismissive gesture with his hand, sounding impatient. At the very least he was distracted, and not as deferential to her as he should be.

"Not the fire. The goddess's return. Not all the Godseekers are aware of it yet. Too many of us are spread throughout the northern mountains, and are isolated."

"When you say *goddess* are you referring to the thief from the mountain?" Mamna asked. "The one the Demon Slayer was hired to bring to justice and now refuses to release to me?" She curled her lip in disdain. "She's no more a goddess than you or I. She's the demon spawn of a priestess."

"I've seen her," Pillar said. "I know a goddess when I see one. Female spawn don't exist."

Mamna pressed her palms flat against the tops of her thighs to resolve any telling movements that might reveal her intentions. Or her lies.

"How can you be so certain female spawn don't exist?" she asked. "I agree it's very unlikely for any spawn to survive beyond childbirth, and those born in mortal form would be an even greater enigma. But do you really think a priestess wouldn't be made aware of a goddess's presence? That the goddesses wouldn't speak to me?"

Worry lines dragged at Pillar's brow. Stubbornness remained. "I no longer know for certain what to think, other than that I saw a goddess with my own eyes."

"You saw a spawn," Mamna said. "You have been with a goddess, Pillar. You know what their presence is like, and how it feels to be touched by one. A demon is not so very different. This female spawn will have her father's immortal presence to her. It's part of what makes her dangerous, especially to mortal man."

Pillar finally gave her his full attention. "The Slayer believes she is special."

She kept the excitement from her expression. He had not quite accepted her argument, Mamna thought. Not yet. But he was close.

"She is special," she replied, "and the Slayer knows why that is. The Demon Lord himself claims to be her father, which was why the Slayer was hired to bring her to me. I was then to turn her over to the Demon Lord."

"If that's true, why would the Slayer be willing to follow her?"

Real doubt entered his manner. She could hear it in his voice, and see it in the way the question filled his eyes.

"Is she beautiful?" Mamna asked.

Pillar nodded once, although as if reluctant to acknowledge it. "Exceedingly so."

"The Slayer is mortal." She pressed her advantage. "Is it so strange to think he, too, might fall under the spell of a beautiful woman, especially one who is half demon?"

"What if you're wrong? What if she really is a goddess, sent by the others to lead the Slayer and the Godseeker army?" Thoughtfulness eased some of the worry lines around his eyes. "Have you seen her? How can you be so certain she's a demon's spawn?"

She was very close to success now. She pretended to examine a tear in the faded wallpaper, as if unwilling to concede he might be correct.

"No, I haven't seen her," she admitted. "But I'm certain if I did, I would know. I served the goddesses."

"As did I." Pillar again looked through the shutter's slats into the courtyard, lost in thought. Mamna waited, careful not to push, allowing him to come to his own conclusions. "What if you saw her for yourself?"

"Impossible. The Slayer knows it's the Demon Lord who wants her, and he made it very clear to me just this morning that he'll protect her at all cost, even from the priestesses. It's unfortunate that he shows so little faith," she added. "The priestesses serve the goddesses. If he believed in her, he wouldn't be worried."

A few more moments of indecision settled over him before Pillar made up his mind.

"I can arrange for you to see her," he said. "If you swear to serve her as a goddess once it's determined for certain."

Mamna smiled. Perhaps all was not yet lost to her. If she could convince the spawn it had been betrayed by the immortals, then it might be persuaded to restore and invoke Mamna's amulet. If not, then Mamna would kill it and at least have some vengeance on both the Slayer and the Demon Lord.

"If the Demon Lord has no claim on her, then I will gladly serve this new goddess," she said.

• • •

Airie helped Sapphire serve coffee to the men who had come to speak with Hunter and Blade.

She agreed to do this to help Hunter, but she did not like being presented to people as something she was not. Serving them was a silent act of rebellion, to let Hunter know this was a part she played, and that she disapproved of his plan.

It amused him more than anything. Though he avoided looking in her direction, she could tell by the set of his mouth. It was not as harsh as usual.

The men sat in half-circles at the round tables they'd drawn together in the saloon, all facing forward so that they could see and hear. She thought there might be fifty men in total, maybe more. Most were Godseekers, but some were locals, according to Sapphire.

Hunter, Blade, and a Godseeker sat at a table before them. The Godseeker was quite a bit older than Hunter and Blade and seemed to be in charge of the northerners. *Pillar*, she heard someone call him. Airie remembered him. He was the one who had threatened Hunter.

The two men appeared to bear each other no ill will over the incident.

The curious scrutiny of the strangers present left her uncomfortable as she moved in and out of the room, but she wanted to hear what was being planned and so did not rush.

"The Godseekers have a system for communication set up throughout the city," Pillar said, speaking loud enough for everyone to hear. "There are plenty of men who will fight demons if we call them. More will fight if they believe the Demon Slayer does, too." His eyes slid to Airie, then away, but he made no mention of goddesses.

"The demons will attack from above, and they'll use fire," Hunter added. "Every available man or woman who can use a bow and arrow or sword should be positioned on the rooftops inside the city, and the walls surrounding it. Only the best shots should be using rifles. The chance of ricochet is too high."

Pillar agreed. A number of other heads nodded, too. "Those who can carry water for fighting fires should do so. We'll need access to private wells, including the one in the temple. I can arrange for that." He exchanged a long look with Hunter. "More rain would be helpful."

"I'll see to that." Hunter leaned forward in his chair, resting his forearms on his thighs. "We don't want the demons to accurately guess our numbers. Let them think we're paralyzed with fear, which is what they'll expect. They haven't met with organized resistance in three hundred years. We'll draw them in as close as possible, then let the sharpshooters take over. Demons are most vulnerable here, here, and here," he said, indicating points on his body. "That's where the joints in their bone plating are."

"What will you be doing?" someone asked, directing the question at Hunter.

Airie was curious about that, as well. The way his mouth hardened indicated he was no longer even faintly amused, and that had her worried. So did the way he still refused to look at her, despite her having chosen a position near the center of the room and in his direct line of vision.

"I intend to challenge the Demon Lord," Hunter said. "If we take away their leader, they'll lose any semblance of an organized attack. Demons don't have much more liking for one another than they do for us, and they don't fight well together. That's our real advantage."

Her concern had been justified. The walls and the ceiling of the saloon rippled and danced, leaving her dizzy and grasping at the back of a chair for support. Thankfully, the copper tray she carried was empty.

Hunter had seen her reaction. He partly rose in his chair, caught himself, and shifted the action so as to turn and lean across the table and whisper something to Blade.

Airie returned to the kitchen behind Sapphire, and with a tinny clatter, tossed the tray on a counter.

Sapphire turned to her.

"Pillar, the Godseekers' leader, would like to speak with you privately," the blonde girl said. "He said to say you would remember him because you set his boots on fire." Fair eyebrows lifted in an unspoken query, but she did not ask about it. When Airie did not explain either, she continued. "He says a priestess wishes to join the battle against demons as your servant. What should I tell him?"

"Do you know the name of this priestess?" Airie asked.

"No."

Loyalty to Hunter warned Airie she should send a refusal. This felt too clandestine. Only the possibility that the Godseeker and this priestess might seek a better solution, one that did not involve him behaving so foolishly, had her agreeing to it instead.

The goddess had said she would need to earn her place in this world. She would not earn it by pretending to be something she was not, or by bringing death. She did not want anyone to die. But it was Hunter she feared for the most, and she would do what she could in order to protect him.

Despite her prayers, the goddess remained silent. Speaking with a priestess, one who was willing to help, might give her the guidance she sorely needed right now.

"Ask the Godseeker when and where we can meet."

• • •

The city gates remained closed, although a carefully screened few were allowed to pass.

Demons had not been idle the past few nights, and several settlements near the goddesses' mountain had suffered heavy losses. Survivors had trickled into the city, seeking protection, and the guards at the gates were not without compassion.

Therefore, no one paid more than cursory attention to a lone man on foot entering through the city's gates shortly before sundown. The Demon Lord drew the hood of his oilskin slicker forward, placing his face in shadow.

Come night, he intended to burn Freetown to the ground. Before he did that, he had to find the spawn. Once he located her and prevented her from calling the goddesses' rain, he would set the city on fire from the inside.

As he moved through the streets, the inconsistencies surrounding her continued to eat at him. She was female. She could summon goddess rain. If she were his as well, spawn or not, it meant she was an immortal.

The Slayer would then have two things that belonged to him. That amulet he wore was the other. The existence of both caused the Demon Lord deep humiliation and pain.

He had crafted that amulet himself. He had given it to a goddess out of love so she would have added protection against his kind, and in return, she had discarded both the amulet and their child.

Now, the Slayer used his amulet to slaughter demons, which

meant the Demon Lord owned the burden of those deaths. The Slayer would use his daughter against him, too, if given the chance.

The Demon Lord gravitated toward the city center and was rewarded with bits of conversation overheard in the streets. Mortals were rallying and mounting a defense.

The Slayer would be part of it. He would lead the Demon Lord to the spawn.

He found the saloon where they gathered to plan their strategy by following others. He then waited across the street from the saloon in the shadows, his hat pitched over his eyes so his face could not be seen. Only two mortals would recognize him in this form—Mamna and the Slayer. Neither would expect him here.

The sun set, and the shadows lengthened. Men came and went. The taste of their fear was what demons relished about battling mortals the most, and Freetown was thick with it tonight.

Suddenly, he straightened. A figure, tall and too slender to be a man, and wrapped to the boot tops in a long, hooded cape, slipped through a gate at the far side of the saloon and glanced furtively up and down the emptying street. She turned to her right and headed in the direction of the city's outer wall.

The Demon Lord could not see her face.

But he did know that whoever she was, she was not mortal.

• • •

Hunter walked the walls of the city, staring at the night sky and waiting for demons, making certain to be seen by everyone who had turned out in defense of Freetown.

Godseekers had spent the remainder of the day going door to door, spreading a wide net throughout the city in order to recruit as many as possible who were willing to fight.

The numbers had been both surprising and heartening. The Godseeker, Pillar, had been correct. Word of Airie had spread, and with the Demon Slayer to fight for her, hopes had risen.

Hunter had not made amends with Airie before he left. He had not liked the way the men in the meeting had watched her—as if she, too, might be for hire—and he had not dealt with it well. Too many things could happen to her without him or Blade there to guard her. But she had promised him she would not leave the city, and he had also asked Ruby to watch over her for him because he did not completely trust that she would be safe.

Anticipation hummed through him. While he hated demons, and feared for Airie, he loved what fighting them did to him. He felt more alive. Invincible.

If he killed the Demon Lord, the remainder would have no leader, and he could hunt them to extinction.

He refused to think of what might happen if he did not win.

"Make sure the archers and the sharpshooters take careful aim," Hunter said to the captain of the guards. "I'd hate to be shot by accident."

The captain was a heavyset man, with a broad face and thick, fierce black eyebrows that met across the bridge of his nose. He was not in favor of Hunter's plan. "The archers aren't the ones you need to be worrying about."

An alarm sounded as the first demons appeared on the horizon. Within minutes they circled overhead, well out of range of the weapons. High above, one demon broke away, diving swiftly at Hunter.

Hunter's amulet flared a warning, but as he swung his sword, a volley of flaming arrows streaked trails of orange and yellow across the sky. The arrows bounced off the demon's plating, showering thousands of rainbow-hued sparks in their wakes before falling harmlessly to earth.

It was enough of a display to show that the archers were as good as their word, and Hunter would have adequate protection when he faced the Demon Lord.

Hunter searched the sky.

Where was he?

Chapter Seventeen

Guilt lashed at Airie for slipping away from Hunter yet again without telling him where she was going, or why. He would not approve and would try to forbid it.

But Sapphire had promised to cover for her, and if Airie could help Hunter even in some small way, then it was worth the risk.

She had been told to meet Pillar near the tunnel entrance. When she got there, she saw that the guards, in position earlier that day, had now vanished. Uneasiness whispered cold words of warning up her spine. The street was dark here, and very empty. None of the city's night watchmen walked the walls above. The demons were not expected to attack from this side of the city, so the men had been concentrated nearer the gates.

She heard movement behind her and turned, fists clenched, prepared to defend herself.

A small figure hobbled toward her. At first, Airie thought it was a child. Then the figure lifted the hood of its cloak, and she saw a telltale shaven head above a plain, broad-featured face. This, then, must be the priestess she had been asked to meet.

But where was the Godseeker, Pillar?

"Priestess?" Airie asked, addressing the woman. "You wished to speak with me?"

The priestess squinted at her in the darkness. Instead of answering, she clutched her chest at the base of her throat. As she did, the same sense of compulsion Airie had experienced the night the Godseekers called to her slammed through her.

Disbelief forced her back a step. The priestess was attempting to use an amulet against her.

Airie's skin began to glow, bathing the ground at her feet in golden light, and the goddess awakened to whisper in her ear. *This one is not to be trusted. You do not ask for her help. You command it.*

No, Airie wanted to protest, but an ugly suspicion had already begun to form. Who was she to command a priestess?

"You dare try to use an amulet of the goddesses against me?" she demanded.

"Forgive me." The priestess lowered her hand from the amulet. "I thought you were a demon."

The goddess went still inside her, and Airie knew she had been insulted.

She stepped closer to the priestess, and the old woman recoiled. She was terrified of her, Airie saw, or rather, of what she believed her to be. But if she believed her to be a goddess, why was she so afraid?

Because she did not believe Airie to be a goddess, as Pillar had suggested. She thought of her as something else.

Airie's hand went to the priestess's throat, and she felt for the chain. She drew the priestess's amulet into her palm and examined it.

Deep, tiny fissures marred the desert varnish encasing it. She could see it quite well in the glow from her skin. The amulet depicted a rainbow on fire, and looked very much like a combination of the ones Airie and Hunter both wore.

Airie did not understand the significance of the image, although she knew it caused the goddess a great deal of pain. She felt it.

She did not release the amulet. "Perhaps I am a demon."

"You are no more demon than goddess," the priestess said. "This amulet protects mortals from them all. With your help, it can be used to free the world of immortals forever."

Don't trust her, the goddess whispered again, with greater insistence.

Airie did not know whom she could trust. Her suspicions were growing stronger, and pointing to conclusions she did not want to reach. She did know that she disliked the feel of the amulet, and did not trust it either. "What would I have to do to help?"

The priestess's eyes hardened. "Heal the amulet. Give it life."

"And who would become responsible for it if I do?"

"I've looked after it for years," the priestess said. "I've used it to protect this city from demons. It belongs to me."

This, then, was Mamna, the one responsible for the desperation on the faces of the women for sale in the market. She had sent Hunter to find Airie, and intended to turn her over to the Demon Lord. Hunter did not like her and called her evil.

And Hunter, Airie trusted. She clenched her fist and the amulet crumpled to dust. She sifted the dust through her fingers and let it trickle to the ground.

Mamna drew in a sharp breath.

"You are free of the immortals, Priestess," Airie said. The goddess's voice echoed with hers, both of them speaking as one. "No one protects you now. Betrayal brings its own rewards. Enjoy them."

The presence of the goddess faded to nothing, along with the golden brightness of Airie's skin.

The priestess's fury, however, lay thick between them. Mamna knotted her fingers in the now-empty chain around her neck.

Pity for her replaced the certainty of a betrayal Airie knew had been committed. Whatever Mamna might have done, she remained a priestess. The goddesses had touched her and claimed her as their own. That would not change.

"If you pray for forgiveness, the goddesses will hear you," Airie said.

The priestess's lip curled in contempt. "You think I am the one who should pray for forgiveness? A demon spawned you and a goddess whore gave birth to you. You are an abomination. The goddesses fear you and the demons despise you. Your death could set the demons free from this world for good, Spawn. Your very existence holds them here. If not for you, they would be long gone, the same as the goddesses." Her ugly face twisted into an even uglier smile.

"But the Demon Slayer never told you that, did he?"

• • •

The words slid easily from her tongue.

Mamna had hated the spawn on sight. Although she had her mother's face, there could be no mistaking who had fathered her. She bore his eyes and, despite the ugly, ill-fitting clothing she wore, possessed his bearing. She was dark-haired, like him.

"My mother was a priestess, the same as you," the spawn dared to say, but Mamna could read the uncertainty growing on her pretty face. This spawn might have the physical appearance of an immortal, but she did not possess their full strength.

She had destroyed Mamna's amulet, however, and with it, any use Mamna might have had for her. "I watched you grow in your mother's belly for months," she said. "I heard the goddesses plan for your birth so that they could use you against your demon father. The priestess who raised you was left to ensure you were delivered to him when the time came. That time was the collapse of their mountain."

The demon-dark eyes turned to red. "She would never do such a thing."

Mamna leaned close, enjoying the pain she was inflicting. "When the Slayer arrived, she turned you over to him immediately, did she not? Did she fight for you? Warn you of danger? Was she faithful? Unwavering in her loyalty to the goddesses?"

"You're lying," the spawn said, but with even less conviction.

"Am I?"

"It's so hard to tell," a deep voice interrupted them from the darkness. "I find it easier to assume you are."

The Demon Lord stepped away from the shadows, and the contents of Mamna's stomach shifted at the expression on his face. Without her amulet, she had not been alerted to his proximity. Neither had she expected to see him here, inside the city walls, when the entire city anticipated an attack by him.

And never in mortal form, with its physical weaknesses.

The fear in Mamna shifted to angry frustration as a tear she could not contain slid down her cheek. She had wanted nothing more from him than that he favor her with a small portion of the kindness he had once shown to a goddess, but Mamna was not beautiful, and he was not kind. He was a demon, with no pity or thought but for his own superficial wants and desires. She had wasted much of her life harboring impossible hopes and dreams.

No more.

Desperation forced her thoughts to coalesce into a plan of action. She did not want to die and she would not make it easy for him. Her hand inched toward the pocket in the seam of her cloak.

"Would you really try to kill me?" the Demon Lord asked. He had flames in his eyes now, fed by unleashed hatred for her. "After everything we've meant to each other?"

He did not know how deeply those words wounded her. That he could speak them to her so carelessly made her hate him even more. He did not deserve her love and never had.

"I've meant nothing to you," she said, "while you were once everything to me. I betrayed the goddesses for you. I would have done anything you asked of me for no more reward than the chance to serve you. Instead, you've spent years blinded by the loss of a whore who cared so little for you that she abandoned both you and your child. Good riddance to her. To both of you."

She fumbled for her pistol.

The Demon Lord raised his hand, palm out, but she managed one shot at the spawn before the flames of his fire engulfed her.

Pain and sheer terror wrenched shrieks from what remained of her soul.

Along with her own screams, she heard those of the spawn. Rain began to fall, faster and harder, and for an instant, Mamna thought it might save her. Then the rain turned to billows of steam, and all she could see or feel was fire.

As death claimed her, she prayed the goddesses would not be waiting for her.

. . .

The Demon Lord watched Mamna burn.

She had never wanted to serve him, as she'd tried to claim. She wished to manipulate and control, and had lied to him about the existence of his daughter for years.

The realization forced him to consider the possibility of other lies he had accepted too readily, and of truths perhaps spurned. He turned his back on the dying priestess to examine his daughter.

She looked so much like her mother that his breath hitched at the unexpectedness of it. Too much of the past had bared itself already today. He did not care to see or hear any more.

The girl needed to be taught her place.

Beyond the wall, near the city's gates, the first of his demons dove from the heavens, a great shadow that plunged in a free fall before twisting to one side and soaring away. An answering wave of fiery arrows from the ramparts dragged streaming tails of yellow across the deepening indigo sky.

The city was undefended on this side, dark and silent. It would not remain so for long, once the attack began in earnest.

The burst of rain had stopped. The Demon Lord tossed back the hood of his slicker. "This is my territory," he said. "You do not call goddess rain here. What is your name?"

She did not flinch away as he'd intended her to. Dark emotions lashed at him instead, overriding the gentler, goddess-driven ones behind her defiant attempt to save the ugly priestess from his fire. *Anger. Contempt.* This daughter despised him, which he found intriguing. Demons did not show fear, and she had none.

Her answer came willingly. "Airie," she said.

Rainbows and lightning. The meaning of her name was a slap in the face. The rainbow pendant she wore around her neck dealt another harsh blow. It had once been offered to him, and he had thrown it back at its owner.

He reached out and touched it now, rubbing it between his fingers, not wishing for her to see how much she'd unsettled him. "Where did you get this?" he demanded.

Her unwavering, fearless eyes held his. "From my mother. She told me to wear it, and to think of her often, and more importantly to remember that I was born out of love." She twisted the pendant from his fingers as if afraid he would somehow taint it, and tucked it inside her cloak. "At least I was born out of love on her part."

His throat ached. Allia had given this token, once meant for him, to their daughter. She'd had some true feelings for him, then, or she would not have done so. Yet she had also allowed the Slayer to take possession of the amulet he had given to her, and that was not to be forgiven.

The west wind had risen with the arrival of his demons, dispersing the remainder of Mamna's bitter, smoldering ashes before it as it wound its way through the narrow streets of Freetown and past the tightly shuttered houses.

At least I was born out of love on her part. He did not dare to dwell on the meaning of those words.

The Demon Lord could not decide what to do with this daughter, and he was not used to indecision. He had planned to kill her. He still might, but his curiosity regarding her was far from satisfied.

"It's possible that it's as the priestess said, and your existence is what keeps demons trapped here within the confines of time." He frowned. "It's equally possible that your death would be my destruction. Her words are not to be trusted."

"No more than yours should be."

Flames rippled beneath her golden skin and crackled in her blazing eyes. Lifting a hand, a great orange and yellow ball of fire formed in her palm. She drew her arm back and released it with a great deal of force.

Well, well. Fire as well as rain. There could be no doubt she had demon in her, and goddess, too. She had been aptly named.

Rather than dodge her fire, he called it to him so that it embraced them both.

With a jolt of surprise, he felt a subtle difference in the fire she wielded. It was almost as if it had been tainted, although that was impossible. Fire was his.

He slowly absorbed its heat until the flames died away and only the golden gleam to her skin remained.

"Never use demon fire against its lord," he said to her. "I own it all, even yours, and I can call it to me as I choose."

She took one step toward him, and bracing her foot, balanced her weight over her bent knee for impetus. She shot a blow to his chin with the heel of her fist that rocked his head back. While he remained off-balance, she followed up with a strike of her other knee to his hip that nearly felled him.

Impressive. She was fast as well as strong, and the blows hurt. Her skirt, however, hampered her. He grabbed her leg, flipping her onto her back on the ground as they both fell, so that he landed on top. He dropped his knee to her chest, then pinned her with one forearm across her throat. She struggled to get her arms between them in an attempt to unseat him, but he blocked that move, too.

If he intended to kill her, now was the time. But what might it mean for him, to own such a death as this?

He did not want her dead. Not yet.

And while he now had his daughter in his possession, he had not forgotten about the Slayer. He wanted his amulet back, too.

The Slayer would come for her.

"I think," the Demon Lord said slowly, "that I'd like to know what other surprises you might possess."

He lifted Airie in his arms, shifting to demon form so quickly she could not react other than to wrap her arms around his neck for safety as he leaped into the air.

He climbed steadily and circled the city. Faint shouts carried to them from the far side of the city, over the wind, as mortals rallied against demons. Archers on nearby rooftops witnessed his ascent from within the city walls and released a fresh volley of flaming arrows. A few struck the buildings. Confusion broke out below as people ran toward the creeping flames, shouting for water.

With his enormous wing muscles pumping, he glided through the skies high above Freetown, then flew off into the desert.

He left the demons behind to do as they wished. Demon fire, however, would not be called again this evening. He did not wish for harm to come to the Slayer.

When it did, it would not be so fast or merciful.

• • •

The Demon Lord had not appeared.

A brilliant yellow dawn blanketed the city. Wearily, covered in soot and sweat, Hunter walked through the emptying streets to Blade's saloon. Mortal losses throughout the night had been heavy and discouraging, but the demons had not burned the entire city, as it had been feared would happen. The fire brigade had performed its duties admirably. Freetown remained standing, although not unscathed.

At midday, the battle's leaders would meet again. In the meantime, he wanted Airie. He craved her smiles and her touch. When she was near him, his world seemed brighter and filled with hope.

Hunter knocked off the dust at the door, then entered the kitchen to find Blade and Ruby waiting for him at the table. Ruby's hair was unbound, and she had been crying. Neither looked as if they had slept. Hunter headed for the back stairs.

"Airie is gone," Blade said.

He stopped at Blade's words, certain there must be some mistake.

"Impossible." She had promised him to be here, and he trusted her.

Fresh tears filled Ruby's eyes. "Sapphire said Airie went to meet a Godseeker last night. I made her tell me who, and where, and I went after her. A priestess was waiting."

Hunter went cold. *Mamna*.

Ruby told him of the priestess's words to Airie, of the terrible things she had said, and of the Demon Lord's appearance.

"After he killed the priestess, he took Airie with him," she finished.

Mamna was dead. The Demon Lord had Airie. That explained why he had not made an appearance last night, then. He had already gotten what he wanted.

The enormity of what all of it meant had not yet fully hit Hunter. He felt frozen inside, and numb to anger. That would change. When it did, he intended to be far from here.

"You should have come to me at once," Hunter said to Blade.

"I only just found out, myself."

Hunter headed again for the stairs.

"Where are you going?" Blade called after him.

"To pack my bags. I've already lost too much time."

His insides thawed a little, heated by spreading panic. The Demon Lord had too great a head start, and could travel much faster than Hunter.

"Wait a minute." Blade surged from his chair. He came to stand by Hunter but did not try to get in his way, which was wise given Hunter's mood. "You need to think about this. You could be walking into a trap."

Or Airie could already be dead. Blade did not say it, and Hunter was grateful. No one else was to blame if she were. He should have protected her better.

His insides thawed a little more. He had to get moving. He wanted to be alone when reality settled in. It would be better for everyone. "I'm not leaving her with demons. Do you know what they will do to her?"

Blade's jaw worked. "Yes. Better than most." He scrubbed at his face. "Did you hear what Ruby said to you? Did you understand it at all? Airie's not mortal, Hunter. Do you really want to involve yourself in this?"

Hunter rounded on him. "I know what she is, and who. She's Airie, and that's all that matters to me. I can't abandon her to demons, any more than I abandoned you—and I knew nothing at all about you."

There was silence. "No, you didn't," Blade said, his voice quiet. "She's certainly worth no less than me."

Ruby inserted herself between them. "I don't think she's dead," she said to Hunter. "She fought him. If he'd wanted to kill her, he could have done so then."

Of course she would have put up a fight. What she could not have done was kill, even to defend herself, as she should have.

How quickly his opinion of her had changed.

But there were other things demons could do to her that were worse than death, and thinking of those did nothing to reassure him as to her safety. As long as the Demon Lord lived, she would never be safe.

A muscle worked at the base of Blade's jaw. "I'm coming with you."

Ruby made a small sound of dismay. Her anxious eyes fixed on Blade, who refused to look at her. Hunter understood what the offer cost his friend and was moved by it.

He would not accept it, however. "Taking a whole army of mortals deep into demon territory wouldn't defeat them, so whether I go alone or with you, it will make no difference. I have some protection, but you have none." He touched his amulet. He could not abandon Airie to demons, and yet here he was, abandoning an entire town. He did not say what they all knew. Come nighttime, Freetown was as good as lost. Airie, however, was not. "Take the boy, and the women, and head to my cabin," Hunter added. "At least there, you'll have some natural protection."

Blade looked from Hunter to Ruby, and nodded, yet Hunter knew what he would do without him having to say it. Blade would take Scratch and the women to Hunter's cabin, and then he would return to fight in Freetown with the others.

Hunter looked in on Scratch before he left. The child was asleep on the floor in Ruby's private bedroom, snuggled into a thick nest of blankets.

Hunter did not wake him. He could hardly explain to a child what was happening.

He closed the door and left the saloon, then made his way out of Freetown through the tunnel. From there, he headed into the desert toward demon territory.

CHAPTER EIGHTEEN

Hunter took a short break to avoid the worst of the midday heat, and awoke to small fingers prying open one of his eyes and a solemn, accusing face staring into his.

He shot upright in a tangle of bedding, his pistol in one hand, his sword in the other, and his heart pounding beneath his ribs like an animal intent on escape.

Scratch.

How on earth had the boy followed him?

He set the weapons down. His heart rate steadied. "Sometime soon, you and I are going to have a little man-to-man talk."

He gave off an air of such innocent satisfaction at having found Hunter that it was impossible to be angry with him. How many people, other than Scratch and Airie, actually sought out Hunter's company for no purpose other than to be with him?

It warmed his heart. One companion had been returned to him. Now, he wanted the other.

He untangled himself from the bedding and stood, tucking in

his shirttail and slipping his suspenders over his shoulders as he did. A quick glance at the sky told him the afternoon was still young.

It was too late to turn back now, and if he did, he suspected Scratch would only come after him again. Hunter had no choice but to keep going and take the boy with him. The prospect should displease him when in fact, he found just the opposite was true. The child's presence brought calm, and Hunter had need for such companionship.

He shielded his eyes and checked the landscape for familiar markings, squinting against the hazy heat dancing in waves off the uneven desert terrain. There were many little dips and valleys, as well as patches of low vegetation and pillars of sand and rock, and it took him a moment to place them.

He experienced a brief moment of disorientation. He'd traveled a lot farther into the desert than should have been possible.

"I don't suppose you'd know anything about that?" he said to the boy. Scratch sat beside a clump of sage, dribbling dirt through his fingers, and didn't answer. Hunter rubbed the top of the boy's head. "Of course not."

A few miles to their east lay a canyon cutting a deep ribbon through the desert. Its nooks and crannies would offer them hiding places from demons in the coming night. Hunter packed his bedroll and settled his hat on his head. Even though he slowed his steps to accommodate the boy's shorter stride, they walked the few miles to the canyon's lip and began their descent to the bottom in what seemed like no time at all.

Midway down, a gently sloping shelf jutted out over the canyon floor far below them. When they reached it, they followed the shelf gradually downward.

Walking was far more comfortable here than above, where they had been exposed to the full heat of the desert, but the comfort would not last.

Late in the day, Hunter noticed that his amulet had gotten too warm against his skin. He looked up.

They were being followed.

He took off his hat and wiped the sweat from his forehead with his sleeve. The canyon now had them at a disadvantage. The sheer walls at this point made climbing ill-advised, effectively boxing them in. If he'd been alone he might have tried anyway, but Scratch, agile as he was, would never make it.

The canyon, however, was not one straight crevasse. The gorge at the bottom, where the floodwaters flowed, was fed by a number of smaller arroyos. Some were dead ends. A few led back to the desert surface.

Hunter would feel more confident facing a demon on level ground than here, where his footing was uncertain. He took the child by the hand and headed into a passage barely wide enough for him to fit through, which would make it even more awkward for a bulkier demon.

The skin between his shoulders prickled, as if it were shrinking.

"We're going back up," he said to Scratch.

The boy bobbed his chin up and down, his eyes widening. He knew, too, that they were being followed, and that their situation was not good.

This was no way for a child to grow up, Hunter thought. The worst thing that had ever happened to him as a child was being forced to play dress-up with his sisters because he'd gotten caught up in some girl game.

Running for his life from demons had come much later on.

The arroyo he chose proved so narrow that Hunter had to turn his shoulders sideways and carry his pack in his hand at one point. It narrowed again so that the sky appeared as a thin blue sliver of ribbon above them. The temperature, however, dropped a few welcome degrees, the thick granite walls dispersing much of the heat.

There had been a rockslide here at one time. Rubble blocked their path, and the opening was too small at the top for Hunter to climb over. The amulet around his neck grew hotter, shining in the gloom, and any hope of escape died.

They could try to outwait the demon by staying in here and hoping it was too large to come after them, but Hunter was not about to put much faith in that approach. Besides, there was always the danger from juvenile sand swifts. Hunter did not much care for that fate either.

"Climb up and tell me if you can get past the rockslide," he said to Scratch.

The child did as he was told, climbing nimbly up the mound of rock and debris. When he reached the top he looked down at Hunter.

"Stay up there," Hunter said to him. "Watch out for anything that moves—and don't touch it." He set his pack against the rubble and withdrew his sword. "No matter what, you don't come down from there until I tell you to."

Hunter tried not to think of what would become of the child—and Airie—if something should happen to him. Instead, he concentrated on the amulet, drawing as much power from it as he could. Then, he stepped back into the open.

And discovered two demons hunting them, not one.

They came at him on foot. Massive, with ugly heads bulging forward from bunched, rock-solid shoulders, their leathery skin and bone plating shone a dull red in the filtered light. Meaty fists hung from heavy arms, and their footsteps shook the ground when they walked. Although their wings were their main weakness in a fight, when not in use those wings furled inside the protective bony humps on their backs, as they were now.

Hunter saw no reason to wait. At least he had the sun at his back, so it would be in their eyes, not his. He rushed forward, a move they did not anticipate, and struck the demon closest to him with an amulet-enhanced, closed-fisted blow to its throat. The demon staggered back from the force of it. Hunter ducked to the side, careful to keep the first demon between himself and the second, mindful of their talons. If blood were drawn, he did not want for it to be his.

As the first demon choked, clawing chunks of flesh from its damaged throat, Hunter followed through with a well-placed knee to its groin. Only then did he thrust his sword into the soft point under the demon's arm, and into its heart. The demon collapsed, then lay still.

Hunter whirled, yanking his sword free, prepared to face bloodlust from the second demon, but this one had greater self-control than the first. That made it all the more dangerous. Regardless, now that there was only the one left to deal with, Hunter's confidence in his chances rose.

It was short-lived, however. A heavy fist connected with the side of his head and his thoughts splintered into pain. The ground and the sky spun together, fading to gray before righting themselves. But, rather than move in to press its advantage, the demon stepped back, looking at a point beyond Hunter's shoulder. While Hunter knew better than to turn to look, the shadow that fell across him from behind made him do so despite his best intentions.

This third demon was even bigger than the first two. Even though he was soon to be a dead man, Hunter refused to give up. He could take at least one more of them with him. What of Airie, he wondered. What of Scratch? Of all the years he'd hunted demons, why had his luck run out now, when others depended on him?

He danced to the side, trying to draw the second demon between him and the third as a shield, but they both circled, flanking him. The third demon's taloned fist shot out, and Hunter thought, *This is it.*

But instead of the crush of those talons around his neck, he felt leathery knuckles brush his skin and the talons closed around the amulet instead. The demon snapped the gold chain, curling the amulet into its fist.

It scooped Hunter up in one arm and in seconds became airborne, carrying him off into the dusky sky.

• • •

Deep in his desert stronghold, the Demon Lord held the recovered amulet in his hand, rubbing one thumb over its jagged surface. He thought of the pleasure on Allia's face the day he gave it to her.

He had it back, but now, it brought him no joy.

He had the Slayer, too, imprisoned in a large metal cage that dangled from a chain in the cavern ceiling near the Demon Lord's throne. The sight of him entertained the demons preparing for another long night of attacks against Freetown.

With Mamna now gone, such organized attacks would not last much longer. The demons would go back to their solitary hunting patterns. And then, Freetown could genuinely begin to worry.

"Fight me, you bastard," the Slayer shouted at him. The cage swayed beneath his shifting weight.

The Demon Lord smiled at the challenge. Mortals would not

have the Slayer to help them, either.

He wondered about the relationship between the Slayer and his daughter. How close it was. And if the Slayer could be used to break her.

"You'll get your fight." The Demon Lord held the amulet aloft. It glittered as it spun on its chain. "But without this, what do you think your chances of victory will be?"

"Equal to, if not better than, yours." The Slayer's fingers ground into the bars of his cage. "That is a toy I found as a boy. Its value to me is sentimental. Do you think I need that trinket to best you?"

For a mortal, and a prisoner, he was arrogant. The Demon Lord enjoyed this lack of fear in the mortal. What would it take to instill some?

"Did you think it would work against me? Did you not know it was once mine? That I crafted it?" He watched the Slayer's expression change to one of caution, and knew he had not. "I know what it is. What it can do. And it's not a toy."

"Not a toy, then," the Slayer conceded. "But I found it in a stream, buried in the mud, so it's something someone discarded as having no value to them, either."

The game lost a bit of its pleasure. The Demon Lord closed his fist around the amulet. "My daughter was discarded as well, yet you seem to find value in her. Why did you not turn her over to the priestess as you were hired to do?"

The Slayer continued testing the bars, searching for weaknesses. "I have a liking for women. I wouldn't turn the worst of them over to demons."

"She is a demon."

"I hear she's as much goddess." The Slayer's grin filled with insolence. "Mamna likes to talk. Sometimes she even tells the truth."

"Not often. Besides, Mamna is dead. And we'll see how much demon is in her when I have you torn apart in front of her eyes." He leaned forward. "Blood tells, Slayer. In more ways than one. Do you think she can resist the smell of yours when it's spilled?"

The Slayer held onto his grin, but with a more visible effort. "I think," he said, his words slow and deliberate, "that you have no idea what she is, or what she can do. You know nothing about her."

"I know she was born inside of time, which gives her limitations that make her of little use to me alive." He watched the Slayer carefully. "But not, perhaps, to one of my demons." The slight heave of the Slayer's chest and his quickening breath gave away a satisfying depth of anger, but his ability to hide his fear was more impressive. The threat of being torn apart by demons had not caused even a minor tremor in him.

"Ask the last demon who dared touch her what her limitations are," the Slayer said.

So. Agares had tried to tempt her and she had resisted.

Unfortunately, it was impossible for the Demon Lord to kill him twice. And while the Demon Lord already owned that death, he did not plan to struggle with one over an answer he could easily find out for himself.

"I would prefer to discover her limitations—and her strengths—on my own." His daughter would join him, or she would die. She could not survive among demons if she could not defend herself. The Demon Lord spoke to the demon standing closest to his throne.

"Bring my daughter to me."

• • •

The room where Airie was imprisoned contained sparse, bulky furnishings, and no natural light. Demon fire burned in sconces carved to represent nude figures in impossible and confusing sexual positions.

She lay on an enormous bench that doubled as a bed and stared at the stone door.

The door opened by using a single word of command, which she had been given. It was not entirely accurate, then, to claim she was a prisoner, but the one time she had ventured from her room, the number of demons roaming the halls had not encouraged her to wander far. A spawn as well as a woman, she was an anomaly to them.

None of them approached her, however, unlike the demon she had encountered outside Hunter's cabin. These knew to whom she belonged.

And what the Demon Lord would do to them if they touched her.

She, on the other hand, had no idea what the Demon Lord intended to do with her. She did not expect a loving family relationship to develop, nor did she want one. She certainly did not feel safe here.

More than anything, she felt anger and worry. Her anger came from the number of lies she had been told, particularly the ones by Hunter. He had known who—what—she was, and who had fathered her, yet he had not communicated any of it to her.

The worry was for precisely the same reason. Hunter had known, yet he continued to protect her. By now he would have discovered she was gone, and he would come for her.

What would the Demon Lord do to the Demon Slayer when he did?

She tucked a hand beneath her cheek and wondered, too, if the priestess's words were true, that she had been intended as a weapon to use against demons. Perhaps that was why the goddesses had watched over her all these years. She had hoped it was because she was loved. The possibility of being nothing more than a tool chilled her and left her feeling more alone than she had since her mother—the one who raised her—had died.

But what of the mother who gave birth to her? What if she watched over her, too?

Please. Airie whispered a soft prayer. *If you are my mother, speak to me now.*

A soft voice whispered back. *Are you ready to hear what I wish to say to you?*

The question gave Airie pause.

She had not wanted to hear Hunter's reasons for coming to the mountain, and he had obliged her by keeping them to himself. Desire had raised her, and would always be her mother. Airie had never wanted to know more than that, either.

But Airie had another mother, too, and it was time to acknowledge her. She could not blame others that she had never asked enough questions or pushed for the truth.

Yes.

A gleaming golden shadow appeared in the room with Airie.

"My name is Allia," the goddess said. "That is what my loved ones call me."

This, then, was her mother.

Allia was as beautiful as Airie remembered from their first meeting, in the rain at Hunter's cabin. The realization was bittersweet. Years had been lost between them, and Airie discovered she resented them.

"Is it true?" she asked. "Was I created by the goddesses to be used against demons?"

The goddess clutched her hands to the slender waist of her gown. She appeared to choose her words carefully.

"You need to understand the relationship that exists between them. Demons search the universe for the other half of their souls. Goddesses bring life to the universe, but also restrict demons' movements within it. My sisters wanted to craft an amulet that would bind demons to us and give us more freedom from them, and I was part of that plan. But the moment your father first touched me I knew I was the one he searched for, and that we were meant to be together. You are the result of that." A wistful smile lifted the corners of her lips. "No one planned your birth. You were created from love." Her smile warmed. "And you are loved still."

Airie wanted to believe her. She could not, however, forget Mamna's ugly words. "If you are the other half of his soul, why did he accept a priestess's lies?"

"Because the priestess did not lie to him," the goddess said. "She simply did not tell him the whole truth." Deep, beautiful blue eyes met Airie's. "I was meant to betray him. In the end I couldn't do it, but how was he to know that? Neither one of us trusted the other enough to be honest. We share the responsibility for the death of our love. And now you are caught between us. You were born to immortals, but inside of time. You are bound by its laws. So is your father through you, and through him, the demons."

Airie's stomach tightened. While she wanted to believe she had been born of love, that was not what her birth had meant to either of her parents. She represented betrayal and punishment. She had no place in the mortal world, and none among the immortals. It would have been better for everyone if she had never been born. "I would like to release you from me."

Allia touched a finger to Airie's cheek and her love flowed

between them. "Our bond is different. I would not give it up."

Airie was not certain how she felt about that connection. She had heard of the bond between a priestess and the goddess she served. Even Desire, who loved them, had agreed they made demanding mistresses.

"What do you want from me?" she asked.

"Not *from* you, *for* you," Allia gently corrected her. "I want you to be free. I want you to find the kind of love your parents should have treasured, but did not. I want both you and your father to find peace. I can help you."

It was difficult for Airie to think of the Demon Lord as her father. She had seen him burn a priestess to death before her eyes, and the reminder that she had the capacity for the same sort of violence made her afraid—not for herself, but for others.

Not much wonder Hunter had been repulsed by her when they first met. He, more than anyone, knew what a demon could do.

Allia smoothed her palms over the folds in the front of her gown as if nervous. "A priestess once had enough faith to stand by me when everyone else abandoned me," she said. "She loved you enough to ask me for your life, and I gave it to her, even though we both knew you are half demon. She reminded me you are also half goddess, and swore to me she felt nothing but goodness in you. She was right. For her sake, can you trust me with your life now? Can you be strong enough to do what must be done?"

No one had ever loved Airie as much as Desire. No one had possessed as much faith in the goddesses, either. To know she had asked her mistress for Airie's life made Airie's heart ache with love for her in return, because the request would not have been made lightly.

She could do this one last thing and give the goddess her trust, not for herself or the immortals who had created her, but to honor Desire's memory and what she would have wanted. Desire would have wished to repay the goddess for the trust placed in her to raise a half demon in a mortal world.

Airie thought of Hunter, of where he might be, and her worry for him expanded. She might willingly put her faith in Allia, but he would not trust her life to anyone else. Not even a goddess.

She did not want him to be a part of this. If she were to do it, she had to do it now.

"I will trust you," she said.

The goddess glimmered brighter, as if some long-lost hope had been restored to her. "The Demon Lord will send for you. When he does, permit me to face him on your behalf."

The summons came a short while later.

Airie prayed for a fast resolution as she allowed her goddess mother to take her place.

• • •

His daughter entered the main cavern, her footsteps a faint brush of sound against the dirt floor in the otherwise heavy silence.

The demons gathered in the hall watched her walk the length of the large room. Several shifted away as she passed so as not to come in contact with the golden light enveloping her.

The amulet slipped, forgotten, from the Demon Lord's fingers. If not for her dark hair and eyes, he would have thought it her mother drawing near. He could not tear his gaze away.

Before long, he knew with certainty, one of his followers would challenge him for the right to claim her. More demons would die. Was this, then, another facet of the trap the goddesses had planned for the demons? To have them kill each other in their desire to possess something so lovely?

She stopped in front of him. Her eyes did not hold flame, as they had last night. Instead, they were deep, vivid pools of blue. He had seen them often in his dreams, and now, seeing them in his daughter's face, he could not speak.

"Why?" she asked him. The golden glow of her skin shone so brightly it burned like the sun, forcing those standing closest to her to abandon demon form and back even farther away. "Why did you turn your back on the one who offered you the other half of your soul?"

This voice, too, he had heard in his dreams.

"Allia?" He whispered the name, hardly daring to believe it was true. He could see her now, in the faint shadow of gold surrounding their daughter.

Her face tightened, reminding him too much of how stricken she had looked the last time he saw her. He had been cruel to her, his words harsh in the backlash of her betrayal, although he could no longer recall all he had flung at her.

"Don't call me that," she said. "You have no right."

He'd once had every right to use her given name—the one only her sisters had known. Had he truly thrown that right away?

No. His gaze sharpened. Allia had fled the mortal world with her sisters a long time ago. The blame for the bitterness of their final parting was not his. This girl before him now was a spawn, preying on the weaknesses of her demon father, and yet another trick of the goddesses. He should strike her down and be done with their games.

But he could not do it. What if Allia truly spoke to him through her?

He could not stop himself from pursuing the possibility, any more than he could squelch the swell of hope it raised that she had returned to him.

If so, she would have to earn his forgiveness.

"You plotted against me," he said.

Her chin lifted. "Until the first moment I set eyes on you, that night by the pool in the desert, and I knew we were meant for each other. After that, I was yours."

He had always known their first meeting was not by chance — just as he had known she was his, in spite of the circumstances. But to admit that would mean to accept guilt, and he was not to blame for this. The goddesses were. That meant Allia was, too.

"Our daughter is another part of your plot."

"Never," she said. "I swear to you, no one anticipated her." The golden light around her grew brighter still. "I gave up everything for her at the time of her birth. She now owns the soul you refused to accept. I am hers to command."

It took two breaths of time for him to understand what she was saying to him. Even then, he was unprepared for the desperate sense of loss and the bone-chilling despair that accompanied the knowledge.

A part of him had assumed he would one day find Allia again. He had nursed thoughts of revenge, and of how he would make her pay for her betrayal. Those thoughts had all involved her belonging to him.

She would never be his again.

He closed his eyes against the pain. She had been so beautiful and gentle. He had not wanted her dead.

And now, he had no idea what to do with their daughter. If she was what kept the demons trapped in this mortal world, then by rights he should kill her.

Her death would release Allia as well. He sat back in his throne with one leg extended. "If what you say is true, then I could free you," he said.

"What will my freedom change for you and me?" Allia asked. "I do not want it. Not at her expense. You and I are responsible for the death of any love between us. We alone own that. She is the true innocent in all of this. But you can set her free if you choose. She was born inside of time, but immortality can be hers if she wants it."

He should have known the bond to the mortal world would work both ways. His daughter's death would free him. His would free her. And yet, either way, they would remain connected to each other forever.

"You hate me so much?" he asked the golden goddess who stood with their daughter against him.

Allia's eyes gentled, and for the first time since the burning of the mountain, he thought perhaps she had loved him a little.

"I would see you at peace," she said.

Bitterness burned at his throat like hot bile. What was peace to him now, when he could have had so much more than that?

He hated the priestess who had lied to him. He hated the goddesses who had used Allia against him. He hated, too, the daughter responsible for the death of the one woman he had been meant to love and protect for eternity. Because of her, Allia was lost to him forever.

And a tiny part of him hated Allia as well. She should have told him of the plot from the very beginning. If she had, things would have turned out very differently for them. This was as much her fault as anyone's.

He gripped the arms of his throne, his thoughts conflicted. If his daughter wanted a place among the immortals, she had to fight for the right to claim it. If she did not earn it, then she would die.

And he would own her death.

He did not know what that might mean for him, or to the others he commanded. Was this yet another part of the goddesses' plot against demons? Was the risk worth it to him?

Knowing Allia was finally free might give him a very small measure of that peace she claimed to want for him. Owning their daughter's death seemed a small enough price for him to pay.

"If she wants immortality," the Demon Lord said, the challenge ringing clearly throughout the cavern so that all in attendance could hear, "she will fight me for it."

. . .

Hunter stayed still for as long as he could and listened to the talk around him, anxious to find out what would happen to Airie.

The cavern was high-ceiled and relatively narrow, tapering to a single entrance through which faint light could be seen, so it must be day, although he could not begin to guess at the time. Torches provided the room with smoky light, illuminating striated walls of red sandstone.

He peered through the bars of the cage, making no sudden movements, careful not to draw unwanted attention. No matter what else might happen, he would find a way to kill any demon to touch her.

He watched her walk, golden and beautiful, through the crowd of demons and straight to the Demon Lord's throne. All eyes remained on her, including Hunter's.

Not once did she glance at him.

He wanted to rip apart the bars of the cage and rush to protect her. Blood pulsed at his temples. He had never in his life wanted to kill demons more.

He promised himself he would have the opportunity soon enough.

But for now, he forced his mind to separate rational thought from emotion. He would be of no help to her if he could not pay attention and form a plan. She was alive and unafraid, and although that calmed him somewhat, he knew that she was far from safe even if she did not.

A small sound beside his cage, a slight shuffling, caught Hunter's attention. He dared not turn his head, but from between the slats of his prison floor, he saw the top of a child's head.

Scratch.

The boy had crossed miles of desert and walked through a den of demons, avoiding all observation. Even now, no one seemed to pay the boy the slightest attention.

The child was not mortal.

Acceptance slid through Hunter with an ease that he did not question. He found he could no longer summon the hatred he had once felt for all demon offspring. Whatever Scratch was, he loved Airie as much as she loved him. There was no threat in the boy, only the same innocent kindness Airie possessed, and that was all that mattered to Hunter. He had come to love them both.

Scratch stood on his toes and slid an object into the cage, pushing it under Hunter's hip and out of sight. Familiar warmth spread through him. His amulet.

A spark of relief ignited. If he put up enough of a fight, he could force them to kill him rather than have them tear him apart and eat him alive. He did not want either Airie or Scratch to witness that.

Hide, Hunter mouthed to the child.

Scratch disappeared from his line of vision and Hunter again tried to hear what was happening with Airie.

Immortality can be hers if she wants it.

He had missed important information. What did that mean? What else had been said?

If she wants immortality, she will fight me for it.

No.

Hunter surged to his feet, hurling his whole weight at the bars of the cage, again and again, the rage pounding against the inside of his skull matching his frantic efforts to free himself.

CHAPTER NINETEEN

Airie had drawn on a lifetime of faith by granting the goddess permission to speak through her, but as fire sputtered in the sconces anchored high on the soot-streaked cavern walls, doubt squeezed her heart.

The sight of Hunter in a suspended cage in the demon-filled hall, and the whispers of those demons and their plans for him, meant that Hunter's life was also at stake now, and suddenly, Airie was no longer willing to rely solely on the faith she'd been raised with.

She resolved that he would not suffer because of her. A goddess had claimed her as her daughter. Airie had demon blood in her, too. Surely she possessed some of their strengths.

Release me, she urged the goddess, *so I can accept the challenge.*

Her request, however, went unanswered.

The Demon Lord came around to the front of the platform and stood not five feet from her, staring at her face as if searching for something familiar in it.

Again, the goddess addressed him through Airie. "I demand the right to fight for my daughter's freedom."

His eyes shuttered. "You cannot."

"I can if someone will fight on our behalf." She looked to Hunter, wild now inside the swinging cage, his chest heaving with an enormous anger that threatened to burst loose at any second. "The Demon Slayer wears protection that was once mine. He is my chosen. If he wishes, he can fight for Airie and me."

Inside, Airie screamed for him to refuse. This was not his battle.

She, however, was trapped as effectively as he was, and every bit as angry—because she had agreed to this, although naively. She had trusted the goddess with her life, but hers was not the one most precious to her. She had not thought to safeguard Hunter's and would never forgive the goddess for this betrayal.

Hunter's knuckles gleamed stark white against the bars of his cage as he tried to bend them with his bare hands. "I do wish it. I want to fight."

"Very well," the Demon Lord said to the goddess. Cunning entered his expression. "But remember, Allia, this is your proposal. If he wins, he will not be the one to own my death."

He turned to his throne as if in search of something.

At the same time, Hunter stooped to retrieve an object from the floor of the cage. It dangled from a gold chain snarled around his fingers, and flushed a dull red in the firelight when he straightened.

"Looking for this?" he asked, holding the amulet up for the Demon Lord to see before fastening it around his neck.

"How…" the Demon Lord recovered from his surprise. "So be it, then. Slayer!" he roared, his demon voice shaking the cavern. The cage swayed on its chains as the gathered demons roared in anticipation. "Fight me!"

And Airie, helpless through her own ill-conceived actions, could do nothing but watch.

· · ·

The cage dropped to the stone platform, and Hunter exploded from inside, ready to fight anyone who approached too near to Airie.

As he leaped to the ground to stand between her and the press of demons, thrusting her behind him, the rumble in the cavern rose to a level that shook the earth beneath his feet.

He did not fully understand what had just transpired between Airie and the Demon Lord. The conversation he'd overheard had been confusing at best. All he knew beyond any doubt was that Airie had been threatened, that she was in danger, and that he was going to kill the demon responsible for it.

Yet he despaired of Airie getting to safety when it was finished. He calculated at least a hundred demons present, which meant most, if not all, of their numbers, so the odds were hardly in his favor. His weapons had been confiscated.

A memory of the poor young woman he had buried from the ill-fated wagon train filtered into his thoughts. Grimly, he acknowledged the reality of their situation and its inevitable outcome, and that a dark decision had to be made. Even if he won this challenge as planned, he could not protect Airie from the remaining demons.

Better for her to receive death by his hand than face these monsters alone. He did not want her to witness what they would do to him either.

First, however, a challenge had been issued and accepted, and Hunter would take the Demon Lord and as many more of the hated immortals with him as he could.

The touch of the bright golden halo of light surrounding her calmed Hunter. With one arm he groped behind him to catch her around the waist and draw her to his side, careful to keep one of his hands free and not to turn his back on the demons, and took one last look at her face, hoping she would recognize in his own some of what he was thinking.

There was so much he wished he had said to her—words of the profound love he held for her but had refused to recognize until too late. He wished he had been kinder and gentler with her. It was hard to know that the last thing he might ever bring her was death.

She met his eyes.

"I have one more thing I wish you to wear," Airie said to him.

As she lifted the rainbow amulet from her own neck to place it around his, it struck him that something was not right about her. He stared harder into her face.

Her eyes were blue now, not brown, although familiar gold fire flickered in their depths. In his rage he had, indeed, missed important information.

If he wishes, he can fight for Airie and me.

Whoever this was, it was not Airie.

She smiled at him, an apology in the soft arc of her lips, and with a politeness of manner, she extricated herself from his embrace.

"Be quick," this Airie-Who-Was-Not advised him. "I can't hold her back for much longer. She's very angry." Her voice grew wistful. "I hope someday you can convince her to forgive me."

Immortality can be hers if she wants it.

Understanding edged past his confusion, like the sun sliding from behind clouds. Airie was the child of two immortals, not one. A goddess did, indeed, walk with her. She did not have to die by his hand. As long as he won this fight, she would have immortality to save her.

His relief was followed by another, more painful, awareness. When this was over, whether he lived or died, he would lose her.

Regret stung at the backs of his eyes. He had wasted their valuable time together by worrying over things that did not matter. It was Airie, the woman, he loved. Would always love.

While Airie the immortal could never be his.

"Whether she forgives you or not," he said, his throat thick, "know that I thank you for this. She could never have killed him, not even to save herself."

"She would have, for you." The goddess's smile filled with sadness. "But she does not yet understand the consequences of it. And she would never have forgiven herself. He would not forgive himself either, if he harmed her. I would rather they both be unable to forgive me."

She took both amulets in her hands and in a sweet, rich voice, so much like Airie's it made his chest ache, she offered him her blessings. Then, with glowing fingers that trembled slightly, she fitted the amulets together, just as he had once done with them.

"Goddesses offer a different type of strength," she said to Hunter. She leaned closer to whisper in his ear. "When the Demon Lord fights, he does not fight only you. He battles the demons whose deaths he owns, because they fight him for their freedom, too."

She drew away before Hunter could ask her what she meant.

"Slayer!" the Demon Lord shouted. "I grow impatient."

Hunter lifted Airie—and the goddess—onto the low platform and out of harm's way.

Then, as he turned to face his opponent, he put them firmly from his thoughts. He had a fight to win.

The demons had begun to assemble into a tight half-circle around the front of the platform, forcing the Demon Lord and

Hunter into its center. Many wore their demon forms. Hunter chose not to dwell on what would happen when first blood was spilled, only hoped it was not to be his.

He held his hands low and ready, prepared to defend himself against attack, and breathed deeply as he blocked out everything except for his opponent. This was the Demon Lord he faced, and not to be taken lightly.

He had chosen to fight Hunter in mortal form, stripping down to expose a broad, bare chest, wearing nothing but a pair of faded trousers. Thick black hair, shot through with threads of gray that glinted red in the fire from the sconces, swept his shoulders.

While impressive enough, this was not the form Hunter would have preferred to confront. He meant to goad the Demon Lord into using his greatest strengths first, so that the amulet could absorb and transmit them to Hunter.

"You seem to excel at fighting women," he said. "A goddess, a crippled old priestess, and now your own daughter. I hope a mortal man won't prove too much of a challenge for you." As he spoke, he watched carefully for any opportunity to strike.

The demon's face darkened. "Her goddess mother was a pleasure-seeking, faithless liar. Did my daughter tell you she loves you, as her mother once swore she loved me? Can you imagine how great a liar she must be, too?"

"You should be more concerned with why I'm known as the Demon Slayer," Hunter said. "When I kill them, they die screaming."

"We'll see if my daughter screams, too, when she dies," the Demon Lord said. "Although you'll already be dead, so you'll never know for certain." He smiled. "You'll have to imagine it until then."

Hunter did not like the image, and could not shake it off as easily as he should. He realized he had chosen his weapon poorly, and that Airie was his weakness, not her father's. The Demon Lord cared nothing for her, but only for himself.

And, perhaps, for the goddess. Certainty made Hunter smile, too. The demon spoke of her with too much anger and contempt for it to be otherwise.

"I wonder if her mother also died screaming," Hunter said, and saw at once the barb had gone true. He had little time to prepare himself against the furious response.

A shimmering ball of searing flame the size of his head caught him high in the chest, igniting his shirt and hurling him into a living wall of demons.

Blinding pain scorched through Hunter so that it was all he could do to keep from screaming, himself. His amulet compensated, caught the power behind the demon fire, and sent it through him. The flames died. The pain, too, ebbed away as fast as it had risen.

Rough hands and grasping demon claws thrust him back to his feet. Hunter's shirt now hung in smoldering tatters from his body, but other than that, he was unharmed. He wondered why he should feel such surprise that a goddess's stone did so much more than enhance the power of its demon counterpart when Airie, too, could heal with a touch.

The Demon Lord walked the edges of the semicircle, pumping a fist in the air while the crowd roared, but his complete attention was not on the fight, Hunter saw. His eyes drifted to the platform.

Hunter, seizing an opportunity to use the distraction against him, rushed at his swaggering opponent.

The Demon Lord whirled, dropping into a crouch. In a blur of speed, one fist shot out.

Hunter blocked it and ducked, following through with a foot to the back of the Demon Lord's knee that spilled him to the ground.

Another roar rose from the spectators.

The Demon Lord, however, surprised him again, and Hunter found himself on his back, looking up at a ring of faces—too many of them demonic now, not mortal, as they shifted in reaction to the fight.

The Demon Lord's knuckles slammed against Hunter's cheek, narrowly missing his nose, and for a second, Hunter thought his cheekbone had shattered. Agony blossomed in his eye socket and through his temple before his body absorbed it to turn it to strength.

But the Demon Lord had not gotten as much force behind the blow as he'd intended. The flash of awareness in his eyes as his glance flickered to the dual amulet on Hunter's chest said he understood why, and that he had not expected something he had crafted to work against him.

Now that he knew it would, once he got over his shock, he would find a way to circumvent it.

Hunter had to draw blood while he still had a chance.

He hooked his feet into the Demon Lord's hips to lock him in place, then grabbed the amulet in his fist and used its edge to gouge at the Demon Lord's face.

A thin line of red streaked from the demon's left eye, down his cheek, to the corner of his mouth.

He bellowed in outrage and pain. He tried to shift, but the amulet had drawn too much from him so that he could not do so completely. Claws sprouted from the tips of his fingers.

Those were enough to be deadly.

He slashed at Hunter's throat, and thick spurts of warm, copper-scented blood sprayed out to stain the Demon Lord's face and bared chest in reward. Still straddling Hunter's body, both his fists flew high and his shouts of victory rang off the cavern walls.

A woman's screams pierced through the howls of the demons as Hunter's hands went to his torn throat in an effort to stop the heavy flow of blood. He fought to stay conscious, fear for Airie the only thought in his head.

The Demon Lord had drawn his hand back, prepared to deliver a second blow to Hunter's chest to tear out his heart with his claws, but the attempt to shift had cost the Demon Lord more strength than he seemed to realize.

Hunter's amulet shot out great streams of blinding golden light that flung the Demon Lord several feet backward. He struck the edge of the stone platform and slumped to the ground in a daze. A chunk of rock the size of a demon's fist split away and toppled past his bent head.

As Hunter struggled to right his blurring vision, the bleeding at his throat stopped and the sting of the cuts disappeared. A sense of urgency, and of time slipping away, roused him to action. The amulet, too, was growing weaker, every time it had to heal him.

A larger threat lifted its head.

Hunter froze in the act of rising, one hand on the ground and legs bent at the knee, and looked up. The demons closest to him had caught the scent of his blood. Hunger glittered in their red eyes.

Hunter dared to steal another glance at Airie, who had fallen to her hands and knees when the Demon Lord struck the platform's edge, and saw she was no longer alone. Beside her, outlined in gold light, stood the faint silhouette of a second woman. Her lips moved as she spoke soothing words to Airie he could not hear, and she placed one hand on her arm in an attempt to stop her trembling.

His heart went still. If not even Airie's goddess mother could contain her when she was this agitated, it would not be long before she threw herself into the fray. Airie possessed no natural fear for herself, and would let nothing stop her from coming to his aid.

He did not trust goddess light to protect her from blood-frenzied demons. Not when the goddesses had been unable to defend themselves against the fury of the Demon Lord as he burned their mountain.

The Demon Lord was on his feet again, although staggering as if drunk. A bluish green haze enveloped him.

Hunter blinked, thinking at first that his vision had been damaged by one of the blows he'd received, but then the haze wavered and separated into a number of shadows.

The goddess's words returned to him.

He battles the demons whose deaths he owns, because they fight him for their freedom, too.

Hunter had often wondered why demons who enjoyed hunting mortals had not killed each other off a long time ago. The answer was that they paid too heavy a price for it.

It meant the Demon Lord was weak, and the change in the tone of the crowd's rumbling told Hunter the others knew it, too. The cheers for their leader died away.

Their thirst for blood did not. Both the Demon Lord and Hunter were coated in it, and Hunter watched warily as their attention shifted between them, trying to decide which of them was the weaker.

He could not claim to be in the best of shape. Much of the strength he had gained was lost in his healing, and while one demon he thought he could manage, a hundred would be ninety-nine too many.

Low chanting began, gradually gaining strength and momentum. *Blood. Blood. BLOOD.*

Pushing and shoving from the spectators at the back triggered a brawl as they tried to move to the front. One sledgehammer-sized fist missed its target and pummeled a hole into a cavern wall. Another demon slammed headfirst into a stone pillar. Fine cracks splintered upward and fanned across the ceiling in intricate, spidery webs. Without their leader to keep them in check, whatever discipline remained to them was about to be lost.

The fire guttering along the cavern walls gave Hunter an idea. Airie needed something to do that would be of benefit to them both, yet also keep her from harm.

"Airie!" he shouted to her. "Surround us with fire!"

. . .

It had taken all the strength Airie possessed to disentangle her thoughts from the goddess's, and she'd had to draw on her demon birthright to do so.

She could not stand back and do nothing. If the Demon Lord fell, the others would tear Hunter apart. Bloodlust already consumed them.

Please, she begged the golden figure, now still as a stone statue beside her. *Release me from our agreement. I have to help him.*

The goddess turned tragic, sorrow-filled eyes on her. Her lashes lowered, and it was clear her attention was not on Airie. *I am your servant. Yours to command. I cannot hold you if you don't wish for it.*

Anger at this admission of another lie and betrayal, offered so casually, pounded inside Airie like a heavy fist on an already fragile door. She had been raised to respect the goddesses, and helped her mother serve them her whole life. She had stood back while Hunter accepted a challenge on her behalf because she had trusted a goddess to deal fairly with her, but had not been told she did not need to agree to it.

Her faith and very existence were founded on lies.

Airie tried to think past her boiling anger and growing desperation. Hunter could not fight them all. She searched around her for a weapon, but came up with nothing.

The Demon Lord was back on his feet now, a writhing, blue-green haze churning, snakelike, beneath his glowing skin, and while that slowed the tide of demons, it did not stop them.

Hunter was shouting something to her, his words barely understandable over the rising chants for his blood.

"Airie! Surround us with fire!"

CHAPTER TWENTY

Hunter was pointing at the sconces on the walls.

Of course.

Airie's hopes lifted. Fire was her weapon.

The last time she called it the Demon Lord had wrested it away from her, but this time, as she held out her hands, she was better prepared and more confident in her abilities. Her demon instincts, straining against the confines of a goddess upbringing and the will of her Demon Lord father, told her all she needed to know. What she held was hers, not his, the same as rain. She had been born with it, and it came to her from the world around her.

She was the Demon Lord's daughter. If she wished, she could call his fire to her, too.

She did.

It danced up the walls in great ropes of yellow flame, twisting and swirling along the rifts in the cavern's ceiling before dropping to form a thick sheet of fire between the two combatants and the mass of demons.

As it fell, Hunter shot from his crouched position like a bullet from a gun, ramming his shoulder into the Demon Lord's chest and bearing him to the ground.

Both were on their feet again in an instant. The Demon Lord grabbed Hunter by the arms, then grimaced and could not seem to retain his grip as blue-green shadows undulated and writhed beneath his flesh. Hunter took immediate advantage, and brought his head forward to smash it into the demon's face before driving a knee into his groin.

Bloodied and weakened, doubled over in pain, the Demon Lord's eyes went to the golden figure of light on the platform beside Airie. Loss and sorrow crossed his face, followed by resignation.

Airie knew he was beaten, and moved to shield her goddess mother from the sight of what was to come.

The Demon Lord wiped at the blood streaming from his nose and mouth with the back of his hand as he squared off against Hunter to deliver one last taunt. "My demons won't be held back. Will you battle them all, Slayer? Is she worth that much to you?"

"Yes," Hunter said.

He shot his fist into the Demon Lord's broken face, knocking him down one final time.

Then, he crushed his throat beneath his boot.

A thick, blue-green haze slid from the fallen Demon Lord to Airie, through the pores of her skin, its weight and a sick comprehension driving her to her knees on the platform. She owned her father's death now, as he would have owned hers if he had won the challenge instead of Hunter, and her demon instincts whispered that it would not be as easy a one to bear as her mother's.

The sound of the goddess's sobs echoed in the otherwise silent cavern as the demons watched their leader fall.

As Airie dealt with the death she'd absorbed, and the weight of its strength shifting to her, the wall of fire she had summoned at Hunter's request faltered and slipped from her grasp.

She lifted her head.

The mood in the cavern had shifted from ugly anticipation to even uglier threat. Hunter stood to her right. Blood stained his tattered clothing and smeared his skin, but for all that, he appeared unharmed. He swung sweat-dampened blond hair from his eyes and glared around, chest heaving, primed for the next demon to step forward and challenge him.

Despite the freedom the Demon Lord's death brought them, the demons were not departing, Airie also saw. Instead, they divided their attention between her and Hunter, as if deciding which of them to pursue first.

Raw anger exploded inside her. She would not own the Demon Lord's death for nothing. She possessed fire. And rain. If demons would not leave peaceably, she would kill them all, one by one if she had to.

She dragged herself to her feet, then the edge of the platform, as the goddess's sobs turned to screams.

No, Airie. This is not the way!

Ignoring the warning, Airie leaped to the ground to meet the first of those demons brave enough to approach her.

Hunter started forward to protect her, his expression murderous, but she would not have him facing more danger on her behalf. Stronger now, and becoming acquainted with the additional weight of the death she bore, she reconstructed the wall of fire around them.

Four demons, however, had gotten too close to her and were now trapped inside it. She slapped her palm to the bone-plated arm of the first one to reach her, and mixing her fire and rain together, drove them deep. Steam billowed beneath her touch. The demon shrieked in agony as it boiled from the inside out. She had to turn her face from the stink of cooking meat.

The demon fell to the ground, clouded eyes staring upward. The haze of death rose from its body to settle around Airie, coating her skin in a sickly light. In her head, she knew horror. This, she realized, sick at heart, was her first step toward immortality, although she had taken it in a direction she had never intended.

She did not want to be a demon. Neither did she want for Hunter to die.

She brought the flat of her hand against a second demon, sending another burst of fire and water into its flesh. More screams, and a second blue-green haze joined the first.

This death was stronger, and the weight of it sent Airie to her hands and knees again so that the wall of flame faltered, but she could not stop now.

She groped blindly for a leg and caught it above the ankle. The thick, clinging haze of this one's death drove the others a little deeper into Airie.

Hunter fought the fourth demon.

Panic scalded her. She did not know if she could carry the weight of too many more, yet she had to find a way to drive them from the world so Hunter would have a chance to escape, and she could think of nothing other than to kill them.

Then her mother was at her side, draping Airie in golden goddess light, but even that could not displace the eerie glow of the ones already dead and clinging to her.

"Listen to me," the goddess said, her voice cracking with unspent grief and a rising urgency. "You were meant to have a choice, and you hurt only yourself this way. You own your father's death, and therefore his strength. That will be enough to protect you from demons if you choose them. Or you may send for the goddesses through me and take my place with my sisters. They will welcome you." Her cheeks sparkled beneath golden tears. "But choose quickly, while you still can. They won't wait for you. Now that the demons are freed from the boundaries of time, the goddesses will go back into hiding."

Airie's attention was divided. The demon Hunter fought was weakening. The desire to help him was strong, but he did not need it and would not thank her. She would be nothing but a distraction to him.

She turned her face away so she could not be tempted. They both needed the help of her mother if they were to survive this.

"And if I don't make a choice?" Airie asked her. "What happens then?"

The goddess wiped the tears from her cheeks. "The number of deaths you own will decide the matter for you."

Cold prickled her skin. That was why her mother had tried to stop her from fighting them.

Already, Airie felt the enormous surge of power that full demon immortality would bring her. It was heady, and difficult to resist, and she knew it would not be long before she could not. She tried to organize her thoughts, and examine her options so that she made a decision that was of benefit to others, and not herself. It had to be something her mother—her priestess mother—would have approved of. She had been loyal to her goddess, but also to her own mortality. And she had loved Airie more than either of them. She had not feared the demon in her, but always encouraged her to do what she believed was right.

If she chose to take her goddess mother's place, the goddesses would flee the demons and she would go into hiding with the others. That was of harm to no one. If she chose to be demon, however, she could stay here with Hunter. He did not fear them either, and would never fear her.

But if she did that, it meant demons would retain a link to this world through her. Where there was one immortal there would be others.

That was true, too, of the goddesses, and neither goddess nor demon had ever been of true benefit to mortality. The world did not need them.

She could not decide.

"You say you are my servant," she said to her mother, leaning close. "Yet you used me to get Hunter to agree to fight in my place when it wasn't necessary for him to do so. It was not his challenge to accept."

Fresh tears sparkled in her mother's eyes. A shaking hand went to her lips. "Forgive me. I could not bear for the two people I love to harm each other."

She had also said she was Airie's to command—and something else. About a bond between them...

The words fit into their proper context with startling and painful clarity. "I own your death, too," Airie said. "That's the bond between us, and my other claim to immortality."

The goddess did not deny it. "Because of that, he won't fight you for his freedom if being a demon is the immortality you want. He won't do anything more that might harm me or cause me pain."

Airie reconsidered the choices she had been given. Choosing either immortality meant her parents would never be free again. She would own their deaths forever.

Pity stirred in her. If that was her price for immortality, she did not want it.

She found she could not remain angry over events that might someday bring peace to two tormented souls, not while Hunter still lived. In her heart, where her immortality spoke to her, she knew with absolute truth that he held the other half of her soul. She could search for all of eternity, from one end of the universe to the other, and never again find his equal.

The immortals alone did not determine her future, any more than they did their own.

"I have a third choice," Airie said. "You once told me if I wanted a place in this world I would have to be welcomed to it. But even if someone does welcome me, I don't want my place here to be as an immortal."

"Even though you'll live inside of time and be subject to its laws, you can never be truly mortal," the goddess warned her. "Because of that, you cannot give up the deaths you now own. They will be with you throughout your lifetime. And you will not get to make another choice if this one is rejected—it will be made for you." Her eyes were anxious. "Think carefully. The goddesses will accept you. So will the demons. Are you as certain of your welcome here in the mortal world?"

Airie thought she was, at least by one person. If not, the demon deaths she owned would guarantee the immortality thrust on her. She could feel it tugging at her already.

She hesitated. She did not want to be demon, but if that was to be her fate, she would never forget the teachings of her priestess mother. She controlled her own actions and owned responsibility for them.

But it was Hunter she truly wanted.

"Yes," she said. "I will risk it. But no matter what happens to me, immortals will never be welcome here again."

Their fingers touched, a brief clasp, her mother's little more than a soft stirring of air against Airie's skin.

Golden light laced with streaks of vivid blue-green shot through the cavern as her mother's image was joined by the shadowy haze of another, larger one. While Airie might command her demon father's death, and have his protection, it was the goddess he would forever follow. Perhaps his defeat was more of a kindness to them both than she'd understood. They did not have immortality. But this was not an end for them either.

Her throat tightened, and she looked away from them to find Hunter.

More blood had been spilled, she saw. He had won this fight, too, but he would not win many more. Agitated beyond reason now, on the other side of the wall, several dozen demons hurled themselves into the fire in an attempt to get at him. More had scaled the cavern's walls to the cracked ceiling, thinking to break through at the top.

Yet Hunter, with one knee on the ground and breathing in deep, heaving gasps, his body battered and bloodied, his face dripping in sweat from the heat of the blaze around them, had eyes for no one but her. He pressed his hands to his thighs and pushed to a standing position.

Airie ran into his arms.

He cupped her face in his hands and scanned her anxiously from head to toe, then finally, satisfied she was unharmed, kissed her. He paid no attention to the shadowy forms of her father and mother standing close by, or the demons roaring for the Slayer's blood.

"Surround yourself with fire," Hunter said to her. "While I fight them off, I want you to run. When you get outside, call on goddess rain. That will protect you." As long as she had water, she could survive in the desert for days. His mouth settled in grim resolve.

"If they want the Demon Slayer, they can die fighting him."

• • •

Hunter did not know how she had killed the demons. It was enough for him that she could defend herself against them. But it tore at his heart to think she had been forced to do something she did not believe in because he had not been strong enough to protect her from it.

That did not mean he was sorry they were dead. If he could, he would kill them all. Since he could not, he would rid the world of as many as possible and die content knowing Airie, at least, was safe from them.

She met his eyes. Hers were brown again, he was thankful to note, warm, and filled with emotion.

But not the emotion he was seeking. His contentment turned to worry.

"I'm not running from them," Airie said, standing straight as she curled her fingers to fists and took a step back. Her eyes flashed with fire. "From now on, they are running from me. Fire and rain alone won't be enough to rid the world of them, but I know of something that is."

Gold and blue-green light encased her. The wall of shimmering flame she held curled inward as it collapsed, then ran like fingers of fire along the ground. A roar came from the mouth of the cavern, building in intensity. At first, Hunter could not place the source. Then he recognized the pounding of heavy rain.

A wide stream of water gushed toward them, forcing demons

into the air. Those who did not take to wing immediately found they did not have room to spread theirs out, and screamed in agony as the water washed through, ankle deep, to flood the floor of the cavern.

The fire met the rain, and the cavern filled with thick, scorching steam. Sweat streamed down Hunter's face.

Scratch.

His heart pounded. He could scarcely believe he'd forgotten him. Airie did not know that he was here, and Hunter did not know how demon flames and goddess rain might affect him. He glanced around frantically, trying to find his hiding place, and shouted for him, hoping to be heard over the rain and fire and demon cries.

The child crawled from under the platform, near Hunter's feet. Hunter snatched him up in his arms, turning his body in order to shield him from the spreading mist. While Hunter was mortal, and the mist did not appear to cause him any significant or lasting harm, he was not willing to take any risks with Scratch's well-being.

It was the steaming mist, however, that drove the demons from the cavern. It penetrated every corner, every crack and crevice, making it impossible to escape its touch.

And outside, in the desert, they would find no protection from the rain unless they took to the skies above it.

Something hard pressed against Hunter's chest, and Hunter looked down to see what it was. Scratch had what at first looked to be a rock in his hands. It was egg-shaped and rough, colored a drab shade of green similar to the areoles of cacti, with a pin at the top to lock its detonator. Hunter's heart pounded harder. He could not believe the boy had not killed them all before now.

But he could think of a use for it. With the bomb cushioned against his chest, and Scratch in his arms, Hunter grabbed Airie by the hand and ran, following in the wake of the demons as they fled.

The rain continued to fall, but thankfully, had no effect on the child. It ran down Hunter's face and soaked his tattered clothing. Blood trickled in thin rivulets from his chest and arms to drip to the ground in pale, watery splotches. He set Scratch on his feet and eased the bomb from his tiny fingers.

Hunter examined it. It fit the curve of his palm, and was heavier than he'd expected. The head of the pin was round, as if meant to fit a man's finger. He wondered whether it was still live, and if so, how stable the detonator might be after all these years.

He did not want either Scratch or Airie near him when he pulled the pin.

"Stay right here," he ordered the boy. He took hold of his chin and looked into his face to make sure he had his full attention. Rain clung to the boy's lashes. "And I want to be able to see you. No hiding. No more touching things you find if you don't know what they are. Do we understand each other?"

Scratch nodded, and Hunter ruffled his wet hair. "Sit down and cover your head until I tell you it's safe to move."

He jogged a short distance away, then closed his eyes and prayed as he yanked the pin.

Nothing happened.

He threw the bomb into the mouth of the cavern. Again, nothing happened. Less than ten seconds later however, the earth shook, knocking him to his knees.

The mouth of the cavern had crumpled. Then, as he watched, the cliffs above it collapsed inward. Streams of smoke intermingled with steam drifted up through fallen rock and rubble. Hunter wiped mud from his face, grimly satisfied.

That was for Airie's priestess mother. The goddesses' temple was gone. The Demon Lord's hole was, as well.

Airie was searching the sky for signs of demons, but as near as he could tell, they were gone. Rain slid down her hair and off her cheeks, like teardrops that sparkled as they fell. Mud spattered her slim, bare feet.

Hunter checked on Scratch, who was sitting where he had been told to wait. Then he went to Airie, who had not yet released her hold on fire and rain. The steam billowed into the sky and rolled through the yucca trees, twisting around and under everything it touched, layering the desert in a thick, hot fog.

The flames in her eyes were gone, leaving them soft and beautiful, and shining with flecks of light. He read anxiety in them and reached for her, wanting to hold her tight and reassure her that all would be well, but he could not be certain of that yet.

He did know, however, how much he loved her. She had fought demons for him, and for the world. She would always do so, and it was best to accept it. They would fight them together.

She stepped away from him and would not let him touch her. His heart retracted into his throat.

"Time has run out for me," she said to him. "I have to choose now."

At first he didn't know what she meant. Then he saw the entire situation with greater clarity, and a part of him died. She was an immortal, but she could be only demon or goddess, not both. There seemed little contest in that decision.

Or consolation, for that matter. Either way, he had lost her.

"I understand." He swallowed hard. "No, I don't."

"There can be no place for me in this world. Not as an immortal." The fire in her eyes disappeared, replaced now by gleaming tears of gold that made him ache for her.

Her place was with him, he wanted to say, but how could he

want what was best for her, and yet ask her to give up immortality?

He would not cry, and he would not beg her to stay.

"I love you," he said. "Immortal or not. I thought you should know that." He cleared his throat, embarrassed by the emotions he could not hold back. He could not stop his next words either. "Please don't make me live without you. But I'll understand if you must."

A smile lit her face, and hope flickered to life in his heart.

"What do you want?" she asked.

"You," he replied without hesitation. "I want you."

She was in his arms, hers tight around his neck, a sodden bundle who kissed his rain-washed face over and over. "I want you, too," she said. "I love you. Wherever you are, that's where I belong."

The sun peeked out through the rain. A rainbow, brilliant and multihued, arced across the desert from one end of the horizon to the other.

He hated himself for asking the next question. He would have hated himself more if he didn't. "Will you have to give up immortality in order to stay?"

She took the back of his head in her fingers and drew his mouth to hers, then pressed her face into his neck. The golden sheen she had worn since their first lovemaking began to diminish, slowly fading away beneath the steady patter of rain.

"What good is immortality to me," she said, the rapid flutter of her eyelashes caressing his skin, "when my heart remains mortal?"

EPILOGUE

It was three days before the heavy mists dissipated and the sun returned. By that time, everything in Freetown was sodden. Nothing had escaped its touch. It flowed under doors and through the tiniest of cracks.

On the fourth night, Hunter heard the sound of a door opening and closing a floor below him and was instantly awake.

It was nothing, just one of the saloon's restless residents, because Airie still slept—she would have awakened otherwise—but the stealth in the movements he'd heard made Hunter uneasy.

She had said that the demons would not return, that the goddesses kept them away, but he had fought them too long to feel as certain of that as she was.

He slipped from the bed, careful not to awaken her. She rolled over in her sleep and flung her arm over his still warm pillow, pulling it close to her, and he smiled in the moonlight.

Blade was right. He was a lucky man. More so than he deserved.

He found his friend in the kitchen, filling a large pack with canned goods and utensils. He was dressed for travel.

Blade looked up when Hunter entered, his face shadowy in the glare of the single lantern hanging from the ceiling joist behind him. "Sorry if I woke you."

Hunter sat down at the long wooden table and watched him as he continued to work. "Going somewhere? Without saying good-bye?"

"I don't like good-byes."

Neither did Hunter. But forgoing this one didn't feel right. Packing and leaving in the middle of the night indicated to Hunter that Blade didn't intend to return.

"Where are you going?" he asked.

"Not sure."

So his friend was running away from home. Granted, Hunter had once done the same thing, but he'd been a kid. Blade was a little old for that. And settled. With Mamna gone, he had a real chance for his business to grow.

Hunter waited for Blade to elaborate. When he didn't, he said, "I guess what I really want to know is, why?"

With the pack bulging, Blade flipped the canvas flap closed and tightened the leather straps. He lifted a careless shoulder, not meeting Hunter's eyes. "Now that I have my leg back, I'm restless to see the world." He sighed and looked at the ceiling, then finally at Hunter. "I asked Ruby to marry me and she said no."

"I see."

And he did, far more than Blade likely yet had. Hunter knew his friend, he knew Ruby, and he knew something of women. The two were not suited to be more than friends. Perhaps with a bit of distance between them that might change. If not, it was never meant to be.

"You can come with us to the Borderlands," Hunter said.

"No offense," Blade replied, shrugging into the pack's shoulder straps and tying it tight around his waist, "but it's hard enough to get any sleep when I'm one floor below the two of you. Trying to share your campfire at night would scar me for life. Do me a favor, though. Make sure Airie understands that this isn't a bad thing. She's given Ruby and me a chance at new lives."

"What *about* Ruby?" Hunter asked. "And the others?"

Blade tapped an envelope on the table behind Hunter. It had Ruby's name on it.

"She'll run the saloon. As long as I own it, at least in name, she should have no problems."

So that was that, then. Blade was a grown man. Hunter wasn't about to try to change his mind.

But he was going to miss him far more than he'd expected. When he'd decided to take Airie back to his home, he hadn't thought he'd lose all contact with his closest friend. Now, he wouldn't know where he was.

Hunter held out his hand. "If you're ever in the Borderlands, look me up."

Blade's grip was solid and familiar, and far too brief. "I will. And I'll be hoping that by the time I do, Airie will have gotten tired of you."

"No chance of that," Hunter said smugly.

Blade clapped him on the shoulder. "I'm going to miss your misguided self-confidence."

He let himself out through the kitchen door and was swallowed by the night.

Hunter continued to sit, thinking back over their years of friendship. Blade had provided him with a place to return to. A temporary home. Now it was time for him to make a real one with the woman he loved.

He extinguished the lantern and went back to bed, and to Airie.

• • •

Normally Airie loved this time of day, when night turned to morning and both the moon and the sun touched the sky. It spoke to both parts of her nature and fused them in harmony.

But she cried when the last signs of the collapsed mountain disappeared from view on the desert horizon behind them.

She couldn't help it. She didn't want to leave her mother, but she didn't want Hunter and Scratch to see her cry either.

Hunter, who was walking, drew Sally to a halt and eased Airie from the saddle. She slid to the ground with Scratch in her arms. Hunter took him from her and set him on his feet. Then, he pulled Airie close.

He knew immediately what was wrong.

"She wouldn't want you to feel this way," he said. "She wanted you to be safe and happy. That's why she asked me to take you with me before she died. I promise you, we'll come back to visit her."

Airie rested her head against his chest, feeling the steady, reassuring beat of his heart. He meant well, and he intended to keep his promise, but it was a trip that took at least several months when traveled both ways. She knew they would not be back for a very long time, if at all.

She was leaving her home for the unknown, and while Hunter and Scratch both loved her, she worried what his family would think of his choice in a mate. She would never be truly mortal. And she possessed demon deaths, although her father fought them for her. He remained with her, as present and as silent as her mother, content, it seemed, to wait out her mortal life in order to win his freedom.

When he did, she hoped he and her mother found it together.

"What if your family hates me?" she asked. She wanted to add, *because of your sister*, but she didn't have to. Again, he understood her concern.

His arms tightened. "It was a long time ago. My family will look at you and see someone I love, and they'll love you, too. Besides," he added, "no one could have a better reason to hate demons than Blade, and he wants you to keep him in mind if you ever get tired of me."

She hadn't wanted a reminder of Blade. She'd tried to speak with Ruby about him before they left, to say she was sorry for causing her pain, but Ruby had refused to listen to any apologies.

"You gave Blade back something that was worth far more to him than I was," she'd said, offering Airie an overly bright smile. "And I deserve better in a marriage than a comfortable friendship."

Scratch tugged on one leg of the trousers she'd worn for travel. Hunter had bought her clothes and boots that fit. The little boy, too, was comfortably dressed, although no matter how hard she tried, she could not seem to keep him clean. And although he had been warned time and again not to pick up things he did not recognize, they did periodic and thorough searches of his pockets.

She bent to receive the grimy kiss he offered her, then looked up at Hunter. "He's the same as me."

While it was unlikely his mother was a goddess, there could be little doubt that his father was demon.

"We'll worry about that if there's ever a need to," Hunter replied, his tone light. "Until then, who better to be his parents than us? He's ours now, and that's all that matters. We'll give him a new name. A good one. We'll raise him right."

She could not help but worry. "What if there are more people like us?"

"The world should be so lucky. Don't borrow trouble, Airie." He pointed to Sally, who was impatiently flicking her tongue. "It's time to move on. Saddle up."

She curled her fingers in his shirtfront and pressed her lips to his.

"I'll never get tired of you," she said. "I love you, and I'll follow you to the four corners of the earth if I have to."

His eyes were a deep, startling blue in his suntanned face.

"I know," he said, a satisfied grin creasing his cheeks.

Airie swung into the saddle and settled Scratch in front of her, feeling better already because in her heart, where it mattered, both of her mothers smiled, too.

Turn the page
for a special look
at the next book in the Demon Outlaws series,
Black Widow Demon
by Paula Altenburg

Coming soon from Entangled Select

CHAPTER ONE

Tidy towns often concealed dirty secrets. And this small mining town was too tidy for Blade's liking. It was nothing like he had expected.

Nestled amongst the foothills of the Godseeker Mountains, it suffered from too-uniform construction and a general lack of aesthetic design. But after several months of crossing the desert alone, Blade's standards were not all that high. He wanted a bath, a hot meal, and a soft bed.

A bed he could wake up in alone. The two-foot goldthief, one of the more dangerous variety of snakes in these parts, he had found in his blankets that morning had been an unwelcome surprise. Fortunately, Blade was neither a restless sleeper nor easily startled and possessed a great deal of natural patience. Once the sun came up on the desert, the well-rested serpent had slithered off on its own without incident.

Blade studied the mining settlement deep in the valley below from the outcropping of weathered sandstone. Layers of desert dirt coated the rooftops, painting the entire town a dull shade of gray.

Beyond it, the hills rose to flat peaks of a vast rocky mountain range, sparsely forested with juniper and yellow pine. Narrow ribbons of silvery water streamed down to filter through sand dunes on the valley floor and irrigate the town's gardens, ones that were now spent and shriveled by this time of year. Behind and above, past the top of the mesa, stretched the desert.

This bold new settlement had sprung up arrogantly close to what had, until recently, been demon territory. It possessed no protective ramparts, something Blade thought a serious oversight on the part of its founders. Demons might be gone, yet the world contained any number of mortal dangers.

When he considered his near-empty pack, however, and that this was the first sign of civilization he'd come across in several weeks, its proximity to evil and its underwhelming neatness was not enough of a deterrent. He did not know for certain what had drawn him back to this land of his youth, anyway. He'd had no particular destination in mind. Perhaps, after more than a decade away, it was time to lay old ghosts to rest.

He patted down his clothing to confirm that his knives were secure and at hand. He doubted if he would be recognized here, or if it would mean much to anyone anymore if he were, but he'd already received his second chance in life and he intended to treat the gift with respect.

A slight breeze stirred the warm, late afternoon air and he made a face—he stank, no doubt about it. If he did not get that bath, he could forget about finding the hot meal and soft bed. Although waking up alone would be guaranteed.

As he turned, he detected movement at the far edge of the town, near the dunes. From this distance it was difficult to say for certain, but it looked as if they were building a very large bonfire.

He wondered what they were celebrating.

Shrugging his pack higher on his shoulders, he picked his way off the outcropping. Once on the valley floor, he carefully circled the town to approach via the main street that cut through its heart. It was time to go home.

. . .

Fair trial, be damned. Without the arrival of some sort of miracle, come nightfall the townspeople intended to burn Raven at the stake as a spawn.

She sat in a makeshift jail cell on the edge of a rough wooden bed, its wool blanket scratchy beneath her flattened palms, and her feet dangling well off the whitewashed pine floor. The jailor's chair and a desk with a crooked leg were the only other furnishings in the room, and were well out of her reach on the other side of the iron bars.

For the hundredth time she mentally raced through her options. All of them involved killing her stepfather. But her first attempt was what had gotten her into this trouble.

She toppled to her side and tucked her clasped hands beneath her cheek, staring at the bars. It was his own fault that she'd stabbed him. He had slipped his hand down the front of her dress. When she defended herself, he'd had the nerve to blame her for his wrongdoing. He claimed she had tempted him.

Then, he'd told others her mother had slept with a demon and that Raven was nothing more than spawn.

The injustice of her situation quivered through her slight frame. She was not a whore, and she would rather be burned as a spawn than become one for him. If Creed knew how her stepfather had touched her, he would kill him on her behalf. Her friend, however, was miles away and knew nothing of this.

Time crept by as the shadows deepened.

The front door of the jailhouse creaked open and she sat up with a start, her heart hammering in her chest. She blinked her eyes against the sudden stream of light from outdoors.

Justice appeared before her—Justice in the form of her stepfather, and not any sudden righting of wrongs. Hate unfurled in her stomach at the sight of him.

She rose from the bed and stood at the bars of her cell. His gait was stiff as he walked into the room to set a lantern on the desk. She had jabbed the knife into his thigh and that the wound pained him filled her with joy, although he had been lucky. That was not where she'd aimed.

"There is still time to change your mind," he said to her, speaking softly so as not to be overheard in case anyone lurked outside the jailhouse door. "I can help you exorcise the demon in you."

Raven met his eyes. It was a talent of hers that she could sometimes read people's darkest thoughts, particularly when emotions ran high, and his were darker than most.

She no longer had any reason to disguise her contempt for him. "You would love to see me humiliated, stripped naked, and flogged to within an inch of my life. Then you would take me. Afterward, you would drink my blood because you believe what it contains can give you a demon's strength."

His face flushed with anger. He had been a handsome man once. Still was, in fact, despite the silver threads lacing his brown hair and the deep creases around his eyes and mouth. He had a presence about him that commanded a high level of respect. But Raven saw the ugliness simmering beneath the surface. Her mother had died a broken woman because of him.

Hatred and fear fed her strength. She gripped the cell bars so tight, she knew when she released them the imprints of her fingers would remain.

You could break free if you choose.

That inner voice terrified her far more than the man who faced her.

Her stepfather's eyes followed hers to the bars that contained her. "That's it, little demon," he taunted, his words soft. "Show the world what you are. What the blood you say I'd love to drink contains. How far do you think you could run then? How safe from the Godseekers' assassins would you be?"

That was what stopped her. She did not want people to think of her as a demon spawn. She did not want to be hunted, nor for Justice to be proven right in anyone's eyes. She had to find another way to escape.

When she did, she would kill him.

"There are some who suspect you for what *you* are," she said in return. "If I burn, more will begin to doubt you. They will watch you." Her glance flickered to the amulet he wore around his throat. "And eventually, when the goddesses fail to return, no matter how many so-called spawn you torture and kill, the people will turn from you."

Justice hooked the wooden jailor's chair with his foot and swung it around, favoring his injured leg, then sat with his arms folded across the chair's spindled back as if he had all the time in the world. He planted his chin on the crook of one elbow and studied her.

She had never fully understood the way he watched her until a few short nights ago. Now, she read raw hunger in his expression and thoughts. Her dinner rebelled at the memory of his touch on her bare flesh.

"It seems people have already turned from you," he observed.

He, too, spoke the truth. Raven had not believed that people she'd known her whole life would go through with his plan. She had hoped they would see the wrongness of it long before now. Sundown, however, had already passed.

Despair settled in with the night. No one had come to her rescue. Creed, her only real hope, was far away, and oblivious to her situation. If she chose to save herself, it meant releasing a presence inside her she had never before allowed to be free.

The thought frightened her. There would be no turning back from it if she did.

The ugliness of her stepfather's thoughts decided it for her, though. She would not burn, and she would not live in fear. She would not be broken by him as her mother was.

She would save herself.

She wore the same dress he'd deemed indecent two nights prior when the nightmare began. Tracing a finger along its prim neckline, she let her eyelids droop to examine him from beneath a dark fringe of thick, curling lashes. Her golden-toned skin gleamed in the lamplight as she pressed against the bars of the cell.

Justice swallowed, then with unsteady fingers gripped the amulet he wore around his neck. Once, a long time ago, he had been a goddess's favorite. The amulet protected him from the seduction of another immortal.

But it did nothing to protect Raven from him.

"Whore," he spat at her, and with that single utterance, she knew she had lost.

"Enjoy your final moments of glory," she said, dropping her hand to her side. "Women cannot all be whores and spawn, and

Faith will not remain silent forever. Not after tonight."

It had been a wild guess on her part, based on what she'd read of his ugliest desires, but her words struck home. His face reddened, then paled.

Fear flamed in her chest—not for herself, but for the frail, timid woman she had named.

What had she done?

"Undertaker!" Justice shouted, half turning toward the door. It opened at once, and a tall, gaunt man stuck his head into the room. "It is time."

Raven watched her stepfather lift a heavy black key from a hook on the wall behind the desk, then move to insert it in the lock on the cell door. She held her breath, waiting for the right moment to strike.

Justice drew his hand back without unlocking the cell door and regarded her thoughtfully. He turned back to the battered desk, then rooted around in a drawer. He hauled out a shining pair of handcuffs crafted from silver metal that had been mined in the nearby mountains and hardened with a special alloy. "Hold out your hands."

She did not want to be bound. If she were, she would be twice as helpless. "No."

"If you do not,"—his tone was harsh and deliberate, his eyes hard—"I will burn the jail down around you."

She felt the truth in him. He would do it. Stunned into obedience, she held out her hands and he snapped the cuffs in place. Then, he opened the cell door.

Undertaker reached in to capture her arm.

"Don't touch her!" Justice snapped, slapping the other man's hand aside. Undertaker turned to him, his bushy black eyebrows raised in silent surprise. "She's a spawn. If you touch her, she can claim you."

The lie came so easily to him.

And yet, it was not quite a lie. Raven could not claim a man. But she could cloud his thoughts long enough to defend herself from him. Justice had the knife wound in his leg to prove it.

"Ask him how he knows that," she said to Undertaker, her gaze never leaving her stepfather. "Ask him how he touched me, and for what purpose."

Justice slapped her hard across the face, and her head snapped back. Pain blossomed, blinding her. The world darkened.

"You disrespect your mother's memory when you speak like this. She was an innocent, lured by a demon—just as you tried to lure me. She raised you to be better."

Raven's eyes watered, the pain now more than physical, but she refused to shed tears. He had not married her mother out of love or respect for her innocence. She had been a beautiful woman, a master artisan and an asset for him to own, nothing more, and he had destroyed her.

Raven touched the back of one shackled wrist to the corner of her mouth and wiped away a trickle of blood. It left a dark smear on her skin in the fading light. Undertaker had given her candy when she was a child, yet he'd neither made a move to protect her from Justice's blow nor uttered one word of protest against it. Pity for him displaced the hurt in her heart. He was simple-minded and easily led. She read no malice toward her on his part.

Her chin went up and she gazed steadily at both men. "There is no need for either of you to touch me. I will walk on my own."

She displayed all the dignity she possessed as she crossed the small jailhouse and stepped into the cool embrace of the night.

Inside, she was shaking with anger and fear. She did not want to die.

But living would come at a heavy price.

• • •

He had been wrong. No celebration was planned.

With his angular face freshly shaven, shoulder-grazing black hair damp and tied back with a worn leather thong, Blade noticed the increased activity in the dusty, darkening street the instant he stepped from the bathhouse.

He'd bought a change of clothes to wear, leaving what he already owned behind to be laundered. A wool-lined coat of soft, supple leather that fell to his hips, allowing for easy access to his knives, was his one major investment. Cold ruled in the mountains.

While he was happy to be clean again, he disliked the feel of his knives in their new and unfamiliar hiding places. He especially disliked it now, when night was falling and people had gathered in tight little groups, their hushed voices filled with unmistakable tension.

Years of training, received long ago but never forgotten, had him react to it out of instinct. He inched the knife in his sleeve closer to his palm as he pressed deeper into the shadows. Invisibility was an assassin's greatest weapon.

He eavesdropped on the conversation of three men who were standing around the corner of the building from him, on the street.

"She has always been strange."

"Perhaps," a second conceded. "But being strange does not make her spawn."

Blade's interest spiked. The goddesses had disappeared from

the world nearly thirty years before, and more recently, demons had been scoured from the earth. During the years in between, the shapeshifting demons had ruled the desert, luring mortal women to them for pleasure. Half demon spawn, like their fathers, were male—monsters born in demon form to mortal mothers who had not survived their delivery. Demons, in turn, killed spawn at birth. Blade knew of only one true, living female spawn in existence—and her mother had been a goddess, not a mortal woman.

"She bewitched my son," the first man complained to the second, defending his stance. "If not for Creed's interference, he'd be her slave now. With Creed gone, I don't know what will happen to him. He has started to follow her again."

"Creed thrashed your son to within an inch of his life for following her around like a pup in the first place," a third man pointed out. "He claimed your son tried to touch her against her will."

"Creed spread that lie because he is already bewitched by her."

"If he is bewitched, how could he leave her for training?"

"Who says no to assassin trainers when they are recruiting?"

No one could deny the truth of that observation, Blade thought. Those who declined recruitment ended up dead.

The second man spoke up again. "I'm not certain luring a man for pleasure warrants burning a woman at the stake."

The third man murmured an uneasy agreement.

"It's not the pleasure part that warrants it," the first one insisted. "It's the bewitching. Raven enslaves men. You've seen how the young ones look at her, and how she pretends not to notice. People always said her mother slept with a demon," he added. "But when it was a girl that was born, and the birth didn't kill her, everyone thought they were wrong." A note of worry crept into his tone.

"Who knows how many more spawn there might be? What if there are more like her?"

Blade, from his hiding place in the shadows, propped his broad shoulders against the wooden wall of a building and tipped his head back to stare at the emerging stars, lost in thought.

Women had only the protection of men in this world. Some men were better protectors than others. Many were no protection at all. But who was he to judge?

He had once been an assassin, although he had never worked in the service of the Godseekers. He had been strictly for hire, killing men, women, and children alike, without the luxury and freedom of choice. Once he had reached a level of skill that let him name his own price, he had become more selective in the work he accepted.

Even at his lowest and most desperate, however, he had never deliberately made anyone suffer. Whether the woman named Raven was spawn or not, he wanted no part of this.

What was happening here was not his problem....

ABOUT THE AUTHOR

Paula Altenburg lives in rural Nova Scotia, Canada, with her husband and two sons. Once a manager in the aerospace industry, she now enjoys the luxury of working from home and writing fulltime. Paula also co-authors paranormal romance under the pseudonym Taylor Keating. Visit her at www.paulaaltenburg.com.

And don't forget to check out these dangerously delicious titles,
exclusively from Entangled Select

Devil May Care by **Patricia Eimer**

Being the Crown Princess of Hell has its drawbacks. For one, it makes falling in love with an angel named Matt a teensy bit tricky. It's even more complicated if his heavenly ex and devious, haloed mother are hell-bent on breaking up the new couple. When the matriarch of Heaven declares war on Satan's royal family and kidnaps Faith's brother, there's nothing Faith can do but risk it all—including her heart—to restore peace between Heaven and Hell.

Out in Blue by **Sarah Gilman**

In a violent world where fallen archangels are hunted for their valuable plumage, Wren knows one thing for certain: the human woman who saved him from a poacher attack will die if she stays with him. The demon responsible for his parents' gruesome deaths pines for the chance to rip apart any woman who stands under Wren's wing. And when Ginger reveals a unique talent of her own and discovers the truth about Wren's father's disappearance, Wren must confront his demons to save his father—and the most courageous woman he's ever known.

Kiss of the Betrayer by **Boone Brux**

For fifteen years, mix-blooded Bringer Luc Le Daun has blamed himself for the death of his beloved. But he isn't the only one who carries hatred deep down in his soul. Jade Kendell has been seeking revenge on him for years and is finally armed with a plan. But when her plot goes awry, Luc and Jade must plunge together into the dangerous world of the demon Bane, and as the peril of their journey grows, so does the fire between them.